Anne Wyn Clark was born and raised in the Midlands, where she continues to live with her husband, a sweet-natured cat, plus a chinchilla with attitude. She has three now grown-up children and six grandchildren. Much of her formative existence was spent with her head in a book, and from an early age, she grew to relish the sheer escapism afforded by both reading and writing fiction.

She has a love of antiquity and a penchant for visiting old graveyards, often speculating on the demise of those entombed beneath.

The Shadows of Hill Manor is her fourth novel.

You can follow her on X @EAClarkAuthor

Also by Anne Wyn Clark

Whisper Cottage
The Last House on the Cliff
The Secrets of Mill House

ANNE WYN CLARK

The Shadows of Hill Manor

avon.

Published by AVON
A division of HarperCollins*Publishers* Ltd
1 London Bridge Street
London SE1 9GF

www.harpercollins.co.uk

HarperCollins*Publishers*
Macken House, 39/40 Mayor Street Upper,
Dublin 1, D01 C9W8, Ireland

A Paperback Original 2024

First published in Great Britain by HarperCollins*Publishers* 2024

A catalogue copy of this book is available from the British Library.

ISBN: 978-0-00-861414-0

Typeset in Sabon Lt Pro by HarperCollins*Publishers* India

Printed and bound in the UK using 100%
Renewable Electricity at CPI Group (UK) Ltd

For my grandma, Gladys Mary Fry.
A truly good soul.
xxx

In this hollow I do grieve
For all the things that cease to be.

Angie Weiland-Crosby

Prologue

April 2007

Something about the woods had felt different that day. Or at least, with the benefit of hindsight, Nathan had convinced himself that must have been the case. The whisper of wind between the trees; the ominous bird call echoing through the branches above their heads.

He shuddered as he stared out through the window, now that night had eventually fallen over the spinney; the same veil of darkness which seemed to have enveloped the whole estate in an eerie, menacing cowl. The dark silhouette of Hill Manor loomed like a sentinel above it all. It was still the same place he had grown up, where he and his younger brother had hitherto enjoyed a carefree, unrestricted childhood; but right now, he felt he didn't really know it at all and he wanted to get as far away as he possibly could. Tomorrow pictures of their home would be splashed all over the newspapers and television, the name to be forever synonymous with unnatural death and crime of the worst kind.

Forever overshadowed by the old house and the terrible secret thrown up by the same soil supporting its foundations.

*

The Laurels, marketed originally as "a modern residential development in a prime suburban location", stood just four miles north of Oxford. Constructed in the mid-1970s, it was the epitome of the boxy architecture that was so popular during the decade that taste had somehow bypassed. The settlement commandeered the former grounds of an eighteenth-century mansion house, the now sadly dilapidated Hill Manor, though sprawling woodland still remained at its periphery. It was close enough to the housing estate for the residents and their children to explore, and particularly popular for those with trail bikes but the house itself was a no-go area. Much of the high wall surrounding the once grand building had begun to crumble, its tall, rusting gates propped permanently open between worn stone pillars. The huge sash windows were now boarded up, the rafters exposed in many areas, with slates lying smashed on the overgrown terrace beneath.

Hill Manor's last inhabitant, Eustace Hill, elderly great-grandson of the original owners, had died alone in the house, penniless and reclusive, over seventy years earlier. Said to have lain undiscovered for weeks, his body had made a meal for rats and visiting foxes, and little of it remained to bury by the time it was found by local police.

With no offspring to whom Eustace could leave the house, the place had gradually been reclaimed by nature and was now home to bats, nesting birds, and various rodents. The rotten floorboards were a potential death trap to anyone who might be foolish enough to venture over the threshold. But despite the numerous warning signs hammered into the ground, some of the older local kids would dare one another to enter, particularly around Halloween. Stories of the grisly demise of its former owner stoked their imagination and the thought that his restless spirit paced the rooms at once thrilled and terrified them. Plans to demolish the building imminently had made it even more of a draw of late and parents lived in fear of someone having a serious, if not fatal, accident eventually.

The Easter holidays were coming to a close, the weather warming nicely towards a promising spring. But after a fortnight of constant bickering and treating their home like a refuse tip, the boys at Number 14 had finally pushed their mother to her limits.

"Right. That's it. You're driving me up the bloody wall. Out – *now*." She jerked the leads from their respective PS3s, holding out a hand for the controllers.

"That's *so* unfair. What are we supposed to do?" Nathan sat back, his mouth gaping in indignation.

"Use your imagination. You're *kids*. Just stay away from the old house unless you want to break your necks." She narrowed her eyes in warning and watched with folded arms as the two boys slouched out of the front door, then she dusted off her hands and closed it behind them.

"Cow." Sulkily, twelve-year-old Nathan steered his cobweb-bedecked BMX out of the shed. "Come on then, moron."

Daniel followed, sticking up one finger belligerently behind his older brother's back. They wheeled the bicycles out of the cul-de-sac and Nathan paused for a moment.

Daniel puffed out his cheeks. "Where we gonna go? Hey, why *don't* we go up to the Manor? It would really piss her off . . ."

Despite feeling like defying his mother, Nathan had the good sense to heed her words. Hill Manor gave him the creeps, anyway.

"Nah. Charlie Nolan reckons it's full of bat shit. We'll do a few laps of the spinney instead. Bet I can get round in half the time it takes you."

"That's not fair – your bike's better than mine. And you're bigger, too."

"Excuses, excuses." Nathan grinned smugly. "You know what they say, squirt: a bad workman blames his tools. And size has nothing to do with it, anyway – I'm just better than you at everything. *And* you know it."

"Huh. We'll see about that."

As they entered the copse, Daniel leapt astride his bike and began to pedal for all he was worth, leaving Nathan standing.

"Oi, you little git! I never said you could have a head start."

Daniel laughed gleefully. Sticking his feet out to the sides, he freewheeled erratically over the well-beaten downward slope, disappearing into the heart of the woods. Nathan glanced over his shoulder briefly at the crumbling building looming behind him. He thought of the other stuff Charlie Nolan had said about the place and shuddered. He for one wasn't going to be checking it out any time soon. Mounting his BMX, he gave chase.

"Holy shit!"

Nathan slammed on his brakes as Daniel, a few yards ahead, jarred suddenly and went flying over his handlebars. He smacked to the ground with a thud. The younger boy groaned, hoisting himself into a sitting position. He appeared dazed, and looked round as if unsure quite what had happened.

His irritation replaced by concern, Nathan dropped his own bike and ran to his brother's aid.

"Y'all right, squirt?"

4

Daniel rolled up his tracksuit bottoms and inspected his grazed knees. His palms smarted. Tentatively, he put a hand to the side of his face. It was stinging a little, but there appeared to be no major damage.

"Yeah, think so. The stupid wheel got caught – must've been a tree root, or something. I didn't see it."

Nathan picked up the bike, straightening the handlebars, and propped it against a tree. He scoured the ground where Daniel had fallen for evidence of the cause of the mishap. The light levels were dim, owing to the dappled shadows thrown by the thick canopy above, which shielded them from the brightness of the afternoon sun. Something black and shiny, no more than three inches wide, was jutting from the hardened soil next to his brother's extended leg. Nathan prodded the slightly curved surface cautiously with the toe of his trainer.

"What's that?" Daniel's eyes were drawn to his brother's foot.

"Dunno, but it's definitely no tree root." Nathan cast around for some sort of implement. Picking up a stone, he began to scrape the soil from the half-covered item. He peered at his discovery and frowned.

"Weird. Looks like one of those old-fashioned door handles."

He continued to rake at the ground and suddenly hit something solid, but hollow-sounding.

"Hey, look at this."

Daniel brushed himself off and rose to his feet. He bent down and stared at the ground where his brother was pointing.

"It's a bloody door!"

"Give us a hand." Nathan gestured beyond where Daniel was now squatting. "Grab another stone or something."

Their interest piqued, the two boys scrabbled at the earth,

eventually revealing a full-sized wooden panelled door, the type typically found in early twentieth-century terraced houses. It was attached to the round Bakelite handle that Nathan had initially uncovered. They looked at one another in eager anticipation.

"D'you reckon there's something underneath it, or is it just an old door someone's buried for some reason?" Daniel's eyes shone. The discovery was almost worth his fall.

"Only one way to find out." Nathan twisted the handle, but unsurprisingly the door didn't yield. He thought for a moment. "Here, you take that top corner and I'll pull from the bottom. Let's see if we can lift it up. On the count of three . . ."

Together, the boys gave one almighty heave and the edge of the door gradually started to rise. The surrounding earth beneath began to fall away, causing a mini-landslide to trickle into the huge aperture revealed below. With another final supreme effort, they pushed the door wide open. It crashed against the ground. Nathan stood back, wiping his hands on his jeans. Gingerly, he leaned forward. Wooden steps led down into the hollow they had uncovered, which disappeared at an angle deep into the ground. His eyes widened.

"Looks like some kind of den."

Daniel peered down into the darkness. His face lit up.

"Shall we . . .?"

Nathan thought for a moment. He was curious about the hole but common sense told him they needed to be mindful of the terrain. They didn't want several tons of earth collapsing on top of them.

"Okay, we'll have a proper look. Better get a torch, though. It's pitch black. I want to see where I'm treading."

"Wait here. I'll fetch one." The trauma of his earlier fall apparently forgotten, Daniel grabbed his bike and pedalled furiously back through the spinney. Within minutes he had returned, brandishing a flashlight.

Nathan held out a hand. "I'll go first – check it all looks safe and that."

Daniel looked on expectantly as Nathan inched his way down the steps, clutching the torch as he ducked beneath the low timber lintel bracing the entrance. Once at the bottom, he played the beam round the dugout.

"What can you see?" called his brother from above.

Nathan's eyes were beginning to adjust to the darkness. The space was probably big enough to accommodate six people – eight, at a push. He scanned round, absorbing the arch of the roof, the dirt floor. Suddenly remembering a documentary he'd watched about people uncovering a tomb in Egypt, he felt a frisson of excitement. Maybe he'd find some priceless artefact. But the dank, foetid air was almost enough to make him gag, and on closer inspection, there seemed to be little of interest. The contents were sparse and looked decades rather than centuries old: an ancient oil lamp sitting on a small wooden table just inside the entrance, a filthy tin chamber pot tucked beneath it on the ground. A slatted wooden bench ran the entire length of the wall adjacent.

"Looks like an old air-raid shelter. Just think – I might be the first person down here for about sixty years! Yeah, pretty sure that's what it is. The walls are made of that corrugated iron stuff. There's a couple of old bunks and a bench. And it *stinks* down here, man. I s'pose people must've just used the corner to piss in."

The rusting frame of bunk beds lined the wall opposite the bench, their mattresses absent, revealing the unforgiving metal mesh which would have supported them. It had been bad enough when he and Daniel were forced to top and tail at their cousin's house last summer. He wondered how anyone could possibly have slept on such things, especially with the threat of being bombed at any moment.

The air in the shelter was icily cold. Nathan's breath was visible in the rays cast by the flashlight. Something caught his attention from the depths of the bunker. He had the sudden sense of a pair of eyes observing him and felt strangely discomfited, gooseflesh rising on his arms. Peering into the gloom, he grew rigid with fear. There, in the gap between the bench and the beds, stood a small but unmistakably human form. Nathan caught his breath. He could make out no words, but could have sworn he heard someone whispering. His imagination began to run away with him. Heart racing, he stumbled backwards, almost missing his footing.

"Shit!"

Daniel, who had been hopping from one foot to the other above, could contain himself no longer.

"What's up? Here – I'm coming in." He clambered down the steps, shielding his eyes from the torch beam as Nathan turned it towards him.

"Point it the other way, you idiot. I can't see a thing." Daniel backed towards the bench on his left, screwing up his face. "Eugh. You're right, it does stink."

Daniel's foot caught on something poking from beneath the bench. Freeing his trainer, he peered down to see what looked like heavy-duty, translucent polythene sheeting.

"Hey, they never had plastic during the war, did they?"

Nathan shrugged. "Search me. Why?" His heart still hammering, he looked around uneasily. He could have sworn there was someone down there, watching him – but how could there be? He'd been reading too many Point Horror books. He felt foolish now. Thankfully Daniel didn't seem to have noticed how spooked he'd been or he'd have had a field day telling his mates.

Daniel tugged at the sheeting. It seemed to be caught on something.

"Here, give us a hand. There's something under the seat."

Nathan propped the torch on the upper bunk, creating a fan of light on the opposite wall. The two boys pulled at the thick plastic, which after its initial resistance suddenly jerked free.

The smell released was pungent, sulphurous: something akin to rotten eggs.

Daniel let out an involuntary squawk. They both recoiled simultaneously in shock. Nathan inadvertently knocked the torch from where it had been balanced. It clattered to the dirt floor. There was an ominous click and the boys were left in what felt like a thick black void.

"*Nath!* What the—! I can't see a thing." Daniel's voice was reduced to a whimper.

"'S okay, 's okay . . ."

Nathan dropped to his knees, his heart hammering. He groped around before eventually managing to locate the torch. With trembling hands, he fumbled with the switch to restore illumination, but his fingers seemed to have lost all coordination and the torch fell from his grasp. It rolled across the floor, spinning and landing in the perfect position to highlight what lay beneath the bench.

Time seemed to stand still. Scrambling to retrieve the flashlight, Nathan drew back, grabbing his younger brother reflexively by the arm. The two boys were rendered momentarily speechless as they stared down in horrified disbelief at their discovery.

There was no question. The plastic had been wrapped around the badly decomposed body of a child.

9

Chapter 1

April 2007

The morning air was cool, but watery sunshine had gradually started to seep through the clouds. PC Simon Warner had parked his vehicle in Winchester Road. Turning into Lime Tree Avenue, he walked slowly, scanning the numbers on the doors. It was a pleasantly quiet suburban road of neatly maintained post-war terraced houses, lined with brutally pollarded lime trees; evidence of nature fighting back could be seen in the form of fresh green shoots, sprouting from the spindly twigs emerging haphazardly from their tops like fledgling dreadlocks. The street ran perpendicular to the Woodstock and Banbury Roads. Number 37 stood out from the rest for all the wrong reasons, just as his DI had predicted it probably would.

"Mr Painter's been through a hell of a lot. Don't be surprised if you find him a bit prickly. My predecessor did nothing to improve his opinion of us, I'm afraid. Tread carefully," she had warned him.

Looking more like an adolescent choir boy in fancy dress than a bona fide police officer, the young constable creaked open the rusty gate apprehensively, picking his way through the tangle of weeds pushing up between the paving stones. He paused to collect his thoughts, before pressing the doorbell. Its tinny ring could be heard echoing through the hallway on the other side. He stood stiffly, hands half-covered by his sleeves, mentally rehearsing what he was about to say. The occupant's silhouette came suddenly into view through the filthy frosted amber window at the top of the door. Warner could hear him fumbling with the chain. A dog barked briefly from within, but was silenced almost instantly by a surly utterance from its owner.

A thin, grey-haired man screwed up his eyes against the daylight as he opened the front door, its faded, peeling paintwork and cracked glass a further hint of what lay within. The man was tall but stooped with age. He peered in blatant irritation at the slight, youthful stranger standing on his step, his eyes travelling from Warner's head to his feet and back, clearly noticing the new jacket, which was at least two sizes too big.

The moment of truth. PC Warner's palms were sweating. He rubbed them against his trousers.

"Erm . . . Mr Painter?"

"Who wants to know?"

"I'm PC Warner, from St Aldates Constabulary?" Warner shrivelled inwardly as he thought how ineffectual he must sound. "Erm . . . I have some news for you." There was an awkward pause. He couldn't deliver this bombshell on the doorstep. "Could I—? I wonder if I might come in, please?"

The old man narrowed his eyes. "Got any ID?"

Warner recalled his DI's warning about Painter being potentially uncooperative. He'd heard the stories of the man's hopes having been raised and repeatedly dashed over the years. It was understandable that Painter wasn't welcoming him with open arms, but this wasn't making him feel any better about the information he had to impart. He hated confrontation.

Flustered, the young officer rummaged in his inside pocket and eventually produced an identity badge. He looked at Painter hopefully. The man shrugged, gave an exaggerated sniff, and, turning on his heel, shuffled back into the dingy hallway. Warner hesitated.

Painter called over his shoulder gruffly. "Well? You coming in then, or what?"

The little terraced house was dimly lit and offered little in the way of creature comforts. The plastic light shade dangling from the vestibule ceiling was cracked and laced with cobwebs. A threadbare carpet led the way into a poky living room, which was sparsely furnished, with a bulky old-fashioned TV set in one corner. The air was thick with the odours of stale cigarette smoke and dog, the ceiling and walls stained yellow with nicotine. A thin, gangly mongrel with a rough grey coat – almost a canine version of its owner – was sprawled on the filthy hearth rug. The animal lifted its head and emitted a warning growl as they entered the room.

"Shut up, Tucker," grunted Painter. Obligingly, the dog flopped back down but continued to watch the intruder in his home mistrustfully.

"'Scuse the state of the place – afraid I've let things go a bit, as you can probably see." The older man rolled his eyes resignedly. It was an apology he was obviously used to uttering. He pointed to a battered, dog-hair-smothered armchair, its cushions peppered with cigarette burns. "Have a seat."

PC Warner thought it impolite to decline and, giving the dog a wide berth, lowered himself gingerly onto the edge of the proffered chair. At least he had a spare pair of trousers; these would have to go straight in the wash when he finished his shift.

Painter ensconced himself on the settee opposite and eyed his visitor with some curiosity. After running a hand through his greasy, thinning hair, he pulled a cigarette from the packet in his shirt pocket. Flicking a lighter, he lit the cigarette and inhaled deeply.

"What's this all about, then?"

The young policeman's heart quickened. "There's been . . . a discovery."

How the hell should he phrase this? He took a deep breath. He just needed to spit it out.

"That is to say, the remains of a young girl have been found."

PC Warner wanted to kick himself. It had all come out in a rush. Every muscle in his body tensed as he watched for Painter's reaction.

Painter nodded slowly. He spoke through the fog of smoke he was generating, the vapour pouring from his nostrils like a world-weary dragon.

"And I s'pose they think it could be our Kimberley?"

"It's a distinct possibility, yes. I'm sorry, I know this can't be easy for you. I'm aware your hopes of finding her have been falsely raised in the past and understand your relationship with us has been, well, a bit strained."

Painter spluttered a huge guffaw. "Huh! You can say that again. Did that arsehole Bennett send you? Didn't have the nerve to come here again himself, I dare say."

"It was before my time, but I believe DCI Bennett took early retirement – quite a few years ago now."

"Well, good riddance to bad rubbish, if you ask me. A right friggin' chocolate teapot he was – him and that drippy sergeant . . . what was his name? Henderson, wasn't it? Neither use nor bloody ornament, the pair of 'em."

Warner didn't acknowledge this last remark. It would be unprofessional to pass comment on a senior officer, whatever the rumours may have been. He cleared his throat.

"Sergeant Henderson moved from the area not long after DCI Bennett left. The case has been re-assigned to DI Shelley, but she's on annual leave at the moment." He thought of his DI and for the first time that morning felt the corners of his mouth lift into a smile. "She's *very* good . . ."

"*She?*" Painter looked incredulous. "They've got a *woman* in charge now?"

PC Warner bristled. He hated misogyny anyway, but had nothing but admiration for his DI, who was always fair and measured in her approach – more so than many of the male officers he'd come across so far. In fact, secretly, he had a bit of a crush on her, despite the fact she was old enough to be his mother.

"I can assure you, Mr Painter, that DI Shelley is a first-class officer, with an excellent track record. If anyone can solve a cold case, she's your man – if you see what I mean." He groaned inwardly at his clumsy choice of phrase, his cheeks colouring.

Painter sat back, frowning. "So, they've found a body, you say?

"Yes. They're carrying out a fingertip search of the surrounding area in case there are any more out there. There are several unsolved missing child cases in the Oxford area going back quite a few years, and this could be the breakthrough we've been waiting for. It's a pretty densely wooded location, though, so it may take some time to do a thorough search."

Malcolm Painter nodded, slowly absorbing this information. "And what exactly makes them think it could be Kimberley?"

Warner blanched. A single bead of perspiration trickled

down his temple and he raised a hand to swipe it away. His eyes were drawn suddenly to the framed photograph in the centre of the mantelpiece. He'd seen the photo from the case file, so he knew what she'd looked like. But seeing the same picture in the house where the little girl had actually lived really brought it home to him. His stomach clenched as he remembered the shocking sight of the tiny, angular skeleton forced into the foetal position, its fragile limbs contorted unnaturally. Even in his personal life, he'd been fortunate enough to have no first-hand experience of death thus far, and had found his encounter with the remains of such a young child deeply disturbing. It would be burned into his consciousness for eternity. How those poor kids who'd found her must be feeling, he couldn't imagine. It was the stuff of nightmares.

Warner swallowed down the knot which had risen in his throat.

"I'm so sorry. I'm afraid the body has decomposed too badly for visual identification. Further tests still have to be carried out. But there were certain items accompanying the . . . the remains . . . that might be recognisable. If you feel you could accompany me to the station, maybe you might be able to identify—"

Painter stubbed out his cigarette in the ashtray beside him and eased himself to his feet. He nodded solemnly. "Okay. I'll get my coat."

PC Warner glanced back at the sad little house as they made their way along Lime Tree Avenue towards where he'd parked the patrol car. So that was where she'd spent her short life, poor Kimberley. He knew in his gut it must be her. She'd be almost thirty now, if she'd lived – about the same age as his older sister. The whole thing had really got to him and he hoped fervently that with time he'd get used to dealing with cases like this.

Because, being realistic, he knew that sadly there would surely be more.

Sudden movement in the upstairs window drew his attention.

Was that—? Had someone been looking down at them? He pulled up sharply, trying to focus beyond the grimy glass. A cold feeling crept along his spine.

"Mr Painter, was there anyone else in the house with you just now?"

"Nope. Just Tucker. He's my only company these days."

Painter shot a look over his shoulder, following the trajectory of Warner's gaze. His mouth spread slowly into a smile. He turned back to face Warner, fixing him with a strange look.

"Well, most of the time, anyway."

*

St Aldates Station was only a relatively short drive away, but for Painter the journey seemed interminable. The morning traffic was heavy, and the young police officer drove at a steadily sensible twenty-five miles per hour, stopping all too frequently to allow other drivers right of way.

Not bolshy enough to abuse his blue lights yet, Malcolm concluded.

He glanced sideways at the constable, who was sitting bolt upright behind the wheel. Feeling the weight of Malcolm's stare, the lad smiled nervously, shifting a little in his seat. There was a huge gap between his neck and the collar of his shirt. He looked barely old enough to drive, let alone be involved in a murder investigation. Bitter experience had made Malcolm cynical of the police and the tendency many of them seemed to have of exploiting their status, not to mention treating everyone as a potential criminal.

He sat in silence, staring unseeingly through the car window, contemplating what might confront him upon arrival at the station. He'd waited for so long to bring his daughter home and hardly dared hope that she had, indeed, been found after all these years. Years of anger, frustration, and heartache had taken its toll on his health and marriage, and ultimately sent his wife to an early grave. He was too tired now to care much about his own life, but knew he'd never give up entirely until Kimberley had been found and laid to rest. That was the one final purpose of the pitiable existence he now led. In truth, it was the only thing keeping him going.

Though he had never told anyone, Malcolm was convinced he felt Kimberley's presence everywhere in the house. It had started after Mary passed away. He was sure he had seen her on several occasions: a fleeting shadow moving through the hallway; a glimpse of movement from the corner of the room, which would quickly vanish as he turned to look. He'd come to recognise when she was drawing close. Immediately beforehand, the distinctive aroma of rain-soaked soil would permeate the air. It was very odd. But he wasn't unnerved by it. He actually found it comforting.

It hadn't been the same when Mary died; it was as if once her life had been extinguished, nothing of her remained. But Kimberley's soul was restless. She had unfinished business. Malcolm had convinced himself that she'd never find true peace until her earthly body, or what was left of it, had been returned to him and given a proper burial. He'd never been a believer in the hereafter before, always scoffed at the notion, if the truth be told, but Kimberley's loss had made him think otherwise. It had given him hope that one day they'd be reunited.

The unwelcomely familiar smell of the police station hit him as he followed the young constable through the double doors: cleaning fluid and vending machine coffee. It wasn't a

17

particularly offensive odour, but its grim associations were. Like the overpowering aroma of lilies in the florist's, all it ever conjured up now was the painful recollection of Mary's funeral, and would always send him plummeting to the depths of despair. Funny how scents, good or bad, could instantly transport you to another place or time.

Malcolm's stomach churned. A wave of nausea surged through him, and he raised a hand to his mouth as he felt bile rise from his gullet, its bitter tang hitting the back of his throat. In his mind, he replayed his visits here all those years ago. Those ridiculous allegations and the lengthy, distressing questioning at the hands of Bennett and his bumbling sidekick.

He looked about him. Things hadn't altered much, although the aluminium ashtrays were no longer a fixture, he observed. The unnaturally white glare of the fluorescent lighting showed up the stains on the polystyrene ceiling tiles.

Obligatory Crimestoppers posters, with telephone numbers inviting dutiful members of the public to report wrongdoings, adorned the wood-panelled walls. All that appeared to have changed was the inclusion of a web address. A couple of dubious-looking individuals sat waiting on rickety plastic chairs, scowling first at one another, then at the unsmiling desk sergeant, who seemed to be deliberately avoiding eye contact with them.

The sergeant, ostensibly absorbed by the paperwork piled up on the counter, looked up sharply as they entered and nodded to PC Warner. Without a word, he indicated a doorway leading off the main reception area. Malcolm was shown into a small side room. Several items had been laid out on a trestle table, everything meticulously labelled and placed into clear plastic evidence bags.

"Take your time, Mr Painter," said PC Warner, studying

Malcolm's face as he led him into the room. "Have a good look."

Painter sent him a withering glance, then began to examine the exhibits. His eyes darted about as he tried to take in what was spread out before him: various scraps of shredded, dirty fabric; a cherry-red hair-slide; a child's multi-coloured plastic bracelet; a battered navy-blue shoe . . .

The old man's pulse began to race. The air suddenly seemed to crackle with electricity; the scent of damp earth that sometimes filled his home flooded his nostrils. Malcolm's head swam, his vision blurring.

"It's her." His voice was barely more than a croak. He choked back the bile that threatened to resurface. "That's her shoe. I used to clean them for her every Sunday evening. I'd know it anywhere."

He staggered a little and stepped backwards, clutching at the edge of the table for support. Painter looked up at the young officer, tears welling in his eyes. "Where was she found?"

PC Warner shifted his weight awkwardly from one foot to the other.

"An abandoned air-raid shelter. In what used to be the grounds of a mansion house called Hill Manor. About three miles from here." He hesitated. "A couple of young lads from the housing estate nearby were riding their bikes in the spinney, and . . . well, they saw something sticking up out of the ground and came across the entrance—"

"*Kids*, you say?" Malcolm snapped back his head, his eyes widening in anger. "Kids found her? And your lot haven't managed to uncover anything for nearly *twenty years*? *Unbelievable*. Absolutely fucking priceless."

"Mr Painter, I realise this must all come as a terrible shock to you—"

"A *shock*? You've no idea at all, have you? How could you? You're no more than a lad yourself. I'd just about given up any hope of ever finding her. And by the sound of things, it's no thanks to the boys in blue she's eventually turned up. My life's been ruined. People pointing fingers; whispering behind closed doors. You know what they say: *no smoke without fire*. I've been to hell and back, d'you realise that? All I want to know now is when I can take my daughter home and give her a proper burial."

PC Warner's cheeks flushed crimson. "I'm terribly sorry, Mr Painter, but that may not be possible for some time. I'm afraid we'll have to wait until all the forensic test results come back. But I can assure you we're doing our utmost to push everything through as quickly as we can. I appreciate how long you've had to wait already . . ."

Malcolm Painter gave a derisory snort. It wasn't the lad's fault – he knew that. But after the initial shock, the feelings of sheer frustration and rage, knowing Kimberley had been so close and the police had failed to find her, that he *himself* had failed to find her, made him want to punch something. How he wished Bennett was still around. At that moment, he'd have been happy to be up on an assault charge if it meant he could wipe the floor with the incompetent idiot. Nothing would have given him greater pleasure.

"That's no more than I'd expect from your lot. I suppose I can wait. I haven't got much choice, have I? What's another few weeks after all these years? Now I'm sure it's really her, at least I know I'll be able to reunite her with her poor mother." He paused. "But is your new woman – Shelley, or whatever her name is – ever going to nail the bastard that did this to my daughter? Or am I going to die like my wife, without ever seeing justice served?"

20

Chapter 2

Saturday, 9 June 1990

The two police officers had, in fairness, arrived quite promptly. The call came through to the station at 7.45pm, shortly after WPC Alessandra Cano had started a late shift, and she and her colleague were standing on the Painters' doorstep within the half hour. She had begun to regret having such a large portion of her mother's signature cannelloni dish before leaving the house, and it sat now in her stomach like a brick.

The earlier deluge had abated, leaving the streets shrouded in a light mist, blurring the outlines of the trees and buildings. There was a strange stillness in the air, an almost eerie absence of life. The only occasional sound was that of a solitary blackbird, emitting a few melancholy notes before the day's end.

Detective Sergeant Henderson was a thin, moustachioed middle-aged man. WPC Cano had accompanied him on only a handful of occasions since starting at St Aldates, but had quickly gleaned that he was equally short in stature and wit. She had yet to find anyone within the department who seemed to be on her wavelength, and as the new girl, had attracted sly glances of both admiration and mistrust from the male officers. There had been more women on the team at Kidlington and she'd felt less exposed there, in a way. But as ever, Alessa had soon begun to feel like a misfit. And from everything she'd heard, a move to St Aldates might offer more wide-ranging experience in the long run, so she'd put in for a transfer. Even though she was starting at the bottom of the ladder, she was determined to make a go of things and prove her worth. Still in uniform and honing her skills, she aspired to become a detective. Alessa had realised, quite recently, that somehow she had grown attractive – a fact which had come as something of a shock, since she'd always felt plain and dumpy as a child. Rather than enhance her appearance further, at the station she tried for the most part to hide her trim figure beneath the buttoned-up jacket; no make-up, sensible shoes. Her approach continued even outside work, much to her mother's chagrin.

"Why don't you make the most of yourself?" Greta had asked one day, smoothing the curtain of her daughter's dark bob from her cheek. She had thrown up her hands in a gesture of exasperation. "You have such a pretty face – you should be proud of it. You'd have those boys queuing up to take you out."

With a glint in her eye, she'd proceeded to regale Alessa with tales of romantic encounters that she herself had enjoyed as a young woman, before she'd met and married her errant husband, Jorge. At times, Alessa found her mother's anecdotes a little too candid and would have been happier if she'd kept some of the details to herself. But then that was Mamma – once she was in full flow, everything just came spilling out.

Alessa preferred to stay as inconspicuous as possible. It suited her purpose. Her social life was non-existent and she knew that her mamma's main concern was with her finding "a nice young man" to settle down with. Greta reminded her constantly that she had been twenty-three when she'd married Alessa's father. Alessa could have said that, with the way things had turned out, that hadn't exactly gone well, but she didn't. She would smile and tell her mamma that, for the moment anyway, she was intent on focusing on her new placement and was living and breathing the job. She was only twenty-four – she had plenty of time ahead of her.

Alessa watched in exasperation as DS Henderson entered the Painters' hallway self-consciously, apparently nervous of eye contact, concentrating his efforts on repeatedly and unnecessarily wiping his feet on the doormat. The man was obviously out of his depth and looked as though he'd rather be anywhere else than in the Painters' home. He said very little and when he did speak it was barely more than a mumble, then he would sniff occasionally and scribble copious notes as he hovered awkwardly in the living room doorway, whilst the young police officer tried her utmost to allay the overwrought Mary's fears.

A missing child was always taken seriously, although Alessa knew even from her limited experience that, ninety-nine times out of a hundred, the disappearance could be attributed to some event within the home, and the situation would, more often than not, culminate in a tearful reunion between the parents and their sheepish, if not always contrite, offspring. But with a recent spate of abduction attempts of young girls in the area, such a report was a red flag and not something to be taken lightly. Alessa hated these situations. They always brought *the* memory to the fore – the awful, gut-wrenching recollection of something she'd prefer to bury forever. It was like continually picking at an old, painful scab.

Of a sensitive disposition probably ill-suited to her role,

Alessa was still finding it hard to remain detached on such occasions. She had already been out on a few "death knocks", as they were somewhat irreverently referred to at the nick, and kept telling herself it would get better with time, but she was beginning to doubt it. But this wasn't a death knock. At least, she prayed that wasn't where it was heading. They couldn't rule out the possibility of the local would-be kidnapper having finally been successful.

She cast an eye around the small living room. Everything was spotlessly clean and tidy, and it had a pleasant, homely feel. A child's crayoned picture and a clumsily painted cardboard elephant were proudly displayed next to a small vase of freesias on the window sill. Knowing first-hand how little it could take for a family's domestic bliss to be shattered, Alessa was consumed with a feeling of dread.

The little girl's mother was distraught, her eyes red and swollen from crying. Mary Painter was painfully thin, her short, greying hair dull and dishevelled. Alessa couldn't be sure of the woman's age. She might have been anywhere between forty and sixty. She wore a drab, shapeless cotton shift dress and battered bedroom slippers, neither of which would have looked out of place on someone the wrong side of ninety. Alessa's heart went out to her. Mary's hands lay clasped in her lap around a scrunched-up tissue, the knuckles raw from what Alessa suspected was years of exposure to harsh cleaning products, the nails ragged and untended. Her time was clearly devoted to the maintenance of her spotless home, rather than her personal appearance.

Alessa thought of her own mother, who, despite the fact that she rarely went out, always made an effort to look well-groomed and smart. But then, that was how she'd been raised, and part of who she was and always had been. That was the face she wanted to show the world. Even before Alessa's younger brother Joey died and Alessa knew she'd been up half the night tending to him, her mother was always coiffed and made up at breakfast, ready to face the day. Greta Cano was a formidable woman. She was strong – and God knows she'd had to be. Whatever life had thrown at her, and at her children, she'd always managed to rise to the challenge. Joey's death, whilst not entirely unexpected, had cast a shadow over them both, and sometimes Alessa would hear her mother crying during the night. It broke Alessa's heart to think how devastating it must have been for her mamma, losing her only son. But Greta got on with things. There was always someone worse off than herself, she declared. Life was too short to wallow in self-pity.

It occurred to Alessa that Mary Painter lacked both confidence and self-esteem, and she worried that the woman wouldn't have the resilience to cope in a crisis. She seemed fragile – as though it would take very little to tip her over the edge. Even from this short encounter, it was obvious to Alessa that Mary's identity was shaped by her role as mother and housewife, her whole life revolving around what lay within those four walls. And now there was the possibility that her existence was about to be ripped apart. It was too cruel.

The steady ticking of the wooden mantel clock was almost hypnotic, like a metronome. In spite of herself, Alessa's mind began to wander. Suddenly she found herself propelled back in time, back to that place she never wanted to revisit. Her stomach lurched.

Catching sight of her own reflection in the mirror above the fireplace, she realised her memories were reflected in her haunted expression. She darted a look at DS Henderson but he appeared oblivious, staring from his post by the door towards the window as though willing someone to come and rescue him.

25

Clearing her throat, Alessa tried desperately to focus once more on the here and now. At least *one* of them needed to look as though they were being proactive.

"Mrs Painter, was everything all right when Kimberley left your house this afternoon?" she asked gently. "There hadn't been an argument? I mean, she hadn't been told off, wasn't upset about anything?"

"No, definitely not. Malcolm told the policeman over the phone what happened. He dropped her off at her friend Faye's house, then went back to collect her after tea, as arranged. But they said she'd already left for home."

"You say she's asthmatic? But you're certain she has an inhaler with her?"

"Yes, she always takes it everywhere. We're very strict about it." Mary Painter began to weep once more. "But what if she's lost it? What if someone's taken her and she has an attack? She's only ten – she really shouldn't be out there on her own. Oh God, I can't bear it . . ."

By now it was almost nine o'clock and daylight was beginning to fade. Malcolm Painter paced the living room floor like a caged animal, his hands clasped behind his head. His wife watched him. Her tears had been replaced by bubbling anger, thin lips merged into a hard line. An invisible finger of blame was wagging in the air.

"I had a bad feeling about all this, even before she went out. I should *never* have let her go. I should've put my foot down." Mary glared at her husband, her eyes narrowing. "Something's happened to her – it must have. She would've been home hours ago, otherwise. Oh God! Oh God, let her be okay . . ."

She began to rock back and forth in the armchair, her arms wrapped tightly across her chest, a wail rising in her throat.

Malcolm stared helplessly at her.

Mary held him responsible; he knew it. She was making no attempt to conceal the fact. He wanted to say something to placate her; something that would make everything all right, but words failed him. He had a terrible sinking, nauseous feeling in his gut. Every time he thought of Kimberley his chest grew tight and heavy. It was common knowledge that someone had been trying to snatch children in the area, and Kimberley had been missing now for more than four hours. She was never allowed out alone as a rule and wasn't a robust child. The poor little kid hadn't the stamina to run any distance. Should she be pursued by someone with evil intent, she could never escape. He knew that. He wanted to be optimistic, but knew he must prepare himself for the worst.

But he mustn't cry. What sort of message would that send to Mary?

He had to be the strong one but was struggling to keep it together.

It was a complete nightmare.

*

Alessa felt useless. She was irked that DS Henderson, despite being her senior officer, was doing precious little to inspire the Painters with hope, whether there was any or not. She crouched beside Mary, placing a hand gently on the woman's shoulder.

"We're doing all we can, Mrs Painter. We've got officers out looking for Kimberley all over the local area, and . . ."

She paused, distracted momentarily by the photograph of a smiling, elfin-faced child given pride of place on the mantelpiece.

27

Her thoughts drifted suddenly to another little girl, also fair and petite. Kimberley Painter would probably be around two years younger. The realisation made her shudder. She checked herself and resumed:

"Forgive me. My mind was wandering there for a moment. D'you think . . .? Could I have a look in Kimberley's bedroom, please? I know it might sound strange but it's possible, if she *has* wandered off, even if you think it's unlikely, there could be something that might give us a hint where she's heading. Another friend's house, the park, a favourite shop, maybe?"

Mary nodded to her husband who shrugged slightly and headed for the door. Hesitantly, Alessa followed him up the stairs. The whole house was so immaculate, she was almost afraid to place a hand on the banister. Her shoes were quite clean, but she felt she ought to have removed them at the front door. The quest for seeking out dust and grime was one Mary clearly took very seriously. As if reading her mind, Malcolm looked back over his shoulder.

"The house has to be kept very clean – Kimberley's asthma, you know. Mary's worried sick in case anything sets it off. She spends hours every day damp-dusting and vacuuming." He fixed her with a look of sheer desperation. "Kimberley's welfare is the most important thing to her. To both of us."

The little girl's room was equally pristine. Decorated with pink rosebud wallpaper, not a thing was out of place: a child's white wooden wardrobe and chest of drawers; white-painted shelves full of neatly arranged story books, a glass-topped dressing table with ceramic Mickey and Minnie Mouse figurines and a small brush and comb; a little wooden rocking chair with a beautiful hand-painted china doll. Dainty framed miniatures of fairies in flight hung on the walls. The bed was made up, with an obviously much-loved teddy bear lying atop the pink floral duvet cover. No clues to anything here, except a very well-cared-for child.

A muffled, throaty cough could be heard from the other side of the wall.

"That's Bernard – the old chap next door," explained Malcolm. "We hear him now and again – not that he makes much noise."

He squeezed out a small smile, but his heart clearly wasn't in it. The anguish behind his eyes was painful to see.

Alessa nodded mutely. She looked around the room.

"Is there something of Kimberley's we could borrow, please? An item of clothing, say? It would be helpful for the dogs – you know, if they could pick up on her scent. Something she's worn recently would be best."

Malcolm's brow creased. Without a word, he went to the small wicker linen basket in the corner and pulled out a child's hand-knitted pink cardigan, lifting the garment to his face before thrusting it towards her.

"This do?" he enquired abruptly. "Mary's washed most of her stuff this morning – not that it needed it. Nothing stays grubby five minutes in this house."

Alessa indicated the basket. "D'you use that just for Kimberley's clothes – no one else's?"

Malcolm nodded miserably.

"Yes, that should be fine, then. Thank you." From her cross-body bag, Alessa produced a brown paper carrier, opened it up and held it out. Malcolm hesitated briefly, then dropped the cardigan inside. Alessa thought for a moment, her eyes settling on a small square picture stuck to the dressing table mirror. "Is that a recent photograph?"

Malcolm followed her gaze. He leaned over and peeled off

the picture, picking a piece of folded Sellotape from the back, and handed it over.

"It's a proof of her latest school photo. Take it – we've got a large one being framed. Just waiting to collect it from the shop."

He stared desolately at the image held between Alessa's fingers.

"You don't think something bad's happened to her, do you? It's just . . . you hear such awful stories, and this is so unlike her . . ." A lump moved visibly up and down in his throat.

Alessa felt wrong-footed by the man's directness. The quaver in his voice was heart-wrenching. She made a weak attempt at what she hoped was an encouraging smile.

"Kimberley's only been missing a short while, Mr Painter. There's every chance she'll turn up safe and well. Please don't distress yourself."

"I hope you're right, miss. It'd kill Mary, you know, if anything . . ." He trailed off. "I can't tell you how much she dotes on our Kimberley. She's her whole life. Mine too." The break in his voice suddenly gave way to a sob and he turned away, clapping a hand to his mouth.

Alessa stared at the cardigan and felt a pang. The tiny garment reminded her once more that this was a vulnerable little girl who was out there alone somewhere and quite possibly scared witless.

Or worse.

*

The officer in charge of proceedings was Detective Chief Inspector Bennett. When the call had come in to St Aldates earlier to say that Kimberley had gone missing, he'd instructed Alessa to accompany DS Henderson to the Painters' address, whilst he

30

himself went to question Kimberley's friend, Faye Greene, and her family. Officers had immediately been deployed in the area to search for the missing child, but with the imminent fall of darkness, their task would inevitably be hindered and time was of the essence.

Alessa was only too aware that Bennett had regarded her with disdain from day one. He rarely made eye contact and any time he'd had occasion to speak to her at the station, he'd been unsmiling and brusque, verging on rude.

"You'll need to keep an eye on that one," she'd overheard him telling Henderson under his breath, as they left the station. "Can't see her holding it together in a crisis."

She found her new boss loathsome. His attitude had put her back up from the outset. Alessa had joined the force straight from university, full of enthusiasm and with the best of intentions. She'd always worked hard, was never less than conscientious, but once she'd joined B's team it soon became apparent that she would never get the recognition she deserved. The ethos within the department was generally lazy, not to mention chauvinistic, and Alessa was quick to realise that the tone was definitely set by the slap-dash, but moreover self-serving, attitude of the man at the helm. Bennett was all about statistics – making sure everything looked good on the surface and maintaining his reputation for closing cases quickly, even if it meant sweeping things under the carpet; or at least that was how it seemed to Alessa. Things needed to change for the better and she was determined to maintain her own high standards, whether or not her colleagues followed suit. At the moment, she still felt very much like an interloper.

After obtaining the Greenes' version of events, DCI Bennett had appeared at the Painters' front door around an hour or so after the other officers, looking as if he meant business. In his mid-forties, of average height and build, with thinning dark hair, his aquiline features were etched with a permanently sour, cynical expression. He sported a well-worn, crumpled 1970s pale blue polyester suit, and his cheap aftershave did little to mask the lingering smell of the moth balls used to preserve the time warp his wardrobe represented.

At once, the hitherto inert Sergeant Henderson stood bolt upright, nodding deferentially as his superior entered the room. It was the most animated he'd been since his arrival. From Malcolm's stony expression, it was evident to Alessa that he'd taken an instant dislike to both of her colleagues.

"Mr Painter, are you *quite* sure that all was well with Kimberley at home?"

Bennett screwed up his eyes when addressing Malcom. He'd seemed hostile from the minute he walked through the door. Painter stiffened at once, folding his arms defensively across his chest. At above six feet, he stood at least four inches taller than Bennett and the DCI appeared to be trying to maximise his own height by lifting his chin and pushing out his chest.

"That she wasn't in any trouble?" Bennett continued, his tone infuriatingly sing-song and patronising. "Or could there have been some other reason she wouldn't have wanted to come back here? Has it occurred to you that she might have run away?"

One by one, he began to pick up and replace the ornaments from the mantelpiece, frowning as he examined them, as though they might miraculously throw up some useful clue. His eyes lingered on the smiling image of Kimberley, captured on a family holiday, with sunlight in her wispy golden hair and an impish grin, about to devour an enormous ice-cream. He emitted a small, forced cough.

"Well, Mr Painter?"

"Listen, mate," – Alessa could see that Malcolm's hackles were rising – "we've already told the young lady here that there was nothing wrong at home." He spoke through gritted teeth. "Kimberley had been round at her pal's, they had a falling-out for some reason, and she left. I went to pick her up, but she wasn't there. That's exactly how it happened."

Bennett gave a half-smile, his eyes narrowing. "Well, Mr Painter, according to the Greenes, Kimberley wasn't entirely happy at home." Bennett's tongue explored the inside of his cheek as he studied Malcolm.

"*What?*" Malcolm's pupils grew large, his mouth falling open.

"Apparently, she told their daughter, Faye, that you and her mother made her life a misery. That you wouldn't let her do anything, or go anywhere, and kept her locked up like a prisoner. Is this true?"

"That's complete *bollocks!*"

The rage that Malcom had so far managed to suppress came spilling out. He was leaning towards Bennett now, his hands balled into fists at his sides, knuckles white. Alessa was startled, and for a moment she thought he was actually going to hit her boss.

"*For God's sake!*" Malcolm was getting even louder. "You've only got to look at them – the way they're dragging that girl up – what the hell would *they* know about anything? Leaving the kid to fend for herself most of the time . . . They're a bloody disgrace!"

Mary began to weep quietly, burying her face in her hands.

"Malc, *please*," she sobbed. "This isn't helping."

Bennett drew himself to his full height, squaring up to the irate Malcolm. He spoke in a low voice, but the slight quaver betrayed a hint of fear.

"Mr Painter, I don't believe it's Mr and Mrs Greene's parenting skills that are in question here, and if you have such a low opinion of them, why on earth would you allow your daughter to spend time in their home?"

Malcolm's eyes grew wide, his face reddening. "How *dare* you! The way you're carrying on, anyone'd think *we'd* done something to Kimberley."

Alessa rose to her feet, trying to maintain a calm façade. Whether he was her DCI or not, she couldn't stand by and listen to this any longer.

"Sir, Mr and Mrs Painter have had a terrible shock. Their daughter's missing, and I don't think—" She stopped mid-sentence, realising from his expression that she had crossed a line.

Bennett turned to her, his jaw muscles twitching. "You don't think *what*, WPC Cano?" he hissed. "What pearls of infinite wisdom were you about to impart, with your wealth of knowledge and decades of experience in such matters?"

Alessa felt heat rush to her cheeks, quickly regretting her outburst. "I don't have— What I meant was—" she faltered.

Bennett's mouth twisted into a smirk. "No, you don't, do you. I think you should quit while you're ahead. Leave the tricky stuff to the big boys, there's a love." He rolled his eyes in an exaggerated gesture of irritation, turning to the now grinning DS Henderson, who appeared to be positively basking in this rebuke, since he was usually the one on the receiving end of Bennett's put-downs.

"Yes, sir. Sorry, sir." His words had felt like a very public slap in the face. Berating herself for letting the idiot get to her, she cast her dark eyes downwards, afraid he might see that they'd filled with angry tears.

*

Malcolm was incensed by Bennett's arrogance and disgusted with the condescending way in which he'd spoken to the young WPC, who may have been a touch wet behind the ears but clearly had more about her than the moronic inspector and his uncharismatic bagman put together. He turned to the policeman, trying to keep his tone measured now and regaining some outward composure.

"Right. If you've nothing useful to tell us, I think you'd better leave."

"I beg your pardon?"

"You heard. Mary and I haven't done anything wrong and you're talking as if we're under suspicion. You're upsetting my wife and I don't care for your attitude."

Full of indignation, Bennett opened his mouth to speak, but Malcolm was already holding open the door. The sniffling Sergeant Henderson had sidled off into the hallway and seemed to need no further persuasion as he hurried out into the cool night air. Alessa gave Mary's hand a reassuring squeeze and promised her that they'd be back in touch as soon as there was any news. Clutching the photograph and the bag containing Kimberley's cardigan, she followed her colleague out to their vehicle.

Bennett hung back, affronted by this untimely expulsion from the Painters' home. He wasn't accustomed to being spoken to in such a manner.

Malcolm gestured wildly. "Go on. You heard me. *Piss off!*"

"I'll let that go, just this once. You're obviously overwrought." Bennett was on the back foot as he addressed the wild-eyed, puce-cheeked Malcolm. "We'll be back to see you again soon. In the meantime, I suggest you calm down and think long and hard if there's anything you've omitted from your statement. It's not . . ."

The ensuing response was the front door being slammed in his face. Malcom had no desire to listen to the inspector's whining voice any longer. He'd had quite enough of coppers for one evening.

*

Deep into the night, Malcolm paced the living room floor, desperate for news of his daughter. He had lain awake, tossing and turning, watching the staccato movement of the bedside clock's luminous minute hand as it ate up the hours. Excruciatingly long hours during which Kimberley was being kept from them. He felt exhausted but his mind was whirring.

He went into the kitchen and rifled through the drawer for a cigarette. He lit it from the stove and went out into the garden, drawing in the smoke as if his life depended on it, then blowing it skyward. He'd always kept a packet, even though he'd given up when Kimberley was a baby. It had been a sacrifice he'd made willingly. Since her arrival, their whole life had revolved around their daughter and her needs. He was her father and he should have kept her safe.

He looked over the fence into Bernard's garden. His neighbour's curtains were closed, but the living room light was still burning. He wondered if the police had called on the old man to question him. Ruefully, he remembered their conversation about Kimberley's friend, Faye. How Malcolm wished now that he'd heeded Bernard's warning.

The night air was chill, but Malcolm was oblivious to the cold. He was numb. He felt beyond helpless. The police were out looking for Kimberley, but he had little faith that they were doing all they could with someone like Bennett in charge. Malcom felt he should be out looking for her himself, but *where*? Where to even start? It would be like looking for a needle in a haystack.

Someone must have taken her. That bleeder who was plastered all over the news . . . He felt suddenly queasy, and stubbed out his cigarette on the wall, dropping the dog end into the dustbin.

Please God, let her be all right.

He couldn't bring himself to contemplate the unthinkable. But he was only too aware that the longer she was missing, the more the chances of her being found alive and well were fading. And what of Mary? What was all this going to do to her? A locum doctor had called to give her a sedative at his request. There had been no pacifying her and her anguished cries had been more than he could bear.

And it was *his* fault. All his own stupid, bloody fault. If only he could rewind the clock.

Chapter 3

Tuesday, 12 June 1990

Seventy-two hours had passed and with it no clue as to Kimberley Painter's whereabouts. That morning, DCI Bennett had organised a press conference, which had seemed, as far as Alessa could tell, more about blowing his own trumpet than anything else. There was a constant stream of hot air coming from his mouth and he personally didn't appear to be doing anything constructive towards finding the little girl. There had as yet been no useful information coming in, and the odd phone call from people living in the area had been fruitless.

It had just turned 9.30pm. Another futile round of trudging door-to-door behind them, Alessa and DS Henderson had returned wearily to the station. Alessa had, as usual, been left to do most of the talking. She was finding it increasingly frustrating that the man was supposed to be a higher ranking officer, yet was happy to hang back and let her do all the work. She might as well have gone out on her own.

The office was quiet, with only a couple of weary-looking PCs sitting side by side at their desks beneath the window on the left, discussing something in low voices. They glanced across briefly as Alessa and Henderson walked through the double doors, then resumed their conversation. Alessa could see DCI Bennett at the far end of the room, through the glass wall of his office. He looked up from his desk and, seeing her, his face crumpled into a scowl. Alessa's heart sank. She knew he'd been waiting for their return, impatient for some news that meant the case was approaching being wrapped up in one way or another. She wondered if she was being uncharitable, but had begun to suspect he was less worried about finding Kimberley alive and more concerned with his own reputation. The man was still full of his first encounter with the Painters and she knew he was desperate for something that would point to Malcolm Painter's involvement.

"Erm, I'm just getting a drink," muttered Henderson. "You carry on." He turned briskly and went back out into the corridor.

Still clutching a notepad and pen, Bennett emerged from his office, raising his eyebrows questioningly.

"Anything?"

Alessa shook her head.

"Afraid not, sir. But we'll keep plugging away. I'm sure—"

Bennett shook his head in evident disgust. His gaze travelled to the image of the smiling child, blown up from the tiny proof to A4 size, now pinned to the incident room's notice board. His eyes narrowed. *"I've seen too many children snatched from the street by some pervert or killed at the hands of those they trust most, the latter being more often the case."* Alessa had heard his spiel several times now. The DCI was evidently cynical and suspicious of almost everyone he encountered.

"Well, you know what I think. My money's on the father."

He stared down at the lined page he'd been scribbling on, brow creased, flicking his biro absent-mindedly against the notepad. His tongue probed between his teeth, creating a bulge in his cheek, a habit which hadn't gone unnoticed by the other officers in his department, some of whom had irreverently (and privately) dubbed him "Blow-Job Bennett".

Alessa gritted her teeth and made no comment. She took off her cap and made her way to the small desk allocated to her in the corner, then logged on to her computer to revisit a file she'd picked up on that morning, praying it might give them some sort of lead.

DS Henderson reappeared, clutching two plastic cups containing murky-looking coffee. He slopped one down on the table next to the DCI. Bennett looked down and then back at him in some irritation.

"White, two sugars, sir, just how you like it." The hapless sergeant smiled amenably.

Bennett sipped the liquid and winced theatrically as it burned his mouth. "*Jesus Christ!* You bloody idiot! You could have warned me it was so flaming hot."

Henderson blushed, glancing sideways at Alessa to see if she was paying attention. She pretended to be engrossed in something on her computer screen. Though she wasn't a fan of Henderson, she understood the humiliation that came from a dressing-down in front of another officer, especially a junior one.

"Do you have any thoughts on the matter? *Well?*"

"About the coffee?" The man looked perplexed.

"No, you *pillock*. About the missing girl's father. Shifty as hell, if you ask me."

"Oh, right." Henderson considered for a moment. What few cogs he had in his brain were clearly turning. "Yeah. Yeah, I bet you're right, sir. The bloke wanted rid of us, that's for sure."

"Hmm, something odd's gone on there. I'd put money on it."

Alessa had to bite her tongue. She kept her head down, feigning disinterest in their conversation. What she really wanted to say would have probably cost her her job – or at least meant a disciplinary. They were imbeciles, the pair of them. How they'd ever attained their ranks was beyond her. Bennett was inept and Henderson was no more than a yes-man. The only conclusion she could draw was that they must have friends in high places. Freemasons, probably. It was well known that there was a culture of mutual back-scratching in the force in some areas. Alessa was incensed by the ethical questionability of it all.

She didn't believe for one moment that Malcolm Painter had had anything to do with his daughter's disappearance. She suspected that, as usual, Bennett was simply eager to draw a line under the case as soon as possible, regardless of whether it had actually been solved. His attitude was quite bizarre. Rereading the reports of the recent attempted abductions of children in the town, she'd grown more concerned than ever that Kimberley Painter had become the first true victim of the "Oxford Snatcher", as the man was being referred to in their office. From the picture that had emerged, it seemed to her that Kimberley was a fragile, sickly child, not worldly in the slightest. She'd have made an ideal target. It turned her stomach to think that, at that very moment, the little girl could be enduring a terrible ordeal at the hands of some twisted bastard.

Alessa took a deep breath. She needed to share this. She'd been scrolling back through the file she'd located earlier and the information – plus the mugshot in the accompanying paper file she'd dug out – looked promising.

"Sir? I've just been going through the information about our would-be kidnapper again. From the description given by two of the children he tried to grab, he sounds remarkably like a man called Jerome Wilde. He's got previous – a spell in HMP Bullingdon for child abduction, and a pretty nasty sexual assault on an eleven-year-old girl, back in '86. He was only released a few weeks ago. It ties in with when these kidnap attempts were first reported."

Bennett nodded, looking thoughtful. "I remember the Wilde case, now you come to mention it. Right piece of work, he was. No harm in bringing him in, I suppose." He glanced sideways at Alessa, his eyes narrowing. "You've got an address, I take it?" His tone was sharp.

"Yes, sir. The man's living in a bedsit, just off the Cowley Road. He's only served half an eight-year stretch. The balance of his sentence is under the licence of the probation service. He's supposed to check in with his allocated officer on a weekly basis."

Bennett peered at his watch. It had just turned quarter to ten. He blew out his cheeks, looking slightly pained. "I suppose we ought to pay our Mr Wilde a visit, then. No time like the present – and nothing like the element of surprise, eh, Sergeant?"

He turned to Henderson, who seemed to shrink a little. "I did tell the wife I'd be back at a reasonable time this evening, sir, and it's already . . ." He trailed off, his cheeks tinting red.

The look of disgust Bennett fired at his sergeant warranted the man having emitted a noxious odour. A confirmed bachelor, it was well known that Bennett had neither patience nor empathy when his officers let their home life impinge on their commitment to him.

"Well, far be it from me to interfere with your domestic arrangements." His lip curled into a snarl. "You run home to wifey, then. I'm sure WPC Cano and I can manage on this occasion."

"Well, I s'pose I could—"

Bennett raised a hand and halted him mid-sentence. "No, I insist. Never let it be said I'm not a reasonable man. As you know, I'm all for promoting the fairer sex in our job. Give the young ladies a chance to prove their mettle, that's what I say."

He smiled joylessly at Alessa. She averted her eyes and clenched her teeth.

"Looks like it's just you and me, then." He tossed her the car keys. "What are you waiting for? Let's go."

*

They crossed Magdalen Bridge and headed off the roundabout towards the Cowley Road. It was buzzing with activity, the usual Saturday-night clusters of rowdy, drunken youths spilling out onto the streets. A short distance from the city centre, the area's clientele seemed to comprise more locals than those frequenting the bars nearer the colleges.

"Town, not gown," Bennett remarked, peering through the car window scornfully. "Pfft." He rolled his eyes, leaning back in his seat.

The pavements shone with rain, reflecting the street lighting and rainbow of neon signs above the multitude of eateries and pubs. The nightlife gradually petered out as they approached the more residential part of the district, passing St Mary and St John Church on their right. Turning into Newcombe Terrace, the road was dingy and deserted. Alessa crawled along in second gear as Bennett craned his neck to look for number 78.

"There you go. Pull in anywhere along here, on the left." He waved a hand imperiously.

The house was in darkness, except for a single upstairs window, through which a dim bare bulb could be seen dangling.

The property was divided into five bedsits. Each address had a separate doorbell, the illegible, rain-blurred names diffusing into their respective plastic holders, which were fitted to a plaque on the wall. Alessa took pot luck, pressing the uppermost bell, then stepped back. Someone peered down from the illuminated window above, then quickly withdrew from sight as she looked up. The hall light was switched on and an elderly man wrapped in a tatty dressing-gown shuffled to the front door. He squinted at them from behind thick-lensed spectacles, looking less than pleased.

"Whaddya want? I was just off to bed."

"We're police officers." Bennett flashed his ID badge irritably. "I'm Detective Chief Inspector Bennett. I believe there's a Jerome Wilde living at this address?"

"Oh, 'im. 'E's upstairs. Number 4." He indicated with an upward rolling of his rheumy eyes. "Wha's 'e done now?"

"That's not for you to worry about, Mr . . .?"

"Sedgwick. 'Arold Sedgwick."

"Well, Mr Sedgwick, we'll carry on up and have a word with Mr Wilde, if that's all right with you. You get yourself to bed. Unless you've anything you want to tell us?"

The old man shook his head, grunted, and shuffled back to the door through which he had appeared, slamming it shut behind him.

Bennett and Alessa climbed the dusty wooden stairs. Every step creaked under their weight. The building had seen better days and was desperately in need of renovation and redecoration. The caustic odour of urine hung in the air, as though tenants thought nothing of relieving themselves before even arriving in their rooms. Alessa found herself shielding her nose with her sleeve.

Bennett rapped loudly on the door marked crudely in chalk with the number four, and waited. There was no response.

"Jerome Wilde? Police. We'd like a word."

The door remained closed. The occupant called from the other side, "Fuck off. I ain't done nothin'. Why can't you wankers leave me alone?"

"Just open the door. We've a few questions we need to ask you."

There was no response. Alessa could see from Bennett's pinched expression that his patience was wearing thin.

He massaged his temples with his fingertips then inhaled, stepping forwards to knock again with the side of his fist, more loudly this time. The door marked number 5 was flung open and a scrawny young woman glowered at them.

"D'you mind? I've got a baby in here. It's taken me two bleedin' hours to settle her down, and you're going to wake her up again with that racket."

Alessa apologised. The woman retreated, muttering to herself.

"Open the bloody door, Wilde. Now. I don't want to have to kick it in or you'll be the one paying for the repair. You don't want that, do you?"

A key turned in the lock and an obviously inebriated Wilde peered round the door. "I told you, I ain't done nothin'."

Bennett pushed past him and Alessa followed. The room reeked: a blend of stale cigarette smoke, beer, damp, and urine. It was a repugnant combination. As on the landing, the floorboards were bare, with only a small, stained rug in front of an old-fashioned two-bar electric fire. A narrow single bed was pushed up against one mould-ridden wall and a moth-eaten armchair stood in the opposite corner. It was a hovel; there was no other word for it. Alessa's eyes took in every detail of the space and the odious Wilde, remembering the shocking information she'd read in his file. She couldn't help but feel it was no more than he deserved.

Bennett's eyes scanned the room with distaste. "We want to ask you some questions regarding your whereabouts on Saturday afternoon."

Wilde feigned innocence, spreading his filthy palms before him. "I was 'ere all day. You ask old Sedgwick, 'e'll tell you."

Wilde had gradually inched his way towards the bed and was surreptitiously trying to push something underneath it with his foot.

"What have you got there, then?"

Bennett shoved the man aside and, sliding his own foot beneath the divan base, revealed a porn magazine. The girl in a compromisingly explicit position gracing the cover was heavily made up but looked no more than twelve or thirteen at the most.

Alessa looked at Jerome Wilde and shuddered. Mercifully she'd had few dealings with sex offenders in her short career, but found those she *had* come across seedy and abhorrent. It was the thought of what they were all about – and what was evidently uppermost in their minds. While she knew that paedophiles came in all guises, Wilde seemed to fit what she considered an almost exactly stereotypical image: unshaven, malodorous, skinny, and with straggly, combed-back grey hair which sat on dandruff-peppered shoulders. His long fingernails were encrusted with grime and curled over at the ends. Each time he opened his mouth, it revealed a set of stained, crooked teeth. The man was repulsive.

"Never mind what else we've come about. You're nicked, you scumbag."

"What for? I ain't even done nothin'."

46

"You're in possession of pornographic literature depicting underage girls. That's quite enough for starters."

Before Wilde could protest further, Bennett yanked the man's right arm upwards behind his back and produced a set of handcuffs from his jacket pocket. Unsure what to do, Alessa looked on as he pushed Wilde out onto the landing and manhandled him down the stairs, delivering a swift but vicious kick to the back of the man's legs as he did so. Ordinarily she might have objected, but Wilde deserved no sympathy. The thought that little Kimberley Painter could have been preyed upon by him – or one of his kind – sickened her.

And the thought that there were many like-minded fiends out there, responsible for the abduction and even murder of so many other innocent victims, made her fear for the safety of children everywhere.

*

Alessa felt exhausted. That night before bed, she sat at her dressing table to brush her hair, mulling over the day's events. She stared absently at the ephemera she'd accumulated over the years. The Pinocchio puppet, sent by her Italian godparents for her seventh birthday, still dangled from the wall above the mirror by its strings. A faded castanet-wielding flamenco doll, brought back by Uncle Rob from a trip to Majorca, stood at the back of the glass-topped surface behind the other paraphernalia.

She was nearly in her mid-twenties, but because she still lived at home, was conscious things hadn't moved on much from her teens. The surface of the dressing table was littered with dried-up cleansing wipes and a flaking metal tube of Clearasil spot cream – she was thankfully long past that miserable stage; an ancient pot of strawberry lip gloss, the lid encrusted with shreds of tobacco from a brief dalliance with smoking; glitter eyeshadow – when was she ever going to wear *that* again? A faded photo snipped from *Smash Hits* magazine of Spandau Ballet still Blu-tacked to the mirror. She didn't even remember liking them that much. She really needed to have a clear-out.

Alessa stiffened. Something about the room felt different suddenly. Although Alessa couldn't put her finger on it, there was a tangible shift in the atmosphere, a discomfiting feeling that she was no longer alone. A ripple of movement from behind made her look up sharply. Alessa caught her breath as she saw what looked like the faint reflection of someone standing in front of the window, illuminated by the soft amber glow of lamplight passing into the room. Pulse racing, Alessa whipped round. A dim, amorphous mist, silent but shimmering like a swarm of translucent bees, hovered just above ground-level. She could make out no features but had the definite sense of being observed. Alessa squeezed her eyes tightly shut. When she opened them again, the haze had vanished. The only clue to anything untoward was the gentle rise and fall of the curtain, as though something – or someone – had passed through the window and melted into the night. And the room felt suddenly several degrees colder.

As though glued to the padded stool, Alessa sat rigidly, trying to collect her thoughts. She took deep breaths, and gradually her heart rate began to return to normal. But the possibility that there could have been some sort of unearthly presence in her own bedroom had unnerved her. She felt shaken. She'd lived in that house her whole life and nothing like this had ever happened before, despite rumours of a young pupil having fallen to her death into the stairwell in the early 1900s when their home had been a private girls' school. Greta had kept the story from her until she was an adult, fearing it might frighten her. But apart from the tragedy of it, the notion had never troubled Alessa – she wasn't really sure she believed in ghosts.

This was plain silly. She tried to rationalise. She was overwrought because her sleep pattern had been all over the place since beginning work on the Painter case. Maybe she was hallucinating because of sleep deprivation. Or maybe the apparition had been some sort of manifestation caused by everything that was going on at work.

Maybe she needed to go back to her therapist.

Chapter 4

Wednesday, 20 June 1990

Known as Milford Academy in a former incarnation, the Cano family home had been renamed Squitchey House in the late 1930s. Situated towards the top of the Woodstock Road and around two miles from the city centre, the building, despite its outward grandeur, had seen better days. And now a cloud of gloom seemed to have descended over its residents.

Alessa had become subdued and uncommunicative. She couldn't help it. She was trapped inside her own head; seeing things that clearly weren't there. And the vivid nightmares had begun again. The dark emotions they invoked had begun to plague Alessa day and night. In spite of everything, she'd become drawn to the battered cardboard box of memorabilia kept in the heavy oak chest at the foot of her bed. Old photographs, birthday cards, and something that, in spite of everything, she'd felt compelled to keep.

She felt conflicted. Although desperate for Kimberley to be

found, at the same time she was beginning to dread going into work, where no one talked of anything but the Painter case. There was no respite from it.

"Still no news of the little girl?"

Her mother's voice cut through her thoughts and Alessa looked up blankly.

Come Saturday, a whole fortnight would have passed. Though Alessa had deliberately said very little, it was impossible for her eagle-eyed mother not to have noticed the impact the investigation was having on her. Greta was studying her across the breakfast table, her brow creased with concern. Alessa's brown eyes were encircled by dark rings, and recent weight loss had carved hollows beneath her cheekbones, making her pretty heart-shaped face gaunt and angular. She looked careworn and not at all her usual bubbly self.

Gazing unseeingly at her bowl, Alessa absently stirred the sea of milk in which sodden cornflakes were now bobbing. The realisation that little Kimberley might never be seen alive again was going round and round her head. And the thought of what the ten-year-old's fate might have been was too horrible to contemplate.

"No. Nothing. It's as if she's vanished into thin air."

"That's terrible. Her poor parents."

Her poor parents, indeed. Alessa was frustrated and angered by Bennett's clumsy, insensitive handling of the case. Since Kimberley had gone missing, in tandem with the investigation into Jerome Wilde's movements, the DCI had already brought Malcolm Painter in for questioning – out of no more than sheer spite, as far as she could see. There was nothing to indicate that the poor man had had anything to do with his daughter's disappearance, yet for some inexplicable reason, Bennett seemed intent on pinning it on him. In the last few days, he'd even deployed officers to observe the Painters' home for signs of comings and goings. It seemed such a waste of resources when there was a child missing. She was powerless to oppose him, but the injustice and absurdity of it all was wearing her down.

Greta placed a steaming cup of tea before Alessa, who had pushed aside her cereal and was now flicking through the newspaper in a vain attempt to distract herself. Greta pulled up a seat next to her.

"And what of that awful man you arrested? They charge him with anything yet?" She leaned across and gently lifted a strand of her daughter's glossy, dark hair away from her troubled eyes.

Alessa looked up and smiled wearily. "Come on, Mamma. You know I'm not allowed to talk about it."

Her mother threw up her hands theatrically in response. "But it's only *me*. I'm the soul of discretion, you know that. My lips? Sealed." She mimed a zip crossing her mouth.

"Yes, but I'd be compromising my position if I discussed it with you in any depth. And it could jeopardise the investigation if you said something to anyone outside the house, without thinking." Alessa arched a knowing eyebrow.

Greta snorted. "Hmm. I get it. You don't trust me." She rose from the table, brusquely removing Alessa's cereal bowl and marching across to the sink, where she began to scrape the cornflakes noisily into the bin beneath then rolled up her sleeves, ready to wash up. Alessa sighed.

"Mamma. Don't be silly. It's just . . . I'm not supposed to discuss it with people outside work, that's all. And believe me, you really don't want to know about that . . . that disgusting little creep, anyway."

Alessa shuddered as she remembered her encounter with the odious Wilde. She glanced up at the clock and gasped. "Oh

God, I'm going to be late if I don't get a move on. And Bennett just loves to have something to whinge at me about."

Greta put down the scouring pad and turned to face her. "Hmm. He sounds like a nasty piece of work, that man. You want I get your Uncle Rob to have a word with someone about him?"

"*No*. Definitely not. He doesn't know who I am, and I'd rather it stay that way. I want to stand on my own two feet, not have people saying I'm taking advantage of my connections."

Her mother shrugged. "Okay, okay. Just thought I'd ask. I hate to think of some woman-hating little *idiota* making life miserable for you, that's all."

Greta and her younger brother Roberto had emigrated to the UK from Italy with their parents as children. Rob had worked his way up from waiting tables to owning several restaurants in the area, the most exclusive, Ristorante Roberto, being extremely popular and highly regarded by more well-heeled clientele from both the local area and further afield.

Alessa adored Uncle Rob. Ever since her father had callously walked out on them, returning to his native Spain when Joey was still a baby, her fiercely protective uncle had made sure that his older sister and her children wanted for nothing. Owing to Joey's health issues, much of Greta's time had been taken up with his care, which meant Alessa had often been left to her own devices. It was Uncle Rob who'd made sure she never felt excluded when she was young and who had taken her to the park and museums, fostering in her a love of history and culture. He managed to make everything educational but fun. Alessa especially loved the Pitt Rivers Natural History Museum, its glass cases filled with artefacts from all over the world that offered glimpses into the past. Her imagination had been captured by the dinosaur bones and mummified remains from Egypt, but most of all by the shrunken heads, which stopped her in her tracks every time. On one occasion, during the summer holidays when Alessa was about nine and old enough to understand, Uncle Rob had explained their origins.

"When we first came to Oxford, when I wasn't much older than you are now, our *papà* took us – me and your mamma – to the museum sometimes on a Saturday. He taught us it's important to understand the past, how people lived. How they did things and what they believed. To learn from their good ideas – and sometimes very bad mistakes." Uncle Rob had crouched beside the saucer-eyed Alessa, taking her hand in his own as she stared in horror and fascination at the tiny heads, which were no bigger than oranges. "These heads belonged to the Shuar and Achuar peoples from South America. They died in battle. They killed one another, each tribe believing they could get power from the other's souls, which they thought were inside the heads. And then, well, I won't go into it but it wasn't nice, how they made the heads small. That's something for another day." He pulled a face.

"So, they just killed each other because they thought it would make themselves powerful?" Alessa was appalled. She hated the idea that the heads displayed in the cases had belonged to real people with families and feelings, that they'd been subjected to violent deaths and then mutilated. It gave her a peculiar feeling in her stomach.

"Uh-huh. They believed if they rubbed the skin with charcoal, the soul couldn't see out, and they sewed up the lips so it couldn't escape, too. Pretty silly, eh? And this went on until not that long ago. I think it only stopped in the 1960s. Imagine that!" He shook his head. Alessa thought she saw tears in his eyes. "One day, a long way into the future, everyone living now will be in the past, and other children like you will want to know how *we* all lived. And hopefully they'll have learned that some things people got very wrong and aren't acceptable at all. Even things that are happening nowadays." Uncle Rob straightened, clearing his throat. "Come on. Enough now. Let's take a walk into town and get an ice-cream."

Alessa had been glad to get out into the fresh air. Soon the memory of the unfortunate little heads was behind them. The sun beat down as they wandered down the Banbury Road from the museum, turning right to eventually head past the Bodleian Library and up to the High, then meandering down St Aldates to Christ Church College. It felt to Alessa like they'd walked miles. An ice-cream van was parked a short distance inside the tall black gates. Uncle Rob bought two huge cornets with chocolate flakes and they sat down on the grass to eat them in the sunshine. The area was full of people, students and families with children alike, many with picnic blankets spread out on the lawns, others strolling past on the path between and disappearing through the trees towards Christ Church Meadow. The river was only a short distance away and Uncle Rob had promised they could have a boat ride later.

"This is the life, eh." Uncle Rob closed his eyes and tilted back his face, soaking up the warm rays. "We could almost be back in Italia."

"Do you miss it?" Alessa asked, licking the drips from her cone. Her mamma often talked of home, sighing wistfully when she spoke of the olive groves; the way the light caught the trees and buildings; the winding, cobbled streets and the deep, rhythmic toll of the church bells.

"I missed my friends when we first came. And my cousins. But we were very poor. That was why Mamma and Papà wanted to come to England. To make a better life for us." He turned to Alessa, smiling. "Oxford isn't so very different – when the weather's good. It's a beautiful place. And I have the best life now. I can afford to take holidays, and—"

He stopped mid-sentence. Alessa followed his gaze, noticing a young, handsome man with floppy, light brown hair and wearing an open-necked shirt, staring at them from the bench where he was sitting, beneath a tree near the path. He rose, folded his newspaper and approached them, his face widening into a grin.

"Rob! How the hell are you?"

Uncle Rob seemed to grow rigid. His smile faded. He sat up, pushing his hair from his blue eyes. "Stefan. I'm good. You?"

"Yeah, great. Erm . . . I was wondering why you hadn't been in the club lately? I've been looking out for you. You didn't leave me your number. Was it something I said?" He gave an odd, nervous-sounding laugh.

"I've been busy." Uncle Rob's voice was strained. "This is my niece, Alessandra." Alessa glanced up and noticed that Uncle Rob was fixing Stefan with a cold stare. There seemed to be some unspoken communication.

The young man puffed out his cheeks. "Ah. Well, better be off. Things to do, you know. Maybe see you around some time."

He turned and walked away. Alessa watched as, nearing the college entrance, he glanced back over his shoulder at them. Uncle Rob had his face turned in the other direction and it seemed deliberate. Alessa thought Stefan looked confused.

"Uncle Rob, who was that man?"

Uncle Rob sniffed. "That," he explained, "was someone I used to know. We aren't such good friends now." His closed expression invited no further questions. But Alessa felt a bit bad for Stefan. She wondered what must have happened for them to fall out. Uncle Rob was usually so friendly. It wasn't like him at all.

It was only years later that she understood about her uncle's sexuality. Greta had explained that he'd been very fond of Stefan but discovered that his new partner liked to play the field and hadn't made his intentions clear. Uncle Rob was looking for a proper relationship, she'd said. Not just a flash in the pan.

Even now, Uncle Rob was striking. His hair, though no longer dark, was still thick, his eyes wide and clear. He was tall and carried himself well, as though he was comfortable in his own skin. And his taste in clothes was impeccable, tailored and classic. Often when they were out, Alessa noticed him receiving lustful glances – from men and women of all ages. It made her smile. He'd had a string of partners over the years, but they always seemed to fizzle out for one reason or another. He seemed restless sometimes and she wished he could find someone to make him happy. To make his life complete.

*

A small flurry of crumbling plaster suddenly drifted to the floor in the corner of the room. Water had leaked through from the hot water cylinder upstairs some weeks earlier, creating an unsightly brown patch which both Greta and Alessa were doing their best to ignore. One more job to add to the ever-increasing list – and despite Alessa's pleas to allow Uncle Rob to help them out, Greta refused point blank. Sometimes her pride was exasperating.

Alessa gestured upwards, her eyes travelling anxiously to the ceiling. "I'm worried the whole lot's going to cave in one of these days. We really need to get it sorted, Mamma."

Greta shook her head and dried her hands, smiling wearily. "It's not so bad. It's drying out now. Look, I promise I'll ask Uncle Rob if it gets any worse. But let's wait a while, okay?"

Alessa's conscience pricked her as, in spite of her mother's ever-immaculate appearance, she realised how tired she'd started looking lately. Older, too. The house was too big for just the two of them, and there was so much to do to maintain it. But however much Alessa tried to persuade her, Greta wouldn't hear of selling, even though it would be the most sensible option. She was too attached to the old place. It held too many memories. It would break her heart if she had to leave, she'd said.

Alessa could understand. Since Joey had died two years earlier, even with all its flaws, it was as if the house had become a sort of comfort blanket for Greta, as if some part of Joey was woven into the very fabric of the building.' Alessa felt she ought to be at home more to keep her mamma company, but her job was important to her. Especially now.

Greta's voice cut through her thoughts. "Hey, you'd better get yourself to work. You don't want to keep your nasty boss waiting. But don't forget what I said – if you'd like me to have a word . . ."

Shaking her head adamantly, Alessa slipped on her jacket, planting a kiss on her mother's cheek and squeezing her hand. She felt torn in the knowledge that, now she didn't have Joey to care for, Greta would be rattling around in the house all day with nothing to do but clean and think about what to prepare for dinner.

Alessa missed Joey, too. So much. But now that he was gone, it was as if Greta had lost her main purpose in life. Alessa hated to think of her being lonely and miserable.

"No. I appreciate the offer, really I do. But I'd rather put one over on Bennett without any help – it'd be much sweeter that way. Got to go. *Ciao*."

*

Disappointingly, they had been unable to connect Jerome Wilde with Kimberley Painter's disappearance. Despite his insistence that he'd stayed at home all day, CCTV footage had shown Wilde entering a pub on the Cowley Road during the early afternoon of the day that the little girl had vanished. He had remained there until about 9.15pm, at which point he could be seen, clearly the worse for wear, staggering back to his car. He had driven back to his bedsit, unarguably well over the limit, but unquestionably alone.

But there was little doubt that, over recent weeks, he had made numerous attempts to lure young girls into his vehicle. The car, a battered red Vauxhall Chevette with a distinctive taped-on wing-mirror and broken number plate, had been clearly described by one of his would-be victims, along with a damning and uncannily accurate photo-fit picture. This, combined with his previous criminal record, would be sufficient to secure a conviction. A thorough forensic examination of the car had, however, thrown up no evidence of anything linking him to Kimberley. Wilde was indisputably a seedy, perverted individual, but it appeared that, with regard to their missing child case, he wasn't the man the police were looking for.

"Well, looks as though WPC Cano may just have come up trumps," Bennett announced somewhat begrudgingly to the small clutch of officers gathered in the office. There was a low rumble of congratulations and half-hearted applause. Alessa looked round to see DS Henderson muttering something behind a cupped hand to the weasel-like PC Morris, who looked pointedly in her direction and sniggered. Bennett cleared his throat and glowered at them.

"We can safely say the 'Oxford Snatcher' will be off the streets for the foreseeable. More brownie points for the department, so we can all give ourselves a pat on the back. Wilde's been charged and will remain on remand until the preliminary court hearing in a fortnight. But we're still no nearer to finding any sign of Kimberley Painter. And with time ticking by, I think it's pretty safe to assume when we do eventually find her, it's more than likely going to become a murder investigation."

He stood before the link chart on the bulletin board, probing his cheek with his tongue. The blown-up version of the little girl's school photograph stared out at them from its centre, around which headings had been bullet-pointed and arrows drawn to various bubbles of salient information.

"Kimberley was last seen here." He indicated a street map studded with numerous coloured drawing pins, showing the bus stop at the end of Faye Greene's road. "The Greene girl claims Kimberley left their house around five o'clock. Unfortunately, her parents appear to have been too pie-eyed to notice whether she was there or not." He rolled his eyes skyward.

"We did a thorough house-to-house in the area, but nobody remembers seeing a child out on their own that day. The weather was so bloody awful, anyone with any sense wouldn't have gone out anyway, unless they'd really had to. One bus driver thinks he remembers a girl fitting Kimberley's description getting *off* the bus here at around 4.45pm, which doesn't quite stack up. Although it's possible Faye could've been confused about the time, why would Kimberley have been getting *off* the bus in that location if she was heading home?" He drummed his fingers repeatedly on the chart as if hoping for divine inspiration.

"Where was the bus coming from, sir?"

Alessa looked round to see PC Shelley, a recent addition to the department, raising his hand. She'd heard through the grapevine that they were getting a new recruit. He was tall, with tousled dark hair, and had startlingly blue eyes, which landed suddenly on her. He gave Alessa a warm smile. She felt heat creeping up her cheeks and turned back sharply. She was sure she could feel his eyes on the back of her head and stiffened.

"Back from the Acacia Hill estate, apparently. If it's true, it doesn't bode well. But I'm beginning to think it may be a simple case of mistaken identity. From everything we've heard about Kimberley, I can't see her going anywhere on a bus on her own, let alone to such a dicey part of town. It's in the news almost daily for something or other. Anyway—"

"Maybe we should launch a TV appeal for witnesses to come forward, sir? Or to track down the girl on the bus, if it wasn't Kimberley – just to rule her out?" PC Shelley was apparently keen to get himself noticed. He smiled at Alessa again, winking one eye slightly. *Winking*? Eugh. Cheesy. She dropped her gaze.

"What's your speciality, sonny? Stating the bleeding obvious?" Bennett looked scathingly at the young officer, who appeared unperturbed. "Before I was so rudely interrupted, I was about to say we've got another press conference lined up this afternoon. We're not involving the parents at this stage – the mother's in a bit of a state and unlikely to be coherent. And Painter's being decidedly uncooperative. However, we *will* be issuing a statement on their behalf. The regional news people will be there filming for this evening's bulletin. It's scheduled to broadcast nationally tomorrow. Obviously, the more help we can get from the general public, the better. In the meantime, we're still keeping the house in Lime Tree Avenue under surveillance. I want Painter questioned again; keep the pressure up, see if there's anything he or his wife have neglected to mention. I've a feeling we'll trip him up, sooner or later. Softly, softly, though, eh?"

He looked pointedly at Alessa.

"Perhaps you'd like to take our new boy here along with you. I'm going to be busy preparing my own statement for later." He adjusted his tie, smiling conceitedly to himself. "But see to it you're both back here for the press conference at one-thirty. We want the full complement present. It's important they see we're not holding back on manpower. We want the public to think – to *know* – we're doing our job properly."

Think was definitely the more appropriate word. Bennett's chaotic handling of everything left a lot to be desired.

The group of assembled officers gradually dispersed as Bennett drew the meeting to a close. Alessa groaned inwardly. Bennett was, as ever, insufferably full of his own self-importance. And now she was going to be saddled with this keen newbie who appeared to be trying to flirt with her. She rose from her chair but PC Shelley was at her side before she could approach him.

"Jason Shelley. Pleased to meet you properly at last." He extended a hand and Alessa shook it somewhat warily. "I know who you are, WPC Cano. Your reputation precedes you."

She couldn't help but smile at his apparent enthusiasm. "Alessa," she countered. "Pleased to meet you, too. Didn't realise I had a reputation, though – you've got me worried now."

Jason's generous mouth curved into a grin. There was a brief beat of silence as they appraised one another. Alessa found herself mesmerised by his eyes. His lips were full, his teeth white and even.

Oh God, what was she *thinking*?

"Are you new to the job?" Alessa asked eventually, averting her gaze to place her cap on the table beside her. She twirled it round pointlessly.

He shook his head. "Transferred from the Met. I've been in the force six years now. I'm from Headington, originally. My mum's ill, so I wanted to be a bit closer to home."

"I'm sorry to hear that. About your mum, I mean."

"Thanks." Jason paused. "She's got a pretty nasty form of rheumatoid arthritis. Hit her quite young." He pulled a face. "She's wheelchair-bound and very up and down, mood wise, as well as physically. It was in remission for a while, but she's gone downhill this last couple of months. My sister emigrated to Canada ten years ago, and Dad's not coping too well, so . . . well, you know." He shrugged slightly. "I know London's not that far, but it was difficult to come home every day. So I traded offices and moved back in with them last week." He smiled resignedly but his eyes had clouded.

Alessa felt a stab of empathy. She nodded. "Sounds tough. Not the same, I know, but my younger brother had a severe brain injury and it was really hard on my mum, caring for him round the clock. My dad left us years ago. I always tried to help out as much as I could, but I still used to worry she'd work herself into the ground. He passed away though. Almost two years ago now . . ." She swallowed down a lump as she remembered her mother's face earlier. The empty feeling as she closed the front door behind her.

"I'm so sorry. That must've been awful – for both of you." Jason paused. "So . . . you still at home, too, then?"

"Yep. Can't see myself moving out anytime soon, either. Even if I could afford it, I couldn't even think of leaving my mum all on her own now." She hoped the desperation wasn't evident in her voice. Clearing her throat, she picked up her cap. "Right then, we'd better make tracks. I'll fill you in on the way, but sounds as if you're pretty much up to speed with everything anyway. I take it you've been following the case?"

Jason nodded solemnly. "I'm afraid the guv'nor, even if he is a bit of a plank, may be right. You know, about it being a murder. I can't see the poor little kid turning up alive now, can you?"

Alessa hesitated. Whatever her gut feeling, she didn't want to appear negative and certainly didn't want to dash any hopes the Painters may still have.

"Stranger things have happened. I reckon we should keep an open mind at this stage. Anyway, come on." She dipped into her pocket and tossed him a bunch of keys. "You can drive."

*

It was past 11am, the sun bright and the sky clear, but the drapes were closed as they pulled up outside the house in Lime Tree Avenue. Alessa noticed an elderly man in the adjoining property peeling aside the net curtain to peer through his living room window as they walked up the path. He smiled tightly and disappeared.

Malcolm Painter looked exhausted and unkempt as he opened the door. He bristled immediately, filling up the space as he glared past Alessa and Jason at the patrol car parked outside. It was clear they weren't going to be invited in.

"What d'you want now? I've had a bellyful of your lot."

Alessa fired a grimace at Jason, who raised his eyebrows, nodding to spur her on. She drew herself upright.

"I'm really sorry, Mr Painter. I know you've been having a tough time. We're not here to interrogate you. We're just trying to do our job – and the more information we can gather, the better our chances of finding Kimberley."

Malcolm's shoulders slumped. He let out a long breath. Stepping aside resignedly, he ushered them into the living room, explaining gruffly that his wife was unwell and still in bed.

"Mary's taking this all very badly, as you can imagine. She's been given tranquilisers. You still have no news for us, I take it?"

"I'm afraid not, Mr Painter. Erm . . . this is PC Shelley. He's just joined our team."

Malcolm nodded vacantly, barely acknowledging Jason's presence.

"What are your lot actually doing? It's been nearly a fortnight. Your boss is a complete knucklehead. How the hell can he think I'd have had anything to do with my own child vanishing like that? It's ludicrous. I can't sleep for the worry; can't eat. And poor Mary's going out of her mind."

He crossed the room to open the curtains, then stared helplessly through the window. His face looked almost grey.

Alessa shot a look at Jason. He remained silent, clearly observing Malcom, his eyes scanning the room. She wondered if he just wanted to be sure there was nothing in what she believed to be Bennett's ill-founded suspicions.

"I'm really sorry. We're doing everything we can. The whole team's been out knocking on doors and appealing for witnesses. Please don't take it personally – it's just that DCI Bennett's trying to cover all possibilities."

"Take it *personally*?" Malcolm's voice raised an octave. "I should think I'm taking it *very* personally. How d'you expect me to feel, being treated like a suspect when my daughter's missing? The man needs his bloody head looking at."

She couldn't have agreed more, but daren't admit as much. Bennett was just waiting for her to slip up, and if anything negative she'd said about him or his investigation got back to him, he'd make her life hell; she was sure of it.

Jason cleared his throat. "Mr Painter, we've had officers with dogs combing the whole area for evidence. There's going to be another press conference this afternoon and they'll be giving an update on the evening news later, too. We're trying to establish whether the child seen by the bus driver *was* Kimberley or just someone who looked similar, so we can eliminate her from our inquiries."

"But it makes no *sense*. Kimberley's never been on a bus on her own. Even if she did catch one for whatever reason, what the hell would she be doing getting off by Faye's house? It doesn't stack up." Malcolm sank onto the sofa, burying his face in both hands.

Jason persisted, firing a glance at Alessa. "Look, if she definitely wasn't heading in the direction of home, we need to explore the possibility that Kimberley could've run away. Is there anyone – family, friends – that she might have been trying to reach?"

"No!" Malcolm raised his head, his eyes flaring. "For Christ's sake, man, I've told your lot all this already. I don't believe for one minute my daughter's done a bunk. There's nothing more I – we – can tell you. If you need to question anyone, surely it's the Greenes. They were the last people to see her, as far as we know. How d'you know *they* haven't got something to hide?"

Alessa felt uncomfortable. She took a step forwards, placing a hand gently on Malcolm's tense shoulder. "No one's accusing you of hiding anything. But it's just— We've got so little to go on at the moment. Any piece of information, however irrelevant it might seem, could be useful."

He let out a sigh, dropping his head. "Look, speak to young Faye Greene. No one got to the bottom of why she and Kimberley fell out. Maybe if you pile on the pressure, you'll get some answers from her. I reckon she knows more than she's letting on."

"We'll speak to Faye again, yes. But we need to tread carefully. After all, she's just a child."

Malcolm lifted his face towards her, incredulous. "You have *met* the girl, haven't you? You must've formed an impression of her. I should've listened to my gut instinct – and Mary's. Stopped our Kimberley seeing her. Oh, she may only be a kid, but she's worldly, that one – and bloody wily with it, make no mistake. What you lot always seem to overlook is that children grow into adults – and they're just as capable of anything. I've got a nose for these things. And I'd bet my bottom dollar she's not telling the truth."

*

Alessa followed Jason from the house, Malcolm's parting words echoing in her ears. Was Faye Greene withholding information? As she turned to close the gate, Alessa's eyes were drawn to the window above. A silhouette hovered in the gap between the half-opened curtains, apparently watching them leave. Sunlight reflected on the glass, making it difficult to discern the person's identity.

Assuming Mary must have finally got up, she raised a hand to wave. But the gesture was not returned and the figure quickly receded from view.

And despite the increasing warmth of the day, Alessa felt suddenly, inexplicably cold.

Chapter 5

Saturday, 19 May 1990

From her bedroom window, Kimberley Painter stared down at the group of dishevelled, laughing children playing kerby as they ran in and out of the parked cars along Lime Tree Avenue. To anyone looking up, they'd have seen a solitary, hollow-eyed little figure, forehead pressed up against the glass, gazing longingly out at the world like Rapunzel imprisoned in her tower. It was a pitiful sight.

What had been a gloriously sunny day had given way to a pleasantly warm, balmy evening. But another asthma attack that afternoon – only a mild one, but enough to send her mother into a flat spin as always – meant she'd been confined to the house again, and Kimberley resented it bitterly. She breathed onto the window pane and drew a down-in-the-mouth stickman in the steamed-up patch, then quickly rubbed it away with the sleeve of her cardigan. Her mother would be cross if she made a mess of the recently polished glass.

"I'm all right now, Mum, really I am," she'd insisted earlier, hovering in the kitchen doorway as her mother stood pressing shirts. "Didn't the doctor say it was good for me to be out in the fresh air?"

Mary sighed. She rested the iron on its board and crossed the kitchen to slip an arm around Kimberley's slender shoulders. "Listen, love, me and your dad aren't trying to be mean. It's . . . well, you'd be out there, tearing around – and it's no good saying otherwise—" She raised a hand firmly as Kimberley opened her mouth to protest. "You know you wouldn't be able to just watch, with your pals all dashing about like lunatics. You've had a nasty turn and you could easily get another one."

"But—"

"No buts, young lady. You know as well as I do that it's risky. We don't want you being carted off in an ambulance, do we? Have a bit of a rest this afternoon. With any luck you'll be okay to join in with your friends by tomorrow."

The irony in her mother's words wasn't lost on Kimberley. She *had* no real friends, apart from Faye. There was little danger of her being invited to join the others even if she *were* allowed to go outside. It would have been enough to just sit and watch them, though, listening to their chatter, even from a distance, rather than being cooped up in her room again.

One more seemingly endless afternoon had eventually given way to evening and the hours were dragging painfully. Kimberley's ill-health was a source of constant anxiety to her parents, but she was beginning to feel stifled by their over-protectiveness. Her bond with Faye Greene was the one bright spot in Kimberley's existence. When Faye had been moved into Kimberley's class in Year 4 and assigned a seat next to her, she had given her new friend the nickname "Peanuts" because of her initials – KP. Kimberley's parents found it an irritation, but for Kimberley it was a sign of acceptance; affection, even. She looked up to Faye – she was just so *cool*. Good at sports, not afraid to backchat the teachers, and always wearing the latest fashions. She was at once popular and slightly feared by a lot of the other kids, and Kimberley could hardly believe Faye had chosen *her* as a friend. She wasn't sure what had drawn Faye to her in the first place, but didn't want to question it in case the girl changed her mind.

Faye's parents let her do pretty much whatever she wanted. She could stay out late and went home whenever she felt like it – even during the winter, when it was dark. She had her own front door key, in case her parents were out when she got back. They even let her get the bus into town on her own – something Kimberley could only dream of doing. Faye seemed so confident and streetwise, and it made her feel silly and babyish by comparison.

"We'll let you go when you're older," her mother had promised her. "Personally, I think Faye's mum and dad are irresponsible. Well, let's face it, they're hardly more than kids themselves, are they? Her mum can't be more than twenty-five, and with a ten-year-old daughter! They let her run round like a street urchin. It's no way to bring up a child, if you ask me."

But Kimberley longed to be permitted the lack of restrictions that Faye enjoyed. Her own parents seemed so *old*, with old-fashioned values; not laid-back like Faye's. They were strict and there were just too many rules she had to abide by. It seemed so unfair. And in spite of her mother's misgivings, she liked Faye's parents. They were friendly and asked her to call them by their first names, Laura and Mike – not Mr and Mrs Painter, as her own parents liked to be addressed. *Malcom and Mary*. Even their names were old-fashioned. They seemed so stuffy compared with Faye's mum and dad. Mike was Faye's stepdad. Faye had explained that her own father had died when she was a baby and Faye never knew him. She'd always called Mike "Dad", and from what Kimberley could gather, they seemed to get on really well. He treated her more like an adult than a child. It only accentuated the silly way Kimberley's own father spoke to her, and Kimberley often felt embarrassed by it when other people were around.

Kimberley remembered the time she'd gone to Faye's house for tea during the last summer holidays. Her parents weren't keen on her going round there; it seemed to Kimberley that they weren't keen on her doing *anything* without them. But after days of pleading and sulking, her mum had reluctantly allowed her to go. Laura and Mike hadn't arrived home from work yet, and it was exciting that there were no adults in the house to tell them what to do. Her own parents would have gone berserk if they'd known. Her dad had dropped her off as always, but was in a hurry and hadn't come to the door on that occasion, thankfully. The two girls had watched *The Goonies* on video and played *Super Mario Land* on Faye's dad's Nintendo Game Boy. Kimberley had never even *seen* a Nintendo before, let alone played on one.

She'd been amazed, too, that Faye actually knew how to cook, when she demonstrated her ability by making fish fingers, oven chips, and baked beans for them both. Her own mum wouldn't let her anywhere near the stove, in case she burned herself.

"When will your mum and dad be back?" she had asked Faye. The girl shrugged indifferently.

"Whenever," she'd responded casually, as she stood at the sink, washing up their plates. "Sometimes they meet up at the pub on the way home. Why? Does it matter?"

"No, course not. Just wondered, that's all. My mum and dad never go out. Well, not very often. I s'pose everyone's different."

Faye laughed.

"Yeah, my mum and dad are pretty cool. I'd hate to be kept on a lead like you . . . Sorry, Peanuts, I didn't mean it like that," she added, screwing up her face. "It's just, well, your parents don't really let you *do* much stuff, do they?"

Kimberley had to admit that they didn't. And her stupid asthma didn't help matters at all. She lived in hope that, as the family doctor had implied, it might be something she would grow out of. But at the moment she felt – yes, Faye was right – as though she were being kept on a lead. And she didn't appreciate it one bit.

Kimberley felt suddenly defiant. Next time her mum and dad tried to stop her doing something, she was going to stand up to them. They had to realise she wasn't a baby anymore.

If she wanted to be taken seriously, she'd have to do something to prove them wrong.

Chapter 6

Friday, 22 June 1990

Thirteen days after Kimberley's disappearance

Faye Greene paced the floor of her room. Through the window, she'd just seen a patrol car pull up outside yet again. Kimberley had turned out to be a proper wimp and a goody-goody, and now on top of it all, she'd landed her right in it. She couldn't tell anyone that they'd been in Acacia Hill, not even her parents. It would open up a whole can of worms and she could get into real trouble. Her mum and dad had been furious with her for bringing the police to their door. The atmosphere at home was tense and she hated getting the silent treatment.

She felt conflicted, but more than anything, she was furious with Kimberley. This was all her stupid fault! She shouldn't have got so wound up over nothing. Where was this all going to end up?

The doorbell rang. Faye's heart began to race. She looked

down to see the dark-haired policewoman who had visited last week, accompanied by a different, much taller policeman this time, standing outside. What did they want now? A few minutes passed. Hopefully they'd leave soon. She sat on the bed, straining to listen to what was being said. She could hear her dad talking to them in the hallway.

"Faye? You'd better come down here. *Now.*"

Her stomach dropped. She knew from his tone that he wasn't pleased. Mike was generally a reasonable man and fairly easy-going, but he wasn't nice to be around when he was angry.

"*Faye!* Get down here."

She peered cautiously around the bedroom door. The policewoman was looking up at her, smiling.

"It's okay, Faye. We'd just like to ask you a few more questions about the other Saturday. Shouldn't take long."

Faye reluctantly descended the stairs. Her stepfather glared at her. He turned back to the officers.

"You'd better come through."

He led the way into the living room where Faye's mother was watching television. She looked up and gave a half-smile.

"You don't mind if I carry on watching, do you? I'll turn it down a bit." Her eyes went straight back to the TV set in the corner. Faye noticed the policeman look at his colleague with widened eyes, but they said nothing.

Faye sat down on the settee next to her mother. She perched on the edge of the seat, eyeing the police officers warily.

"What d'you want to know?"

"Faye, we're trying to understand why Kimberley might have been getting off a bus at the end of your road. We don't know for certain that it was her, but a bus driver says he thinks a girl fitting her description was on the bus coming from the Acacia Hill area. Does that make any sense to you?"

Faye shrugged, pushing forth her lower lip.

"Dunno."

She wriggled uncomfortably. A sideways glance at her mother, who was engrossed in her TV programme, told her that Laura hadn't heard the policewoman's question. Her stepdad had spread himself out in the armchair opposite and appeared to be studying the newspaper. He didn't look up. She relaxed a little.

"Maybe. Maybe after she left, she got lost, so she had to get the bus back to where she started from."

The policewoman nodded encouragingly. She seemed to agree.

"Can you . . . would you like to tell us what the two of you argued about?"

Faye swallowed. She'd thought long and hard about their falling-out since Kimberley's disappearance. She knew she couldn't divulge the real reason and had her story ready.

"She kept nagging me to give her my denim jacket. For keeps. *And* my baseball cap. I told her she couldn't have them and she went off in a mood."

Faye's mother turned round suddenly. "You never mentioned that before."

Faye could feel heat rising in her cheeks. "Yeah, well, I thought it might make her sound like a brat. I didn't want to say anything bad about her – you know, because she was missing and everything."

The police officers exchanged glances again. Faye noticed the man's eyes narrowing. He pursed his lips, looking at her with his head to one side as though he thought she might be lying.

"I see." The policewoman was doing all the talking, but Faye was beginning to feel as though they were both backing her into a corner. "And – think about this carefully because it's important – are you *sure* about the time she left here that day?"

Faye hesitated. She racked her brains to think what time Kimberley had left her grandmother's house. It took about ten minutes to get back home on the bus from Acacia Hill, and the buses ran every quarter of an hour . . .

"I told you – I think it was about five o'clock. Yeah, that'd be right, because we were just gonna watch the film starting on TV when she decided to clear off."

"Did you watch the film in the end, Faye?"

"Huh? Oh, yeah. Got a telly in my room."

"What was the film?"

Faye felt flustered. She shot an anxious look at her mum, whose face had hardened. Laura turned to the policewoman abruptly. "You sound like you're giving her the third degree! Christ, she's only ten. Anyone'd think *she'd* done something to Kimberley, the way you're grilling her."

"Not at all, Mrs Greene. We're simply trying to establish exactly when Kimberley left in order to find out if it was, in fact, her that was seen by the bus driver."

The policeman spoke next. His tone was stern and Faye felt a bit scared of him. "Mrs Greene, this is a very serious situation. A young girl is missing and we have very little to go on. The more information we can gather, however trivial it may seem to you, the better. We'd just welcome some cooperation, that's all."

The policewoman raised her eyebrows. Her mouth twitched. Faye thought it looked like she was trying not to smile. She turned back to Faye once more.

"D'you remember what the film was?"

Faye felt a flutter of panic in her chest. "Erm . . . yeah,

something about a horse, I think. Can't remember what it was called. I . . . I didn't like it much."

"Thank you, Faye. That's been very helpful."

The woman motioned to her colleague and they both headed for the door.

"Don't get up. We'll see ourselves out. Thank you very much for your time."

Moments after they had left, Faye sidled out of the room, hoping to avoid further questioning from her parents. She'd stay up in her bedroom for an hour or so. Out of sight, out of mind – that's what her mum always said. Hopefully by the time she came down again, they'd have forgotten all about it. And hopefully the police were satisfied with everything she'd told them too, and wouldn't bother them again.

After all, she didn't have anything to hide. Well, not really.

*

Alessa and Jason sat in the police car for a moment, looking back at the house. Jason turned to Alessa.

"You thinking what I'm thinking?"

"I expect so. I'd put money on it. The World Cup's in full flow, and the football monopolised the telly most of the afternoon last Saturday, right until the middle of the evening. Unless she's got a video player in her room – and how many kids her age have? – I reckon the little bugger's lying through her teeth."

"She was doing plenty of squirming, that's for sure." Jason chewed his lip, tapping a finger on the car door as his eyes travelled to Faye's bedroom window. "Yep, she's hiding something. But what?"

Alessa recalled Faye's fidgety body language, her faltering speech. What if the girl had actually played some part in Kimberley's disappearance? The thought made her stomach roll.

"We'll let her stew a bit, then maybe we ought to have another word." She puffed out her cheeks. "I really hope she's got nothing to do with it."

Jason grimaced. "You and me both." He glanced at the clock on the dashboard, his eyes widening. "Shit. We'd better make tracks – Bennett wanted all hands on deck for the press briefing and it's almost 1.15. Shall I blue light it?"

Alessa drew in her chin and looked at him in mock horror. "PC Shelley, I can't believe you'd even suggest such a thing. Just get a shift on – we should be okay. I doubt he'll notice if us minions are there or not, anyway."

Jason flashed her a grin as he turned on the ignition. And for no obvious reason, Alessa felt something flutter in her chest.

*

The press conference lasted only around half an hour. The station's meeting room was oppressively hot, heaving with sweaty-faced journalists, their cameras clicking incessantly. The TV news team had its sights set firmly on Bennett, who sat facing those in attendance with a simpering expression, extolling the virtues of his team and stating without foundation that he was certain they were on the verge of a breakthrough. Alessa and Jason hovered at the back, glancing sideways at one another in exasperation as the preening Bennett puffed himself up, his sickly smile reminiscent of Dickens's revolting Uriah Heep, all for the benefit of the various media in attendance.

As the crowd eventually dispersed, Jason beckoned to Alessa.

"*Jesus Christ*," he said in a low voice. "Thank God that's over. It was painful. D'you want to grab a coffee from the canteen before we go back to the office? I need something to pick me up after listening to that idiot spouting bollocks. That was the biggest pile of egocentric crap I've ever heard."

Alessa gave a wry smile. "Lead on."

Several other members of their team also headed for the canteen, and somewhat annoyingly beat them to the front of the queue. The room was filled with talk of the conference and what they were all going to look like on TV later that evening. How pathetic most of them were, Alessa thought, as she sat waiting at a table by the window for Jason to join her. A child was missing, and all they could think about was whether they'd look good on the small screen.

Eventually, Jason arrived with two large cappuccinos. He put them down and pulled up a chair, looking round to see who was close by before launching into a tirade about Bennett and the way he was handling everything. Alessa was relieved to realise she wasn't alone in her low opinion of their DCI.

"Bloody waste of space." Jason grimaced. He ran a finger along his top lip to remove the froth, grinning as he licked it off. "Anyone'd think he'd got it all sewn up the way he was carrying on in there. What a joke."

"Excruciating," admitted Alessa, grateful she could share her thoughts for once. She lowered her voice. "God knows what the public are going to think – or the poor Painters. I'm concerned he's given a completely false impression of how well the investigation's going."

"The man's a bloody clown. Hopefully it might drum up a bit of public sympathy when they see what the rest of us poor sods have to put up with on a daily basis." Jason sighed. "And as for the Painters, they must be out of their minds with worry, knowing someone like him's in charge of looking for their daughter. What an absolute shambles."

They both exhaled in mutual frustration. Time flew as they shared their concerns and Alessa suddenly noticed that, one by one, the other officers had gradually drifted back to their desks.

"Hey, I think we'd better make a move. Wouldn't want our illustrious leader to think we're slacking."

Back in the office, there was a noticeable buzz in the air. Alessa detected a hush descending as she and Jason entered. Bennett rose immediately from his seat and crossed the room briskly towards them. His expression was almost triumphant.

"Ah, WPC Cano, glad you're back. In your absence, you've created something of a stir. A package has been delivered – with your name on it. That is, I assume it's for you. We don't have any other officer by the name of Cano – but strangely the initial is 'S'." He placed a finger on his chin, jutting his lower lip as though it was a real conundrum. "Anyway, we thought it best if you opened it, as you're more than likely the intended recipient."

Alessa was taken aback. She stared at Bennett and then looked round the room at the intrigued faces of the other officers. Who could possibly be mailing her something to the station? She felt a sudden rush of panic.

Bennett was impatient.

"Come on then! We haven't got all day! We're all agog here and dying to see what's in your mystery parcel. So do the honours, will you? Put us out of our misery."

He handed Alessa a rectangular package, roughly twelve inches by six, bound neatly in plain brown paper. From the clearly stamped postmark, it had been mailed the previous day from Reading. The name and address label was written in bold, rather wobbly capital letters. Alessa stared at her name uncomprehendingly. Everyone looked on as, with trembling fingers, she tore at the wrapping, revealing a blank, plastic case for a VHS film. Inside was a video tape. On a strip of masking tape along the outer edge it bore the hand-scrawled words:

Jessie Lockheed News Footage.

"Jessie Lockheed. Jessie Lockheed? Where do I know that name from?" Bennett scratched his head. He raised a finger, his eyes widening as light dawned. "Missing child case, late 1970s. An attempt was made to snatch her and her friend, but the other girl managed to escape. They never found the perpetrator and it was all over the news for months."

He waved a hand impatiently. "PC Morris, there's a VHS player knocking about over there somewhere. Bring it here and hook it up to the TV, will you? Let's all have a look at the contents of our colleague's surprise present."

The team crowded eagerly around the table as PC Morris set up the video player and Bennett slid the tape into the machine. There were probably no more than fifteen officers present, but to Alessa it felt tenfold. The walls seemed to be closing in around her. Her chest tightened. She wanted to run from the room, to scream at the top of her voice. She felt completely vulnerable, as though exposed for her part in some terrible misdemeanour. But she remained rooted to the spot, her fists clenched, nails digging into her palms. Her cheeks burned and cold beads of sweat studded her forehead. She could feel scrutiny from every direction. Suddenly, the room began to sway. The voices of the newsreaders coming from the TV monitor seemed to echo in her head and she felt her legs buckle. Then everything went black.

*

"Give her some room, for God's sake!"

Alessa gradually came to, finding herself propped on a hard plastic chair near the opened window, a sea of curious faces leaning in and staring at her. Jason Shelley's arm encircled her shoulders, supporting her. He raised a plastic cup of cool water to her lips.

"Here, drink some of this. It'll help."

She sipped gratefully, her head still swimming. "I don't know what happened. One minute I was . . . The next . . . Oh, Christ—"

Without warning, Alessa vomited over his extended arm.

"I'm *so* sorry." Mortified, she stared at the speckled sleeve of his jacket. "I've never passed out before, and . . ." She began to retch uncontrollably and was violently sick again.

Jason pulled a tissue from his trouser pocket and mopped at his arm. He seemed unfazed.

Bennett had paused the tape. He was staring at Alessa with narrowed eyes, studying her now as if seeing her for the first time.

"*Ah.* WPC Cano, are you otherwise known as Sandi, by any chance?"

A Mexican wave of whispers passed through the group. Stunned, Alessa gave an almost indiscernible nod of her head. The weight of every pair of eyes in the room was upon her. She felt trapped.

"Yes." Her voice was barely audible. "I'm Sandi Cano." She felt suddenly very small, almost as though she'd regressed. Despite Greta still calling her by her pet name, she always introduced herself as Alessa these days. It was her therapist's suggestion to reinvent herself in order to help shake off the past and it had worked, to an extent. But of course it had come back to haunt her eventually.

Jason pulled back a little, shooting her a surprised look. "Are you—? Were you the other girl involved in the Jessie Lockheed case?"

She straightened almost defiantly, looking him straight in the eye. "Yes. Jessie Lockheed was my best friend."

Glances were exchanged but no one said a word. The gleeful Bennett was the first to break the silence.

"Well, WPC Cano— Alessa— Sandi . . . whatever you're calling yourself these days, I don't see that your friend disappearing without a trace over a decade ago has any bearing on this case – unless there's something you're not telling us. But enough surmising – let's watch the rest of the footage. We might learn something interesting." He arched an eyebrow, a smirk twitching on his lips.

Alessa dropped her eyes. She wanted the ground to swallow her. The last thing she needed was to see any more of the video. She knew the contents by heart already.

Jason leaned in towards her. "D'you want to get some air?"

She looked up, disorientated, barely registering what he was saying. He looked genuinely concerned.

"That must've been a hell of a shock for you. Take some deep breaths. Can you stand?"

She wiped her mouth on the back of her hand and nodded feebly. The other officers moved aside to allow them to pass. Bennett shot her a derisory look.

"I've said it before and I'll say it again. If you can't stand the heat—"

Jason turned and glared at him. "I think that's uncalled for, don't you? *Sir*?" He enunciated this last word with ill-disguised disdain. Bennett looked slightly uncomfortable and made him no response. He adjusted his tie, cleared his throat, and pointedly addressed the remaining officers as Alessa and Jason left the room.

"So, does anyone have any thoughts – possibly a link to the Painter case? Some marked similarities, I'd say . . ."

His voice faded as the double doors swung to behind them.

Once outside, a hint of colour began to return to Alessa's cheeks. Jason held her arm firmly, watching her carefully for any further signs of keeling over. Taking gulps of fresh air, she attempted to regain some vestige of composure.

"You okay now?" Releasing her from his grip, Jason stood back.

"I'll be fine. It was just so . . . so unexpected, you know?"

He nodded. "Well, you're outed now. Not that it makes a blind bit of difference to anything."

She looked up at him, her brow creasing into a frown. Her stomach felt like a lead weight.

"Who the hell could've sent it? That's what I want to know. Someone who wanted to see me squirm, that much is obvious."

"Well, if you can't think of anyone who bears a grudge against you . . . May have been some con you've upset in the past? Even someone in the office you've pissed off . . .?" He screwed up his face, obviously realising that this might not be a comforting notion. "No; no, it wouldn't be that," he added hastily, placing a hand on her shoulder. "Anyway, it's not as if it's a bad revelation. I mean, you haven't actually done anything *wrong*, have you?"

Alessa cast her eyes skyward. She'd been over and over this with the therapist, but still her sense of guilt was deep-rooted. She turned suddenly to look Jason straight in the face, her expressive dark eyes locking with his. "It was because of all that – what happened with Jessie, I mean – that I joined the force. I wanted to make a difference; to stop vermin like that

84

from walking free. I felt I owed it to her. I was 'the one that got away', after all."

"And thank God for that."

Colour suddenly flooded Jason's cheeks. He attempted to backtrack. "I mean, you're a great copper, by all accounts. We need more people like you, people who genuinely want to improve society. There are too many just looking to make a name for themselves and claw their way to the top, by fair means or foul. Like . . ." He tipped his head towards the building, his eyes narrowing.

"Hmm." Alessa nodded, her thoughts still very much on the sender of the tape. She'd only been in her new job five minutes – not nearly enough time to make enemies. At least, she hadn't thought so. Until now.

"He'll come unstuck sooner rather than later. No one can get away with it indefinitely," Jason ranted on, his mouth setting into an angry line.

Seeing his expression, Alessa tuned back in to what he was saying with interest.

"Do you know something I don't?"

Jason hesitated. He dropped his gaze, implying he'd instantly regretted this little outburst, then blew out a long breath.

"Let's just say there've been rumours flying about . . . From what I've heard, Bennett's track record isn't all it's cracked up to be. Lots of shit swept under the carpet and decidedly dodgy convictions."

Alessa rolled her eyes. "I've gathered that much already."

Jason looked round, lowering his voice. "Sounds as though he's got friends in high places. Friends who are prepared to back him and turn a blind eye."

"So you think he's only got to his current position because of who he's tight with? Sounds about right." Alessa reflected on

Bennett's ineffectual, not to mention illogical, approach. She'd had her suspicions and wasn't at all surprised, but it riled her.

"Look, I probably shouldn't be saying this, but I think that's *exactly* why. I've heard Chief Superintendent Walker is his cousin, and I'd put money on it he'd never even have reached the rank of sergeant if it weren't for his family connections. Keep it under your hat, though."

Alessa pursed her lips. "If that's true, it stinks. I joined the force back in '87, but I was based in Kidlington before. I've only been in this department a couple of months. Don't know too much about him, other than that he's clearly a sexist knobhead. And he definitely likes to take the easy option all the time. Plus he seems to surround himself with yes-men. But I don't see as how there's a fat lot we can do about it at our level – especially if he *is* related to one of the top brass."

Jason leaned towards her conspiratorially. "Yeah, but the current Chief Super's due to retire next year. And I've met the guy in the running – he's a superintendent at the Met. He's bloody dynamic and straight as a die – and well known for not taking any crap. I don't think Bennett'll be around much longer once he takes over."

"I do hope you're right. In the meantime, we've still got a missing child, and with Bennett in charge, I think she's likely to stay that way."

Jason screwed up his face. "I can't help thinking she won't be found alive now. On that score, I'd have to agree with the halfwit."

"Well, we can't just go on that assumption." Alessa felt a sudden surge of anger. It seemed everyone, including Jason, had given up on poor Kimberley. "Christ, if we were that defeatist we'd have just thrown in the towel from the word go. And I, for one, am not prepared to do that."

"Well, whether I'm hopeful of a good outcome or not, I'll back you all the way." He looked up at the station building. "Ready to go back in there, then?"

She thought of half-baked Henderson, the corrupt Bennett, and the general lack of integrity within the department. But then she reminded herself that there was a vulnerable little girl out there somewhere, and she had a job to do.

Lifting her head, she stuck out her chin defiantly.

"Yep. Fuck the lot of 'em."

Chapter 7

Friday, 22 June 1990

Bracing herself, Alessa walked back into the office with Jason at her side. The sight of Jessie's smiling face on the screen was enough to make her legs quiver once more. It was *that* school photograph – the one engraved on her memory; the one they'd used in all the papers and news bulletins. Her resolve began to falter. She clutched Jason's arm.

"I can't do this," she whispered.

"Course you can. Just tell them what you told me. They'll understand."

"Ah, WPC Cano, glad to have you back with us once more. We've just been watching you on the telly – my, haven't you changed." Bennett's sneer was enough to bring Alessa's anger to the fore. She wrestled the desire to hurl abuse at him but managed to push it down.

"Yes, Jessie was my friend. And of course I've changed – I was only twelve when— Well, when it happened. I didn't see any reason to advertise it, and I don't see what difference it makes to anything now. I've done nothing wrong. But if anyone has a problem with who I am, they'd better come right out and say it." She looked around challengingly.

A murmur passed through the assembled officers as everyone shook their heads. Bennett looked irritated. "Well, I don't suppose it's a problem," he said curtly, "as long as it doesn't impact our investigation. But clearly someone out there knows who you are." He gave her a long, hard stare. "So perhaps you should watch your back."

His expression made her shudder. But much to Alessa's relief, he switched off the video.

"Right, we can't stand around here all day. Time to pull your fingers out and get some real work done." Pointedly ignoring Alessa, he addressed Jason. "Did you get anything useful out of Painter earlier?"

"Not really, sir." He shifted awkwardly, glancing apologetically at Alessa. "But he was quite insistent we needed to question Faye Greene some more. And the girl did seem pretty cagey, to be fair."

Bennett harrumphed. "She's a kid – what d'you expect? Notoriously unreliable witnesses. And as for Painter, he's obviously trying to throw us off the scent." He turned to Henderson. "Since we've ruled out Jerome Wilde's possible connection with Kimberley's disappearance, I want Malcolm Painter brought in for questioning again."

Alessa's hands tightened into fists. She shot a look at Jason, who merely shrugged and rolled his eyes.

"On what grounds, sir?" The words came out more forcefully than Alessa had intended.

Bennett's jaw clenched. "On the grounds that, in around ninety-five per cent of these cases, it's someone the child knows who's responsible for their demise. We know from what the Greenes told us that young Kimberley wasn't happy at home. Apart from that, I don't like the man. He's hiding something; I'm sure of it. And if anyone can get to the bottom of it, it's me."

Alessa felt in her gut that Malcolm Painter had done nothing wrong, but she didn't want to attract further attention right now. She inhaled deeply, swallowing the urge to tell Bennett exactly what she thought of him.

"Sir, when we visited the Greenes earlier, PC Shelley and I both got the feeling Faye wasn't telling the truth. Maybe we should concentrate on trying to get more information out of her?" She spoke through gritted teeth.

Bennett rounded on her. "Listen, *love*, I was a copper while you were still in nappies. I can sniff out a lie and Painter's not telling us everything, I'm certain of it. I intend to find out what he's been up to. We saw what a temper the man's got. My bet is he's lost his rag with the child and she's finished up dumped in a ditch somewhere. All a bit too convenient, her clearing off on her friend like that, if you ask me."

He smirked, blatant contempt for Alessa written all over his face. "By all means, you go off and interrogate the little Greene girl some more, if it makes you feel better. Bless you; you could do with a nice easy one, after the shock you've had today. Henderson and I are off to pick up Malcolm Painter."

Alessa opened her mouth to protest, but thought better of it. She bit down on her lip and watched as Bennett, hotly pursued by Henderson, disappeared through the double doors.

"What a complete tosser," Jason muttered under his breath, managing to raise a smile from the quietly seething Alessa. Even if the rest of her colleagues were sheep, at least she appeared to have one ally.

"Come on," she said. "Let's go and lean on Faye a bit more.

I know we've only just spoken to her, but we've got no other leads right now. I've got a strong feeling she knows *something* about all this. I'm sure if we suggest bringing her down to the station, she'll spill the beans. Nothing like the threat of arrest to aid cooperation."

*

They found Faye at home alone. She answered the door with caution, peering through the gap created by the security chain.

"Mum and Dad've just gone out."

Alessa turned sharply to Jason, her eyebrows raised. Strictly speaking, Faye should have an adult present if they were to question her, but she had a gut feeling that the girl wasn't going to tell them anything in front of her parents. Jason hesitated, then gave a brief but definite nod, which Alessa took to indicate approval.

She cleared her throat and turned back to Faye. "That's okay. It's you we've come to talk to."

"Mum says I'm not to let anyone in."

"You can make an exception for us – we're police officers."

"Mum doesn't trust the police. She says I need a grown-up with me if I speak to you. She says—"

Alessa was losing patience. "Look. I think there's something you're not telling us. And I'm sure you'd rather answer our questions in the comfort of your own home, rather than in an interview room down at the station."

Sullenly, Faye unlatched the chain.

"Come in, then."

Alessa and Jason exchanged glances as they followed her into the living room. The smell of marijuana lingered on the air. Alessa watched as Faye crossed the room, hovering uncertainly

91

by the window. The net curtains were almost brown, bathing everything beyond in a sepia mist.

"Faye, I want you to think very carefully about what happened the day Kimberley left here. We know you couldn't have been watching a film at the time you stated because the football was on. You did say you were watching a film on TV, didn't you?"

Faye was quick on the draw. "I remembered after – it was a video. Dad hired it from the shop on the corner."

Alessa threw Jason a sideways look. "Oh, that explains it, then. And you still can't recall what the film was?"

"I told you, it was about a horse. I don't remember what it was called. I watch lots of films."

"Maybe they'd have a record of it in the video shop?"

"Nah – they don't keep records in there. Once you've taken the film back, that's it."

"Oh. Right."

"Is that all?" Faye brightened, her relief palpable.

"I think so." Alessa turned as if to leave, then stopped. "You're a lucky girl, having a video player in your room. I haven't got a telly in my bedroom, even now. D'you think we could go up and have a look?"

The girl's cheeks flushed crimson. She dropped her gaze. "I haven't. Got a video player."

"But I thought you were watching the video upstairs. At least, that's what you told us."

Faye looked slightly startled. Her eyes landed on the VHS player beneath the TV stand in the corner of the room. "I-I made a mistake. We-I must've watched it down here."

"But I thought you were upstairs when Kimberley left? Your parents said they were downstairs the whole time and hadn't realised she'd gone."

"I-I'm not sure . . ." The girl's eyes darted from Alessa to Jason, whose face was stony. She'd dug herself into a hole and was clearly racking her brains for a plausible explanation.

"I don't think you've been completely honest with us, have you, Faye?" Jason decided to add to the pressure. "Were you telling the truth about what happened when Kimberley left? Or was that a lie, too?"

Without warning, Faye buried her face in her hands and began to sob. "I never meant it. Really. I just didn't want to get into trouble."

Jason drew in a breath. "I think you'd better sit down and tell us the truth. This is very serious, Faye. You could be charged with wasting police time . . ." He locked eyes with Alessa briefly. "I want you to think very carefully about what actually went on that Saturday. Try to remember everything that happened – and this time, tell us the whole story, please."

Faye sank into the armchair, her eyes fixed firmly on the floor. Alessa actually felt sorry for her, but held her tongue. She was hopeful they were on the verge of a breakthrough.

"We went out after lunch," Faye said with a sniff. "We were gonna go into town, but I wanted to see my nan first, in Acacia Hill. We caught the bus there. Then Kimberley got in a strop and said she wanted to go home. I know I shouldn't have, but I was annoyed so I let her go on her own. So that was why the driver saw her getting off the bus at the end of our road."

Alessa was perplexed. "I don't understand why on earth you didn't just tell us this in the first place," she said, exasperated. "We'd have widened our search right from the start. You do realise this is very important information, don't you?"

"I'm sorry. I didn't want to say I'd been to my nan's house. Mum doesn't like me going there. She's my *real* dad's mum, you see." Her hands twisted in her lap. "He's in prison."

Jason darted a look at Alessa. "Okay. So, you both went to Acacia Hill," he said slowly. "What time *did* Kimberley actually leave you?"

"About twenty past four, I think. We hadn't been there very long."

"And why did she clear off like that?"

Faye paused. "I dunno. She's a bit spoilt. Got a habit of going all huffy." Avoiding eye contact with both of them, she began to pick at a thread on her cuff. Alessa noticed that her fingernails were badly chewed. "Her mum and dad always let her have her own way, I s'pose that's why."

"Hold on. Didn't you say before that they don't let her do what she wants a lot of the time? I thought she was fed up at home?"

"Yeah, well, sometimes, they don't. I dunno, do I?" Faye had begun to fidget in her seat, her bottom lip wobbling once more.

Alessa sighed. "Okay. I don't suppose it really matters. What we really want to know is if that was her on the bus, and it looks as if it must've been. I think you've confirmed what we thought – that Kimberley left you much earlier than you originally said."

"Will I get into trouble?" Faye tilted her face, looking pleadingly from Jason to Alessa. "I never meant any harm. I just didn't want to be landed in it with my mum and dad. Will you have to tell them?"

Alessa glanced at Jason, arching her eyebrows a fraction. "I think you've learned an important lesson here. Honesty is always the best policy."

Faye looked anguished. "What d'you mean?"

"She means, young lady, that you should always tell the truth," Jason interjected. "Or it'll come back and bite you on the bum. D'you understand?"

94

Faye nodded solemnly.

"It might be better if you just come clean and tell your parents where you went. But that's up to you. Just make sure you don't go telling the police fairy stories in future, got it?"

Alessa puffed out her cheeks. She glanced across at the house as they made their way back to the patrol car. Faye still hadn't told them everything, she felt certain. She wondered why the girls had fallen out. She thought of herself at that age; of how things could be sometimes with Jessie. Their arguments had been infrequent and trivial as a rule, and blew over pretty quickly. But whatever the cause, it had usually been Alessa who was the peace-maker. Jessie could be stubborn. Faye reminded Alessa a little of her friend in some way. She wondered if the dynamic between Faye and Kimberley had been similar to that she and Jessie had shared. From everything she'd learned about Kimberley, it seemed likely that Faye was the dominant one: she could imagine that little Kimberley would have followed her lead like a faithful puppy. Her stomach dropped as she remembered how sometimes she would go along with Jessie's plans rather than risk her friend's disapproval. But she liked to think she'd have had the good sense to dig her heels in and refuse if it had been something serious. She wondered if Kimberley had the maturity to do the same.

Alessa could see Faye's outline, watching them from the window.

"I bloody knew it." Jason smacked the steering wheel in frustration. The sound of the horn sent a cat that had been sitting on the pavement fleeing for its life into someone's front garden. They sat in silence for a moment as he watched the house in the rear-view mirror, then pulled away slowly.

He turned to Alessa as they rounded the bend. "Fuck's sake. We've wasted precious time because of that silly little— *Pfft.*

At least we've roughly confirmed the time Kimberley went missing and possibly her whereabouts. If I'd known she'd gone to Acacia Hill, I'd have put money on her going missing somewhere round there. But it definitely sounds like she caught the bus back to nearer home. I reckon she must've tried to walk back from Faye's road. So where the hell did she actually vanish from?"

"Sounds as if it must've been within yards of Lime Tree Avenue. And a good three hours *before* her father realised she was missing." Alessa shook her head. "A lot can happen in that time."

Jason chewed his lip. "Hmm. Unless she *did* arrive home and got into big trouble? It would've been the perfect cover for Malcolm Painter, pretending he thought she was still with Faye . . ."

"No." Alessa shook her head. "I just don't buy that. You didn't see the Painters when they first reported it. I really felt for them. That little girl's the centre of their universe. No. Someone else is responsible for this. I'm sure of it."

"I hope you're right. I don't want that berk Bennett crowing over us with his hunch turning out to be right. He'd be intolerable."

*

Enraged and frustrated, a pale, unkempt Malcolm Painter sat at the Formica-topped table in the windowless interview room, arms folded tightly across his chest. His eyes were puffy and red-rimmed from lack of sleep and the frequent bouts of crying that he succumbed to privately when alone.

He tapped his foot on the tiled floor now, staring straight ahead at the "Lock It or Lose It" poster on the notice board, avoiding eye contact with Bennett and his sidekick. A third officer, a tall, unsmiling man introduced as PC Morris, stood staring down with disinterest at his own shoes, ostensibly guarding the door.

Malcom was in turmoil. He could hardly believe it when the coppers turned up at the house again. Mary had been beside herself when he'd had to leave with them. He'd tried to reassure her that there was nothing to worry about; that it was all just procedure. But he had a terrible feeling he was in real danger of having something pinned on him, just so that Bennett could tick a box. It was beyond belief that the imbecile appeared to be focusing all his attention on him when the real culprit was still at large.

And Kimberley, his beloved Kimberley, was out there somewhere, possibly being kept prisoner and enduring God knows what at the hands of some deviant. It didn't bear thinking about. Every time he thought of her, his stomach lurched. It always made him feel sick, any time he'd heard about a child going missing and turning up dead. How the poor families' lives would have a shadow cast over them for evermore. And now he was living in real fear that he and Mary were about to join their number. Stupidly, he kept turning over the grisly details of previous prominent child murders that had hit the headlines over the years, his imagination going into overdrive. It was sheer torture.

"Why are you wasting time like this?" he burst out suddenly. "This is bloody incredible. How the *hell* can you believe I've got anything to do with my own daughter vanishing into thin air? It's sheer fucking incompetence, that's what it is."

"Mr Painter, you aren't doing yourself any favours." Bennett sat opposite him, along with DS Henderson, looking self-important as he operated the cassette recorder. "We'll get to the bottom of it all sooner or later. It'll help you in the long run if you just cooperate. I'll ask you again: what have you done with your daughter?" He leaned back in his seat, an infuriatingly smug expression on his face.

Shoving back his chair, Malcolm jumped to his feet, fists clenched, his bloodshot eyes wild. "For Christ's sake! How many times have I got to tell you? She left her friend's house and God only knows what happened next. I'm going out of my mind with worry. Mary's on tranquilisers; neither of us has slept in nearly a fortnight. How the hell can you think there's even the remotest possibility it's got anything to do with me? With either of us? This is a bloody farce! And *you're* a disgrace to your profession."

Bennett cleared his throat nonchalantly. "Mr Painter, sit down. You're becoming irrational."

"*Irrational?* I'm being accused of something unspeakable here, and I'm being *irrational?* How the hell d'you expect me to behave?"

*

An ill-timed knock made Bennett grimace. He stiffened, indicating to Henderson to pause the tape.

"Come in," he grunted irritably.

Alessa peered tentatively round the door. "Can I have a word, please, sir?"

Bennett sucked air through his teeth, and rose from his chair, scraping it across the floor. He left the room, closing the door behind him. Malcolm sank back into his seat, burying his head in his hands. Henderson looked uncomfortable. He cast his eyes downwards, then up at the clock on the wall. PC Morris stretched his hands above his head, revealing huge sweat patches around his armpits. He coughed loudly in an attempt to attract Henderson's attention. The two men exchanged a brief nod of shared ennui as he motioned with a hand towards his wristwatch, pulling a face.

Out in the corridor, Bennett appeared ruffled. He glared at Alessa, folding his arms across his chest. "This had bloody well better be good. You've ruined the continuity of my interview."

"We've just come from questioning the Greene girl, sir. As we suspected, she wasn't telling the truth last time. It seems she and Kimberley caught a bus to visit Faye's grandmother in Acacia Hill. There was some sort of disagreement between the girls and Kimberley left the house alone. The bus driver who thought he'd seen her must've been right. Faye admitted that Kimberley left her at about four-twenty. So it sounds as if Kimberley might've caught the bus back to Faye's road, then attempted to walk home from there."

Bennett looked almost gleeful. "It gets better," he declared, rubbing his hands. "So she might well have gone home and got it in the neck from her dad for not staying put at the Greenes' house. We know her parents didn't allow her out unsupervised. And she would've been completely drenched with all the rain that afternoon."

Alessa tried desperately to think of an alternative explanation. Instinctively, she knew that neither of the Painters would ever have laid a finger on their daughter, but persuading Bennett of the fact seemed like an impossibility. The man had an irrational fixation with Kimberley's father and there was no reasoning with him.

"I don't think we should jump to conclusions, sir. It's more than likely someone abducted her on her way home. The Painters are quite clearly devoted parents—"

"And what the hell would you know about it?" Bennett turned to her, his head wobbling condescendingly from side to side. He reminded Alessa of one of those ornamental nodding dogs people sat on their parcel shelf. "You don't have the years of experience of dealing with the general public that I do. People can put on an Oscar-winning performance when it's called for. I've seen it many a time. No, I reckon we can wrap this one up nicely. I'm going to charge Painter with the murder of his daughter. I had an inkling right from the start that he'd done it. Who knows? The mother might've had a hand in it, too."

Looking triumphant, he began to march back towards the interview room.

"You're forgetting something quite crucial, sir."

Bennett stopped in his tracks. He twisted round to face Alessa once more. "Oh? And what would that be?"

"We don't have a body."

"Only a matter of time, Cano. Only a matter of time."

Chapter 8

Sunday, 27 May 1990

"I don't like it, Malcolm." Mary Painter's brow folded into a frown as she watched her daughter playing in the street from the living room window. She put down her duster on the sill. "Our Kimberley's got far too friendly with that Greene girl. You mark my words, she'll be trouble in a year or two. I can see it coming. She's heading that way already. No proper parental guidance. It's a recipe for disaster."

"Hmm?" Her husband peeled over the page of his newspaper, his thoughts very much on the article he'd just been reading. There had been yet another attempted abduction of a young girl in the city centre, which had made the front page. They'd got a good description of the culprit this time, at least. It made Malcolm's blood boil to think there was some depraved bastard on the loose in his home town, preying on innocent children. And even if the coppers caught up with him, more than likely all they'd probably give the swine would be a slap on the wrist and a couple of months in some cushy detention centre with a load of other perverts, only to let him out to do it again. The world had gone mad.

"For God's sake, Malcolm. *That girl*. Doesn't it worry you that Kimberley's palled up with someone who could lead her astray?"

Malcolm let out a sigh. Putting down the *Mail*, he rose from his armchair. He patted his wife gently on the back as he looked through the bay window himself, smiling at the sight of their daughter, pale but carefree and laughing as the Frisbee she had skimmed through the air landed in next door's front garden. Bold as brass, Faye Greene strode through the gate and, trampling across the well-tended border, retrieved it from Bernard's immaculate lawn, blithely ignoring their irate neighbour as he raised his net curtain and rapped loudly on the window. The girl turned slowly and waved impudently at the elderly man, grinning and winking at Kimberley as she did so. She stood head and shoulders above Kimberley, who was small for her age, her dark hair cropped into a spiky urchin cut which made Faye look older than her years. They made an unlikely pair.

"Just *look* at her!" Mary sounded exasperated. "She's got the cheek of the bloody devil. No respect whatsoever."

"She's just a kid, Mary." Malcolm was less concerned. He'd been a bit of a tearaway as a lad and knew it was something most kids grew out of. He felt a bit sorry for Faye, all things considered. She didn't seem like a bad child at heart, and she certainly wasn't to blame for her parents' lackadaisical attitude.

"Our Kimberley's a good girl. Minds her p's and q's and knows how to behave herself. We've brought her up properly. Hopefully it might just rub off on young Faye, eventually. She can't help it if her parents are half-soaked."

"I hope you're right. I don't want my daughter being dragged down by a little" – she waved a hand, searching for a suitably derogatory adjective – "a little . . . *toerag* like that."

"Oh, come on, love. She's not that bad. She's just a bit more . . . streetwise, I suppose you'd call it, compared with Kimberley. Look, they'll be at the big school come September next year. Probably make a load of new friends, the pair of 'em. Tell me honestly, how many of your old pals did you keep after you started high school?"

Mary huffed. "I do hope you're right. I don't want to stop Kimberley seeing her friend, but it worries me Faye'll be a bad influence. I think we're hard enough on Kimberley as it is, sometimes. I'd like to be able to give her a bit more freedom, but . . . she's so precious to me, Malcom. I couldn't bear the thought of her ever coming to any harm." She finished her sentence with a sudden quaver in her voice, covering her face with her hands as her eyes flooded with tears.

"Hey, where's all this coming from?" Malcom turned Mary to face him, placing his hands on her shoulders. "The doctor told us the asthma's not that bad. As long as we keep an eye on things, she should be fine."

Mary shook her head. "It's not that," she sniffed, blotting her eyes with a tissue. "I just had the most awful dream last night, Malc. It's proper shaken me up. I don't even want to tell you what it was about. Saying it out loud would seem even worse, somehow – as if it might make it actually happen. I know it was only a dream, but it's really disturbed me. She's my whole world; I don't know what I'd do without her."

Malcolm looked at his wife, not knowing how to respond. Her distress was palpable. In the harsh light of day, she looked every one of her forty-nine years. Any vestige of the lovely, vivacious young woman he'd fallen for all those years ago had long since been eradicated. Her short, mouse-brown hair was streaked with grey, and dark shadows framed her troubled blue eyes, the vertical lines between them giving her a permanently cross expression. Throughout their marriage, Mary had endured more than her fair share of pain and disappointment, and over time it had become etched into her face. He was only too aware how much their daughter meant to her; fifteen fruitless years of trying for a baby, and Kimberley had been their only success. They both wanted to wrap her up in cotton wool, but for Mary it had almost become an obsession. His brow puckered into a worried frown as he contemplated the possibility.

"Look," he said eventually, "this isn't like you, getting all irrational. It's usually a sign you're heading for a relapse. What d'you say if I try to get you in at the doctor's on Monday?" He gently smoothed a lock of hair away from her tense forehead. "Maybe you could do with some more of your pills. We don't want you sliding back into the doldrums again, do we?"

Mary stiffened. She sniffed back her tears and responded brusquely.

"I'm fine. Really. I told you – it was only a bad dream, but it's set me to thinking, that's all. I was just having a moment. It's passed now." She extricated herself from his grasp and walked purposefully towards the door.

"I'll get the lunch on. I suppose we'll have to ask that Faye to stay, seeing as she's come round." Mary rolled her eyes. "Don't imagine that mother of hers will have left her anything decent to eat. From what our Kimberley says, the girl seems to be left to her own devices for much of the weekend. It's a bloody disgrace, it really is."

*

They sat in awkward silence around the kitchen table, eating the plates of egg, chips and peas that Mary had prepared. Only the occasional word was spoken and the atmosphere felt tense. Malcom began to wish Mary hadn't suggested inviting Faye to stay. But the girl cleared her plate and said thank you when she'd finished, then rose from the table and cleared away the plates unprompted. She filled the sink and set about doing the washing-up.

Malcolm looked on with interest, noticing a shift in Mary's demeanour. His wife's face seemed to have softened and she leaned back in her seat, eyebrows slightly raised. Whatever she may have thought about Faye's parents, Mary seemed impressed with the girl's obvious domesticity. Maybe she had realised she'd been a bit hard on Faye. He hoped she could at least *try* to like the girl, for Kimberley's sake. After all, it wasn't *her* fault that her parents were useless. And then again, there must clearly be *some* form of discipline in the home, if she'd been shown how to carry out household chores . . .

"We'll have to get Faye to show you how to wash up, won't we, Kimberley?" Mary said suddenly.

Kimberley looked taken aback.

"But you'd never let me before," she protested. "You said I might break something."

"Yes, well, you're a bit older now. It wouldn't hurt you to learn how to do a few things around the house. I'm not getting any younger, after all. A bit of help from time to time might be nice." She winked at Faye, who looked somewhat startled.

Malcolm smiled to himself. Perhaps it had been just a momentary blip earlier – Mary seemed more like her old self now. But he'd have to keep an eye on her, just in case. He wasn't sure he could cope if the depression returned. Last time it had very nearly ended their marriage.

Kimberley's face lit up. "Will you let me go into town with Faye, then, if I'm a bit older now, as you say?"

"One thing at a time, young lady. When you're at secondary school—"

"But that's over a year away. That's like . . . forever!"

"Don't exaggerate," Malcolm chipped in, seeing Mary's face grow stern once more. "It'll come round soon enough, believe me. There are a lot of odd people out there. I mean, it's even in the papers at the moment, some creep's been trying to snatch little girls off the street. You need to know how to look after yourself. A year or so will make all the difference."

"But I *do* know how to look after myself! I—"

"That's *enough*, now."

Kimberley's pale cheeks flushed. Her lower lip jutted petulantly, but she said no more.

Faye made no comment. But a strange little smile twitched at the corners of her mouth – subtle, but sufficient not to have escaped the notice of the sharp-eyed Malcolm. Soon enough, that smile would come back to haunt him.

If only he'd known then what lay behind it, how very differently things might have turned out.

*

"Listen," said Faye later, when she and Kimberley were alone in Kimberley's room. "I'm going into town next Saturday. I've got birthday money from my nan and I want a new top. Why don't you come with me? We'll just say you're coming to mine for the day. Tell your mum and dad you're staying for tea. They'll never know. We'll make sure we're back by whatever time they tell you."

Kimberley was hesitant. She didn't want to lie to her parents, but above all else feared the repercussions if they should catch her out.

"I don't know. What if—"

Faye smiled. "Don't worry, Peanuts. How will they find out? My mum and dad definitely won't say anything – I told them how yours don't let you go anywhere or do much. They think it's really stupid. Go on. It'll be a laugh."

"But I'd have to ask for spending money – and bus fare. I haven't got much in my piggy bank. I spent most of my savings on Mum's birthday present."

Faye waved a dismissive hand. "Just hang on to your dinner money. You take that in to school on Mondays, right? You can share my sandwiches this week – I make my own, so I'll make enough for both of us."

Kimberley considered the invitation for a moment. She felt a sudden tingle of excitement. How *would* her parents find out? They never usually left the house on a Saturday. And she'd be able to prove to herself that she was capable of doing something on her own; that she *wasn't* a baby. In spite of what her mum and dad might think.

"All right then. I'll do it!"

Faye jumped up and down, clapping her hands in anticipation. "Yay! We'll have a fab time, you'll see. We can go to the Covered Market for some Ben's Cookies – they're *gorgeous*."

Kimberley grinned. Her stomach fluttered with nerves, but at the same time, the idea of doing something forbidden was liberating. She could hardly wait until the following Saturday. Drawing a star on the calendar hanging on her wall in red felt-tip, she stared at it, her eyes shining with excitement. She felt a rush of optimism. What her mum and dad didn't know wouldn't hurt them. It was going to be a day to remember.

It was going to be *wicked*.

Chapter 9

Friday, 22 June 1990

Thirteen days after Kimberley's disappearance

Bernard had seen Malcolm being carted off earlier that day in a police car. He knew this wasn't the first time they'd had him down at the station. Bernard wondered what on earth was going on and it was playing on his mind. Malcolm was a good man; Bernard hated to see him looking so anguished.

Bernard had just made himself a cup of tea and was about to turn on the evening news when he heard a vehicle pull up outside. Peering through the nets, he could see Malcolm, head drooping, making his way slowly up the path next door. Bernard put down his cup and hurried from the living room.

Malcolm was about to turn the key in the lock when Bernard opened his front door.

"Everything all right, Malcolm?" He hoped he didn't sound too anxious. "Any news?"

Painter shook his head wearily. "Nothing. The tossers have just had me in for questioning again. Can you believe it? All the time they're focusing their efforts on me, the real culprit's still out there. And so's my little girl." Bernard detected the catch in Malcolm's voice as his neighbour averted his eyes, clearing his throat.

Bernard was incredulous. "For God's sake! I'll vouch for you. I know you and Mary are devoted to Kimberley. You just tell them to come and speak to me. I'll put 'em straight."

Malcolm smiled sadly. "That's very good of you. Thank you. But the joker in charge has got it in for me. Christ knows why."

"What's wrong with the idiot? What the hell does he think you've done with her? It's *unbelievable*." Bernard's cheeks flushed with anger. He wrinkled his nose in agitation, pushing back his glasses with a forefinger.

"Let's just hope they get their act together soon, eh. I don't know how much longer we can go on like this. It's making Mary ill." Malcolm pointed to the house and grimaced. "I'd better get back in and see if she's okay. She was in a right old state when they took me in earlier. I'll keep you posted if there's any news. But thanks very much for your support, Bernard. I appreciate it."

The old man watched as his neighbour disappeared through the front door. His heart went out to the Painters. If only there was something he could do to help. He felt useless.

No. More than that.

He felt culpable.

*

Back at St Aldates Station, Alessa was about to leave for the day when Jason collared her by the exit.

109

"Don't suppose you fancy going for a drink, do you?" He smiled uncertainly. "Just a quick one . . .?"

She hesitated. She'd always thought it unwise to get involved with a colleague, but he seemed really nice and they'd hit it off. After the day she'd had, she could do with a little light relief. Alessa glanced at her watch.

"Okay," she found herself responding. "But yes, only a quick one. Lead on."

"I'll take the car. It'll be easier for me to head home straight from St Giles later and the parking's free in the evening, anyway."

Within ten minutes, they were wending their way in a roundabout loop towards the city centre in Jason's old Austin Montego. At the start of Walton Street, Jason veered right, and drove via Beaumont Street, passing the Ashmolean Museum. He found a space and parked the car where the Woodstock and Banbury Roads converged at St Giles, a stone's throw from the steeple-like Martyrs' Memorial, its steps streaked white with pigeon droppings but nonetheless popular with tourists for photo opportunities. They wandered past the mellow, honeyed limestone buildings of St John's College and the omnipresent row of bicycles chained to the railings beyond the public conveniences, passed a queue of buses belching out diesel fumes at the terminus, then turned left along Broad Street, well-named with the wide expanse of road between the opposing pavements. It was a pleasantly warm evening and, despite the shops being closed, plenty of people, many of them tourists, were still milling about. An expectant and slightly nervous-looking group were assembled next to a sandwich-board emblazoned with the words "Ghost Tour", outside the tall gates to Trinity College, where a man dressed in a black top hat and cape was trying to drum up further trade.

Alessa threw Jason a grimace. The pair quickly crossed to the other side to avoid being collared. They passed the architectural splendour of Christopher Wren's Sheldonian Theatre and the History of Science Museum, from where the majestic Oxford Emperors, seventeen bearded stone busts, stared straight ahead with bulging eyes from atop their pillars. They were blackened with grime, making them look like chimney sweeps. Alessa thought it a shame. She had been fascinated, if not a little scared, by the heads as a child. She imagined them coming to life during the night and wreaking havoc. Whenever they went into town, Uncle Rob would hoist her onto his shoulders as they walked down the Broad, so that she could get a closer look at their faces, each one totally unique.

"Why do they look so cross?" she'd asked, staring at their solemn expressions.

"It can't be much fun, being stuck up there all the time," he'd quipped. "You'd probably be pretty fed up, too."

Crossing the road via Catte Street to the bustling King's Arms, Jason stepped back to allow Alessa to enter first, following closely. As she stepped over the threshold, Alessa glanced into the small reading room on her left and was arrested by the sight of DCI Bennett huddled in a corner, deep in conversation with an unlikely and dubious-looking drinking companion. Alessa's mind began to whirr. What the hell was Bennett up to, fraternising with someone she recognised as a well-known local petty crook? It was possible the man was an informant, but they were laughing from time to time and looked a little too friendly. Thankfully Bennett didn't appear to have noticed them. She nudged Jason.

"Look who's at quarter to nine," she said in a hushed voice, inclining her head in the direction of the open doorway. Jason whipped round and scrutinised the pair for a moment. His brow furrowed.

"Our boss keeps unsavoury company," he remarked, glowering in the DCI's direction. "Come on. Don't fancy bumping into him at the bar. Let's get out of here."

As they left the building, Jason turned to observe Bennett and his acquaintance for a moment longer. It felt as though he was making a mental note of something, Alessa thought. *Something for later*, was what sprang to mind. But he made no comment and she dismissed her notion as imagination.

They went back out into the street and looked around. Jason suggested trying the White Horse across the street on the Broad, a small but pleasant old pub, which was often relatively quiet during the week. This being June, however, the students were out in force celebrating their end of year exams. A group still in subfusc decorated with confetti and silly string were crammed around the window seat, their raucous laughter spilling through the open doorway.

The girl pulling pints nodded in greeting as Alessa and Jason came down the short flight of steps from the entrance and into the pub. More high-spirited students occupied the seating towards the back, chattering noisily between much swilling of ale. Alessa found a table opposite the bar, while Jason went to order the drinks. A pair of New Age hippies in their middle years were deep in conversation at the next table. The man's silver tresses were scraped back into a ponytail and his female companion had wispy lilac-rinsed hair. The woman lifted her eyes and smiled briefly as Alessa squeezed past them and sat down. Alessa smiled back, then glanced towards the window which looked out onto the street, watching as people walked past and taking in the buzzing atmosphere.

It felt good to be out, not as a police officer for once, but as just another member of the public enjoying a quiet evening socialising. She wished she wasn't wearing her uniform and slipped off her jacket, undoing the top two buttons of her shirt as she leaned back against the panelled wall.

Alessa observed Jason as he stood at the bar and found herself admiring the ample width of his shoulders and the way his dark hair sat above his collar, revealing a glimpse of tanned neck. A tingle of warmth crept up from somewhere inside her. As he turned from the bar carrying their drinks, they locked eyes and Alessa felt her pulse bounce.

"So, tell me more about yourself then, WPC Cano." Jason grinned disarmingly as he placed the glasses on the table, lowering himself onto a stool.

Oh God, what was she *doing*? She realised that he'd noticed her staring at him and dropped her gaze to focus on her wine, shifting self-consciously in her seat.

"What d'you want to know?" She hadn't intended it to sound so sharp, but didn't feel like relating her life history. Jason looked vaguely amused. "Well, what d'you like to do with your free time for a start?" He took off his jacket, leaning across to place it on the bench next to Alessa.

"Free time? What's that?" She gave a hollow laugh. "You're a copper, you should know. I'm pretty much married to the job."

"True. But you must have interests – and we're not at work *all* the time. I mean, what d'you enjoy doing, given the chance? D'you like going to the cinema . . .?"

Alessa's stomach felt suddenly heavy. She had no social life; no circle of friends. Ever since the hard time she'd been given at school, she had withdrawn and kept herself to herself. More owing to pressure from her concerned mother, she'd made a bit of an effort when first starting university, but the handful of dates she'd had amounted to nothing, and she eventually decided the best course of action was to keep her head down and focus on her dissertation. To admit she had no friends might make her sound dull – a bit weird, even. But maybe it was better to be upfront.

"I've never really got out much, to be honest. Things are . . . well, complicated." She paused. She couldn't blame everything on the situation with her mamma and Joey. "I've always been a bit of a loner, I suppose. And I hated school. You know, after Jessie and everything . . ." She dropped her eyes. "Later, I was pretty focused on getting through my degree and never really mixed much. I did try to fit in at Kidlington, but I didn't really enjoy going out on the razz and after a while, well . . ."

Alessa fiddled with the spare beer mat on the table, avoiding his gaze. She must sound like a real barrel of laughs. She thought back to when she'd first started work at Kidlington. There was one girl, Shoba, she'd palled up with, but the friendship had been short-lived, and invitations to the pub had eventually dried up as Alessa kept bowing out for one reason or another. Truthfully, she could have gone along most of the time, but persuaded herself that staying at home was preferable to making excruciating small talk with people she barely knew. She remembered overhearing Shoba telling one of their colleagues that she was a dead loss and it was pointless trying to get her to do anything outside work. It had felt hurtful at the time, but she knew herself it was true enough. She also had to admit she could have tried harder.

Jason was watching her intently, nodding from time to time, his head cocked to one side. "Well, it's not the be-all and end-all, going out all the time. Even when the opportunity arises, I'm too tired to be arsed these days, to be quite honest. Got it all out of my system during my wild and hedonistic youth!" He laughed. "Nah, not really. I like a quiet couple of pints but I've never been a hardened drinker. There's more to life than getting pissed and clubbing, isn't there?"

"Exactly." Although, the job aside, she wasn't sure what else there was at the moment.

"So what d'you do to unwind, then?"

He obviously wasn't going to let up. Alessa considered briefly.

"Never have time for the pictures these days. My uncle used to take me a lot when I was a child. I used to like listening to music, though. Prog rock, mainly. Some classical, too."

Uncle Rob had fostered a love of opera in her from when she'd been small. It had become a tradition that he'd take her to a performance in Covent Garden every January. The last time it had been to see *Madam Butterfly*. It had probably been too soon after Joey's passing and she'd bawled her way through most of it.

Joey was seventeen when he passed away. He was such a handsome boy. Ironically, he had been the image of their father, with his huge brown eyes and thick dark lashes. She remembered the initial excitement of having a baby brother, and then the worry that quickly followed. Alessa was only five years old when he was born and her mother was seriously ill after the traumatic delivery. Thankfully, Greta had regained her health within a few weeks. But soon it became apparent that all was not well with Joey, and that his recovery wouldn't be quite so straightforward. He'd spent his first four months in intensive care. Alessa learned years later that the doctors had told her parents bluntly that he'd be incapable of normal development; that it was highly probable he wouldn't live beyond his first year, and even if he should survive, he would have no quality of life. As he grew up, Joey's world remained small, his existence so limited. Alessa had often wondered if he was really happy, or whether he had enough cognition to appreciate how restricted his life actually was. The seizures he was prone to could be violent and would leave him completely wiped out for days. It was a distressing thing to witness. There were times when she'd wondered if it mightn't have been kinder if he had slipped away as a newborn baby, but the resultant guilt she felt from such thoughts made her squash them at once. She couldn't allow herself to think of him now. It hurt too much.

"Used to?" Jason looked at her questioningly.

"Yeah. Well, still do, I suppose." Music, especially classical, seemed to bring out her deepest emotions and Joey's death was still raw. She needed to change the subject.

"And I read, when I get the chance," Alessa went on, smiling tightly. She thought how staid this all sounded and groaned inwardly, worried Jason might think she was a bit of a nerd. It dawned on her that she actually cared about the impression she was giving him, and she felt slightly confused about it.

"What d'you like to read?" He sipped his pint, studying her. He looked genuinely interested.

"Crime fiction, mainly." Alessa rolled her eyes. "The irony. Busman's holiday, I s'pose."

"Ha. I guess so."

"I did my degree in Criminology at Oxford Brookes, so you could say I'm a bit obsessed."

"Well, you're obviously very dedicated." He grinned. "But you need to let your hair down once in a while, you know." He sat back in his seat and looked her straight in the eye. Alessa felt heat rush to her cheeks.

"So, no boyfriend on the scene at the moment, then?" The words came out in an obvious rush, as though he'd been building up to them. He ran a hand through his hair self-consciously.

She smiled to herself. "Men aren't really my thing, if you

know what I mean. Didn't anyone tell you?" She paused, her expression deadpan, waiting for a reaction. Jason's face clouded. He looked crestfallen.

Alessa burst out laughing. "I'm kidding. I just haven't met the right guy yet, unfortunately. I did go on a few dates at university, but nothing serious."

She thought about the one lad, Pete, whom she'd seen for a couple of weeks not long after she started uni. It was the longest she'd ever been with anyone. When he'd asked her to go for a drink, she'd said no initially, but he'd been persistent and, thinking it would get her mother off her case, she relented. She didn't find Pete particularly attractive, but he had a good sense of humour and seemed nice enough . . . until she invited him back to the house one evening. Joey had been in the living room in his wheelchair, gabbling as he always did in his own unique way. Pete had perched himself on the edge of his seat in obvious discomfort, looking everywhere but in Joey's direction. He'd said very little, answering Greta's polite questions with monosyllabic grunts, and eventually made some lame excuse about having to get home to feed his cat. After that, whenever she saw him at uni, Alessa realised Pete was deliberately avoiding her. She wasn't upset so much as disappointed that someone she'd thought decent was clearly pretty shallow. It had made her question her own judgement and left her wary of accepting invitations from anyone else. But she was older and wiser now – at least, she hoped she was.

"And since I've been a copper, well, I'm sure the uniform puts some people off," she went on. "I know women often find men in uniform attractive, but believe me, it's different for a female officer."

"Well, I happen to think it looks very good on you. If you don't mind my saying."

117

She found herself blushing once more. She never knew quite how to respond to compliments; they made her feel awkward. Anxious to change the subject, she glanced around. The lilac-rinsed woman at the next table caught her eye, and threw her a mischievous wink and a smile. She must have overheard them.

Alessa cleared her throat and turned back to Jason. "Anyway, what about you? How do you spend your days off?"

Jason sighed ruefully. "I did used to like running. It's great to clear your head – you know, especially when there's a pile of shit going on at work. But I injured my knee a few months ago and it's only just getting back to where it was. Bit out of shape at the moment." He grimaced.

Alessa thought he looked in pretty good shape, but refrained from telling him as much. She simply nodded. "Was there a lot of crap to cope with, working for the Met? Bad enough here, but I should think it must be pretty heavy-going in London at times . . ."

"Let's just say Oxford seems less frenetic. As a rule." He arched an eyebrow, turning his attention to his glass. He looked suddenly subdued.

There was a beat of silence. Alessa thought about Kimberley Painter and realised that, wherever the location, nothing could be more stressful than a missing child case.

"Erm . . . have you got a girlfriend, then?" Alessa picked at the beermat, her eyes on the table. She had to ask, even if she didn't really want to know the answer.

He gave a bitter little laugh. "Pfft. I thought I had. Until I came home early after a night shift to find a strange bloke enjoying breakfast in my kitchen."

"Oh." She felt a ripple of disappointment. He was on the rebound, then.

"But that was well over a year ago now," he added. "Water under the bridge." He leaned back on his stool. "Actually, she did me a favour. We'd only been together about a year and I'd realised we weren't on the same page not long after we moved in together. She hated my taste in music, for a start. Couldn't be with someone who didn't appreciate Bowie. It was doomed to failure."

Jason smiled as she raised her eyes to meet his. Alessa felt a warm glow as she smiled back. This was reassuring to hear.

"Another drink?" He swilled back the remainder of his beer and stood up, raising his glass hopefully.

"Okay, thanks. Same again, please."

After one pint of Hobgoblin, Jason moved onto orange juice as he was driving. Alessa found herself throwing caution to the wind and knocking back more Sauvignon Blanc than she was used to, feeling contentedly relaxed. They decided to order sandwiches and a bowl of chips to share, although Alessa wasn't really hungry. The conversation flowed and she found Jason easy, agreeable company. She couldn't remember the last time she'd enjoyed herself so much.

But as she glanced towards the window, it suddenly dawned on her that it was now properly dark outside. Alessa looked up at the clock and gasped. It was 10.30pm.

"God, is that the time? I'd better get home. I need a decent night's sleep – we've got another round of door-to-doors in the morning. I want to be firing on all cylinders."

Jason stretched his arms casually above his head, then reached for his jacket from the bench and got up. "Come on, then. Better get you home before you turn into a pumpkin."

She gave him a wry grin. "Glad to know you don't think I'm one already."

The bar area was cramped and the tables packed closely

together. Jason squeezed past two men sitting at the bar and headed for the door. As Alessa rose to follow him, she inadvertently knocked a packet of cigarettes from the next table onto the floor. Stooping to retrieve them, she apologised as she handed the box back to the lilac-haired woman who had smiled at her earlier.

"Thanks, love."

Taking the packet from Alessa, the woman lightly brushed her hand, and then recoiled, almost as though she'd just received an electric shock. Alessa felt something, too – maybe they'd exchanged a surge of static? But the woman stared at Alessa as though she was seeing something startling, her mouth falling open and her green eyes studying Alessa's face. The intensity of her gaze made Alessa uncomfortable. As she moved away from the table, the woman called her back with some urgency.

"Please, wait a minute. Listen, I'm sure you'll probably think this a bit strange, but I think I may be able to help you." Her voice was gravelly, clearly courtesy of the filter-less cigarettes she favoured, with a distinctive Oxfordshire brogue.

Her liver-spotted hands heavily adorned with mystical-looking rings, the woman delved deep into a turquoise velvet handbag and fished out a business card. Alessa looked down at the card and frowned. It was extremely detailed: a print of a naked woman with swirling golden tresses, pouring water from a ewer she was carrying aloft as she paddled through a rippling brook with a backdrop of silver stars in a midnight blue sky. Behind her was a small sailing boat. Beneath this unusual image were etched the words, "Carmel, Uncannily Accurate Tarot Readings and Advice on All Things Spiritual" and a phone number.

Alessa blew out her cheeks and was about to hand the card back, but the woman pressed it firmly into her open hand. "I know lots of people scoff, but I really think you could do with some advice. Forces are at work around you that I don't think you fully understand. Please, do call me. I feel very strongly about it."

The woman seemed pleasant enough, and although tarot readings and fortune telling in general really weren't her thing at all, Alessa didn't want to cause offence. She smiled and accepted the card.

"Thank you. I'll have a think about it."

"You do that, love. I'll be waiting to hear from you. There's some— Well, some stuff I'd like to talk to you about. Help things make a bit more sense. Take care, now." She nodded her head and grinned hopefully.

Alessa wished her goodbye. The woman stared after her unnervingly as she climbed the steps onto the street.

"What was all that about?" Jason, who'd been waiting on the pavement outside, peered over her shoulder.

Alessa screwed up her face. "Some lady who clearly thinks I'm lacking spiritual guidance." She flashed Jason the card and he nodded knowingly.

"Eugh, right. One of those."

Alessa smirked. No more was said on the matter, although the encounter had left her slightly uneasy. She felt oddly singled out and the woman's words rang in her ears.

Forces are at work around you.

What on earth did she mean?

*

Pulling up on the gravel driveway outside Alessa's imposing detached home, Jason's eyes widened. A brand-new, white Fiat Panda was parked in front of the house.

"That your car?"

"Yes. A birthday gift. From my uncle."

Jason peered through the window at the green and red stripe along the side of the vehicle, with the little *Italia 90* footballer motif, caught in the glare of his own car's headlights.

"Wow. It's the special edition, isn't it?"

"Yep. Well, it's the World Cup this year – and he's a huge *Italia* fan . . ."

"Generous uncle."

"He's great. I haven't used it much to be honest, though. I usually catch the bus into work."

Jason nodded. "Easier than fighting for a parking space."

He looked up at the house, appraising the width of the frontage, and whistled. "Nice pad."

She bristled suddenly. "Yes, but it's not *my* 'pad', as you put it. It's my mum's. And appearances can be deceptive. It's a money pit."

Jason's face fell. "I didn't mean anything by it. I was just saying it looks like a lovely house. I'm rather jealous."

Alessa sighed. "Sorry. I just . . . well, I get a bit defensive sometimes. Ignore me."

"I find it very hard to do that." He leaned towards her without warning and, cupping her chin in his hands, planted a kiss full on her lips. It almost took her breath away.

Alessa felt suddenly light-headed. She drew back. She couldn't let this go any further – not now. She'd had a few drinks, but was sober enough to know she didn't want to do anything she might regret in the morning.

"Thank you for a lovely evening," she said hurriedly, climbing from the car. "I'll see you tomorrow."

Jason's brow furrowed. "Did I do something wrong?"

"No, I— It just took me by surprise, that's all." She hesitated. "I'd ask you in, but it's a bit late on a school night." She gave him a reassuring smile and he relaxed visibly.

"See you in the morning, then. Goodnight."

Alessa closed the front door of the house behind her and leaned against it, exhaling deeply. Her whole body was glowing from the inside out. It was a lovely, unfamiliar sensation.

"That you, Sandi?" Her mother's anxious voice from the living room shattered her reverie.

"*Ciao*, Mamma." She put her head round the door, smiling at the sight of Greta in her dressing-gown and hairnet.

"You're very late. I was getting worried. Everything all right?"

"Yes. Sorry – I should've called. Everything's fine. I've been, well, I *think* I've been on a date. And it – he – was very nice. His name's Jason Shelley. And he's a policeman."

*

Lying in bed that night, Alessa found that sleep evaded her. The evening had given her food for thought. After the initial thrill of the kiss had worn off, she was beginning to wonder if she was doing the right thing. Jason was lovely, but up until now, she'd always considered getting involved with a colleague a complete no-no. But the more she reflected on the relaxed few hours they'd spent, the more she persuaded herself that she needed to be less uptight. She enjoyed his company and he seemed really decent, so where was the harm? They had a lot in common. He clearly shared her dedication to the job, and she knew he was as serious about finding Kimberley Painter as she herself was. And she found him undeniably attractive.

She lay staring at the ceiling, the events of the day turning through her mind. Suddenly, a cool breeze passed over her face. She sat up sharply, her attention drawn towards the partially opened curtains, which billowed gently with the draught. Alessa caught her breath as the security light's beam strobed through the gap between the drapes. A scuffling noise beneath the open window alerted her to someone or something moving below, close to the house. Peering at the bedside clock, she saw that it had only just turned 1am. Gripped by fear, Alessa inched herself from the bed, and padded across to the window. Her heart thudding, she twitched the outer edge of the curtain aside.

A man – she was certain the figure was male; even through the darkness, its lumbering, hooded form looked unmistakably masculine – sidled along the high hedge that bordered the driveway and back towards the road, disappearing round the corner. The light which had illuminated the forecourt snapped off once more, leaving everything in eerie shadow.

Alessa stood, rooted to the spot for a moment, trying to collect her thoughts. Her breath came in rapid gasps, adrenaline coursing through her. Had someone been trying to break in? She grabbed her dressing-gown from the hook on the door, eased it open, and made her way downstairs as silently as she could. Fumbling with the chain, she unlocked the front door and, grabbing the huge umbrella her mother kept in the hallway, stepped outside. The light was immediately activated again. She scanned round sharply, her heart hammering. The driveway was definitely empty. Alessa hurried towards the main road and looked both ways. Although the street was fairly quiet, still an occasional car sailed past in either direction. It had only been minutes, but the prowler was clearly long gone, whether on foot or in a vehicle. She shuddered to think that someone might have been trying to gain access to the house.

Finally satisfied that the unwanted visitor was unlikely to return anytime soon, Alessa went back inside, bolting the door and fastening the chain once again. After taking one last look through the window, she tiptoed up the stairs and climbed back into bed, pulling the covers tightly around herself. Squeezing her eyes shut, she began to focus on her breathing, gradually growing calmer. Tomorrow she would need a clear head and she couldn't allow herself to be distracted. She wouldn't mention the intruder to her mother for fear of unnerving her, but made a mental note to speak to Uncle Rob about installing security cameras. As long as Mamma was safe, that was all that mattered.

Chapter 10

Saturday, 23 June 1990

Fourteen days after Kimberley's disappearance

Alessa's first port of call the following day was to the Painters' neighbour, Bernard Stephens. The old man had telephoned the police station in an agitated state, saying he had important information for them.

He ushered her eagerly into his living room and offered her a seat, lowering himself into an armchair. Alessa shot a look around Bernard's spotless lounge. French windows at the far end opened out onto an impossibly neat garden. A handful of evenly spaced china ornaments adorned the mantelpiece, with a brass carriage clock in the centre. Opposite the writing bureau in one corner stood a highly polished sideboard, displaying a selection of framed family photographs. In contrast to the Painters' home, the room felt strangely clinical.

Noticing her taking everything in, Bernard was quick

to indicate the pictures. "That's my wife, Jean. She passed away . . ." His face clouded, and for a moment Alessa wondered if tears might follow, but he seemed to give himself a little shake.

"I'm so sorry." Alessa's sentiment was genuine. She thought suddenly of Joey, and the empty space he'd left in both her own and her mother's lives. Though his death was something she'd been expecting for as long as she could remember, nothing could have prepared her for how she felt once it actually happened. A jumble of memories passed through her mind: times she'd sat talking to him and showing him picture books, the classical music to which he seemed to react so positively; the broad smiles and excited hand gestures she'd been able to raise from him when he was tiny. Despite his being unable to vocalise his thoughts, they'd shared a definite, special bond. And now her memories would forever be overshadowed by the sight of Joey's limp, lifeless form as they'd found him in his bed that terrible morning. His cold, unyielding cheek as she'd pressed her lips against it for the last time.

As it always did when she remembered her brother, a deep ache formed in her chest.

"It's been two years, now – still feels like yesterday." Bernard's words cut into her thoughts. He shook his head, clearing his throat as he turned his attention to another of the photographs. "And there's an old one of our lad, Derek."

Alessa drew herself up, shifting her focus back to the here and now.

"He's got a great job, you know," he went on." Takes him all over the world, so I don't see much of him these days. Oh, to be young and carefree again . . ." Bernard smiled wistfully. "Can I get you anything? Cup of tea, perhaps?"

"No thank you, Mr Stephens. I understand you've something to share with us, about Kimberley Painter's disappearance?"

The old man shuffled to the edge of his seat. "Yes. Well, I hear you've had poor Malcolm in for questioning. I just wanted to tell you I know he couldn't possibly have anything to do with his little girl going missing. She's the apple of his eye." He lowered his voice. "Look, these walls are very thin. I hear a lot of what goes on next door – not that I'm listening in on purpose, you understand," he added hastily. "Only, you can't really help hearing what's being said. You couldn't ask for better parents than the Painters, and to suggest Malcolm could've done away with her, or whatever it is he's being accused of, is ludicrous."

"I see." Alessa's heart quickened. What could the old man have overheard that he considered so significant? She prayed that this might at least eliminate Malcolm from their enquiries. "Do you have concrete proof then, that Mr Painter had nothing to do with the little girl vanishing?"

Bernard's brow knitted into a frown. He seemed frustrated. "Well, erm, no, not exactly . . ."

She felt deflated, her hopes dashed. Bernard was clearly a lonely old man. Maybe this was just an opportunity for a bit of interaction to lift his day.

"But . . . but I've seen how he behaves towards Kimberley," he continued earnestly. "How protective he's always been of her. There's no way he's faking how upset he is over all this."

Alessa studied Bernard closely. He seemed oddly jumpy. She wondered what was behind his demeanour.

"I quite understand what you're saying, Mr Stephens, but unfortunately we need more than a glowing character reference. Even the best people are capable of terrible deeds in certain circumstances. Not that I'm implying Mr Painter has done something bad; far from it. It's just the law's very black-and-white. We have to go on facts, I'm afraid, not hearsay."

Bernard was insistent. "But I *know* Malcolm. I know how

devastated he and Mary are. He wouldn't harm a hair on that child's head." He paused. "Have you spoken to that Greene girl? The one Kimberley knocks about with?"

"We *have* spoken with Faye Greene, yes." Alessa looked curiously at the old man, whose eyes had begun to dart wildly. This sounded more promising. "Was there something else you wanted to tell me, Mr Stephens?"

Bernard pulled himself to the edge of his seat. "Look. I heard them talking, her and Kimberley. The Greene girl was persuading Kimberley to go into town with her; to lie to her mum and dad about where they were going because she knew they wouldn't let her go. I always thought she was bad news, that one."

Alessa sighed. She'd been hoping for something more momentous. "Faye *did* eventually admit she and Kimberley were heading into town. A pity, though, you didn't tell us sooner, since you knew about it. It might've saved a few precious hours when Kimberley first went missing. Or made a difference in the search."

Bernard looked anguished. "If I'd told her parents about it in the first place, they'd never have let her go – and she wouldn't have gone missing at all. I keep thinking about it. I feel so guilty. I just thought they'd think I was a nosey old so-and-so, listening through the wall. But I'm not like that; really I'm not." He hunched over, burying his face in his hands. "Oh God, what if something terrible *has* happened to her and I could've prevented it if I'd spoken up? It's too awful to contemplate."

Alessa's heart went out to the old man. She rose from her seat and instinctively placed a hand on his shoulder. "You mustn't blame yourself, Mr Stephens. I can see you were in an awkward position, but I really wish you'd been more upfront with the police. And if there's nothing else you have to tell me, I've got more people to talk to. We have so little to go on and time's ticking by." She turned to leave, firing a last look around the room as she paused at the door. Her eyes were drawn to the photographs and something flickered in the back of her mind.

The World Cup . . . What *was* it about the World Cup?

"You didn't see or hear anything you think could've been significant that Saturday, did you?"

Bernard shook his head sadly. "I was at the social club for a couple of hours in the afternoon, watching some of the football. Then I went for a kip when I got home. I'd only had a couple of pints – I'm afraid I can't take the drink in the daytime like I used to. But I didn't see Kimberley that afternoon at all – only earlier on, through the window, getting into the car with Malcolm before he dropped her off at that Faye girl's place. Sorry I can't be more help. She's such a lovely little kiddie. It's a crying shame."

"Thank you for your time, Mr Stephens. If you remember anything else, anything at all, please be sure to let us know. Bye for now."

Alessa turned to look back at the house as she closed the garden gate. Poor old soul. He had the best intentions, she was sure. She looked at the list of street names that she needed to cover, and her heart sank. It felt like a thankless task, knocking on doors to ask for information from members of the public who had already been approached. Possibly as a result of the heavy-handed and interrogative manner fostered in the team by DCI Bennett, the police seemed to have put many of the local residents' backs up, and from everything reported back, no one was being particularly forthcoming, whether they knew anything or not. It was going to be a very long morning.

*

Later that afternoon, while Jason was called to investigate a break-in near Summertown, Alessa had decided to retrace

130

Kimberley's last-known journey. Bennett had mentioned the idea of a reconstruction of events, but hadn't been very proactive about organising anything as yet. She wanted to see for herself the route the little girl would have taken – and hoped it might give her some hint they hadn't considered as yet.

She drove to Acacia Hill, parked the car in a lay-by, and walked across to the bus stop nearest Faye's grandmother's road. Soon, a bus loomed into view and ground to a halt where she stood. Alessa climbed on board, made her way to the back and waited for a few moments until it pulled away. There were only a handful of other passengers: a young woman with a small boy, a scruffy teenage youth and an elderly couple, who were sitting a short distance in front of her. As they began to move, she observed the run-down surroundings: the dirty-grey concrete; the graffiti and litter which were prevalent everywhere. The boarded-up windows. It was a far cry from Kimberley's pleasant suburban home environment. She could imagine the child being really scared, especially as she was alone. A frightened little rabbit already, and then possibly to end up . . . The thought made her stomach clench.

She alighted at the stop nearest the Greenes' house and slowly began the walk back towards Lime Tree Avenue, scouring the pavements, looking from left to right and walking down the alleyways which were found at the end of each terrace. She knew that her colleagues had already searched this area. But she was praying she'd get some sort of inspiration, an insight into the path Kimberley herself might have taken. A short-cut, maybe. But every alleyway was a dead-end and there didn't appear to be one. Eventually she arrived outside the Painters' house. Despite her hopes that she'd have some sort of lightbulb moment, there had been nothing. She stood for a moment, looking up at the house sadly. *Where are you?*

Alessa's thoughts were interrupted by sudden movement in the front garden. Shifting her gaze, she watched, puzzled, as a small, multi-coloured rubber ball began to bounce slowly, rhythmically, down the garden path, landing at her feet. It seemed to have come from the house. She cast about, but there was no one to be seen. Her eyes travelled sharply upwards and she felt her heart quicken, shielding her brow to look more closely. A shadow was drifting across the upstairs window. For the briefest moment, she thought she saw someone looking down at her. Someone small. The hairs prickled on Alessa's arms. But as she looked again, there was nobody there. Giving herself a little shake, she dismissed it as the reflection of a crow which had been pottering across the lawn, taking to the air. She watched for a moment longer, then picked up the ball and tossed it back into the Painters' garden. Despondently, she began the trudge back to the bus stop. She still had to collect the car from Acacia Hill and return it to the station before she could finish for the day.

All that her little jaunt had achieved was to make her feel more helpless than ever.

*

Before she'd even turned the key in the lock that evening, Alessa was greeted at the door by her mother, who seemed jittery.

"Everything okay, Mamma?"

"A parcel arrived for you this morning. I missed the postman, but it was left behind one of the bay trees by the front door. Were you expecting something in the mail?"

Alessa shook her head. Her mother hovered in the doorway as Alessa walked apprehensively into the kitchen to find a small brown paper Jiffy bag on the table. Staring at the label, a shudder ran through her. The address was written in that same distinctive scrawl. And the addressee: *Miss S. Cano*. Scrutinising the top right corner, she saw that the parcel wasn't franked. It must have been hand-delivered. A shiver ran through her.

Without a word, Alessa went to one of the drawers and, with quivering hands, took out a pair of vinyl gloves from a boxful her mother kept for unsanitary tasks. Cautiously, she peeled open the padded envelope and peered inside. Reaching tentatively into the package, Alessa withdrew a brightly coloured child's hair tie, a few strands of fine, fair hair still entwined with the elastic. She caught her breath, recalling the itemised description of Kimberley's outfit: red hand-knitted cardigan, white T-shirt, cream corduroy skirt; navy-blue shoes and white knee-length socks; red, cherry-shaped hair bobbles . . .

Alessa gripped the back of a chair with both hands, afraid her legs might fail her. She paused briefly, her mind racing. Composing herself, she looked into the bag once more. She was confronted with a faded Polaroid photograph.

The image swam before her eyes. It was as if every nightmare she'd had for the last twelve years had finally come to fruition. The package fell from her hands, the picture fluttering to the floor, as she rushed from the kitchen and into the cloakroom, then vomited with force into the toilet bowl.

Greta's panicked voice filtered through the hallway.

"Sandi, what's happened? Are you all right?"

Alessa flushed the toilet and then resurfaced, her face grey. She moved slowly back into the kitchen, her eyes darting from the empty envelope on the ground to its contents.

"It's Jessie. That . . . that photo. I think the same monster who took her has got little Kimberley Painter. Oh God, Mamma. He must have killed her too."

*

Greta stooped to retrieve the photograph which lay, face up, next to the Jiffy bag on the floor, her eyes widening in horror. Thankfully she froze before her fingers could make contact with it.

"*No*, Mamma! Don't – you mustn't touch anything. There might be vital forensic evidence on it."

Alessa picked up the Polaroid by one corner, forcing herself to look more closely at the appalling image.

In death, the little girl was still recognisable: pale and fair, her blue eyes partially open; the unsmiling, parted lips bloodless; her cheek smeared with grime. Tears sprang to Alessa's eyes and a sob escaped from her mouth.

Wrapping her arms around the shaken Alessa, Greta held her daughter tightly, rocking her like a babe in arms.

"It's all right, *tesoro*," she soothed, her voice calm and measured. "We've known for a long time that Jessie was no longer with us. You've had a nasty shock. I'll get you a brandy; help settle your nerves. And then we'll call the station and tell them what's happened."

Alessa nodded mutely, clinging to her mother like a limpet. But what the hell did all this mean? Her stomach was still churning with the thought that the freak who had murdered her friend had suddenly resurfaced.

And the fact that somehow he knew their address chilled her to the core. It was too much of a coincidence: the arrival of the video at the station, the prowler; and now this sickening, obscene package. It *had* to be the same man. She was, after all, the one that got away.

Now he'd tracked her down, was he finally returning to finish what he hadn't managed to do all those years ago?

Chapter 11

Saturday morning, 9 June 1990

"But you *said* I could go!"

Kimberley looked completely crushed. She turned imploringly from Mary to Malcolm, who was wrestling with his conscience, knowing how excited she'd been about going round to Faye's house. But Mary had been concerned ever since Kimberley had said she wanted an early night – unheard of behaviour from their daughter – and was adamant.

"There must've been something up with you last night. I'm worried you might be sickening for something or there's another asthma attack on its way. And we can't be sure Faye's parents will keep a proper eye on you. You know yourself how risky it could be."

"But . . . but Faye said they'll be at home all day today. And they'll have got stuff in for tea. They'll be offended . . ."

Mary laughed scornfully, rolling her eyes. "Pfft. I *highly* doubt that. Listen, why don't you ask Faye to come here, instead?"

Malcolm, seeing how upset his daughter was, was torn. He didn't want to undermine Mary – they always tried to present a united front where Kimberley was concerned, even if sometimes he thought she was being a bit over the top. But Kimberley looked so crestfallen his heart went out to her.

"Look, maybe we're being a bit hasty here, Mary. Kimberley's been looking forward to going. Tell you what, *I'll* have a word with Mr and Mrs Greene when I take her round. I'll explain a bit more about the asthma. I know we've told them in the past, but I'm sure if I stress how important it is to keep a close eye on her, they'll take heed."

Mary glared at him, her mouth set into a hard line.

"On your own head be it. If she has a bout of her wheezes while she's there, I'll hold you responsible."

"I'll be fine, Mum, really I will." Kimberley pressed her palms together, her eyes wide. "I told you, I wasn't feeling poorly last night, just tired."

Mary sighed. "I hope I don't live to regret this," she said. "Just you mind what you're getting up to, then. No running around and getting yourself all out of breath. Take a couple of your board games with you. I daresay Faye hasn't got much in the way of toys, has she?"

Kimberley opened her mouth as if to say something, but closed it again just as quickly. She threw her arms around her mother's neck in an atypical display of affection.

"Thank you, Mum. I'll be good as gold, I promise."

Malcolm raised an eyebrow. Somewhere inside, he had the niggling suspicion that his daughter was up to something. But one look at the angelic smile that lit up her little face was enough to melt his heart, and he dismissed the notion. Maybe she was just relieved that her outing hadn't been scuppered after all. He would definitely have a word with Faye's parents, though. And it *was* only going to be for a few hours, after all.

Where was the harm?

*

The Greene family lived only about three quarters of a mile from the Painters. Malcolm thought it hardly worth getting the car out of the garage, but Mary insisted that he drive Kimberley there.

"I don't want her getting breathless," she told him firmly. "Besides, there's drizzle in the air. The damp'll get onto her chest."

Grumbling to himself, he went through the alleyway at the end of the terrace and round to the garage at the back of the house, where the car was stored. Bernard was standing under the awning in his back garden, smoking a pipe.

"Morning, Malcolm. Everything all right?" he called.

"Morning, Bernard. Never better. You?"

"Not too bad. Bloody weather's playing merry hell with my arthritis, but the gardens need it. Can't have it all ways, I s'pose."

A knock from Bernard's kitchen window made Malcolm look up. It was Derek, the old man's son. He waved cheerily. Malcolm returned the gesture, paused for a moment, then ambled up Bernard's path to say a proper hello. He hadn't seen Derek in a while.

Derek came out, extending a hand, which Malcolm shook firmly.

"Long time no see! How're you doing?" Derek's mouth was half-covered by recently sprouted facial hair, dyed a shade too dark for his pale complexion, as was his thinning hair. He must have been at least forty now, and was obviously trying to stave off middle age.

"Fine, fine. God, yes, it's been, what? Almost a year, I reckon. You here for the weekend?" Malcolm enquired. Before Derek could respond, Bernard chipped in.

"No, he's just up for the day again. He's a busy chap, aren't you, Derek? Always in a rush." The old man smiled a little ruefully.

Derek cast his father a withering look. "Got to take the work while I can, haven't I?" he said bluntly. Turning to Malcolm, his tone softened. "Always better to be busy though, eh? Bit of a lull now the footy's started, so thought I'd nip back to see my old dad before it's nose to the grindstone again." His lips appeared to curve upwards as he slapped Bernard on the back, though it was difficult to tell through his moustache. The old man flinched slightly and gave a weak smile.

Malcom nodded. "Well, I wouldn't have known you with that beard!" He grinned good-naturedly, his eyes drawn to the girth of Derek's stomach. The man must have gained at least three stone since the last time they met.

Following the trajectory of Malcolm's gaze, Derek patted his burgeoning abdomen. "Fine living," he acknowledged, a little smugly. "And I've always liked my beer. Used to be fit as a flea! I keep saying I'll get back to the gym, but you know how it is – not enough hours in the day."

"How're things on the romance front? Not settled down yet?"

"Nah, you know me. I'm the original wanderer." Derek laughed. "A girl in every port." His eyes darted back to the house suddenly.

"I bet your dad here'd like a couple of grandkids, wouldn't you, Bernard?"

Bernard opened his mouth to speak, but Derek cut across him. "Doubt it'll happen, I'm afraid. Not in the foreseeable, at any rate." He rolled back his cuff to reveal an expensive-looking timepiece, his eyes widening. "Good grief! Is that the time? I'm expecting a business call at midday. No rest for the wicked. Anyway, good to see you, Malcolm. Give my best to Mary and your little girl – Kirsty, is it?"

"Kimberley," corrected Bernard, his eyes narrowing towards his son. But Derek was already retreating through the back door.

"Well, he's a man on a mission," remarked Malcolm, raising an eyebrow.

"He's running some flippin' marketing campaign or other. Never one to let the grass grow . . ." Bernard rolled his eyes. "Great business mind he's got, my lad, but not a bloody clue about cars!" He forced a laugh. "Still brings his motor for his old dad to service. I wonder if I'd ever see him at all, if it weren't for that." There was a definite note of despair in his voice, but he shook it off. "Shouldn't complain, really. I like to keep my hand in, you know. Gives me a sense of purpose, like."

Malcom nodded. "I suppose I'll do something like that, when I retire. Handy, being in the motor trade – or anything where you're using your hands, come to that. I'm glad my old man pushed me into being a mechanic. Still love my job, even after all these years. I'll bet you miss it, don't you? Got to have something to fill the days, eh?"

"Too true. There's only so many times you can read the paper or watch the news and most of it's depressing as hell." A shadow crossed Bernard's face. He cleared his throat, nodding in the direction of the garage. "You off out, then?"

"Just dropping Kimberley round to her friend's. It's only

down the road, but Mary wants me to take her. On account of the asthma, you know. A bit of a worry, really."

Bernard nodded slowly. "She's a lovely little girl, your Kimberley. Don't think much of that cheeky little bugger she knocks about with, mind you."

"Young Faye?" Malcolm laughed. "Yes, she has her moments. But she's not that bad really, when you get to know her."

"Hmm. Well, I doubt I'll have that dubious pleasure. But just you keep a close eye on your littl'un – you wouldn't want her being led astray. I've seen it many a time, good kids turned bad by keeping the wrong sort of company. I'd nip that friendship in the bud, if I were you. Before it's too late."

Malcolm asserted that he would indeed keep an eye on Kimberley, and admitted that he, and moreover Mary, hoped the friendship would eventually run its course.

"We've had this discussion many a time. But you can't choose who your kids knock about with, unfortunately. I'm banking on it all fizzling out, once they get up to the big school. Until then, we'll just have to make the best of a bad job, I suppose."

"Like I say, just you keep an eye on your lass. It'd be an awful pity if she were to change because of falling in with a minx like that. I can sniff 'em out a mile off, and she's trouble, that one."

"Thanks for the warning." Malcolm glanced at his wristwatch. "Ooh, best be off – Kimberley's champing at the bit in there. You take it easy now."

Bernard nodded and smiled. "You too. See you later."

*

Bernard stood watching as Malcolm backed the car out of the garage and disappeared up the entry. Tapping out the spent

140

tobacco from his pipe into a disused terracotta plant pot, the old man retreated into the house and closed the door behind him. There wasn't much that got past Bernard, and with the walls between the houses being so thin, he was often privy to his unwitting neighbours' conversations. As much as he wanted to, he couldn't really admit that he'd overheard Kimberley and the other one hatching a plan to deceive Malcolm and Mary, or they'd realise he must have heard several other things, too. It wasn't *proper* eavesdropping – although he couldn't help but listen in sometimes. Since his wife had died two years earlier, he led a lonely life. Derek visited extremely sporadically and would grudgingly run him to the social club if he asked him to, but that aside he rarely saw much of anyone. And admitting that he could hear what was going on next door much of the time, rather than being grateful, well, it might make the Painters think he was a bit of an old nosey parker.

And the last thing he wanted to do was fall out with his neighbours.

Chapter 12

Saturday, 23 June 1990

Fourteen days after Kimberley's disappearance

As soon as she'd managed to gather her thoughts, issuing the anxious Greta strict instructions to bolt the doors and to call 999 immediately should she suspect any suspicious activity, Alessa had driven, hands almost welded to the steering wheel, to St Aldates, the Jiffy bag and its contents sealed in an evidence bag on the passenger seat like an unexploded bomb. Upon arrival, she was grateful to discover that Bennett and Henderson were nowhere in evidence. Neither had seemed very sympathetic about the video.

The duty sergeant, a tall, white-haired officer named Sharman, was avuncular and clearly concerned. He booked in the evidence and made a call to the forensics team with a request for someone to process it urgently, then ushered her through the door into the small office behind Reception and switched on the kettle.

"I heard about the video." He grimaced, handing over a steaming mug of tea as she perched on a stool, shivering with shock rather than cold. "You're not having a good time of things lately, are you?"

Alessa squeezed an unconvincing smile. She didn't know Sharman well, only to say hello to in passing. But right now, she needed someone to talk to. She'd considered calling Jason, but he'd mentioned his mum not being too well again, and she didn't want to burden him further.

"It's shaken me up, to be honest," she admitted. "I'm just hoping there'll be something on the package to point us in the right direction." She paused. "I mean, it could be a coincidence but I'm pretty sure there was someone creeping about outside my house last night, too. I didn't mention it to my mum as I thought it might frighten the life out of her."

Sharman's eyes widened in alarm. "Did you report it, though?"

Alessa dropped her eyes sheepishly. "I thought they'd probably think I was being hysterical. You know, after the video . . . But now this parcel's turned up, I suppose I might sound a bit more credible."

Sharman shook his head, his lips tightening. "You really should keep your colleagues informed, you know. Between you and me, I know Bennett's not the ideal boss, but he *is* heading up the investigation, all the same." He paused. "I remember the Jessie Lockheed case well. Remember you in the papers, too. My own daughter was about the same age at the time. Sick bastard. I'd have liked to wring his neck with my bare hands. Still would."

"I just hope we catch up with him. Before . . ." Alessa

dropped her chin to her chest. She sat with both hands wrapped tightly around the warm mug. Though it wasn't a cold day, the heat was somehow comforting. "I keep going over everything in my mind. He actively pursued Jessie, dragged her off the street. I wonder if he did the same to Kimberley, or if he lured her somehow? No one seems to have seen a thing. It's as if she just vanished into thin air."

"Well however he took her, I'm guessing there'll have been others." Sharman looked grim. "I mean, it seems unlikely he just pops up every decade or so. As you say, we just have to hope he's apprehended before he does any more damage."

"It feels hopeless. We seem to be hitting dead ends with every line of inquiry at the moment."

"Then we just have to hope he's tripped up with this stunt; left fingerprints or DNA evidence. If he's got previous, there'll be something on him."

"I'll get onto it now. I'm praying there'll be a file I've overlooked somewhere."

Sharman cocked his head, studying her face. "D'you think you'd recognise him – after all this time?"

Alessa put down the mug on the counter, casting her eyes to the ceiling. "That's just it. I've got this vague impression, but I can't picture his face. Every time I try to remember, it's just a blank."

"Maybe if you actually saw a photo of him, it'd bring it all back." Sharman suggested. He rubbed a hand across his chin. "In the meantime, let's wait for Forensics to do their stuff and we might nail him like that. And make sure you mention your prowler to your team – before he comes back again." He raised his eyebrows and Alessa managed a solemn nod. The thought made her insides feel as though she was dropping at speed in a lift shaft.

Thanking Sharman for the tea, Alessa headed straight for the archives room in the basement and began to scan the shelves for the box containing Jessie's file. There *must* have been suspects at the time. Maybe the officers working on the case had missed something crucial. Steeling herself once she located the bulging folder, with trembling hands she removed it, clasping it to her chest. Though she probably shouldn't, she decided to take it home. She could be researching and keeping a watchful eye on Squitchey House at the same time. If he returned, she needed to be ready for him.

Alessa spent the following day in a state of heightened anxiety, with frequent bilious attacks. Even in broad daylight, every minor sound sent her leaping to her feet like a scalded cat, terrified that the man had returned and was about to launch an attack on either herself or her mother. Every time she entered a room, she scanned round in case he might be hiding somewhere, waiting to catch her unawares. She couldn't contemplate eating, however much the fraught Greta tried to persuade her that she needed nourishment. Sleep the previous night had been only sporadic, and even then, punctuated with horrific images. She had been through Jessie's file over and over, making copious notes about various suspects interviewed at the time. But nothing jumped out at her. Everyone appeared to have had solid alibis and had been ruled out.

Knowing that Kimberley was no longer living had devastated her. But it was the thought of what her childhood friend must have gone through that was really playing on her mind. That picture of Jessie's grey, expressionless face; those blue-black lips . . .

Alessa couldn't help it. It definitely hadn't been the best thing for her current mental fragility, going back over the key events surrounding Jessie's abduction. It was slightly surreal, reading about what had happened from the perspective of someone who'd recorded the information with no first-hand experience of the whole nightmare. The facts laid out as they were seemed clinical. Seeing the information on paper made it feel almost as though it had happened to someone else. She kept replaying the build-up to the incident, remembering her friend's screams, and the towering figure of the man as she fled down the alleyway. But there was a black hole where his face should have been. The ball that seemed to have formed in her stomach kept growing tighter. She tried to blot out the thoughts with happier memories – good times that she and Jessie had spent together. *Before*.

Right from the first day Alessa and Jessie had started primary school, their friendship had blossomed. Jessie had been a chatterbox, unable to sit still for five minutes; a tiny, beaming bundle of energy. Alessa remembered Jessie catching her by the hand and wanting her to join in a game of 'tag', squealing with laughter as they ran across the playground. She'd reminded her of Tinkerbell from *Peter Pan*, darting here, there, and everywhere. Jessie was easily distracted and often in trouble for not paying attention. But she was an appealing little girl, with her halo of fine yellow hair and bright blue eyes. And she was always fun to be around.

While lively and confident at home, Alessa was always a bit more reserved around other children. But Jessie had enough personality for both of them. Alessa often found herself reluctantly swept along with Jessie's plans, not wanting to question what were frequently daft, occasionally even totally outlandish, ideas. Looking back now, she realised she'd just been glad to have Jessie as a friend and should probably have been a bit more forceful in her opinions at times.

Mrs Nimmo was an elderly widow who lived two doors

along from the Lockheeds' house, just off the north end of the Woodstock Road. She was bad-tempered and seemingly intolerant of everyone, particularly the local children, who had learned to steer clear of her neatly clipped privet hedge, unless they wanted an earbashing.

And cats. She *hated* cats. Jessie told Alessa in disgust that on more than one occasion, she'd seen the woman throwing a bucket of icy water over some poor unsuspecting creature when it dared to wander into her garden. But when the victim had been Jessie's own beloved tabby, Tiggy, that was the final straw.

The incident happened during the February half-term break, the year before the girls were due to start secondary school. They'd been stuck indoors most of the week because the weather had been freezing, with lorries grit-spreading the roads at night.

It was early Friday afternoon, nearing the end of the holiday. The two girls were playing Monopoly, sitting cross-legged on the rug in Jessie's cosy bedroom, huddled in front of the radiator. Jessie wasn't focusing, her eyes still flashing with anger as she got up every now and then to peer down the street at her neighbour's front path. Tiggy had retreated underneath the bed, refusing to be coaxed out after his ordeal early that morning.

"You could tell how cold the water was," Jessie had told Alessa when she arrived. "There was, like, steam coming off poor Tiggy's back. He was all shivery. I had to rub him with an old towel and dry him with the hairdryer, and he hated it."

"That's horrible." Alessa was appalled. She loved Tiggy. He was usually so friendly, and always made a beeline for her lap whenever she visited the house.

"I reckon Mrs Nimmo needs to be taught a lesson, don't you?" Jessie's expression was almost murderous. She went to the window once more. "How about the old bag gets a soaking herself?"

Alessa was hesitant. "What did you have in mind?" She didn't care for Mrs Nimmo any more than Jessie did, but targeting an old lady was something her mamma would frown upon, no matter what the reason.

"Well . . ." Jessie put a finger on her chin as she formulated an idea. Her eyes widened. "I know. We could balance a bucket of water on her porch roof, tie some string to it, and pull it when she opens the door. I've seen it done loads of times on telly." She looked gleeful. "Yep. That's what we'll do. She needs to know she can't keep doing bad stuff all the time without . . . without con-se-quen-ces." She broke the word into its four syllables, nodding to herself. "That's what my dad always says to me."

Alessa thought of the kind of zany, slapstick programmes that featured such tricks. Doing it in real life didn't seem like such a brilliant idea. She considered the repercussions, screwing up her face. "I don't know. What if we get caught?"

Jessie blew out a breath in exasperation. "We *won't*! And even if we did, everyone would think she deserved it. She should be reported – to the RSPCA, or whatever."

Alessa could say nothing to placate Jessie, who was so fired up that they eventually had to abandon their board game. Jessie wanted Alessa to ring the doorbell, then run when Mrs Nimmo answered and she herself would release the water over the old woman, but it quickly became obvious that Jessie's brilliant plan was flawed.

"How are you going to get the water up there without her seeing you? And where would you stand to pull the string?"

Deflated, Jessie slumped back onto the floor, pushing out her lower lip. "Okay, clever clogs. *You* think of something, then."

Alessa considered for a moment. What would needle Mrs

Nimmo without causing any real harm? "We could leave some cat poo on her doorstep," she suggested dubiously.

Jessie pulled a face. "Eugh. But that would mean we'd have to pick it up. No thank *you*."

"Hmm. True." Alessa scratched her head. "I s'pose . . . what if we poured bleach or cleaning fluid or something on her lawn? I remember Uncle Rob being really cross with his friend when he was cleaning the patio and accidentally spilled some on the grass and it went all brown. We could wait till she goes out. She hates anyone going anywhere near her grass. Just think how annoyed she'd be if it all shrivelled up!"

Jessie burst into fits of giggles. "Yes! Yes, that's what we'll do." She clapped her hands. "You are a genius, Sandi Cano. I always knew it."

Soon the pair of them were helpless with laughter, doubled over at the thought of the awful Mrs Nimmo's rage. Suddenly, the bedroom door opened, and Mrs Lockheed peeped round at them.

"What's going on in here?"

Both girls looked at one another, tears pouring down their faces.

"We were just . . . just thinking about . . . doing some . . . cleaning," managed Jessie eventually, between howls.

Her mother raised an eyebrow.

"Really? I'd no idea it could be such fun," she remarked. "Honestly, you two. What a pair." She smiled down at Alessa, who was trying to keep a straight face. "Sandi, would you like to stay for tea this evening? We're having cheese and potato pie. I remember how much you like it."

Before Alessa could answer, Jessie butted in. "Have you made a Victoria sponge, too? It's her favourite." Her laughter had begun to subside now. She winked at Alessa. "You *will* stay, won't you? We've got plans to make."

They never did exact their revenge on Mrs Nimmo that day. Though they watched for the rest of the afternoon, the old woman never seemed to leave the house. They couldn't possibly get into her garden without being seen. Plus, Jessie's mum was in and out of the kitchen all the time and would have demanded to know why they were taking her cleaning products from under the sink.

Just plotting how they could get their own back on the old woman seemed to have been enough to get it out of Jessie's system, however. Often this was the way. She was like a butterfly, flitting from one idea to the next. Sometimes Alessa wondered if her head was full of cotton wool, but it was such an endearing quality.

She thought now of Kimberley; how from everything she'd learned about the little girl, it appeared that in her naivety and eagerness to please Faye, she had allowed herself to become drawn into her worldlier friend's mischief. From her own experience, Alessa understood exactly how Kimberley must have felt. While at that age Jessie hadn't been as mature in her outlook as Faye Greene appeared to be, Alessa herself had found it so hard not to go along with Jessie's whims. She could be extremely persuasive.

But still Alessa wondered what might have happened to prompt Kimberley to leave Acacia Hill alone. Had Faye told her to go? Or had Kimberley walked out of her own volition? Never having been out alone, the little girl must have been scared, but if she'd stood up to the physically bigger, more confident Faye, it demonstrated some strength of character, and enough common sense to catch the right bus back towards her home.

The Painters had stressed how they'd always impressed upon their daughter never to accept lifts from strangers. But was it possible that on this occasion she had dropped her guard – or merely succumbed out of her desperation to get back home? Or, like Jessie, had she been hauled screaming from the street? But somehow the latter seemed the least likely.

No one appeared to have heard a thing.

Monday, 25 June 1990

Sixteen days after Kimberley's disappearance

The first briefing of the week found DCI Bennett in a foul mood. Everyone now knew about Alessa's parcel and the prowler, Bennett seemed irked that he hadn't been the first to be informed. The results just back in from the forensic team were clearly not what anyone had been hoping for. They had, frustratingly, been unable to find any useful evidence with regard to the identity of the sender of Alessa's package. Their suspect had been careful to cover his tracks. It had, however, been possible to verify from a comb supplied by the Painters that the strands of hair belonged to Kimberley.

"Bennett's really pissed off. It's one less solved case to add to his apparently unblemished record – plus, it's shown him up for the total twat that he is," muttered Alessa from behind a cupped hand. "And now everyone's realised how much time and resources have been wasted, all because of his ridiculous vendetta against poor Malcolm Painter. He's had the guy under surveillance all this time and Painter's hardly left the house. He certainly hasn't been sneaking round to my house or popping back and forth to Reading. I never thought he had anything to do with it. Bennett's been pinning everything on Painter being the culprit and now he's been left with egg on his face."

Alessa and Jason sat at the back whilst their puffed-up leader stood, ready to pontificate, beside the bulletin board, his tongue working overtime in his left cheek. She tried her best to avert her eyes from the enlarged picture of Jessie's body, which now featured in the centre of the display. The image turned her legs to jelly. She sat, gripping the edge of her plastic chair, hoping her discomfort wasn't too apparent.

"You okay?" Jason turned towards her, his eyes scanning her face. "If you feel a bit . . . you know, I'll take you outside."

She managed a weak smile. "I'm all right. It's just been a really weird few days, you know? The sooner we find this scumbag, the sooner I can put it all behind me."

"I wish you'd called me. For moral support, if nothing else."

"Thanks. But you've got enough on your plate at home. I thought you could do with a bit of respite – and the main thing was waiting for Forensics to run their checks. Which, as it turns out, hasn't helped a fat lot anyway."

*

Bennett cleared his throat noisily. The low hum of conversation amongst those assembled ceased abruptly.

"The arrival of the package at WPC Cano's home address over the weekend would seem to imply the same offender is responsible for the abductions of both Jessie Lockheed and Kimberley Painter," declared Bennett, in as authoritative a tone as he could muster. "Forensics have confirmed the handwriting on the label had been disguised, its shakiness suggesting it was possibly written with the left hand by a naturally right-handed person, or vice versa. There was nothing remarkable noted about the style, nor the ink. The absence of prints confirmed gloves were clearly worn before handling the Jiffy bag and its contents. Jessie Lockheed's photograph had been taken on an old Polaroid Instamatic camera, using SX-70 film, but given the age of the apparatus and the vast numbers that were once sold, it'll be virtually impossible to track it down." He looked sternly from beneath his eyebrows at everyone. "Hopefully I don't need to stress the importance of keeping this information in-house for the time being."

The team responded with an unenthusiastic mumble. Bennett tilted his chin upwards.

"Good." He adjusted his tie. "At this point we can't positively identify any alleged prowler as being the same individual responsible for sending either the video cassette or the items to WPC Cano's home, therefore we'll just wait it out for the time being – if there is further activity, we may arrange surveillance of the property, but obviously we want to be ninety-nine per cent sure before squandering our resources." He threw Alessa a look of irritation. "We are, in the meantime, going to spread our search further afield. From the first package, we can assume there's a possibility the perpetrator is based in Reading – or has connections in the vicinity – therefore we'll be working in close collaboration with Reading Constabulary. I'm charging DS Henderson here with liaising with some of their officers as soon as possible, to look back over any unsolved missing children cases over the past twenty years. We can leave no stone unturned."

Collective surreptitious eye-rolling ensued amongst the officers gathered for the briefing, but no one spoke. Bennett could be irritatingly theatrical and this was one of his favourite expressions, most notably when things weren't going to plan.

"As you'll be aware, no corpse was ever found in the Jessie Lockheed case, and as such this is our first true confirmation that the girl *is* actually deceased. At this stage, we're not going to inform the families, and I'm sure I don't need to remind you to keep schtum where your own loved ones and the press are concerned. But I imagine you'll have gathered that we're now also treating the Painter case as a murder inquiry."

Sergeant Henderson, who'd been hopping from one foot to the other, clearly itching to share something, raised a hand. "If I might interject, sir?"

Bennett's jaw clenched. He gave an almost imperceptible nod.

Henderson continued. "I was on the phone to Reading Constabulary first thing. One of their officers came back with one particular missing child cold case file almost immediately. An eleven-year-old girl by the name of Sally-Ann Hughes; disappeared, early summer of '86. She'd been on an end-of-term outing from school into Oxford. Went off along Cornmarket to buy an ice-cream and vanished into thin air."

Bennett appeared taken aback and not a little vexed. "That was unusually efficient of you, Sergeant," he remarked, smiling thinly. "Do we have a photograph of this girl?"

"No, sir, not yet. But they're sending one across later today, plus a copy of the file."

Bennett looked almost peeved that Henderson had seemingly made such speedy progress, and on his own initiative. "Good work, Sergeant," he said, somewhat begrudgingly. "Knew I could depend on you to make a flying start." The man's synthetically broad smile belied his rigid body language. His face suddenly stony once more, his tongue began its habitual exploration of the inside of his cheek.

Henderson stood back, grinning like a Cheshire cat. His eyes flicked round the room, apparently making sure that everyone had heard their DCI's rare words of praise.

Alessa and Jason exchanged exasperated glances. A smile twitched at the corners of Jason's lips. "Friggin' hell, it's like watching Laurel and Hardy," he whispered from the side of his mouth.

Alessa snorted. "I think Stan and Olly on the case might be a better bet," she replied in a low voice. "Let's hope the Reading lot are more on the ball."

"Right, then." Bennett clapped both hands together. "Let's get cracking, shall we? There's a killer out there, and we need him off the streets." He dismissed everyone then turned his back and began to talk to Henderson in hushed tones.

The other officers began to disperse. Jason rose to his feet and stretched.

"You doing anything later? After work, I mean?"

Alessa stood up, straightening her skirt. "Nothing planned. I could do with a bit of light relief after this, though. Christ, where's it all going to end?" She sighed. "I've got to be honest, it's really shaken me up to think this weirdo knows where I live. For all I know, he could be watching me right now, even. It feels like I should be looking over my shoulder all the time."

"Don't you worry. I'll look after you." He grinned, winking at her. "Stick with me and you'll be okay."

Alessa laughed. "And who are you, then? My knight in navy blue?"

"That's about it. Yeah, I like that. I can see myself as your appointed protector." He glanced around, then gave her hand a consoling squeeze. "The role'd suit me fine."

Even if she wasn't entirely reassured, Alessa was grateful for Jason's concern. "Thank you. It makes me feel a bit better, knowing you're looking out for me."

"Then come out with me later. I know a great pizzeria in Jericho – d'you fancy it?" He raised his eyebrows encouragingly.

The thought of spending the evening with Jason and having something else to focus on for a while was a welcome one. But she felt guilty at the best of times about leaving her mother all alone, day and night, and after their intruder and now the package turning up, she was really worried. She'd called Uncle Rob and although he was away in Italy, he'd promised to send someone to check on all the doors and windows at the house that afternoon.

"You leave it with me, *piccolina*," he'd told her earlier that morning. She could picture him, stretched out in a deck chair on the sunny roof terrace of his five-star hotel, wrapped in his blue silk dressing-gown, silver hair swept back as he sipped the first espresso of the day. "You want me to come back?" The pitch of his voice and rapid breathing coming down the line betrayed his anxiety. "I can book a flight later today, if—"

"No, no, it's absolutely fine," Alessa had reassured him, though part of her wanted to beg him to jump on the next available plane. "You enjoy your break. You'll be home soon enough. We'll be okay. As long as everything's being checked out by a professional, it should be fine. And you mustn't forget, I'm a police officer now. I can handle myself." If she said it with enough conviction, she might even persuade herself it was true.

"Well, if you're sure . . ." He still sounded dubious. Alessa could hear another male voice in the background suddenly. Uncle Rob must have put a hand over the receiver, as a brief, muffled interchange ensued. He came back on the line more clearly again. "Matteo says *ciao*," he told her, his tone a little lighter.

"Tell him *ciao* back," she said, hoping she sounded confident and cheerful, and not as though she were about to crumble

156

under the weight of everything. "I'll let you go, anyway. Enjoy your day and speak soon."

Even the sound of Uncle Rob's mellow voice had made her feel a bit better. She missed his solid presence and his unfailing ability to make her feel protected and to put things right. She just wished he was coming home a little earlier. But she knew that he could be relied upon to deal with everything. He was arranging for the security cameras to be fitted as soon as possible too, and that would give her greater peace of mind.

But when she thought of the awful contents of that package, Alessa felt her resolve waver once more. What else did the sick creep have in store for her? Or even worse, for her family? She gave herself a mental shake. What was it she'd just been saying? She *could* handle herself – she *had* to. She mustn't let the monster control her life. He'd done that for long enough as it was.

She tuned back in to Jason's words.

"I'd really like that. But it can't be a late one, I'm afraid. I feel bad leaving my mum on her own all the time. Since Joey . . ." She let out a long breath.

"Sure, I understand." Jason offered her a sympathetic smile. "Well, if we go early, you can be home by, say, nine-thirty? I'll pick you up about half six. How does that sound?"

"Okay. Sounds good."

*

The food in the pizzeria was simple, but excellent. The restaurant was a no-frills sort of place: wooden chairs built for function rather than comfort and small gingham cloth-covered tables set with candles in Chianti bottles. An assortment of not very realistic plastic vegetables had been strung around the bay window. It was, however, obviously a popular venue, with a steady stream of customers, and the atmosphere vibrant. But though Alessa tried to relax, her mind was very much elsewhere. She should have known the Jiffy bag's sender would have thought about leaving evidence. He'd planned it all carefully. The man had evaded capture for so long – he wasn't likely to have mailed something like that without being mindful of leaving clues. Jessie's file hadn't contained anything to give her a *eureka* moment, either. She felt sure there must be *something* in the archives on sex offenders or missing children that would set them on the right track – it was just a matter of trawling through it all. But it was all so frustratingly slow.

They had been welcomed warmly by the jovial hostess, a plump, middle-aged woman by the name of Valentina. Her equally lively husband, the portly, flush-faced Alberto, was, it transpired, an old friend of Alessa's uncle.

"I remember you as a little girl!" he'd exclaimed, throwing up his hands in delight. "How's Roberto doing? You tell him to give me a call." He leaned in towards Jason, winking mischievously. "*Che bella ragazza ti sei trovato, figliolo.*"

Jason looked bemused. "What did he just say?" he asked, as the chuckling Alberto left their table.

"Doesn't matter," muttered Alessa, crimson-cheeked. Alberto may have been singing her praises, but she was glad Jason hadn't understood. "Eat your pizza."

She poured herself a large glass from the complimentary carafe of house red that Valentina had brought them, and glugged it back in one. Jason stared at her, his brow knitting.

"*Whoa.* Slow down. That'll go straight to your head – it's about fourteen per cent proof, you know." He reached across the table, taking her free hand in his own.

Alessa dropped her chin to her chest and let out a slow

breath. "I feel . . . I don't know, like I need something to obliterate everything that's going on at the moment. Not that it's going to help." She shrugged helplessly. "I know I have to face up to it, but I keep wondering what the hell he's got in store for me next. And I know I'm being selfish, with what's happened to Kimberley and the sheer hell the Painters must be going through . . ."

Tears pricked her eyes suddenly and she released Jason's hand to brush them away with the cuff of her blouse.

"I'm sorry. I'm not much fun to be around when I'm like this. Maybe this wasn't such a great idea."

Jason sat back in his seat. He tipped his head to one side, studying her with concern. "Don't be daft. You're not being selfish at all. Christ, anyone'd be on edge with what's been going on. But I think this is just what you need – getting out, a bit of normality. And the fucker will slip up sooner or later, you can be sure of it. He's trying to be clever, but sending stuff to your home was probably not his wisest move. I'm sure surveillance could be arranged—"

Alessa shook her head vehemently. "Bennett would never sanction it."

Alessa noticed Jason's hands tighten into fists. He lowered his voice. "Well, he didn't baulk at blowing half his budget on surveilling Malcolm Painter. I could have a word with—" He hesitated. "I mean . . ."

Alessa managed a grateful smile. "It's a kind thought. But how could you – how could *we* – possibly influence Bennett's decisions? The man's a law unto himself."

"Yep, and a danger to every bugger else," Jason muttered, taking a swig from his own glass. His face had hardened. "We need someone like him in charge like we need a hole in the head."

Alessa puffed out her cheeks. "I think the only way the investigation is going to move forward at all is if we're as proactive as possible, even if it means working on our own time."

Jason leaned towards her, lowering his voice. "Definitely. I've been looking into a few more suspects – nothing useful's come up as yet – but it's shocking how many sex offenders are out there in the community. If I had my way, they'd all be forced to wear huge badges."

Alessa gave a small shudder. "I located Jessie's file. There were several interviewed at the time she was taken. But the alibis for every one of them checked out." She chewed her lip. "I mean, it's possible the perpetrator hasn't actually got a record. So even if forensic evidence *had* been found, we wouldn't necessarily have him on file."

"Just so annoying that the door-to-doors haven't given us any clues. It's bizarre she wasn't seen again after getting off the bus. You'd have thought someone would've spotted her."

"Well *someone* clearly did." Alessa played with the stem of her glass. "I'm wondering whether he's just been lying low for the last twelve years or if he's been active somewhere else. There's always that possibility."

"True. We need to widen the search. But how far afield? I mean, he might've even been abroad. Or it's feasible he *is* a known offender and could've been banged up for a lesser offence." He rubbed angrily at his temples with his fingers. "But whatever we propose, Bennett thinks he knows best. It's so fucking frustrating." A muscle began to twitch in his cheek.

Jason had seemed so relaxed earlier. Alessa felt suddenly guilty that her mood was casting a shadow over the occasion. She pulled herself upright, forcing a smile.

"I'm sorry. Let's not talk about Bennett or the case any more. I'll do my best to set it all aside for this evening."

She squeezed Jason's hand and without warning he leaned across the table earnestly and planted a kiss on her mouth, leaving her slightly giddy. He sat back and gazed at her for a moment.

"You are quite the loveliest thing I've ever laid eyes on, do you know that?"

In spite of everything, Alessa felt a burst of pure joy. That one line had been enough to erase every negative thought coursing through her mind. For the time being, at least.

"You're not so bad yourself, PC Shelley."

The conversation quickly turned to lighter topics: favourite foods, favourite music; places they'd visited; embarrassing teenage moments. Alessa considered mentioning the months of therapy she'd been through, but didn't want to put a damper on things, so decided that might be something best left for another occasion. All the time, Jason's eyes barely left hers and butterflies skittered around her stomach.

The evening passed all too quickly. Thanking Valentina and Alberto for their hospitality, the pair stepped out into the crisp night air. Alessa shivered. Jason put an arm around her and rubbed her shoulders to warm her up.

"We could go for another drink, if you like," said Jason, hopefully. "I can ditch the car . . ."

Alessa looked at her watch and pulled a face. "I'd love to, but I really must get home. But thank you, it's been lovely. And a very welcome distraction."

"Okay, no worries." He smiled resignedly. "Another night, then."

They climbed into the car and, considering how well they'd got on, drove in slightly awkward silence back to the Cano family home on the Woodstock Road. As they pulled onto the driveway, Alessa thought for a moment. She turned to Jason coyly.

"You can come in for coffee, if you like."

His face lit up. "Thank you. I'd like that very much. If you're sure it's okay?"

She smiled and stepped out of the car, beckoning him. Jason followed.

Greta must have heard the crunch of tyres on the gravel. She opened the front door and hugged her daughter, then extended a welcoming hand to Jason. Alessa was amused to see a pink flush rise up his cheeks.

"Hello, Jason. It's very nice to meet you."

"Good evening, Mrs Cano. Or should I say, *buonasera, signora*?"

Greta clapped her hands. "Oh, you speak Italian! *Grazie per esserti preso cura di mia figlia.*"

Jason threw a glance at Alessa, a hint of panic in his eyes. "Not really," he admitted. "Just the odd pleasantry, to be honest."

Greta laughed. "No matter. I was just thanking you for looking after my daughter. Come on in, I'm about to make coffee. Did you enjoy your meal?"

"It was really good, Mamma. And the people who own the restaurant are old friends of Uncle Rob."

"Oh? Who would that be, then?"

"Alberto and Valentina? They're from Naples originally. They seemed lovely."

"Oh, I remember them. Yes, very nice people. We used to see them ourselves socially, once upon a time. Before your father—" She broke off, her face tightening as she muttered under her breath and turned sharply towards the door.

162

Alessa fired the baffled Jason a warning look and they followed Greta into the house.

Jason's eyes grew large as he looked round. The hallway was a little dingy, but vast. A huge crystal chandelier hung from the centre of the ceiling, beyond which a sweeping staircase with a wide oak banister led to a galleried landing.

"You have a beautiful home, Mrs Cano."

Alessa looked around dubiously at the cracks in the plaster, the worn stair runner, and the chipped wood along the banister caused by the buckles of her shoes when she'd slid down as a child. It used to drive her mother insane, but Uncle Rob would always wink at her and argue it was crying out to be climbed aboard – and kids needed to have fun. There were still scuff marks along the skirting board from Joey's wheelchair, old-fashioned light switches and sockets that were probably no longer legal, and antiquated, rusting cast-iron radiators that didn't warm up properly. These days, Alessa saw only the problems that the house presented. She tried to view it from an outsider's perspective and thought maybe it wasn't so bad, after all.

"Thank you. But please, call me Greta. You're making me feel like the old retainer." She beamed, all mention of her miscreant husband clearly forgotten, and gestured to a doorway on the right. "Sandi, take Jason into the living room. I'll bring coffee through in a minute."

Jason sank into the faded red brocade settee beside Alessa, gazing round the tastefully if now somewhat shabbily furnished room in ill-disguised awe. "Bloody hell! It's like a stately home."

Alessa felt suddenly embarrassed. Through her job, she had been in enough people's homes to realise that she was incredibly lucky to live in such a large house, even if it was starting to look decidedly neglected.

"You need to close your mouth. You'll be catching flies in there if you're not careful." She tried to keep her tone light. "And trust me – it's a swine to heat."

He grinned. "Sorry. It's just . . . well, it's a hell of a lot bigger than our house. Yeah, I s'pose that's the downside. Mum and Dad's is always nice and warm, being a mid-terrace." He sat slightly awkwardly, hands clasped between his knees, his eyes still drinking everything in. "So, there's no love lost between your mum and your dad, then? What happened there, if you don't mind my asking?"

Alessa let out a long breath. "Papà couldn't cope with my brother Joey. That was the long and short of it. He wanted her to put him into a home. Of course, Mamma wouldn't hear of it. And then Papà started being difficult, staying out late all the time and being generally unpleasant." She paused. "It was a relief when he eventually left, to be honest."

"Where did he go?"

"Back to Spain. Granada. He still had family out there. Clearly they were more important to him than us."

Jason shook his head. "Shit. How old were you?"

"Almost seven. Joey was still a baby. So you see, it was just the three of us against the world for a very long time. Not forgetting Uncle Rob, of course. Mamma's brother. He's been an absolute diamond."

Jason reached over to press her hand.

Alessa gazed into his earnest blue eyes and her whole body seemed to turn to water. Suddenly she wanted to feel his arms around her more than anything. She was about to lean in for a kiss when Greta appeared with a tray bearing a cafetière, a jug of frothy milk, a plate of home-made biscuits and three china cups. She placed the tray on a side table and sat herself down in the gap the embarrassed pair had just created between them.

164

"Well, Jason, tell me all about yourself. Where do you live, then?"

*

Jason remained in their company for just over an hour, then made his excuses to leave. Alessa worried that Greta's incessant questions had frightened him off. She saw him to the door, rolling her eyes.

"Sorry about Mamma. She wasn't really giving you the third degree, you know. It's just her way of being sociable."

He smiled. "Yes, I guessed that. She's really nice. I'd love you to meet my parents too, sometime. You'll have to excuse the state of the house, though. Dad doesn't have much time for cleaning, and by the time I get home I'm too knackered to care." He hovered on the front step, glancing around, his hands thrust into his trouser pockets. "Erm, perhaps we could go for a curry next time, if you like." He searched her face, suddenly serious. "I'm getting ahead of myself. There *will* be a next time, won't there?"

Alessa laughed. "'Course there will. I've had a lovely evening. You were right – it was just what I needed. And a curry sounds good. Thank you."

After a lingering kiss, she watched and waved as he drove away. Her spirits lifted, she took a deep, exhilarating breath. The cool evening air was still and the night sky clear and star-spangled. She gazed upwards, revelling in the moment.

A sudden rustling in the tall shrubs bordering the pavement stopped her in her tracks. She screwed up her eyes to see what was making the sound and spotted what she perceived to be the outline of something – or someone – moving in the foliage. Her heart pounding, Alessa rushed back into the house and, with trembling fingers, bolted the door. She moved the door curtain aside and peered through the glass pane, just in time to see the figure of a stockily built, hooded man of medium height crossing the road briskly away from the opening of the Canos' driveway.

It was pointless calling the station; he'd be long gone by the time anyone arrived. And it would be foolhardy to pursue him alone – there were so many passageways running from the side streets along the Woodstock Road and he could be waiting to ambush her. Maybe that was what he was hoping for. Alessa's mind began to race. How long had he been there? And exactly what was his endgame? He had her at a clear disadvantage – he knew her identity, her home address, and had plainly been watching her comings and goings. She felt suddenly nauseous and bent over to try to get rid of the sensation. When it was gone, she stood up, taking deep breaths as she tried to gather her thoughts. Eventually satisfied that he was unlikely to reappear, she drew the curtain and retreated into the house.

That night, she didn't rest easily. Every snapped twig or crunched leaf, the rumble of an occasional passing car, any slight movement whether outside or in, had her running to the window, her heart in her mouth. She felt certain that he was still lurking out there somewhere; the warped individual who had taunted her with the video cassette and posted that vile package. The same man who had taken and murdered both Jessie and Kimberley.

Watching her home.

Waiting.

But waiting for *what*?

Eventually, after what seemed like hours, she succumbed to restless sleep, tormented by unwelcome thoughts of Jessie's lifeless stare superimposed on the face of little Kimberley Painter.

She woke abruptly, clammy with sweat, shaken from her torturous dreams by something in her subconscious; something that rendered her paralysed with dread.

An unidentifiable sound.

But this time it seemed to be coming from inside.

The house itself was silent and sat in total darkness, except for the occasional muted chime of the hallway clock, which announced the passage of every fifteen minutes. But Alessa had definitely heard another noise; she was certain she hadn't imagined it. Once able to move, she eased herself slowly into a sitting position and strained to listen.

There was someone moving around downstairs. She knew if her mother ever rose for some reason, she would always turn on the landing light to guide her way, but no comforting glow shone through the cracks around the door. Alessa held her breath, her heart banging in her chest. She thought she heard the creak of the bottom stair and waited, fully expecting approaching footsteps to follow. But there was a pause – an ominous stillness, which lasted probably no more than seconds but felt like hours, as though whoever it was might be considering their next move. The stair groaned once more. Alessa could just discern the soft thud of footfall retreating along the hallway, followed by the dull click of the kitchen door, which led to the rear of the house.

Screwing up her courage, Alessa leapt from her bed and rushed out onto the landing, hoping she might be able to see the intruder from one of the windows at the back of the building. The hallway clock chimed four times as she rushed past her mother's room and into the bathroom, flinging wide the large window that overlooked the garden.

But all seemed peaceful outside, the sound of birdsong just starting to shatter the tranquillity. A soft mist hovered above the vast playing fields that stretched behind the houses, as the

167

first stripes of sunlight began to gild the flannel-grey skies in the west.

If indeed there had been anyone there, he was well and truly gone.

*

Returning to her bed, Alessa lay rigidly awake, staring at the ceiling as she turned everything over in her head. Why the hell would anyone have broken in, with the sole aim of putting the wind up her and nothing else? It made no sense. Her mother, who was usually a light sleeper, hadn't stirred.

Was it possible she'd imagined it all?

Eventually, she got up and went downstairs to make a cup of tea. It was almost 5.45am and pointless trying to go back to sleep because she would have to get ready for work soon.

She felt sick with tiredness. She would need an early night tonight; she wouldn't be able to function properly if she carried on like this. Slumped over the kitchen table sipping her tea, Alessa suddenly jolted upright as something occurred to her. The package she'd received the other day had been left behind one of the potted bay trees outside the front door. With mounting dread, she remembered that her mother used to leave a back door key there for emergencies, buried in the soil beneath the top layer of pebbles, after she'd been locked out once. What if . . .?

Alessa felt as though ice was being dripped through her veins. She hurried through the hallway and unlatched the front door. Urgently scrabbling amongst the pebbles in one of the pots, she dug her fingers into the earth.

Nothing.

She caught her breath. Maybe it was the tree on the other side.

Frantically, she repeated the raking of the soil. There was no key in either container. She shrank back against the wall, blood rushing in her ears.

Someone had access to their house – and the Canos had effectively invited them in.

Chapter 13

Tuesday, 26 June 1990

Alessa knew that drastic action was needed. She'd have to ensure every lock in the house was changed, in case he had somehow accessed other keys and was planning to obtain copies. Squitchey House had an antiquated alarm system, but it hadn't been operational in years – she needed to get onto that, too. The CCTV installation – that was all in hand, although sooner would have been preferable.

Her mind was racing. Should she tell Greta to go and stay at Uncle Rob's for a while? But that might send her mother into meltdown. Alessa couldn't seem to hold a thought. She sat at the table with her head in her hands, her pulse throbbing in her temples. *Think*.

She went to the drawer and took out a notepad and pen. If she set everything out, it might help her see the woods for the trees.

The most pressing thing was to find a locksmith. Alessa

fetched the Yellow Pages from the phone stand in the hall and jotted down a couple of numbers. It was too early in the day to speak to anyone yet, but the second they opened she would ring. She leafed through a list of security companies and located one that serviced all types of alarm system. It probably wouldn't be cheap – she wondered if the whole lot would need ripping out and replacing. But so be it. If necessary, she'd have to go cap in hand to Uncle Rob, whether Greta liked it or not. This wasn't a stain on the ceiling – this was serious.

It occurred to her suddenly that if anyone *had* been in the house, there might be physical evidence. Why had she not checked straight away? She got up and switched on the light, then bent down to scour the kitchen floor, inch by inch. Knowing how careful the culprit had been so far, she was certain he'd have worn gloves. But a footprint or two would be useful.

Nothing. After going into the garden on the off-chance he might have walked across the lawn or borders, it became obvious that yet again he'd been scrupulous in his efforts to avoid detection. For once, she cursed the recent drier weather. Wet soil would have been more likely to throw something up. But just as she was coming back in through the outside door, Alessa stopped in her tracks. A thin strip of dark green fabric, around an inch in length, was caught in the splintered edge of the door frame. Her heart quickening, she rushed to get a plastic sandwich bag from the cupboard and, turning it inside out, carefully unpicked the threads from the wood, holding it up to the light. So, he wasn't infallible, then! It felt like a small victory.

She locked the back door, turning the key to a ninety-degree angle and leaving it in the lock, then pushed the rubber wedge-shaped door stopper usually used to prop it open during hot weather beneath. If he should return, that would stop him for the time being. And once the locksmith had been, the worry of their intruder having a key would be eliminated. She looked at her list of phone numbers and blew out a long breath. Having a sort of plan now, she felt slightly better.

In the meantime, she needed to get ready for work. Maybe Forensics could find something from the piece of green cloth she'd trapped in the bag. So far it was all she had to go on.

Thursday, 28 June 1990

Nineteen days after Kimberley's disappearance

Alessa had been on pins waiting for Forensics to come back with the results from the fabric. She'd been a bit vague when she handed it in, but to her shame had used her most beguiling smile and a flirtatious wink to persuade the young, rather spotty technician to run it through quickly and to give the results to her alone. While part of her was desperate to share her concerns about the intruder with the team, still a niggling little voice kept reminding her that she'd been wrong in the past. True: she wasn't taking medication at the moment. But maybe she really ought to see her doctor again. What if she'd imagined it? It wasn't beyond the realms of possibility.

She'd already attracted a few scathing looks from some of the other officers since the video tape arrived, almost as though they thought she was an attention-seeker. Until she knew without a shadow of doubt that there had definitely been someone in Squitchey House, she decided to keep her fears to herself. There was no way she'd share any of it with Bennett. And she certainly didn't want to scare Jason off. If he thought she was some sort of head case, he might run a mile.

It had been three days and Alessa still had no news from Forensics. A frantic telephone call from a member of the public that morning had galvanised everyone into action once more. An excitable elderly woman had rung, recounting how she'd witnessed what she believed to be the attempted abduction of a child outside her home just off the Banbury Road.

Whilst several other officers combed the area, Alessa was tasked with taking a statement from the very animated lady, who went to great lengths to describe the man, and the young boy he'd tried to snatch. A door-to-door along the roads nearby proved fruitless, until the occupant of one house at which she knocked seemed to fit the description of the distinctive man in question – an ageing punk, with his red Mohican hairstyle and numerous facial piercings.

Perplexed by her questions, the man stared at Alessa in disbelief at first, and then, throwing back his head, gave a loud, throaty laugh. He turned and called back into the house.

"Sid! Come 'ere a minute."

A young, dark-haired boy – a miniature but less heavily adorned version of the man – came running down the stairs. Again, he was at once recognisable from the detailed description the woman had given.

"What's up?"

"Tell this nice young lady who I am, will you?"

"You're my dad, of course. Why?"

"And what were we doing this morning?"

"Going to visit Uncle John. Why?"

"And what does Uncle John do?"

"He's a wrestler. You know this! Why are you asking all these stupid questions?"

The man turned back to Alessa. "There you go, love. You

173

can tell the poor old dear she needn't get her knickers in a twist. We were just mucking about. No harm done, eh?"

Back in the car, a smile twitching on her lips, Alessa picked up the two-way radio.

"Another non-starter. Get the word out there to the rest of the team. I'm on my way back in."

The mock altercation between the man and his son, witnessed by the overly vigilant old lady, was the latest of several false leads which had occurred over the last few weeks. Whilst it provided momentary amusement, it still meant that they were no nearer to apprehending the man who had murdered Jessie, and now almost certainly Kimberley Painter. Alessa was becoming increasingly despondent.

As she turned the corner, Alessa's head began to swim. The area had altered a little, but at once, she recognised the stop on the Banbury Road where she and Jessie would wait for the school bus each morning. She knew she should be heading back to the station but felt suddenly, irrationally compelled to revisit their journey. Driving slowly, she began to retrace the route behind a stream of slow-moving traffic until she reached the roundabout at the top and then took the first exit. Soon the road narrowed, the views changing from bricks and mortar to hedgerows and open fields, as she left the outskirts of the city and headed north. Alessa's heart quickened as familiar points along the road brought back memories of things she'd long forgotten. She recalled how she and Jessie would sit huddled together upstairs on the rickety bus, branches grazing the windows and cool air blasting in through the open vents to let out the cigarette smoke the older kids – Jessie's sister Karen among them – were generating from the back seat.

The hedgerows gave way to a development of modern houses

that had sprung up since the last time she'd travelled down the road. Just beyond these, Alessa recognised the cluster of trees bordering The Laurels, the relatively new estate where a couple of their classmates had lived. Hill Manor, the creepy old mansion house around which it was built, surveyed its surroundings from a slightly elevated vantage point, and was just visible from the road. She shuddered now as she thought of the day she and Jessie had taken a detour to get a closer look at the place, after rumours of strange goings-on had started at school when a small group of local boys had ventured over the threshold. Alessa wasn't convinced they were telling the truth, but Jessie had been eager to find out for herself, and had dragged Alessa along. But as they approached the dilapidated, hostile-looking building, Alessa had become increasingly fearful. She could still picture Jessie's wide, shining eyes; could still hear the clear, high pitch of her voice as she stood outside the rotting front door, exhorting her to enter.

"Go on in, I dare you."

But Alessa hadn't dared. One look through the open doorway revealed an enormous rat scurrying towards them, and both girls had run screaming hysterically from the grounds, only pausing for breath when they reached the main road. Neither of them mentioned it to anyone, and Jessie later conceded it hadn't been such a great idea after all, especially when a policeman had come to the school the following day to issue a warning to pupils about used needles and dodgy ex-cons having recently been discovered at the property.

"Just think – we might've had a narrow escape," whispered Jessie behind her hand, grimacing. Alessa had shuddered, grateful it had only been a rodent they'd encountered.

But poor Jessie hadn't been so lucky the next time.

Now, Alessa continued another half mile or so, looking out for the right turn which would bring her journey to an end. And suddenly, there it was. Her old school. The car rolled slowly down the tarmacked dead-end and Alessa found herself, after more than a decade, outside the high metal gates. Staring up at the building, she felt slightly sick. After Jessie's abduction, she had stayed here only six more miserable months. Eventually, Mamma and Uncle Rob had decided that she should move to a small all-girls school slightly closer to home, where the sheltered pupils knew nothing of her identity or, moreover, her connection to Jessie Lockheed.

Alessa pulled up and wound down the window. It was breaktime. The familiar sound of raised voices and mirth spilled through the railings. A group of around six lads kicked a ball to one another across the tarmac whilst others, girls and boys, wandered around aimlessly or stood chatting in huddles, munching on crisps and occasionally bursting into fits of laughter over nothing in particular.

She watched as a couple of girls, age maybe thirteen or fourteen, their arms linked, strolled casually through the gates. They glanced behind them before running to the end of the road and tucking themselves behind the screen of the high hedge that swept round the corner into the secluded, overgrown alleyway: the same alleyway where Jessie's assailant had lain in wait. From her position, Alessa could see one of the girls produce a packet of cigarettes and a lighter from her pocket, then offer her companion one. The girls stood, deep in conversation as they smoked, giggling and peering back through the dense foliage from time to time. They looked carefree and happy, with that lazy self-assured air that many teenage girls seemed to have. Alessa felt a pang. She'd never had that closeness with anyone as a teenager, never felt that sense of belonging. Even after changing schools, her adolescence had been a troubled, lonely time. Everything that happened with Jessie had overshadowed the rest of her youth and continued to do so even now. It made her so angry to think of it. The advice from the well-meaning but patronising Moira, her therapist, to work through her anger using the breathing techniques she'd been taught, had never really helped. How was she supposed to avoid the triggers when they needled constantly inside her own head? The CBT that was supposed to have reprogrammed her emotional responses had done nothing. She found it hard to express her emotions, even to Moira. It had become a vicious circle as she internalised her feelings, comfort-eating and ballooning in weight. Her mother and uncle had done their utmost to bolster her self-esteem, to make her feel pretty and loved, but no amount of praise from home could balance what she was subjected to at school. Of course, she could sit at Joey's bedside and pour out her heart, but even though his expressive eyes would study her face, she knew he couldn't possibly understand everything she was telling him. At times, she had felt so totally, utterly alone.

She recalled one of the cruel taunts from some of the older boys shortly after it happened: *even a nonce didn't fancy you, Cano*. For years she'd hated herself, and since becoming an adult, she'd hated *him*, that evil bastard, even more for what he'd done to the little girl she had once been.

She looked back at the main building now, inhaling sharply as she recalled the vigil that had taken place a fortnight after Jessie was taken, the procession solemnly holding candles aloft as they retraced Jessie's steps for over half a mile from the school as darkness fell, the grief-stricken Mrs Lockheed being almost propped up by her husband. Then there had been that weird séance that had taken place in the school hall. Alessa had heard about it some months after she'd left. There had been a small article in the local paper, and Greta had read it out to her daughter in disbelief. Jessie's older sister, Karen, had arranged it, apparently. She and a group of her friends had broken in one night with a Ouija board they'd procured from somewhere. They were let off pretty lightly, all things considered. The staff – and the police – clearly thought the girls' judgement was skewed. Exactly what Karen had been hoping to achieve, Alessa wasn't sure. But then, she'd lost her little sister – how must the poor kid have been feeling? The whole thing had made Alessa feel like crawling into a hole and never coming out again at the time, and thinking about it now was reviving all those feelings of angst and guilt.

She mentally shook herself. Wallowing in the past was helping nothing. What was she even doing, driving here, raking pointlessly over old ground? Taking a last look at the school, Alessa closed the window and started up the engine, executing a careful three-point turn in the narrow road that ran the length of the metal fence. She had a job to do and she'd allowed herself to become side-tracked. She needed to stay focused.

Arriving back at the station, she was met just outside the entrance by a grinning Jason, who had heard about the wild goose chase but was on his way out again, having been deployed elsewhere by Bennett, who was obviously keen to separate the two of them.

"Listen, there's a band playing tomorrow night, at the Jericho Tavern. We could grab some dinner in one of the eateries on Walton Street first, if you fancy it?"

Ordinarily, Alessa would have jumped at the chance. They'd had such a good time at the pizzeria and she was keen to see Jason outside work again. But she had slept only sporadically since the night she'd been convinced there had been a prowler in her home.

Greta had been concerned by the sudden urgency to call in a locksmith and to have the burglar alarm serviced.

"Why all this now? Is it something to do with that horrible parcel?" she'd asked, her eyes wide, searching Alessa's as she'd hung up the phone from speaking to the security company. "Are you expecting that despicable man to do something else?"

"We've been looking into security measures at work and I realised ours were woefully inadequate. That's all." There was some truth in what Alessa was saying. Their old alarm system had been completely useless. "We've had various people in here helping with Joey over the years who've had keys – supposing they lost them and they've fallen into the wrong hands? Working for the police, it's made me more aware of what's going on in the area. It'll give me peace of mind – especially as you're here on your own all day."

Thankfully, the bedroom doors in Squitchey House all had old-fashioned keys and Alessa had advised Greta to lock her own room at night too, saying there'd been a couple of recent burglaries in the area and it wouldn't hurt to exert extra caution. Greta wasn't stupid. Alessa knew her mother had an inkling there was more to it, but though she seemed anxious, Greta was quite compliant and didn't press her further.

Someone from the company Uncle Rob had contacted was coming to install CCTV for them that coming weekend and it wasn't a moment too soon. In the meantime, even after having the locks changed, she'd been extra careful about securing the doors and windows, even booby-trapping the front and back entrances with string tied tightly across the threshold before going to bed, then removing it before her mother arose in the morning. If nothing else, any would-be intruder would come a cropper, giving her time to ring for help.

All she really wanted was a nice, low-key evening in, a soak in the bath, and early to bed.

"Could we do it another time? It sounds great, but I'm really bushed at the moment."

Jason nodded resignedly. "Okay, no problem." He studied her face, which she'd noticed herself had become even more drawn and sallow of late. "Everything all right at home?" he ventured. "You look knackered, if you don't mind me saying."

The worry about the intruder was still uppermost in Alessa's mind. Yet nothing similar had happened since. She kept turning it all over in her mind, trying to persuade herself that it could have been the result of the constant nightmares; the anxiety and lack of quality sleep, distorting everything. She knew only too well how anxiety had affected her in the past. But she was going round in circles. She had to admit to herself that there had definitely been someone lurking outside on at least one occasion. And however much she tried to squash the thought, she kept revisiting the possibility that there had been someone in the house. That horrible delivery to her home address spoke for itself. Someone had it in for her.

Her stupid, ill-judged pilgrimage to the school earlier had helped nothing, either. Although her gut had been churning ever since, until now she'd just about managed to hold everything together. But being put on the spot, Alessa's eyes began to well.

"It's just . . . I haven't been sleeping brilliantly, these last few nights. I've got loads going round in my head – the Painter case, mostly. It's dragging me down. I'm sure if I could just get a good night's sleep . . ." She felt her lip begin to wobble and bit down hard to stem the tears, digging her nails into her palms to distract herself.

Jason looked at her quizzically. "You sure that's all it is?" His voice was gentle. He placed a hand on her arm. "You seem,

I don't know, really jittery. I'm a bit worried about you, to be honest. D'you think maybe you could do with taking some leave? Give yourself a breather from it all?"

Alessa could hold back no longer. She covered her face with her hands as the tears began to flow, her whole body shaking.

"What is it?" Jason pulled her to him, stroking her hair as she sobbed uncontrollably against his shoulder. "Come on. There's more to this than just the investigation, isn't there?"

Alessa could hardly speak. They stood like that for a couple of minutes, he with his strong arms tightly around her, she a blubbing, snotty mess. Eventually she began to calm, relaxing a little as the tears subsided. She felt drained, but it seemed to have released some of the tension that had been building inside her for so long. Jason released her, pulling a tissue from his jacket pocket.

"Have a good blow," he instructed, handing it over. He smoothed her hair from her tear-streaked cheeks. "You sounded like you needed that."

Alessa felt embarrassed now, realising what a state she must look. She dabbed at her eyes with the hankie, then blew her nose, eventually managing a shaky smile.

"I'm so sorry. It's not just the case, you're right. Although it's all connected, I guess. I never said anything because— Oh, I don't know. It was stupid of me. I suppose I should've told you. The other night, after you left, I thought somebody was watching the house again. I even thought I heard them inside. I mean, yeah, it's possible it was all in my head, but what with everything that's gone on . . . It's really put the wind up me. I haven't slept properly since. I'm worried about Mamma, as much as anything. And after that package, I-I-I keep thinking . . . I don't know. My imagination's running wild right now."

181

Something shrivelled inside her. Alessa thought again about what Moira had said: about how stress could play tricks with the mind. About how the faceless man in her nightmares wasn't really lurking around every corner waiting to make his move.

All her old insecurities had resurfaced. She didn't *want* there to have been an intruder, although she'd feel pretty stupid if it all turned out to be something caused by her subconscious. But whether it had been real or not, it was affecting her badly. Despite her misgivings, she resolved it was better that she'd told someone at last. Moira would have approved.

Jason's eyebrows lifted. He blew out his cheeks. "Jesus. I wish you'd said something before. Have you mentioned this to anybody else here?" He cast around sharply as though wondering if anyone had been loitering, eavesdropping on them. Thankfully the car park was deserted.

"No. I feel such a fool, being scared of my own shadow like this. I've even been keeping my truncheon next to the bed. I'm supposed to be an upholder of the law, not a helpless wimp. Even if it *was* him, what would they do? They can't spare an officer to stand guard outside my door, twenty-four-seven. Bennett'd have a field day if I told him I was frightened. He's got it in for me – for *us* – as it is."

And if it proved to be all in her head, it would be even worse. Alessa groaned inwardly at the thought of the flak she'd receive for wasting resources – not to mention how Bennett would delight in branding her a hysterical female. He'd probably get her the sack.

Jason chewed his lip. "Look, if you don't want to mention this to Bennett, what about me kipping in my car outside your house – you know, so I'm on site and can keep an eye on things? Would that make you feel a bit better?"

Alessa considered for a moment. The prospect of having Jason close by overnight was actually very reassuring. It was really sweet of him to offer. But she couldn't possibly ask him to sleep in his car . . .

"Would you? Really? But what about your dad? He needs help with your mum, doesn't he?"

"She's not too bad at the moment. I could still pop round there first after work, help out with tea and that. But I hate the thought of you being scared – and if that bastard *does* turn up again, I can always call for back-up, if I think I'm going to need it. We'd be killing two birds with one stone, in a sense."

"If you honestly don't mind? I'd be very grateful." She paused. "But I wouldn't dream of you having to sleep outside. We do have a guest room. I can make a bed up for you."

He looked a little surprised, but nonetheless pleased. "Oh. Okay then, if it's no trouble."

"Of course not. It's the least I can do."

"I'll be round about eight-thirty, then. Shall I bring a bottle of something?"

"I'm sure I can find something in the wine rack."

Jason smiled. "Right. Well, I'd better get off to this smash-and-grab in Brewer Street." He rolled his eyes. "I'll see you later, then."

"See you later. And Jason?"

"Yeah?"

"Thank you."

Despite the circumstances, Alessa felt a frisson of excitement as she thought of Jason sleeping just down the landing. Although twenty-four, she had never had a boyfriend sleeping over before.

Although they hadn't been seeing one another for long, she had really connected with Jason and was confident he felt the same about her. There was real empathy there – from personal experience, she understood the responsibility and inevitable restrictions that came with having a family member with a chronic health condition.

It felt good, to think she was now one half of a proper couple. But she'd have to warn her mother that they'd be having an overnight guest first. And not wanting to unnerve her with the truth about the prowler, she wondered how on earth she was going to explain why she had invited him.

Or had he, in a roundabout way, invited himself . . .?

*

Jason had come up with a surprisingly plausible reason for his "imposition". He felt it best if it sounded as though the request was coming from him, rather than Alessa.

"Mrs Cano – erm, Greta – I feel awful about this . . . I wonder if I might be a bit cheeky and ask if I could beg a room for a couple of nights, please? My parents, well, they're having some modifications made to their home to accommodate my mum's wheelchair, and they've got to move out of their bedroom for a while, until the work's finished. The thing is, it's only a poky two-bed house and I haven't really got anywhere to sleep. The couch isn't very long, and I'm a big chap . . ." He'd spread his hands wide, grimacing.

Greta had laughed. "I'd be happy to have you as our guest, Jason. We're rattling around in here, really – there's plenty of room. As long as you abide by the house rules, you can stay as long as you like. I'm sure I can trust you – after all, you *are* a policeman." She gave him a playful wink.

Jason's mouth curved into a grin. "I'll be on my best behaviour. Promise."

"Impressive," Alessa had whispered a little later, once out of earshot of her mother. "You're an excellent liar. I can see I'll have to keep an eye on you."

Jason had rubbed a hand over his chin and laughed – a little nervously, she thought, but he'd said nothing. It made her feel slightly uncomfortable.

*

Jason was a discreet presence at Squitchey House over the weekend, spending a lot of his time in the room allocated to him. He claimed to be catching up on some paperwork. Alessa wondered if he just felt a bit awkward, with her mother constantly asking if he wanted food or something to drink. It was just Greta's way of being hospitable, though Alessa worried he'd find it a bit overbearing, But even if he wasn't visible a lot of the time, it was reassuring to have him around overnight and Alessa felt more at ease than she had for weeks. And there had been the occasional kiss and cuddle when the opportunity arose, which made it even better. While the security cameras were being installed on the Saturday, Jason popped home to check on his parents, giving Alessa the chance to help Greta with a few jobs around the house. But when loading the washing machine, she'd been stopped in her tracks by the sight of one of her mother's old blouses.

"What happened here, Mamma?" Alessa cringed inwardly as she held up the article, guessing the answer before Greta could respond.

"Oh – so annoying. I'll have to darn it. It got caught on that rough bit of wood by the back door. I really need to get a carpenter in, I suppose – I just haven't got around to it yet."

So, the piece of fabric she'd handed into Forensics hadn't

come from an intruder, then. Alessa thanked her lucky stars she'd said nothing to the rest of the team. She'd have looked a total idiot. She would need to buy the young lab technician a few cans or something to thank him for his time. Hopefully he wouldn't ask too many questions.

On the Sunday night, Alessa found herself lying awake once more, worrying about what might happen after Jason returned home. Even though the scrap of cloth hadn't turned out to be anything significant, it didn't necessarily rule out the possibility of an intruder. Suppose someone *was* watching the house and was therefore aware of when she and her mother had been left alone again? Despite all the security measures now in place, the feelings of anxiety were beginning to bubble inside her once more. She was tormented, too, by the memory of Jessie's photograph. Try as she might, Alessa couldn't blot the disturbing image from her mind. What else was the man who could do such a vile, shocking thing capable of?

She stared at the ceiling, lights from the occasional passing car fanning across the walls.

As she lay gazing into space, the atmosphere in the room seemed suddenly to become charged with electricity. There was the scent of something hanging in the air – faint at first, then stronger and more pungent; as though whatever it was, was drawing closer. Like the smell of rainfall on fresh soil. *Petrichor*, she remembered her Classics teacher had called it. It was the liquid running through the veins of the gods in Greek mythology; the stuff of life itself. The word had stayed with her. There was something mellifluous about it.

She couldn't explain this sudden, strange sensation – like a peculiar awareness of something, but she didn't know what. She remembered reading that people with certain mental illnesses started to experience inexplicable sensory disturbances. Hallucinations. There had been that figure she thought she saw that night . . .

A sudden gentle creaking noise to her right made her catch her breath. She pulled herself upright and fumbled with the switch on her bedside lamp, her eyes wildly scanning the room.

The wooden Pinocchio puppet was swinging a little from its tangled strings, its spindly legs tapping rhythmically against the mirror. The head was turned towards her, the painted-on eyes fixed unnervingly in her direction.

It felt as though it was *watching* her. Alessa clapped a hand to her mouth in horror.

For God's sake. She was being ridiculous. She needed to stop thinking like this; it was helping nothing. The puppet must have been caught in a draught coming from under the door or something, that was all. Maybe after everything that had happened lately, she was on the verge of some sort of mental crisis. Her heart had begun to hammer inside her chest, a tight band forming across her forehead. It was like the worst kind of panic attack, and she knew exactly how they felt. She'd suffered a string of them after Jessie was snatched.

She scrambled out of bed and yanked the puppet from its hook, shoving it into the drawer of the dressing table and slamming it shut. The powerful aroma she thought she'd detected a few moments earlier seemed to have dissipated. But regardless, her mind began to fly once again. Gooseflesh rose on Alessa's arms and the back of her neck as for the thousandth time she contemplated what fate had befallen Jessie – and now little Kimberley. She owed it to them and their families to find whoever had committed such terrible acts.

And she owed it to herself for the sake of her sanity.

*

Jason would have stayed longer, but after a phone call first thing on Monday morning to check on his mum, discovered she had been taken ill suddenly. Apologetically, he told Alessa he felt compelled to return home. He was due a few days' leave, so said he was heading into the station just to check in, then would be going straight back to his parents', intending to care for his mum round the clock for a while and lighten the load on his father, who'd admitted to Jason that he was exhausted.

Alessa was reluctant for Jason to leave. But she knew she had no right to ask him to put her needs before those of his own family. The memory of her latest strange "episode" worried her, but she felt unable to share the experience with either Jason or her mother. They had their own worries and didn't need to be burdened with the thought that she might be losing her marbles on top of everything else. As a child, she'd often felt unable to tell Greta everything that was troubling her. Not that she felt her mother would be unsympathetic, but she was always so wrapped up with Joey's needs that the time never seemed right to sit down and talk about anything heavy. If Alessa was upset or had a problem, it was Uncle Rob she would usually turn to – and then, only if it was something she felt really desperate to get off her chest. She had never been one for baring her soul. Moira, her therapist, had recognised this and tried to encourage her to be more open. Alessa knew deep down she'd been right. *A problem shared.* But it was as if it was inherent in her: and as a result of bottling everything up, her concerns often seemed to amplify. Maybe because of the tension in her parents' relationship, she had always been a slightly anxious child and the experience with Jessie had made her even more introspective. There were times when it felt as though her head might actually explode with everything going round in there.

Instead, she attempted to rationalise everything now, trying to persuade herself that she was overwrought and now that the CCTV had been installed and the security system overhauled, everything should be fine. Apart from anything else, sleep deprivation could play havoc with a person's judgement. Maybe if she took some sleeping pills for a few nights, things would feel a whole lot better.

Throughout his stay, Jason had behaved like the perfect gentleman. Alessa knew now that she was really falling for him – and falling hard. Uncle Rob was still holidaying in Italy with his new and much younger Sicilian boyfriend, Matteo, but she planned to introduce Jason to him as soon as he returned. She knew they'd get on like a house on fire. Like her mamma, Alessa's uncle had so often expressed hope she'd find someone decent. Uncle Rob had called at the house briefly the evening she'd brought Pete home and though he'd said nothing specific, she could tell from his rigid body language and tone of voice that he wasn't impressed. When Uncle Rob found out how Pete had reacted to Joey and behaved towards her, Greta told her later with arched eyebrows and one hand over her mouth that he'd called the lad a *cazzone* – an insult he reserved for those for whom he had the utmost contempt. Alessa felt certain his opinion of Jason would be different.

Having already told Alessa how impressed she was with Jason, Greta couldn't resist telling him so too, as he was about to leave. She had followed the pair into the hallway as they were about to say goodbye.

"It's been a pleasure to have you, Jason. I can tell you're a loyal, thoughtful boy. They're rare qualities these days, it seems to me. You're welcome to stay with us again, whenever you like."

Slightly embarrassed, Jason leaned to kiss Greta on the cheek. "Thank you so much for having me, Greta."

"*Ciao*. See you again soon, I hope." Greta made a diplomatic disappearance, as Jason turned coyly to Alessa on the doorstep.

"I'm sorry I've got to go. Ring me if you need anything," he told her, his lips brushing hers tenderly, before climbing into his car. Alessa had thought it wise to continue to arrive at work separately, to prevent any annoying gossip at the station. She was particularly anxious not to alert Bennett to their situation. He seemed to be watching her like a hawk of late, and did nothing to disguise his dislike of either herself or Jason.

"See you soon." She smiled and waved as he pulled away. As if his timing had been planned to the minute, the postman arrived with a handful of letters for the Cano household.

"Morning," he grunted, handing over a small bundle.

"Good morning." Alessa smiled, pulling her dressing-gown self-consciously across her chest. "Lovely day, isn't it?"

"Hmm." The postman shot her a curious look, before proceeding to the neighbouring property.

Alessa closed the door behind her as she leafed through the mail. Bills; a scenic postcard sent by Uncle Rob from Umbria, which made her smile; a bank statement for her mother. But as she reached the bottom of the pile, her brief sense of contentment was replaced by cold dread as she saw something addressed to her.

Miss S. Cano

It was a handwritten brown envelope, her address scribbled in the same wobbly hand, with a Reading postmark. She shouted out to her mother to establish her whereabouts, and a response came from upstairs.

"Yes?"

"Just to let you know . . . we've got a postcard from Uncle Rob," she called back hastily. Quickly, Alessa ran to the kitchen and put on vinyl gloves. With quivering fingers, she tore open the envelope to find a flimsy sheet of white paper, bearing only six words in shaky block capitals:

WE BOTH KNOW WHAT YOU DID.

Alessa felt sick. She tore the letter and its envelope into tiny pieces, dropping them into the waste bin. Her stomach in knots, she went to get ready for work, fearful of what else might be in store for her.

Chapter 14

Saturday, 9 June 1990

Malcolm sighed as they pulled up outside Faye's house just after midday. The net curtains draped randomly at the windows were torn and filthy, and an old pushbike, minus its wheels, lay rusting on the overgrown lawn.

"Is it . . . well, quite clean *in*side?" he asked Kimberley, looking up dubiously at the mid-terraced property, which was letting the side down badly.

"Oh yes. Faye likes to do the cleaning. Says her mum's always too tired after work, so she tidies up and stuff . . ."

He felt suddenly desperately sorry for his daughter's playmate. He wondered what sort of mother allowed her ten-year-old daughter to do all the housework and cook meals. It didn't seem right. Mary would never have *dreamed* of getting Kimberley to act like her skivvy. It made him realise how very different Faye's upbringing was from his own daughter's and how, in many ways, Kimberley led a charmed life. She wanted for nothing and couldn't have been more loved. It was just a shame her health wasn't better.

Kimberley pressed the doorbell. They stood on the front step and waited. Faye came bounding down the stairs and flung open the door.

"Come in, come in!" she gushed, grinning broadly. "I thought you weren't coming." The girl's eyes shone.

Malcolm smiled at her exuberance. "Can I just have a quick word with your mum or dad, please?"

Faye's face fell. "What for?" She darted a look of panic towards Kimberley, who nodded at her encouragingly. They locked eyes for a moment. This brief interchange didn't escape Malcolm's notice. He stiffened, wondering if something was afoot.

"It's not a problem, is it?"

"No, course not. I'll just get my dad."

Mike Greene strolled to the door, still in his dressing-gown, which gaped wide. A glimpse of his well-defined chest suggested that he either liked to work out or had an arduous manual job. He stifled a yawn with one hand, extending the other to Malcolm in greeting.

"'Scuse the attire," he said, grinning. "Had a bit of a late one last night, you know how it is."

Malcolm inclined his head half-heartedly and gave a weak smile. Greene was at least twenty years his junior and clearly still clinging on to his youth. His dark, spiky hair was ruffled and his chin unshaven.

"Good of you to have Kimberley round. I just wanted to say, I know I mentioned her asthma last time we met, but her mum and I are a bit worried she might be coming down with something, so . . ." He produced a slip of paper from his jacket pocket. "Here's our phone number, just in case she has a turn.

She's got her inhaler, so hopefully she should be fine, but if you could give us a bell if she gets wheezy or anything, I'd be very grateful."

"Sure." Mike nodded amiably. "No problem. Well, we'll see you later then?"

"Yes. I'll come and pick her up about seven-thirty – is that okay?"

"Yeah – whenever you like. She's no bother. See you later, mate."

"Bye then, Kimberley."

"Bye, Dad. See you later."

Malcolm planted a kiss on his daughter's pale cheek and released his grip on her hand. He watched as she disappeared down the hallway, laughing at something that Faye had whispered to her. Mike closed the door and Malcom went back to his car, wondering if he was doing the right thing in letting her stay. *Oh well*. It would only be a few hours and then she'd be home again. He shrugged to himself and began to drive away. He glanced back at the shabby little house in his rear-view mirror and shook his head. The way some people chose to live. It was beyond him.

*

The constant drizzle of the early afternoon had given way to a full-blown deluge. Malcolm rang the Greenes' doorbell once more and turned his collar to the water that was dribbling from the portico roof down his neck. Mike Greene appeared eventually, flinging the front door open with unnecessary force. He appeared to wobble a little.

"Sorry, mate, I've got the CD player up a bit loud – didn't hear the door. Come in, you're getting soaked."

194

Malcom hovered in the hallway, wincing. The tuneless boom of some raucous rock band resonated through the house.

"God, really pissing down out there, isn't it?" Seemingly amused by the older man's apparent discomfort, Mike's smile was more of a leer. He looked half cut.

Malcolm was horrified. What kind of a house *was* this? He was in no mood for making conversation and found the overpowering smell of alcohol emanating from Mike repugnant. It was clear now that it had been a big mistake to leave his daughter at Faye's at all. He resolved not to mention Mike's appearance to Mary, but would definitely not be allowing Kimberley to visit Faye in future, however much she pleaded.

"I need to get back, really," he said, tersely. "Is Kimberley ready to come now, please?"

"I'll give 'em a shout." He cupped both hands around his mouth, staggering as he did so. "*Faye!* Kimberley's dad's here."

Faye appeared at the top of the stairs. She looked sheepish. Something about her expression made Malcolm's stomach drop.

"Where's Kimberley?"

"She's . . . not here."

"What d'you mean not here?" Malcolm caught his breath. A sick feeling rose in his chest. "Well, where is she, then?"

Faye's face reddened. She gripped the banister, her body language unwontedly stiff and awkward. "We-we sort of . . . fell out. She said she wanted to go home and she just . . . left."

Malcom's heart began to race. The hallway seemed to be growing narrower, the psychedelic-patterned carpet rising up to meet him. His eyes wide, he turned incredulously to Mike, who shrugged his shoulders.

"Search me," he said. "I thought they were still playing upstairs."

"How long ago did she leave?" The increasing panic was

evident now in Malcolm's voice. He looked again at Mike, who appeared infuriatingly unconcerned, then back to Faye.

Her response was subdued. "This afternoon. About five o'clock, I think."

Malcolm turned to Faye's father in anger. "Didn't it occur to you that you ought to have let us know?"

"Whoa! Hold on!" Mike raised both palms defensively. He sounded suddenly more sober. "I told you, I thought they were up in Faye's room."

"But Kimberley came round here for her tea. How the hell could you not have noticed?"

"Faye was supposed to be sorting their food out. Me and Laura have been in the front room. We like to have a couple of cans on a Saturday – you know, unwind after the week. We were watching the match earlier, and we just let the kids do their own thing. They like a bit of freedom, and from what I hear, Kimberley doesn't get a lot of that at home."

Malcom curled his hand into a fist, but resisted the urge to raise it. Faye's mother, Laura, appeared in the living room doorway, rubbing her eyes.

"What's going on? You woke me up." She sounded dazed, peering blearily at the irate stranger in her hallway. Malcolm couldn't believe she'd slept through the racket that was still pulsing from the living room. "What's the problem?"

Malcolm turned on her. All colour had drained from his face and there was a tremor in his voice. "Well, while you've been having your nap, my ten-year-old daughter, who was left in your care, has walked out. Over two hours ago. It only takes about ten minutes to walk to our house from here, so where the *hell* is she?"

Chapter 15

Monday, 2 July 1990

Twenty-three days after Kimberley's disappearance

The arrival of the letter had sent her into turmoil. Though Jason's presence in the house had helped enormously, Alessa knew that with him gone, she was facing everything alone once more. The sender's timing had been impeccable. She realised, too, that her insomnia would return with a vengeance. And Moira had always told her that, without sleep, her mind could start playing nasty tricks on her. However much she tried to use the coping strategies that Moira had taught her, she couldn't pretend that *everything* was in her head. The letter had been real – and the thought of those mocking words made her feel nauseous. All her insecurities and anxiety were building again. But she felt unable to confide in anyone about it, not even Jason. He was on leave now and she wasn't expecting to hear from him for a while with everything he had going on at home. She assumed he'd be rushed off his feet. She'd been on the verge of calling him a few times that afternoon, but had stopped herself. He had enough on his plate and it wouldn't be fair to add to his woes.

On top of everything else, it had been a gruelling day, combing through yet more files of previous offenders, distressing details that were impossible to forget once seen. Alessa was sickened by what some had inflicted on their victims. She wondered how the children ever got over what had happened to them.

The reconstruction of Kimberley's disappearance, due to be filmed and shown on prime-time television, had finally been arranged for the following Saturday, although Alessa wondered how much use it would be, especially given that the weather had changed so drastically. It would have been so much more realistic in the pouring rain. Bennett had dragged his heels when she'd suggested it initially. She was frustrated, since the incident would have been so much fresher in people's minds a week or two earlier. She just had to hope it would reap more than she was anticipating. So far, every hope she'd had of a breakthrough had been dashed.

Her heart heavy, she'd tried to appear cheerful and engage in conversation over dinner with her mother, but her mind was still on the case. She helped to wash up then went through to the living room, thinking some lightweight TV might divert her for a while. It was approaching quarter to nine when the phone rang out. Greta went to answer it and called Alessa from the hallway.

"Sandi! For you. A gentleman. I think he's in a callbox, so hurry." Greta left the receiver on the hall table and went back into the kitchen, where she was putting away the dinner things and laying the table for next morning's breakfast.

Alessa came through from the living room. She lifted the handset cautiously and listened.

It sounded like someone crooning softly. At first, she couldn't make it out properly and for a moment there was an eerie silence.

But then it began again. Almost like the sibilant rush when you put your ear to a seashell.

A tuneless, warbling male voice, singing quietly.

"Sandy, Can't you see, I'm in misery . . ."

That annoying song from the musical, *Grease*. Some of the boys at school had delighted in teasing her with it and it had always grated on her, especially as they'd usually finish up with horrible, exaggerated vomiting noises. But now, it chilled her to the bone. She stood rooted to the spot, her heart thudding in her ears.

As suddenly as it had started, the singing stopped. A sudden short burst of almost maniacal laughter echoed down the line. In the background, a peal of bells chimed. At once, there was a clatter and the phone went dead. Almost immediately, the clock in the hallway clanged, making Alessa start. With trembling hands, she slammed down the receiver, fighting back tears. She picked it up once more and left it off the hook. She couldn't bear it if he tried calling again.

"Who was that?" called Greta.

Alessa stood with her back to the wall, trying to collect her thoughts. She could hear her mother moving around in the kitchen.

"No one. One of those cold callers trying to flog double glazing."

"Ha. Did you tell him we can't afford it?"

"Pretty much."

"Unusual though, to be doing business from a public phone."

"Hmm. Maybe he's freelance."

199

How the hell had he got their number? They'd been ex-directory for years.

Alessa's mind whirred, her pulse pounding in her throat. A sickening feeling was mounting inside her. She felt like a prey animal, a mouse being toyed with by a sadistic cat before its ultimate demise.

Then something dawned on her. *Those bells*. She knew that, even if she could trace the call, a phone box wasn't going to lead her to the caller's address. But if she could find the location, he might – just might – have left a clue to his identity.

*

The following morning, Alessa had just got back to her desk after yet another pointless early briefing from Bennett and had the beginnings of a headache. Rather than absorbing what was being said, all the time she'd been thinking about the phone call and how she might use it to her advantage. She'd lain awake half the night replaying it through her mind. The more she thought about it, the more convinced she was that, unless she was mistaken and he was calling from another area altogether, it must have been made from the kiosk next to Carfax Tower, whose bells rang out every fifteen minutes. Alessa was racking her brains: she needed to find out who the beat bobbies around that area were currently. *Somebody* must have seen the caller. If he'd been spotted by a copper, hopefully they'd have been observant about his appearance.

She hoped this wasn't going to turn into a migraine. She needed to stay focused. Hunting through her bag for paracetamol, she came across the business card given to her by the lilac-haired woman she'd spoken to in the White Horse. She hadn't given her much thought since their meeting.

But something had stopped her from binning the card.

Maybe she ought to ring her. Just to find out what it was she wanted to say. The woman, Carmel, had seemed sincere – worried about her, even. As a rule, Alessa had no time for those who peddled predictions for a living. She'd always felt they capitalised on people's frailties. After all, no one generally consulted a clairvoyant unless they had some sort of problem or were grieving someone's loss. Nonetheless, she'd been puzzled as to why the woman had singled her out. Maybe – and Alessa couldn't believe she was actually thinking this way – maybe someone with the gift of clairvoyance, or at least some sort of empathy, might be able to shed light on the baffling things she'd been experiencing lately. She'd heard whispers about the police consulting psychics when they hit a blind alley. And even if the woman *was* a fake, right now she would just welcome the chance to offload to a total stranger about all the crap swimming round her head. If nothing else, it might reassure her that her "ghostly" encounters were all something she'd unwittingly conjured up herself because of the stress she'd been under. That would certainly be the preferred explanation.

She popped two paracetamol into her hand from a blister pack and tucked the colourful card into the bag's side pocket where it was visible, making a mental note to act on it later. But right now, she needed to concentrate on checking out her hunch about the phone call.

At lunchtime, she walked briskly up St Aldates, and crossed the High Street. It was a glorious afternoon: the skies were clear and the sun blazing, bringing the shoppers out in force. She hovered outside Lloyds Bank on the corner opposite Carfax Tower, looking round for evidence of a police officer. Within minutes, the familiar sight of a navy-blue dome atop a tall, broad frame lumbered towards her through the crowds along Queen Street. Alessa recognised the man's rounded features but wasn't sure of his name. She dodged a bus that was heading up Cornmarket and hurried across the street towards him, almost careering into a middle-aged woman coming out of the Midland Bank.

"I'm *so* sorry." Alessa felt her cheeks flare.

The woman looked her up and down scathingly, harrumphed and carried on her way.

The officer grinned as Alessa approached, swiping a sheen of sweat from across his brow with the back of his hand. He looked a little younger than her, maybe twenty-one or -two, and had an amiable, pleasant face. "Afternoon. On a mission, are you?" He tipped his head after the woman. "I thought the old dear was a goner there."

"I know – I should've been a bit more careful." She grimaced. "I'm Alessa. Alessa Cano." They exchanged a brief, slightly awkward handshake.

He nodded. "I've seen you at the nick. I'm Jasper. PC Wallace. Can I help at all?"

"I was wondering – is this your regular route?"

"Yep – for my sins. Glad I'm on earlies this week, though – it's a lot less hassle than tipping-out time last thing. 'Specially now the students've just finished their finals – some of 'em can be a pain in the arse when they've had a few." He rolled his eyes.

Alessa puffed out her cheeks and gave herself a metaphorical kick. Of *course*, whoever had been on duty last night would have come off shift first thing that morning. She wasn't thinking straight and hadn't been quick enough off the mark.

"You look as if you've lost a fiver and found 10p," Jasper remarked. "Anything I can help with?"

Alessa sighed. "Probably not, I'm afraid. I was hoping to speak to whoever was patrolling here last night. I'm trying to locate a possible suspect in the Kimberley Painter case and there's a good chance he made a call from that phone box." She waved a hand towards the freshly painted red kiosk next to the tower.

"Really?" Jasper arched his eyebrows. "I've been following the case – he's a real piece of work, that one. I heard about, you know, the Jessie Lockheed connection . . ." He dropped his eyes, dragging the toe of his boot across the pavement. "I was only a kid at the time but I remember my mum wouldn't let my older sister out of her sight for months."

Alessa cleared her throat. "Do you know who was working this patch yesterday evening?"

"Gus. Gus Brown – d'you know him? *Big* guy." He flexed his biceps to demonstrate. "Lovely fella. He's retiring soon. He'll be missed."

Alessa shook her head. "Don't think I've come across him, but I haven't been at St Aldates that long. Is he back on tonight, d'you know?"

"I believe so." Jasper thought for a moment. "Why don't we have a look at the call box, anyway – you never know, your bloke might've dropped something."

He opened the kiosk door and held it wide. Alessa peered inside. Whoever had painted had reserved their attentions for the exterior only. Whilst the smell of paint fumes was still evident, the floor was littered with discarded phone cards, sweet wrappers and cigarette butts. Several dollops of hardened chewing-gum had been deposited on the metal shelf supporting the telephone directory, as if it were a requirement.

"You could take all that lot to Forensics – get 'em to check for prints and stuff?" Jasper looked dubious.

Alessa grimaced. "I'm sure they'd be delighted." She scanned round in the vain hope of finding something, *anything*, that jumped out at her. Her heart sank.

"No, there's no point. It was just a hunch, really. I'll try and speak to – what was his name? Gus? Hopefully he might've seen someone using the phone. Thanks very much for your help, anyway."

Just as Alessa was turning to leave, Jasper called her back.

"Hang on a sec. What's that?" He bent down to look at something. Covering his hand with the cuff of his shirt, he picked up a piece of pale blue paper, screwed up into a ball in the corner of the kiosk and dotted with cigarette ash. Holding it against his jacket, he carefully used the fabric to open it out with both hands. To add insult to injury, the remnants of a crushed can of Coke had been spilled on the floor and the paper was slightly wet along one edge. But closer scrutiny revealed a telephone number scrawled in pencil next to some smudged capital letters.

"What does it say?" Alessa twisted her neck and leaned forwards to see the grubby paper smoothed out against Jasper's sleeve. Her head began to swim.

"Ca – Cano! Oxford 5-1-4-3-6 – 3-6 something. Can't quite make out the last digit." Jasper turned to her, a look of triumph on his face. "Can't be many people round here called that, huh? I take it that's your number?"

Alessa nodded mutely. The man *had* used that call box, then. And here was a piece of potentially useful evidence. She could hardly believe it.

Her hands trembling, she took out a silicone glove and plastic evidence sleeve from her omnipresent cross-body bag, gingerly accepting the paper from Jasper and sealing it inside. She held it up to the light. The crumpled sheet was lined: perforated at the top, and clearly torn from a pad.

"Well, you'd better get that back to the lab pronto. Even if there's no prints, you've got a bit of a proper handwriting sample – and the paper's pretty distinctive, too. Stroke of luck, eh!"

Alessa managed a smile. "And all thanks to you, PC Wallace. I'll make sure you're credited with it, don't you worry."

Jasper's cheeks coloured slightly. He tapped his helmet and gave her a wink. "All in a day's work," he grinned. "Best of luck with it all. Hope you nail the bugger."

"You and me both. Thanks again – I'm really grateful."

*

Alessa returned to St Aldates and booked the evidence in with Forensics, her mind whirring. She would just have to sit tight and hope that the paper offered them some sort of breakthrough. The officers in the lab always worked as quickly as they could, although the waiting felt interminable.

Bennett and Henderson were out of the office, but had left her another heap of folders to work through. Alessa felt restless and it was impossible to stay focused. She was desperate to speak to Jason, but didn't want to seem too needy. Once again, she took out the clairvoyant's business card. There was no harm in talking to Carmel, even if she couldn't help with the case. Alessa was still curious as to why the woman had seemed so anxious to speak to her. And right now, it would provide her with something else to think about.

Arriving home later, she seized her opportunity. Her mother was busy making the dinner, so Alessa lifted the phone from the hall table and, taking it into the living room, closed the door quietly. Taking a deep breath, she quickly dialled the number on the card and waited, her pulse quickening.

"Carmel's Tarot Readings. How can I help you?"

The voice didn't sound anything like the woman she'd met in the pub; it was more clipped and business-like. Alessa hesitated.

"Erm, is it possible to speak to Carmel, please?"

A throaty chuckle came down the line. "That would be me."

Alessa felt tongue-tied. What the hell was she going to say? Maybe this was a mistake. For a moment, she considered hanging up, but then decided that would be cowardly. "I, erm, you gave me your business card when we were in the White Horse a while ago?"

"Ah, the lovely young lady with the soulful eyes. I remember you well. I've been hoping you'd get in touch." Now the burr of her accent became more evident, with its gravelly undertone.

"I don't think we were properly introduced. My name's Alessa, Alessa Cano. I was wondering, would it be convenient to come and see you at some point, please?"

"Of course. Are you busy this evening?"

Alessa's mind began to race. What should she tell her mother?

"You could always say you're meeting a friend for a coffee," came the response, as if Carmel was reading her thoughts. "I assume you're local. Do you know Woodstock?"

*

Greta was already dishing up the *fettuccine ai funghi* she'd prepared as Alessa came into the kitchen. Alessa had little appetite but ate hurriedly, then muttered a garbled excuse to her perplexed mother about needing to speak to a lady about the case she was working on. Without even bothering to change out of her uniform, Alessa went back out to her car and drove away. Inside half an hour, she found herself drawing up in Woodstock's

206

market square in front of a quirky-looking bow-fronted shop with an impressive crystal globe suspended above its doorway. The words "The Magickal Realm" were emblazoned in gold letters above the ebony-framed window.

Alessa looked around. Carmel's premises were a couple of doors along from the pub on the corner. Across the street was the old ivy-clad Bear Hotel, where Alessa remembered Uncle Rob taking her and Greta for dinner on Alessa's birthday some years ago. Greta had been reluctant to leave Joey, but Uncle Rob had arranged for a carer to sit with him for a couple of hours.

The shop seemed incongruous amongst the antique and fine art dealers synonymous with the area, its window display filled with all manner of items pertaining to the esoteric. Books, stones, cards, and ornaments – and not a single one connected to anything earthly or mundane.

Woodstock was a pretty, quaint little town, famous for being on the edge of the Blenheim Estate. Alessa rarely had cause to visit, although her mother had an old friend who lived at the far end of the High Street. She glanced about her, feeling slightly conspicuous given the nature of the establishment she was about to enter. It was almost seven-thirty and the air had begun to cool. A few people were still milling about, but no one seemed to be paying her any attention. The shop was closed, but an old-fashioned bell hung next to the door. Hesitantly, she pulled the cord attached to it, and almost immediately, the clatter of approaching footsteps on stone could be heard from within. A bolt was drawn back and the door opened, announced by a further chiming bell.

"Welcome."

Carmel stood before her, wrapped in a flowing star-spangled black silk robe, her lilac hair unkempt as though she'd just woken up. She gestured towards the interior. Alessa noticed the woman's nails, which were manicured and painted in glittering purple polish. They looked odd next to the mottled skin of her hands.

"Do come in."

The overpowering scent of incense filled the air. The building was centuries old, all dark oak beams and undulating walls. Artificial candles flickered from rustic wooden wall sconces, casting shadows on the shiny flagstone floor. A huge Green Man mask had pride of place on the centre of the wall behind the till, to the right of the shop. A glass case in front of this contained various ornaments and talismans, depicting runic symbols, nymphs, dragons, and other mythical creatures. On the wall opposite hung a colourful pentacle poster, showing the various annual pagan festivals.

The shop sparkled with every conceivable shade of crystal and semi-precious stone, neatly displayed on rows of wooden shelves.

Alessa gazed round the room in wonder. It was like an Aladdin's cave.

Carmel smiled. "We've got some extraordinary pieces, sourced from far and wide. You can choose something to take away with you if you like, before you leave. But, first things first."

She swept back a thick red jacquard curtain, leading to the back of the shop. "Follow me."

In awe and slightly hesitantly, Alessa trailed after her. The shop's theme continued into the small sitting room beyond, which was furnished with multi-coloured floor cushions. A small, squat hexagonal table sat in their midst and a low fire flickered in a blackened cast-iron grate. As they entered, a sleek black cat stirred. She stretched out languorously on the hearth rug, examining Alessa with half-opened amber eyes.

"This is Cerridwen," smiled Carmel, crouching to stroke the purring animal lovingly along the full length of her back. "She knows everything, this one. Like the Welsh enchantress." She indicated an unusual stone carving on the wall showing a woman with wild, flowing hair, the sun at one shoulder and the moon at the other; she was holding up a cauldron whose contents were swirling like a stormy sea, and she was gazing into it. It was mesmerising.

"Cerridwen was a prophet. A very interesting character. So many stories I could tell you about her. But right now, we need to talk about *you*. Please" – she pointed to the cushions – "have a seat."

Alessa lowered herself gingerly to the floor, wondering what she was letting herself in for. Carmel, clearly quite accustomed to sitting cross-legged, positioned herself with ease opposite her. From the pocket of her voluminous robe, she produced a battered pack of tarot cards, which she placed in the centre of the table.

She looked at Alessa, her green eyes suddenly wide and intense, then without warning began to cough suddenly. The sound was rasping, almost painful, and she leaned forwards, clutching at her throat as though struggling to breathe.

"Are you okay?" Concerned, Alessa reached towards her, but Carmel raised a hand and shook her head. Alessa sat rigidly, unsure what to do. It was quite alarming. Within a minute or so, the coughing fit had subsided. Carmel closed her eyes and took a few deep breaths. She straightened once more. "Phew. You'll have to excuse me. It gets me like that sometimes. I really should give up smoking but, well, you know how it is. Old habits die hard."

Alessa studied her uncertainly. "There's help available, you know, to quit. That sounded really nasty."

Carmel's lips curved into a faint smile. "Too late for me, I'm afraid. I'm too long in the tooth. Now then, where were we?" She rubbed her palms together, clearing her throat as her eyes fixed on Alessa's face. "But before we start, I really ought to explain to you what I saw – or rather, what I *felt*, that first time we met. I think you felt something too. I'm right, aren't I?"

Alessa acknowledged this. She had experienced something not unlike a mild electric shock – a peculiar prickling sensation.

"That was me tapping into your energy. Not deliberately, you understand. Happens to me sometimes. Can be useful, but at other times it's a bit of a nuisance. Being psychic, I mean."

Alessa stared at her blankly. She'd never come across anyone quite like Carmel before and realised suddenly just how far outside her comfort zone she actually was. This whole thing was beginning to feel more and more like a weird psychedelic dream.

"It may sound a bit odd, but I felt connected to you in some way, too – if that makes sense. Look, I'll just get to the point," Carmel continued. "I could feel a lot of anxiety coming from you, but more than that, I think someone negative's drawing on your life force. From more than one direction, too."

Alessa pondered this. It was true; she did feel weighed down right now. But it was probably etched into her face and pretty obvious to anyone. She folded her arms. She'd heard about so-called clairvoyants reading people's facial expressions and body language. The very fact she'd sought Carmel out would tell the woman that all wasn't right with her.

"I know this must be hard for you to grasp." Carmel sighed. "I feel something bad's happened in your life, many years ago. But for some reason, after lying dormant, it's suddenly re-emerged."

Despite herself, Alessa found she was nodding in agreement.

Kimberley's disappearance, the resurgence of the memory of what happened with Jessie, the packages – plus the weird sensations she'd had, like that strange smell . . . Maybe if Carmel couldn't help, Alessa really *did* need to see a therapist again.

Carmel regarded her for a moment, her face tilted to one side.

"When I saw you in the pub, I had a brief flash of a little girl, with long, fair hair. Have you lost a child? Or a sister, perhaps?"

Suddenly acutely aware of her quickening pulse, Alessa shook her head. "I'm a police officer. I'm working on a case . . ."

Carmel's eyes widened. She inclined her head and raised a hand. "Tell me no more. I think the cards might lead us in the right direction."

Removing the tarot cards from their packet, she caressed them almost affectionately. "*These*, these are like my babies," she said, her expression suddenly serious. "I have to take great care of them. They've helped me – and many others – so much over the years." She handed the cards to Alessa. "Now. I need you to hold the cards, think about *you* and your life; nothing else. Then shuffle them and ask a question. And then we'll see them work their magic."

Very cautiously, Alessa took the deck from Carmel. This all felt a tad bizarre – if not completely crazy. But the woman was earnest and Alessa felt she should oblige. After all, she was the one who'd instigated this meeting. She held the cards in both hands and closed her eyes. A jumble of thoughts wove through her mind, including all the key events that had dominated her life, both good and bad. It was the weirdest feeling; as if she'd slipped into another dimension. Opening her eyes, Alessa felt slightly disorientated. She thought hard about what she wanted to know, then shuffled the cards, glancing curiously at the unusual image on each as she did so.

"Now, let me have them." Carmel held out an eager hand and Alessa passed the cards back to her. A radiant smile spread across the woman's face.

"Oh yes, they are positively *tingling*. You've imparted much of your essence, my love. Now we'll get a wonderful reading."

Carmel began slowly to spread the cards into a sort of cross formation on the little table, carefully examining each as it appeared before her. She laid out five cards in total. Fascinated, Alessa studied the woman's face as her expression went from eyes wide with wonder, to frown, to smile.

The first card set down was The Fool. "This represents you," explained Carmel. Registering Alessa's alarm, she grinned. "Oh no, that doesn't mean you're an idiot; not by any means. The Fool is wise, all-knowing, the symbol of enlightenment. A new cycle beginning in your life."

Carmel explained that the next card, the Emperor, represented a father figure, a significant male in Alessa's life. "I see an older man, with silver hair and the brightest blue eyes. He's very concerned for your welfare. But not your father?" She raised a questioning eyebrow.

Alessa acknowledged this, slightly unnerved. It was the perfect description of Uncle Rob. How on earth could Carmel have picked up on this?

"Oh, now *this* is a good one to draw. The Lovers." Carmel smiled knowingly. "It can indicate choices. And balance – something we all need in a relationship. Communication, too, which is so important between people in love." She stared at the cards intently, her eyes narrowing slightly. "There *is* a special man in your life, I see. He may not be all you think he is. Just be cautious. But I feel the outcome will ultimately be good. You have nothing to worry about."

Her thoughts drifting to Jason, Alessa considered how little she actually knew about his background. But her gut feeling about him, the way he looked at her, the way he made her *feel* . . . The fact she was being told there was no cause for concern made her push any hint of doubt from her mind.

No. Jason was one of the good ones. She was certain of it.

"Justice – very appropriate, given your job. The scales show the need for balance, and careful judgement." Her face became stony. "I'm getting something else here – a male authority figure; someone in the workplace, possibly. You're in conflict, I see. But don't allow him to manipulate you." She looked up, fixing Alessa with glassy eyes. "Watch your back. He's not a good man."

Alessa's mind flew at once to Bennett. It felt as though a sliver of ice was travelling up her spine. She disliked the man, yes. But the advice to keep looking over her shoulder worried her. Was he capable of more than she'd originally thought? She remembered the man she and Jason had seen him with in the King's Arms. Jason had made some comment – what was it he'd said? Something about Bennett keeping dodgy company, or words to that effect. Maybe the pair of them needed to watch out.

Carmel gave a small gasp. She sat back for a moment, staring not at Alessa but somewhere beyond her, causing Alessa to glance sharply around the room. The woman's pupils had become unnaturally dilated. It was slightly disconcerting.

"Is-is anything wrong?" Alessa swiped away the cold bead of sweat which was trickling from her brow.

Carmel shook her head. Her eyes appeared to grow heavy, her chin lowering to her chest. Suddenly her speech sounded different – slower, deeper.

"Please don't be alarmed, but the little girl I saw – she's standing behind you. I feel like she's trying to guide you, to

213

tell you something. But I can't quite grasp . . ." Carmel's eyes flickered beneath their lids, an anguished look crossing her face. She clenched her hands. "No. I just can't get it. There's a sense that . . . no, I'm sorry. I think with time her message will become stronger. But all I'm getting at the moment is a feeling of terrible sadness. I've no doubt all will become clear eventually."

It felt as though an icy finger was tracing a line along Alessa's vertebrae. She darted a look over her shoulder, but could see nothing. And then she wondered, had Carmel somehow found out about her connection to the Kimberley Painter case? Or worse, to Jessie? There was every possibility this woman had been doing her homework. But the other things she was saying made Alessa consider that she was no charlatan. It was as if she'd genuinely tapped into something. How was that possible? Alessa began to think she'd prefer it if Carmel *were* a fraud. She was finding the woman's observations unnerving.

Carmel shook herself a little, opening her eyes fully once more. She straightened, smoothed her skirts, then resumed the reading.

"Where were we? Ah, the final card. Death. Not something to dread, which is what most people assume straight away. It may be a symbol of fear, but also of change – often for the better. It can mean rebirth or transformation. I think you'll progress well in your job and make a difference to other people's lives. Which I'm sure is why you chose your profession – am I right?"

Alessa smiled nervously. Whether it was Carmel herself or the cards speaking through her, she seemed to have tuned in to Alessa's character with curious accuracy. She wondered what else the woman could see. A tense ridge had formed across her temples. Carmel stared at Alessa, her face lit from within. "This is a very powerful hand. Do you know anything about the tarot?"

Alessa shook her head. She could have said that she'd always thought it all a bit farfetched, but thought that would sound rude. Once more, Carmél seemed to know what was passing through her mind. It was uncanny – and not a little disturbing.

"Oh, plenty of people scoff at what I do – what *we* do, as psychics, mystics, call us what you will. Everyone's entitled to their own opinion. But personally, I swear by the tarot. I'd never make an important decision in my life without consulting the cards first; so I can see the lie of the land, if you understand me. There are seventy-eight in the pack in all. Of these, twenty-two are the major arcana. And every single card you've drawn is one of these, the most significant cards. The odds against that are pretty high, you know."

It was so frustrating. While Carmel was providing an eerily accurate appraisal of Alessa's character and had evidently tuned in to what was happening in her life, there was no really substantial guidance forthcoming. And there'd been no explanation of the origins of the sinister packages, nor what the sender's intentions were. Yet these were the reasons she'd felt compelled to seek Carmel's advice; the only thing that had persuaded her to seek guidance from something she would never ordinarily have considered.

"Yes, but what exactly does that mean? It's all very cryptic. I'm sorry, but I need concrete advice – not *clues*."

"Always trust your instinct, my love. The cards are giving a positive message. You're stronger than you think."

Alessa puffed out her cheeks. "I'm not so sure about that." She paused. "But the little girl you mentioned. Can you tell me anything else about her?"

Carmel sighed. "Only that she's no longer on this mortal plane. The death of a child is always emotive, whatever the circumstances. A young life cut tragically short leaves so much unfinished business. I . . ." She faltered, her lower lip trembling suddenly. It took a few moments until she seemed more composed.

"I'm certain this child died unnaturally. She's clearly found a connection with you and I'm sure in time she'll be able to show you what she's trying to get across. If she only passed over recently, her aura may still be weak. That's my gut instinct – that she's new to the spirit realm. I did get a brief whiff of something – a sort of earthy smell, if that means anything? Other than that, just the sadness. Communication will hopefully become easier for her as she gains strength. Be patient. In the meantime, if you actually see her, let her know you want to help."

Before Alessa could respond, Carmel seemed to jolt suddenly. She gave a small gasp. "Well, well. There's someone else here now. An older boy. He's very dark; the most *heavenly* dark eyes." Carmel fixed her gaze on Alessa, a broad smile spreading across her face. "Oh, there's so much love for you coming through. And he's laughing. It's wonderful. He looks so happy." She nodded, more to the room than to Alessa. "I'll tell her."

"Tell me what?" The temperature had dropped noticeably. Alessa was so absorbed in what the woman was saying that she hadn't realised she was shivering. She could feel electricity in the atmosphere now, almost like the blast of ozone from a waterfall. Cool air swirled around her.

"*Tell Mamma I'm okay now.*" Carmel's brow knitted slightly. "That's what I'm getting. Does that make sense?"

Alessa's eyes swam with tears. "My little brother," she whispered. Frantically she scanned the room, desperate for a glimpse of Joey's sweet face. She had the fuzzy impression of a shadow to her right. But it quickly faded. Warmth was immediately restored and everything felt oddly flat once more.

Carmel beamed. "What a beautiful soul. It's so lovely when

they come through like that. A little nudge to remind us they're still around."

Alessa swiped at her cheeks with the backs of her hands. She was elated and saddened all at once. It was an odd feeling. "Thank you. That's a real comfort. I . . ." She stopped, shaking her head. Alessa couldn't bring herself to talk about Joey. Not now. She would have spent the rest of the reading in tears. But the very thought of him being around her felt as though he was sending a much-needed hug. In her mind, she sent him one back.

She took a deep breath, trying to focus once more on her main reason for seeking Carmel out. "There's something else. I've been receiving anonymous mail. And phone calls – well, just the one, so far. It's obviously connected to the case – but it's also linked to something that happened to me as a child." Thinking of the most recent note, her stomach churned. She looked away. "It's really getting to me. Some sicko out there's watching my movements and I'm losing sleep over it . . ."

Carmel took her silently by the hand, her expression stern now. "You've nothing to fear, I'm sure of it. I think someone's playing mind games with you. And that's all they are. The man responsible's a coward. For whatever warped reason, he's taking a sadistic pleasure in watching you suffer. But to show his face would mean risking capture." She closed her eyes for a moment. "It's odd – I'm seeing a picture of a football. You, know – one of those black-and-white ones? No idea what it means, I'm afraid. I'm sorry to be so vague. It's like that sometimes. But the image is really clear. There's obviously some significance – maybe you can make sense of it yourself?"

Alessa shook her head. A football? What on earth could *that* mean?

"I don't think this character poses any real threat – not to you," Carmel continued. "But there *is* evil at work here. And as you said, it's connected to some event from your childhood. Something very dark." She gave Alessa an almost knowing look. "I feel the truth will out eventually, though it may be a very long and arduous journey until that happens."

Alessa stared at her. All that the woman was saying was making her extremely uncomfortable. Exposed. It was as though Carmel knew everything about her.

Everything?

She felt suddenly cold again.

"How can you possibly know all this?" Alarmed, she searched the woman's face, trying to see what lay behind her expression; how much she *could* actually see.

Carmel grinned. Her eyes glinted with sudden mischief. "I'm a bit of an old witch. Surely you've realised that by now? Oh, don't worry – I'm not one of those satanists or anything like that. Any powers I possess and intentions I may have are for the greater good. I sense you're full of self-doubt, but you're a decent person, Alessa. I pride myself on being an excellent judge of character and I can state that much unequivocally. I knew it the moment I touched your hand. Never forget it. Take what you've learned here and be guided by what the cards advise. And remember what I say – *always* trust your own instinct. No matter what."

Alessa really didn't know what to make of it all. She rose to leave, stooping to stroke the cat, who was now weaving around her legs.

"Well, thank you for your time. You've given me a lot to think about."

Carmel flapped a hand. "Wait. Before you go, I have something for you."

She eased herself to her feet and led Alessa back through the curtain and into the shop, where she began to scour the walls.

218

"Ah. Here it is."

She reached up to lift something from one of the shelves, then turned and pressed it into Alessa's hand. It was a pendant, an unusual blue stone, shaped and polished into a kind of pendulum, attached to a string of twisted black twine.

"It's blue kyanite," Carmel told her. "Wear it always, and it'll protect you from anyone trying to manipulate or undermine you in any way. It's said to alleviate worry. It should also help you think more clearly and may help you understand what your little spirit girl is trying to tell you."

"Thank you. It's very – different." Alessa hoped she looked grateful. "Erm – how much do I owe you – for the reading?"

Carmel shook her head. "You owe me nothing, my love. I approached you first, after all. Sometimes I just need to use my gift to help people. I hope that's what I've been able to do for you." She searched Alessa's face earnestly. "Do remember what I said, won't you – about the man's football connection. I've a strong feeling it will set you on the right track. And please – be sure to pass on the message to your mum. It'll cheer her up no end."

Alessa nodded, smiling weakly. She didn't know how she was going to bring up the subject with her mamma. But she had to agree that it would lift her spirits. Greta put on a brave front, but Alessa knew how much she was hurting deep down.

Casting her eyes heavenward as she left, Alessa thrust the stone deep into her pocket and headed back to the car. Night had begun to fall; the darkening sky was marbled with grey and pink, the air damp and cool. The entrance bell tinkled as the door closed behind her, but she barely acknowledged the sound. Her head was whirring with everything that had happened. It all felt quite surreal. She shuddered, as much from her thoughts as the sudden dip in temperature. The reading had left her more

219

ruffled than reassured. She glanced back at the shop. It was a whole universe away from anything she was accustomed to, and she wasn't sure she was keen to embrace Carmel's other-worldly train of thought. Nevertheless, the woman seemed like a well-meaning soul.

Alessa raised a hand to wave as she drove away, but the lights in the shop had already been extinguished. The Magickal Realm was once again in darkness and apparently deserted. She felt a strange shiver pass through her as she left the market square. It felt almost as though she could have just imagined the whole bizarre encounter.

Maybe Carmel really *was* a witch.

Chapter 16

Saturday, 9 June 1990, 12.30pm

"We'll go into town straight after lunch." Faye looked elated. She jumped up and down on her bed – something Kimberley's mum would never have allowed. For one thing, it would damage the bed springs; for another, the dust it might raise could trigger an asthma attack.

"Mum and Dad won't mind – they probably won't even notice we've gone. We'll be back by teatime. I've got to pop to my nan's first, though. She's still got some birthday money for me, from last month."

"Where does your nan live?"

"Acacia Hill. Only takes about ten minutes on the bus from there into the town centre. Don't worry; we won't stay long. She's as blind as a bat, and deaf, too. But I always get money from the old biddy on my birthday – even if I have to go and fetch it."

Kimberley was a little taken aback. The contempt in Faye's

voice as she spoke of her grandmother was ill-disguised and she noticed her friend's face harden. Acacia Hill was a notoriously dodgy area. There was always some incident being reported on the local news: drunken youths street-fighting and shop windows being smashed; the occasional car set on fire; drug raids in the early hours. But the thought of travelling on the bus was exciting and Kimberley felt sure she'd be fine with Faye, who appeared to know the city and its bus routes like the back of her hand.

Faye was putting gel into her hair in the mirror. Replacing the lid back on the tub, she looked suddenly thoughtful. She glanced at her friend sideways for a moment and then went to her bedroom closet.

"Here, Peanuts, try this on. It's too small for me now."

She tossed her a faded blue denim jacket with a silver star design on the back. Kimberley slipped it on and paraded in front of the mirror that hung on the back of Faye's door.

"I *love* it. Can I really wear it?"

"Course. It looks wicked on you. And there's a matching cap."

Faye rummaged through her drawer, pulling out a denim baseball cap. She turned to Kimberley, frowning.

"Hmm. You need to lose those." She proceeded to slide out the cherry-shaped bobbles which tied her friend's hair into neat pigtails. Kimberley slipped the bobbles into her cardigan pocket, ruffling her wispy tresses into messy, loose waves. Faye then placed the cap on Kimberley's head. She stood back and nodded in approval.

"That's more like it! Just a bit of lippy and that, then you'll be good to go."

Faye unzipped a small patchwork make-up bag, producing a tube of pale pink lip gloss, blusher, a navy-blue kohl pencil and a mascara wand. She proceeded to apply the make-up with expertise to her own face, then handed it over to Kimberley, who followed suit, carefully copying Faye's technique. Kimberley stared at her reflection in the looking glass. She looked older – maybe not as old as Faye, but she was sure she could almost pass for a teenager if she wasn't so small. A quiver of exhilaration ran through her at the thought of leaving the house later in the afternoon. It was going to be *amazing*.

*

It was quarter past three. The rain had become heavier, and as they ran to the bus stop to catch the one due at twenty-five past, the girls were getting wet through. The jacket wasn't the least bit waterproof and Kimberley began to worry that her damp clothes would be a giveaway of their covert excursion, but Faye was dismissive.

"They'll soon dry. We can stick 'em in the airing cupboard when we get back, and I've got a hairdryer. Anyway, your dad's not coming till half seven and we'll be back from town before six – that'll give us loads of time."

They sat at the front of the bus, upstairs. The rain drummed relentlessly on the roof, slanting against the windows. It didn't feel like June. There was one other passenger, a solitary man, who was staring out of the window, seemingly oblivious to their presence. Faye kept getting out of her seat excitedly, jumping from one side of the bus to the other as she pointed out various sites of interest en route. Kimberley was enthralled by her friend's knowledge of the area and hung on her every word.

They passed an old boarded-up church. "See that, Peanuts." Faye lowered her voice. "The vicar was murdered in there last summer. I saw it on the news. Someone smashed his skull in with a brick. They were trying to rob the church one night and he caught them at it. The cleaner found him lying on the floor next morning." Her eyes shone almost gleefully as she shared this gruesome information.

Kimberley looked over at the building and shuddered. She didn't like to think of anything like that taking place so close to home. It was more the sort of thing that happened on TV. Her stomach turned over.

"Did they . . . have they caught the person that did it?"

"Nah. My dad says the coppers are useless. It's like that weirdo going round at the moment, trying to snatch kids. My dad reckons he'll more than likely kill someone before they get him."

Kimberley thought suddenly about what her own father had said; how he'd warned her that she wasn't old enough to take care of herself yet. Maybe he was right in not wanting her to go out alone. It was clearly more dangerous out there than she had really considered. She felt suddenly fearful.

"D'you think we're being wise going into town?" She tried to sound casual but the anxiety in her voice crept through. "I mean, if there's someone going round trying to kidnap children. We're not gonna be able to do much if a grown man tries to grab us, are we?"

Faye stared at her in momentary disbelief, then forced a burst of laughter. Her eyes narrowed.

"I thought you were up for it? Don't tell me you're getting cold feet. I didn't think you were a wuss, Peanuts. Maybe I'd better take you back home to Mummy and Daddy."

Kimberley's instincts told her she ought to let Faye do just that, but realised that to back out now would send her plummeting in her friend's estimation. "*No*. No, I want to go, really I do. I was just saying—"

"Well don't. Just say, I mean. I've been out on my own loads of times and I've never had a problem. We'll have a great laugh. Stop worrying." She nudged Kimberley with her elbow a little too hard.

Kimberley gave her a half-hearted smile and leaned back in her seat. She glanced back over her shoulder at the church and pictured the poor vicar lying there, blood pooling around him. The thought turned her legs to jelly. There was a murderer on the loose. Why, it could be the same weirdo in all the newspapers that was trying to abduct kids. She sneaked a look at the man sitting behind them. He was swarthy with a salt-and-pepper growth on his chin and greasy, slicked-back hair, and was dressed in a charcoal grey anorak. From his reflection in the window, she realised his piercing, dark eyes were staring right at her.

Watching.

Oh God, it could even be *him*.

Kimberley's heart quickened. She gripped the metal edge of the seat and quickly turned back round, trying to shake the idea.

Suddenly, Faye sprang to her feet, pressing the bell on the pole next to their seat.

"Quick, this is our stop."

Careful to avoid eye contact with the creepy passenger, Kimberley hurried down the stairs closely behind her friend. The doors towards the middle of the bus swished open and both girls hopped off just as they pulled into the lay-by. The street onto which they had alighted looked drab and run-down, with litter strewn liberally across the grass verge.

"Where's your nan's house?" asked Kimberley nervously. Her eyes were drawn to movement on the opposite side of the street. Two scruffy-looking teenage boys, hoods up and smoking huge, badly rolled cigarettes, were taking shelter under a tree,

225

watching them. A strange herbal smell was wafting from their direction.

"What you looking at?" One lad stepped forward, staggering slightly. Kimberley froze.

Faye, however, was clearly unfazed. "Not a lot," she retorted. She turned, hooking her arm through Kimberley's.

"Don't worry about *them*. I've seen 'em loads of times. Pair of losers. They're always stoned," she said, grimacing. "C'mon. My nan's is just round the corner." She was almost pulling the reluctant Kimberley along now.

Faye's grandmother lived in a small, dilapidated semi-detached bungalow. One of the windows had a wooden board nailed across it and broken glass lay unswept from the paved area beneath. Many of the neighbouring properties appeared uninhabited. Kimberley timidly followed Faye along the passage at the end of the row and round the back, scanning around her with trepidation as Faye lifted the latch on a rotting wooden gate. It was more of a yard than a garden. The small lawned area was completely bald in places but ridiculously overgrown with thistles and dandelions in others, and bordered by untamed shrubs. The back of the property was protected by a surprisingly high fence, and was therefore quite secluded. They found the door unlocked. Faye walked in without knocking, Kimberley close behind. The pair stood, dripping onto the grimy lino floor. Upon entering the kitchen, they were met with the pungent smell of something decaying. Kimberley covered her nose and mouth with her hand. The sink was piled with filthy dishes and the waste bin was overflowing.

"She's a dirty old cow – my mum's always said so," remarked Faye, looking around in disgust.

Kimberley was shocked. She thought of her own grandmother, who had died two years earlier. She may have been an old battleaxe sometimes, but Kimberley would never have dreamed of speaking about her so disrespectfully. "But . . . I thought you said she was blind. Maybe she needs some help?"

Faye sneered. "Well *I* won't be volunteering. She's never done anything for me."

"I don't understand. I thought you said she always gives you money?"

Faye smiled, but the sudden coldness that filled her eyes was jarring. "It's only what she owes me. You know how I told you Mike's not my *real* dad? I know you thought my dad must be dead and I didn't bother to put you straight. Well, you might as well know. He's not dead. He's in prison. He left my mum when I was only a baby. And she's his mum." She jabbed a thumb with contempt towards the door leading from the room.

Stunned, Kimberley followed Faye into the hallway. She looked on as her friend pushed open the living room door, revealing a dishevelled, frail-looking elderly woman with sparse grey hair who was stretched out across the worn Dralon settee. She was asleep and snoring loudly, her mouth gaping open. Her loose-knit cardigan was filthy and peppered with holes. A half-empty cup of tea and a packet of digestive biscuits sat on the low wooden table in front of her, a pattern of mug rings covering its veneer. The surfaces were thick with dust. Faded wallpaper was peeling from the walls, the paintwork yellow with age. The air smelled sour, with a tang of urine that made Kimberley want to retch. Faye prodded her grandmother, but her action produced no response. She bent down and picked up the battered handbag at the old woman's side.

"What are you doing?" Kimberley whispered.

"Don't worry. She won't hear you. She's half deaf at the best of times, and anyway, she's out for the count."

Faye sniggered. Kimberley watched in horror as Faye delved

into the bag and pulled out an old brown leather purse. She prised out three notes and replaced the purse, snapping the handbag's old-fashioned clasp shut.

"Thirty quid. That'll do nicely."

"Surely you're not going to just *take* it?" Kimberley was aghast.

"Why not?" Faye responded defiantly. "She stopped bothering with me once Mum started seeing Mike. Mum used to bring me to see her when I was little, but she wasn't really interested. I never even got a birthday card or Christmas present; nothing. And then one day I thought, if she doesn't give me anything, and my real dad doesn't either, why don't I just take it? I reckon they owe me that much, considering they've turned their backs on me."

"But it's *stealing*. And . . . and she's an old lady." Appalled, Kimberley backed away from Faye, suddenly afraid. She was beginning to see a side to her friend that hadn't emerged before – and it was a side she didn't like one bit.

The girl glared down at her sleeping grandmother and then back at Kimberley. Her eyes flashed with anger.

"Some mate *you* are. Friends are supposed to stick together. You're lucky to have me. None of the others could understand why I ever wanted to knock around with you. I always stuck up for you. But I'm beginning to think they were right."

Tears sprang to Kimberley's eyes. "I want to go home," she said in a small voice.

Faye laughed mockingly, tilting her head to one side. "Well, off you go, then. No one's stopping you." She folded her arms, filling the doorway as if daring Kimberley to pass.

Kimberley wriggled out of the now sodden borrowed jacket, slinging it and the cap to the ground. She pushed past Faye, her chest tightening. Blundering her way back through the kitchen, she went out into the garden and up the path, looking anxiously beyond the gate and trying to remember where she would need to go to catch the bus. She was cold now, shivering as the rainfall continued its assault. Apart from the trouble she would find herself in with her parents, the realisation that she would have to make her way back alone from Acacia Hill filled her with panic. She thought of the scary-looking youths in the street and the creepy man on the bus. The constriction in her chest began to increase. An unpleasant light-headed sensation was building, making her unsteady, and she put out her arms to save herself in case she lost her balance. Doubling over, she began to cough uncontrollably. Kimberley was gripped by a sudden cold dread. She knew an asthma attack was imminent, and it felt like a bad one.

Not here! Not now!

Fumbling in her cardigan pocket, she realised with sudden horror that she must have dropped her inhaler. Maybe it had fallen out on the bus. The unbearable wheezing was taking hold of her now. Her lungs were heaving and she clutched at her throat as she gasped for breath.

"Help me!" she called out, her voice faint and hoarse. Weakened and desperate for air, she dropped to her knees. "*Please*, help me . . ."

Chapter 17

Wednesday, 4 July 1990

Twenty-five days after Kimberley's disappearance

Alessa wondered how she could ever have missed Gus Brown. She could only assume their paths had never crossed as a result of differing shift patterns. As she walked through the station entrance that morning, she was greeted with the sight of a huge, shinily bald black man, built like a rugby forward. His deep, laughing voice boomed across Reception, as he leaned against the counter in conversation with Sharman. The man's shirt was straining across the width of his shoulders, his arms almost bursting out of the sleeves like the Incredible Hulk.

"Ah – here she is. The lady herself." Sharman tipped his head towards Alessa as she approached. Gus turned and flashed her an enormous grin.

"WPC Cano! I understand you've been looking for me." He held out a hand the size of a dinner plate and shook her own warmly. "Pleased to meet you. I'm Gus, by the way, in case you hadn't realised."

Alessa smiled. "Hello. Good to meet you, too."

"I bumped into Jasper last night as he was coming off shift. He says you were hoping I might've spotted someone using the call box up at Carfax on Monday evening?"

"That's right. I had a – well, a nuisance phone call at home, and it was made from that kiosk." She drew in a breath. "It's pretty likely he was the man who abducted Kimberley Painter."

Gus shook his head, his face suddenly grave. "So I could've been just yards from a killer and not even known it."

Alessa's pulse quickened. "Did you get a look at him, then? It was 8.45 exactly – I could hear the bells going off in the background."

Gus grimaced apologetically. "Sadly not. I was breaking up a scrap between a couple of idiots in the passage outside The Crown at twenty to nine. I noticed the time, 'cause I remember thinking it was quite early in the evening for them to be so pie-eyed. I was back up on Queen Street only minutes later. Must've just missed him."

Her shoulders sagged. "Oh. That's such a shame."

"I'm sorry I can't be more help. D'you have anything to go on, any distinguishing features you've discovered recently we should all be looking out for?"

Alessa thought of everything she knew about their suspect. All in all, it was precious little.

"White, average height. Stocky. Fortyish. That's about it. Like a good chunk of the male population of Oxford."

Gus turned to Sharman. "Well, that's narrowed it down a bit." He pursed his lips. "DCI Bennett's not having much luck then, I take it."

Sharman rolled his eyes. "Personally, I never thought he was the right man for the job," he said, in a low voice, glancing from left to right. "Only on this occasion, I wish he'd prove me wrong."

Gus turned back to Alessa. "I'll keep my eyes peeled for anyone who looks a bit iffy. If he's used that kiosk once, chances are he might be back. Sorry I couldn't be more help."

Alessa managed a small smile. "It's not your fault. And yes, do keep an eye on anyone fitting his description when you're on patrol. He's got to slip up sooner or later."

She wished Gus and Sharman a good day and made her way wearily up the stairs. She'd had another knock-back already and it wasn't even 8.30am.

Alessa was met with raised eyebrows as she walked through the double doors into the room. There were a few sniggers from the far corner as a small group of male constables gathered round one table, talking in low voices.

Immediately, the door of Bennett's office burst open and he came marching towards her, red-faced and waving something in the air. Startled by his demeanour, she realised it was a newspaper.

"What the hell are you playing at, Cano? D'you want to make us a bloody laughing stock?"

"I'm sorry?" Alessa was perplexed. She glanced around at the other officers, who were all watching the live entertainment as it unravelled, some throwing her sympathetic looks, others smothering grins.

"*Sorry*? You damn well should be." He slammed down the tabloid on the nearest table, jabbing a finger at the front page. "What the hell were you thinking – or is there anything actually going on in that fluffy little brain of yours?"

Alessa stared down at the headline:

232

CLUELESS POLICE RESORT TO HOCUS-POCUS IN SEARCH FOR MISSING KIMBERLEY

And there, covering the centre of the spread, was a full-length photograph of Alessa, still in uniform, leaving *The Magickal Realm* the previous evening. Next to the image was a much smaller headshot of Carmel, wearing a star-spangled mauve headscarf and huge earrings. Alessa wanted the ground to swallow her up.

"If I could explain, sir – it was a private visit. Nothing to do with the case." Not strictly true maybe, but it hadn't been on work's time. If only she hadn't been in such a hurry to get to Woodstock. The uniform hadn't been the best idea. Apart from Bennett's ire, the thought that someone had followed and snapped her unawares made her blood run cold.

"Clear up your mess, Cano. You need to ring the paper's editor right now and explain what you were doing there, insist they run another story to correct their inaccuracy. I'm not having my department becoming the butt of the nation's jokes because of some silly, empty-headed—" He stopped short of using a sexist insult and gritted his teeth, his eyes flicking round the room.

"And when you've done that, lie low for a couple of days. There's still a mountain of paperwork to get through. I don't want any more of this sort of embarrassing behaviour bringing shit to my door – am I making myself clear?"

Alessa nodded. She could feel heat radiating from her cheeks. "Yes, sir. I'm sorry. I – I'll put them straight at once."

He retreated into his office, slamming the door behind him.

Alessa looked up to see everyone still staring at her. "Okay you lot, show's over." She attempted a smile, then made her way to her desk, avoiding eye contact with anyone. She felt slightly sick.

"Was she any good, this woman?" one of the men called across, holding a copy of the paper aloft and pointing to Carmel's headshot. "I could do with someone giving me the winning pools numbers."

"Make an appointment with her and find out. But be warned – she's good at sussing out your innermost secrets." Alessa tried to keep her voice light, though her stomach was in knots. "If you've got any skeletons in your closet, you might want to give it a miss. Definitely don't take your wife along, eh?"

The man's face turned crimson and he dropped his eyes. There were a few muted chuckles and Alessa wondered if she'd unwittingly hit on something.

"Yeah, I've seen him chatting up that Sharon in the canteen," said one of the others. "His missus wouldn't be too impressed if she got wind of it, would she?"

Everyone, apart from the blushing joker, laughed loudly. They began to talk amongst themselves and Alessa relaxed a little. Gradually, everyone drifted back to their desks, waiting for Bennett to calm down and come back out to deliver the usual morning sermon.

Alessa found the contact number for the *Mail* and went to use the phone in one of the smaller rooms along the landing. The rookie reporter credited with the piece, a squeaky-voiced man named Sparkes, seemed keen to speak to her.

"So, is it common for the police to turn to alternative sources like this when things aren't going well?" he wheedled. "I mean, I know you must all be under pressure if you're not getting anywhere. Especially your head honcho. I s'pose it's not unreasonable to try just about anything when you're desperate . . ."

Alessa bristled, but she needed to be careful. The man had an agenda and journalists were notorious for twisting things. And he

234

was probably recording their whole conversation. "Look, I just need you to issue a statement to explain my visiting a clairvoyant has nothing to do with the case. Nothing to do with my job at all."

"It was for personal reasons, then?"

She paused. "Yes, I suppose you could say that. Not that it's any of your business."

"And was the clairvoyant able to help?"

Alessa clenched her jaw. "This bears no relevance to anything that's going on with the Kimberley Painter investigation. Nor anything else to do with the police. In fact, it's a gross invasion of my privacy." She thought for a moment. "Has one of your reporters been tailing me? Was it you? Because I have contacts – I'll sue." She had no intention of pursuing litigation, but the mention of the word 'sue' seemed to fluster him.

"No, no; of course not." Sparkes' voice had grown even more high-pitched. "The whole story was based around information from a concerned member of the public. That the police aren't doing a very good job at the moment and they're wasting time."

"And who was this *member of the public*?"

He paused momentarily. "We received an anonymous tip-off, a call from a public phone last night. A local guy, from the sound of his accent. The photo was dropped through our office door and landed on my desk in the early hours – just in time to hit the press."

A sudden coldness crept up Alessa's spine. "The original photo – was it a Polaroid?"

"Yeah. Not a pro shot by any means, but you don't look so bad in it, eh?" He gave an irritating little laugh. "And would you agree – that the police haven't been very on the ball so far with this one? It'd be good to have a few words from someone on the inside."

As much as she'd have liked to slate Bennett, Alessa wasn't

about to be drawn into a conversation about how things were being run. "Just make sure your apology and explanation of all this in tomorrow's edition are just as high profile as today's article. And that Polaroid picture – I need to collect it from you."

"Oh? Any particular reason?"

Alessa could almost hear the cogs turning in his brain. She imagined him scribbling down more sensational headlines. "We want it, that's all. For our files. If a member of the public's been following me – well, we need to warn him off. And please – I expect it's a bit late, but try not to contaminate it. Pick it up with a clean tissue and put it into an envelope. If there are any prints, we need to preserve them."

"Sounds as though it could be important, then?" His voice was eager.

She could picture next morning's front page: *vital evidence uncovered by local reporter*. "No, it's just procedure. And Mr Sparkes, I need your assurance that a full retraction of your piece and apology will be printed. Do you understand?"

Sparkes mumbled grudgingly that he'd ensure something appeared before the end of the week. Alessa hung up.

She made her way back to the office, the thought of having been followed still gnawing at her. She would have to tell Bennett. It was a relief to find she'd missed the briefing, which had clearly lasted only minutes. Everyone was getting ready for their morning's tasks, whether settling at their desks or putting on jackets ready to go out into the community.

Alessa could see Bennett through the glass wall of his room. Steeling herself, she approached and knocked on the door. He looked up from his desk and glowered, but waved her in.

"Did you speak to the *Mail*?"

"Yes, sir. It's sorted. The reporter's printing something by Friday to set the record straight."

236

"Good job, too. Stuff like that could destroy our reputation. I don't know what the hell you were playing at, WPC Cano, but if you're intent on seeing one of these oddballs, make sure you're in civvies in future." He dropped his gaze back to the paperwork on his desk and, without making eye contact, waved a hand as if to dismiss her.

"There's something else, sir."

"What?" He snapped his head back up, scowling. "I'm a busy man, Cano. I've got other things to think about on top of the Painter case."

Alessa felt anger welling inside her. "It was a member of the public that took that picture of me, apparently. He made a phone call to the newspaper and dropped off a Polaroid, but no one saw him."

Bennett sat back, his tongue suddenly poking his cheek from within. "A Polaroid, eh? Are you implying it could've been the same man who sent the packages?"

"That's exactly what I'm saying, sir. I've said I'll collect the photo from the reporter. We can get Forensics to check it out."

Bennett shook his head. "Oh, no you don't. I'll send PC Morris to pick it up. You're staying put for now." He considered a moment. "So he followed you, then, our suspect?"

"It looks that way, yes." Alessa was keeping her fingers crossed behind her back. Maybe he'd offer her some protection now.

"Well, you'll have to be extra vigilant then, won't you? If you clock anyone suspicious while you're out and about, call it in right away." He gave her a joyless smile. "Off you go, then. You must have plenty to be getting on with. Send Morris in to see me, will you. Oh – and shut the door on your way out."

Alessa stood outside his room for a moment, her mind reeling. Even being told outright that she'd been followed, Bennett still wasn't taking it seriously enough. She felt helpless. She would just have to throw herself into her work and hope Forensics had discovered something to help lead them to their man.

Later that afternoon, a report was delivered to the office by the young technician from the lab. It seemed she had an admirer now, as he blushed scarlet and smiled shyly every time she looked at him. She felt a bit guilty and hoped she hadn't given him false hopes after handing over a four-pack of Carling Black Label for his efforts. Maybe it hadn't been such a great idea.

Nothing was coming back from Forensics with the results she'd hoped for. Of course, she knew now that the piece of fabric could be ruled out. Annoyingly, they hadn't managed to get prints from the piece of paper found in the call box, either. It had picked up too much other debris from the floor. But there was the faintest suggestion of writing from the pressure of a pen or pencil that had come through from the previous page of the pad.

A sequence of letters, which appeared to read: *M ay 2 J y D k p s ng t gh*

It made no sense. The only hope was of finding the pad it had been written on – and that felt like looking for a needle in a haystack.

Friday, 6 July 1990

Twenty-seven days after Kimberley's disappearance

Without Jason's presence in the office, the days had seemed even longer and more arduous than ever. Alessa appreciated that he must be busy at home, but the fact he hadn't called at all was beginning to make her anxious. He'd seemed keen enough, the morning he left Squitchey House. But maybe given space and time to reflect, he'd had second thoughts about their relationship. After all, she had a whole lot of baggage – perhaps with everything else he had going on, it was more than he could cope with right now. She couldn't really blame him if that were the case.

There had been no further incidents at home since the phone call and the arrival of the horrible note the previous Monday. She could only pray the evil prick was growing bored with tormenting her, though in her heart knew that was unlikely. The locks at home had all been changed and the burglar alarm system revamped, plus the CCTV cameras were now up and running, which made her feel a little safer. But the fact that she'd been followed to Woodstock had her scrutinising every passing car, every male pedestrian over the age of thirty who looked a likely culprit. Being constantly on high alert was exhausting and it would have been reassuring to have Jason around. Alessa was so looking forward to seeing him again. In the meantime, she couldn't expect him to drop everything and come running to her aid every time something unsettling happened. She would just have to deal with it.

She'd leafed through the *Mail* at breakfast, searching for the promised apology about the article they'd printed. On page three, she found a tiny, small-print paragraph retracting the allegations about the police using a psychic, but barely big enough for anyone without a magnifying glass to have noticed. She should have known. Sparkes had sounded like a weasel. With a heavy heart, she'd caught the bus into work that morning and mulled everything over while she watched the world slide by. Downstairs was heaving, with many passengers having to stand, so she'd made her way upstairs and sat by the window near the front, gazing absently down at the tops of the leafy trees lining the Woodstock Road, as they headed towards the city centre.

Alessa suddenly sat up sharply, catching her breath. The familiar, upright gait of a dark-haired man appeared from round the corner of Rawlinson Road. He was strolling briskly along the pavement, but walking away from the town, dressed smartly in a suit and tie and carrying a briefcase.

It was Jason.

She rapped frantically on the glass, but the sound must have been drowned out by the traffic. His eyes were fixed straight ahead, his expression determined. He glanced to his right and turned onto the driveway of a grand four-storey house. The bus sailed past and Alessa craned her neck, puzzled, to watch as he climbed the steps to the entrance and then disappeared through the huge front door.

She contemplated getting off at the next stop and waiting for him to re-emerge from the building. Although, what would be the point? Apart from anything else, it would make her late. And she certainly didn't want to look as though she were stalking him.

But her mind was racing now. Jason was supposed to be at home, at his mother's bedside, four miles away in Headington.

So what the hell was he doing there?

*

For the rest of the day, Alessa found it impossible to apply herself at work, worrying about what might be going on. She kept thinking about what Carmel had said.

He may not be all you think he is.

Was Jason up to something?

No. She couldn't believe he'd be involved in anything shady.

240

But then again, she knew nothing of his background – not really. Only what he'd chosen to tell her. She hadn't met his parents. Had never been to his home . . .

By the end of the afternoon, a sick feeling was curdling in her stomach. The more she thought about it, the more determined she was to investigate further, even if she didn't like what she uncovered. She had enough shit to deal with; she didn't need Jason not being straight with her on top of it all. She would make a detour on the way home and see if the house he'd entered threw up any clues.

Alessa felt strangely energised as she alighted from the bus at the stop before Polstead Road, crossing the main road to where she'd seen Jason heading that morning. She glanced down Rawlinson Road, wondering whether she might spot his distinctive orange Montego parked somewhere, but there was no sign of it. He was probably long gone by now.

The house had three cars parked on its gravel driveway – two black Range Rovers and a silver Mercedes, each gleaming with pristine paintwork. Alessa stood on the pavement, staring up at the glossy black door. The brass plaque on the wall next to the portico was engraved with something, but she was too far away to make it out. Looking from left to right, she approached with caution, screwing up her eyes to read the inscription.

Dr B. R. Franklin

Below the name was an unusual symbol – a sort of diamond shape, containing the letter 'G'. Perhaps Dr Franklin was a gastroenterologist, or a geriatrician? She was aware there were several private specialist practices in the local area. An old-fashioned, circular push-button doorbell was fixed immediately beneath the plaque.

Alessa stood for a moment, staring at the name. It dawned on her then that maybe this had been a medical appointment that Jason had been attending – or even a meeting about his mum's health. She felt suddenly guilty.

Retreating hurriedly from the driveway, she was about to cross to the other side when the door opened and two men appeared, both immaculately dressed. One was tall and thin, balding and clean-shaven; the other thick-set and shorter, with closely cropped brown hair. The thin man shook the other's hand effusively and waved as his companion unlocked one of the Range Rovers, threw in his briefcase, climbed in and pulled away.

The front door was closed abruptly. Maybe the thin man was Dr Franklin. The other man looked as though he was probably a colleague, rather than a patient, but Alessa was just surmising. She carried on across the Woodstock Road, cursing herself all the way home for playing detective. Jason would have had good reason to be there, she was sure of it. She would say nothing. If he found out she'd been trying to spy on him, even if he hadn't been intending to end things with her, it would probably make him do just that.

Least said, soonest mended.

*

Later that evening, the phone rang. After the sinister call she'd received, Alessa was being extra careful now when answering. She said nothing, merely listened as she picked up, her heart quickening.

"Alessa? Is that you? It's Jason."

Her heart gave a tiny skip. She tried to keep her tone light.

"Hello. I've been wondering how you were."

"All the better for hearing your voice." There was a pause. "Sorry I haven't been in touch. It's been pretty full-on this week, with one thing and another."

"That's okay. I did think you might've been up to your eyes in it."

She could hear him sigh from the other end of the line. "I know, but I should've let you know."

"How's your mum doing?"

"A bit better. But she's been referred to a specialist and given some different medication. It's taking her a while to get used to it."

"Ah." She wasn't about to ask if it was prescribed by Dr Franklin. "Well, hopefully once it kicks in things will improve for her."

"Anyway, how's everything with you?"

"Oh, so-so. Not much happened really." She thought of the disturbing note and her visit to Carmel. Hopefully he'd been too busy to read the newspapers. The heat of shame burned through her as she thought of her little expedition earlier. Things had actually been much more eventful than she'd have liked.

"I'm glad." He spoke softly. "I've missed you."

She felt a warm glow. Thank *God* she hadn't confronted him. Her judgement had completely gone to pot. "I've missed you too."

"See you tomorrow maybe? We could just go for a walk if you want. I'd-I'd really like to see you." He sounded weary; slightly despairing, even. Alessa wanted to reach down the line and hug him.

"Yeah, that'd be nice. Come round about eleven-thirty?"

He sounded a little brighter. "See you in the morning, then."

"See you in the morning." She replaced the receiver, a smile tugging at her lips.

What was it people said? *What a difference a day makes*. It felt as though someone had suddenly switched on the sun.

Monday, 9 July 1990

30 days after Kimberley's disappearance

Jason had returned to work with the bit between his teeth. With little else to go on, he had begun focusing his attentions on researching known sex offenders living in and around Acacia Hill and had uncovered a potential suspect: a forty-nine-year-old man named Colin Bell, who had moved into the area some two years earlier. Bell had previous convictions for flashing young girls in woodland close to his former address – a rented flat just outside Swindon – and one for the attempted abduction of a teenager. Apparently, only a fortnight earlier, a woman had reported him loitering suspiciously near a playground a short distance from Faye Greene's grandmother's bungalow. Infuriatingly, one of the other PCs had answered the call and filed a report, but had immediately gone on sick leave and the information hadn't been fully investigated.

"What d'you reckon?" Jason looked up as Alessa leaned over his shoulder to study the document open on the computer's bulky monitor. "I think we should check him out. He sounds delightful – and he's in the right area."

"Hmm. Definitely wouldn't hurt. I'd like to speak to the woman who called it in, too. Hear what she has to say." Alessa shuddered a little at the thought that this might finally be the man they were looking for. Could Bell be the one who'd taken Jessie? And who'd been targeting her? She felt a spike of anxiety as she considered coming face to face with him. "Is there—? Do we have a photo?"

Jason leafed through the sheaf of papers in the folder on his desk and then withdrew an A4 sheet with a photograph paperclipped to one corner. Alessa stared at the gaunt, unsmiling face looking out at her. She noted the plastered-down hair, the roughly unshaven jaw, and the dead, soulless eyes. The picture had been taken at the time of Bell's arrest four years earlier. He might look quite different now – might have looked *totally* different twelve years ago. Alessa was hoping for *something*, some glimmer of recognition. But her memory had pretty much erased the image of the man who had pursued her and Jessie. Moira, her therapist, had explained that this was sometimes the case; that the brain could block anything that might induce further trauma.

Her monster was a looming, faceless shadow.

Alessa shook away the thought and filled her lungs.

"Looks like we need a trip to Acacia Hill, then."

*

Basia Kowalska, the woman who had contacted the police about Bell, was the mother of two little girls – aged eight and five. She invited Alessa and Jason into her second-floor flat, which looked clean but was shabbily furnished and run-down. She had split from her husband not long after coming to the UK from Poland two years earlier, she told them. She'd been desperate for a better life for herself and her children. Things hadn't begun as well as she'd hoped.

"This all I afford right now." Basia waved a hand, indicating the paper peeling from the living room walls, the patch of mould spreading beneath the window. "I work hard. Save for something better. But it will take long time. But at least we have roof over our head." She gave a brief but slightly sad smile.

Alessa's eyes met Jason's and they shared a subtle grimace. She felt desperately sorry for the woman. She experienced a pang as she thought of the children, having to live in this miserable, damp flat. It wasn't a good way for anyone to start out.

"My babies." Basia's face lit up as she lifted a framed photo from the top of the ancient TV set in the corner, offering it to Alessa.

Two fair-haired little girls in school uniform, one head and shoulders above the other, smiled out at her. Alessa's stomach turned over. She shot a look at Jason, who arched his eyebrows.

"They at school now, but summer holiday soon, and I must work. Is hard." Basia let out a sigh. She was pale and very thin, her fine brown hair scraped back from her angular face. Though she was only about thirty, lines had begun to creep around her eyes and mouth.

Jason offered her a sympathetic smile. "Mrs Kowalska, I wonder if you could tell us what you told the other police officer. About the man watching the children."

Basia stiffened. She replaced the photograph. "I take my girls Sundays, to the swings." She went to the window and indicated the ground below. "Out there."

Alessa crossed to where she was standing and homed in on a small fenced square of grass, comprising two swings, a graffiti-daubed slide, a seesaw and climbing frame. A woman with a pram was sitting on a bench just inside the area, watching a toddler pottering around the play equipment.

"I sit there while girls play. The man, he standing on other side. Looking." Basia shivered, hands wrapped across her chest, rubbing at her thin arms. "But his face. His eyes. They look . . .

246

black." She turned to Alessa and shuddered. "I know something not right."

"Did the man . . . did he actually *do* anything? Approach the girls?" Jason looked hopeful.

Basia shook her head. "He just watch. I see him from up here, too. Watching other kids. Like . . . like he waiting."

Waiting for a golden opportunity, Alessa thought. Something cold seemed to be crawling along her spine. "What did the first police officer you spoke to say about it?" she asked gently.

"Just that he not do much. Not if the man done nothing. He say . . . he give the man a-a-a . . . *gipsy warning*, or something? So he knows police watch him." Basia shrugged. "They must wait he hurts someone. That how it seems."

Alessa was all too familiar with this scenario. It was so frustrating.

"Thank you very much for speaking to us, Mrs Kowalska." She smiled, turning to Jason. "We appreciate it. And please be assured that we'll be interviewing the man. But do keep a close eye on your little girls. It always pays to be cautious."

Basia nodded solemnly. She saw them to the door. As Alessa turned to say goodbye, the woman reached for her hand. "Lady, I think, I think I come to England for my children. I think it good place. Now I not so sure."

Alessa had begun to wonder she was right.

*

Colin Bell's home was situated worryingly close to the children's play area, with only the litter-strewn scrub grass verge and a narrow band of road separating them. He peered round the curtain of his living room as Jason pressed repeatedly on the doorbell to the shabby maisonette. The man glowered at them through the murky glass, then opened the small window at the top of the frame and shouted through.

"What d'you want?"

"We'd like a word, Mr Bell. Open up please."

Jason turned to Alessa and rolled his eyes. She could feel panic bubbling in her chest. Moira's lilting voice filled her head.

"Deep breaths. In, out. One, two."

This felt entirely different from when she'd accompanied Bennett to interview Jerome Wilde. They'd confirmed that Kimberley was in Acacia Hill the day she'd gone missing. And Colin Bell lived just a stone's throw away from where she and Faye had been. He could easily have followed the girl home, lured or dragged her somewhere when she got off the bus . . . Alessa's head began to swim. Had they finally found their man?

Bell opened the front door, but only just wide enough for them to see his face as the security chain hung beneath his stubbly, greying chin. He gave them a look of utter contempt, his deep-set dark eyes narrow, hostile slits.

"This is police harassment, that's what it is. I had another bloke here hassling me only a couple of weeks back."

"We can do this inside, or we can let the whole neighbourhood know why we're here. It's up to you." Jason stood firm, his foot wedged between the step and the doorjamb. He glanced back at Alessa and gave her a brief wink. She felt slightly nauseous in anticipation of what was to come and, without thinking, reached for Jason's hand. He returned a reassuring squeeze.

Bell muttered something that sounded like an expletive and unlatched the chain.

Alessa stayed close behind Jason, still trying to steady her breath. She could hardly bring herself to look at Bell. They followed the man down a short passageway and into a dingy, low-ceilinged galley kitchen, where the otherwise bare work surfaces were covered with coffee mug rings and crumbs. A frying pan containing a dollop of lard and a plastic spatula sat on the scruffy electric hob, an egg and pack of streaky bacon on the worktop next to it, waiting to be cooked. A small drop-leaf melamine table was pushed up against one wall, set with cutlery and a chipped dinner plate, thick-sliced white loaf, and a bottle of HP sauce. There was barely standing room for more than one person, and Jason halted in the doorway. Alessa continued to hang back. She cast around the hall and could see through the open door into the living room, which was empty except for a two-seater wooden-framed sofa with a little side table and an old TV set. The walls were bare, and there were no ornaments. No bookshelves. It felt more like a waiting room than a home.

"Mr Bell, a member of the public has informed us that you've been seen watching the children in the local playground." Jason straightened, drawing himself to his full height and then had to duck to avoid the top of the door frame. He stood a good six inches taller than Bell, who must have been no more than five foot seven.

Alessa turned to look at Bell properly now as he stood, hands at his sides, next to the stove. He was scrawny and smelled unwashed, his lank hair thick with grease. He wore a baggy brown pullover, a dribble of dried egg yolk down its front, and there was a hole in one toe of his threadbare corduroy slippers. His hands looked oddly misshapen, possibly with arthritis. When he opened his mouth to speak, Alessa saw that he had a front tooth missing. He was, she thought now, a pathetic specimen.

"And?" Bell stuck out his jaw defiantly. "You can't arrest me for looking. I've done nothing wrong. Free country."

Jason bristled visibly. His voice hardened. "Can you tell us where you were on the afternoon of Saturday the ninth of June of this year, please."

Alessa kept scrutinising Bell, hoping for a spark of familiarity or recollection, or some clue. But there was nothing that roused any sort of recognition within her. She thought of the hooded figure she'd seen outside Squitchey House. The person had been stocky in build, and square-shouldered. Though she couldn't call to mind the features of the man who'd chased her and Jessie, she had the feeling he'd been bigger, somehow. Bulkier. Of course, she'd been much smaller herself at the time. How she wished she could dig into her memory and picture him clearly.

"Ninth of June?" Bell scratched his chin in mock stupefaction. "Hmm. Let me see. Oh, I was at home, far as I can remember."

"Is there anyone who can verify that?" Jason sounded impatient.

"Erm, not that I can think of. I'm not exactly a social butterfly." He gave a simpering smile. "Sorry. You'll just have to take my word for it."

Alessa was surprised to see that the usually self-controlled Jason was losing his cool. He jabbed a finger in Bell's direction, his eyes flashing.

"Well I'm not prepared to take your word for it, you maggot. There's CCTV in this area – and if you've been doing the rounds, we'll know soon enough. And while I'm about it" – he leaned in through the doorway now, hissing through his teeth – "if you go anywhere near that playground again, I'll have you in a cell so fast your grubby little feet won't touch the ground. Am I making myself clear?"

Bell looked ruffled. He lifted a hand to his throat, his head shaking slightly.

"You-you can't touch me. I haven't done anything," he protested weakly.

"Like I said, if you're not telling the truth, we'll find you out. I've got my eye on you, so be warned. Just keep away from those children – or we'll be letting everyone in the community know who they've got living next to them. And I'm sure you wouldn't want that."

Stony-faced, Jason motioned to Alessa with his head and she turned to leave, slightly stunned by this outburst. Bell didn't seem such a threat anymore, just a horrible, seedy little man.

Bell followed them back along the hallway to the door, suddenly braver now that they were leaving.

"You-you can't speak to me like that. I-I know my rights. I'll—"

Jason pulled up sharply. He was outside now, but spun round to square up to Bell, who took a step back into the house.

"Your *rights*? What about the rights of innocent children not to be corrupted by the likes of you? Don't push your luck, you—"

Alessa saw Jason's hands curl into fists. She gave a small cough, raising an eyebrow in his direction. She was much less agitated now herself, but growing concerned that this might escalate.

"We'll be checking what you've told us, Mr Bell," she interjected, motioning at Jason to carry on back to their car as she stood halfway down the garden path. "As PC Shelley's already told you, owing to the high crime rate, this area's widely covered by CCTV cameras now. So if you *did* leave your house at any point on the afternoon of Saturday the ninth, it'd be wise to come clean now."

"Pfft. I can't be expected to remember what I was doing weeks ago," he snapped, flapping a hand irritably. "One day's much the same as the next to me."

Alessa's thoughts turned to Basia's little girls. She tried to keep the contempt from her voice. "It was the day the World Cup opened. Does that ring any bells?"

The man stared at her now as though something momentous had occurred to him. His eyes narrowed. They seemed to be boring into her, and Alessa found herself backing away, discomfited.

"*You*. I know you from somewhere, don't I?" Bell's mouth morphed suddenly into a peculiar leer.

Jason had stopped halfway down the path. He glanced over his shoulder, firing a quizzical look from Bell to Alessa. Though she was trying to remain composed, her earlier panic began to build once more.

"I don't believe so. We've never met before, to my knowledge. Wh-why would you think that?" She felt the surge of blood pounding in her ears. How could Bell possibly know her?

"Oh, but I *definitely* recognise you. I never forget a pretty face." Bell had obviously realised Alessa was becoming flustered. He was enjoying himself now.

"Ah. That's it. You were all over the news a few years ago, weren't you?" He ran a tongue over his top lip as his eyes travelled lecherously from her head to her feet.

"Sweet Sandi Cano."

Chapter 18

Tuesday, 10 July 1990

Thirty-one days after Kimberley's disappearance

"But we can't hold him here. We haven't got anything concrete to charge him with."

Alessa was worried that Jason was allowing anger to sway his judgement. She thought back to how he'd bundled Bell roughly into the back of the patrol car, almost shutting the man's arm in the door.

"Oh I *do* hope that didn't hurt," Jason had said under his breath, smirking. Alessa had winced. She could see police brutality being added to Bell's list of grievances.

She peered through the glass vision panel in the custody cell door. A night in the cells had left Colin Bell looking even more unkempt, if that were possible. He was sitting bolt upright on the edge of the bunk, claw-like hands twisting in his lap, staring straight up at her coldly. She recalled Basia Kowalska's description of his black eyes – *something not right* – and snapped the hinged cover shut. Her stomach turned over.

"We'll find something. He's done enough stuff in the past. And calling you Sandi . . ." Jason shook his head, his lips pale and tight. He aimed a kick at the rubberised skirting board, looking as though he wished it were part of Bell's anatomy.

"I think, like he told us, it was because he recognised me from the papers," she said quietly. "Look, I haven't warmed to the little turd any more than you have, but I honestly don't think it's him. That man I saw outside the house – he wasn't wiry like Bell. He looked much . . . kind of beefier."

"Well, whether it's him or not, he's not safe to be let loose around kids." Jason exhaled, leaning back against the wall. "You heard what Basia said. Fucking *gipsy warning* – what good is that? I can't believe our hands are tied, pussyfooting round the likes of him until the damage is actually done."

"It's the law, Jason." Alessa gently cupped his face in her hands. "As frustrating as it is, all we can do is act within the guidelines. And hope to God that someone with common sense changes things in the future."

He sighed. "I'll go over the CCTV footage from Acacia Hill, see if Bell's telling the truth about being home all day." He attempted a smile. "It'd be sweet to nail him. But if he *hasn't* done anything, hopefully he'll think twice about hovering around parks now that he knows we've got his number."

He lifted the steel cover over the rectangle of glass and fixed Bell with a hard stare. The man dropped his eyes, his head falling to his chest. Alessa was reassured to see that he looked unnerved. Maybe Jason's size – and obvious hostility – would be enough to deter him from pursuing his revolting urges. She shuddered at the thought of what motivated him.

It transpired that Bell hadn't been entirely truthful. He'd been captured on camera getting off a bus on the afternoon of 9 June, travelling from the city centre and arriving at the terminus in Acacia Hill at around 3.45pm. It was the same bus from which Faye and Kimberley had been seen alighting at the previous stop.

Excitedly, Jason had called Alessa across the office to pull up a chair and view the footage, which they rewound and re-examined repeatedly. But minutes later, Bell could be seen walking slowly from the local corner shop and up his front path, weighed down with two carrier bags. They slowed down and watched the film repeatedly, but he didn't emerge again at all. As Bennett had previously suggested, no one in their right mind would have gone out in that deluge unless they absolutely had to.

"I suppose we'll have to let him go, then." Jason switched off the video player and leaned back in his seat, stretching his arms above his head. He turned to Alessa and blew out a long breath. "Fuck."

Though deflated, in her heart Alessa had known Bell didn't fit with her impression of the man who'd been plaguing her. She squeezed Jason's shoulder and managed a small smile.

"Back to the drawing board, then."

*

Jason had to hurry home to help his dad, who had called to say his mum had taken a fall.

"No bones broken thankfully," he told Alessa breathlessly, as she walked with him to his car, "but apparently it's affecting her mobility badly and she's needing to be helped to the bathroom and stuff. Fingers crossed she'll be a bit better after a few days' rest."

Alessa was disappointed. It was a pleasantly warm evening and she had hoped they could have a night out – or even in – together, but it couldn't be helped. She glanced about her to make sure no one was watching, then kissed Jason goodbye and waved as he pulled away.

She stood for a moment, feeling at a loose end, then decided to take a detour into town on the way home. The whole thing with Colin Bell had left her with a nasty taste and she needed a distraction, or some sort of normality.

She'd managed to get away just before the shops' closing time, so thought suddenly it would be nice to buy a big bunch of sunflowers for her mamma to add a splash of colour to the living room. They reminded her of home, Greta said, and always cheered her up.

Alessa tried to think positively. She was looking forward to seeing Uncle Rob, who was flying home from Italy at the end of the week. The World Cup was over – as, from everything he'd told her over the phone on Sunday evening, was his relationship with Matteo.

"I don't want to talk about it," he'd declared, somewhat melodramatically. "At least Argentina didn't win the final. I couldn't have stomached that after Maradona and his bloody *hand of God* antics in '86. That's been the one good thing about the last few days."

Alessa strolled up St Aldates and turned right up the High, then crossed the street. The Covered Market was due to close, but the gates were still open. Hopefully she would just have time to nip into the florist's.

The lady on the stall was packing up, but happy to serve

her, and even knocked a pound off as it was the end of the day.

"They'd only go to waste," she said with a smile, wrapping the bunch in coloured paper and securing it with a strip of Sellotape. "There you go, lovely. Enjoy!"

Alessa thanked her and made her way back out onto the street. She carried on back up the High, and turned right onto Cornmarket, the main drag leading to St Giles, to head for the bus stop. Though the shops were on the verge of closing, plenty of people were still walking about and the atmosphere was relaxed. Near the bottom of the street, she stopped to look at the window display in Laura Ashley, where she was sorely tempted by a gorgeous pair of pink shoes. But then, they were quite pricey, and where would she ever go to wear them?

It was nice, though, just ambling. Window-shopping. It made her remember that there was more to life than what was going on at work. That there were nice, normal people out there, just going about their everyday business. A week had passed since her visit to Carmel and there had been no further contact from the man in the meantime. Maybe Jason being back on the scene had made him more cautious.

The bus was on time and though it wasn't too packed, she sat upstairs. She liked being high up, having a clear view of the streets below, especially with the trees in full leaf and the gardens in bloom. She opened the window and enjoyed the cool breeze on her face as they travelled along the Woodstock Road. She looked out to the right as they passed Rawlinson Road and Dr Franklin's rooms, wondering once more about Jason's visit to see him. She hoped fervently that it *had* been for his mum and not for him. She couldn't bear it if he were ill and didn't want to tell her. But she couldn't risk asking him. It would surely all become clear, sooner or later.

Clutching the flowers, Alessa alighted at the stop before Blenheim Drive. It was only another hundred yards or so to Squitchey House. She felt tired now, and was looking forward to kicking off her shoes and changing into her joggers and T-shirt. It had been a heavy couple of days and everything seemed to have suddenly caught up with her. She wondered absent-mindedly what Greta might have made for dinner. She couldn't face a heavy meal – hopefully it wouldn't be pasta. Salad might be nice. More than anything, she wanted a nice cold glass of Sauvignon Blanc.

But as she walked, the onset of purposeful footsteps close behind made her heart quicken. She stepped up her pace, but the footfall increased to match her own speed. Heavy, male footfall. Alessa could see the opening onto the driveway now. It was less than fifty feet away. She was almost home. But the person seemed to be closing on her.

She took a breath and stopped in her tracks, preparing to spin round and tackle him head-on.

Maybe this was it.

Maybe someone was actually going to kill her.

*

Alessa wasn't sure what had just occurred.

Dazed, she sat up, looking around. The sunflowers were still in their wrapping and lay on the pavement. A couple of the heads had been snapped from the stems and trodden under foot, whether by her or her attacker, she couldn't recall. It had all happened so quickly.

She tried to collect her thoughts. Slowly, she replayed the incident in her mind.

The footsteps.

The rush of adrenaline that had started to build inside her.

The sudden determination to stand her ground.

Before she could turn to confront her predator, she'd been grabbed from behind. A pair of strong, gloved hands had shoved her to the ground. Her head had been spinning. She had felt hot breath on her face, a scrape of stubble against her cheek. Her knees had slammed against the ground and now they stung.

"*Not very nice, is it, Sandi?*" The words that had been hissed in her ear echoed through her head now.

Sandi.

It *was* him, then. Not just some random assailant. She felt suddenly sick. He must have been following her. He might even have been on the bus. She was so *stupid*. How could she not have noticed?

"Are you all right, miss?" Startled, she looked up to see an elderly man staring down at her, his eyes wide with concern. He bent forward, lifting her by the hand. "Are you hurt?"

"I-I don't think so." Shakily she clambered to her feet, casting around for evidence of her assailant. Her heart was still hammering against her ribcage.

"I saw the swine. He ran off over that way." The old man indicated with a flap of his gnarled hand across the main road. "Stocky, looked a bit of a brute. He was wearing one of those hoodie things. It's not safe for anyone these days – these bloody muggers everywhere. Don't know what the world's coming to. Need eyes in the back of your head." He curled his lip in disgust. "Did he get your purse?"

Alessa delved into her pocket. Her wallet was still there. She dusted off the fragments of grit that were stuck to her palms.

"No. I— Maybe you disturbed him?"

"Maybe. Main thing is you're okay." He studied her. "Have you got far to go?"

"I-I live just here. I was nearly home . . ." She shook her head uncomprehendingly. "It's happened right on my own doorstep."

And in broad daylight. This thought was even more chilling.

The man stooped to pick up the flowers and handed them to Alessa, supporting his back as he straightened. "I'm not as young as I was, I'm afraid. A few years ago and I'd have been after him like a shot. Given him the old rugby tackle." He smiled ruefully. "You sure you're all right?"

He suddenly seemed to register Alessa's uniform. "My goodness. And you an officer of the law. I don't know. You'd wonder how he'd have the brass neck."

Alessa felt ashamed. She was indeed an officer of the law, and yet, despite everything she'd been taught, all the advice she herself had given to members of the public, she'd allowed herself to become a victim. She'd dropped her guard. Especially at a time when she should have been ultra-careful.

She thanked the old man for his help and made her way to her front door. Her hands were still shaking so much, she could barely slot the key into the lock.

Greta called through from the kitchen. "Is that you, Sandi? Dinner won't be long. I've made lasagne. Hope that's okay."

Alessa mustered a mumbled reply. "Fine, Mamma. I'll just get changed." She closed the door behind her and sank to the floor. Every ounce of strength seemed to have drained from her legs. Hot tears coursed down her face as she sat, trying to make sense of what had just happened.

But what was really playing on her mind was what he'd said. In that same mocking voice that had sung down the phone.

She thought of all the time they'd wasted on Colin Bell and her tears were quickly replaced by anger and frustration. She really ought to tell Jason, but she felt too embarrassed. All she could hope was that the new CCTV at Squitchey House had captured an image of her attacker. She hauled herself to her feet and slowly climbed the stairs. She would have to look through the footage herself and hope for some clue that might lead her to him.

Because this, evidently, was her problem and she needed to sort it.

Chapter 19

Wednesday, 1 August 1990

Fifty-three days after Kimberley's disappearance

Alessa had gone over and over the CCTV footage from their home cameras, but could find no trace of the man who'd assaulted her. He had obviously been out of range. Though she'd toyed with the idea of telling Jason days later, she wondered what the point would be. As far as she was concerned, it would only highlight her shortcomings as a police officer, and she didn't want him to think her inept. Also, he still seemed preoccupied, presumably with what was going on at home, and it didn't seem fair to add to his worries.

Days had rolled into weeks, and then passed without further incident, or, for that matter, progress in the search for Kimberley. The reconstruction of the little girl's last movements had generated a handful of calls from the public, but no one seemed able to add anything that they didn't already know. It was soul-destroying.

Although she hadn't been sure how Bennett would react to the news, Alessa had stuck her neck out and contacted a well-respected local criminal profiler, Nerys Armstrong, to see if she could help to build a picture of the man they were looking for. The woman was coming into the office later that afternoon. Combing through files and identifying local paedophiles had so far proved fruitless and she hoped that someone with an understanding of offender behaviour might be able to narrow their search. And if she could relay Nerys's findings to Carmel, too, maybe it would slot another piece into the puzzle.

Rather than seeming annoyed, Bennett was surprisingly accepting of involving Nerys. "You go ahead, WPC Cano. Profiling isn't something I set much store by myself, but heigh-ho. I have an appointment elsewhere this afternoon, so if you could meet the lady and report back, that would be fine. Do tell her she can feel free to use my office."

It was only later Alessa learned that Chief Superintendent Walker enjoyed playing a few rounds of golf with Nerys's husband. No wonder Bennett had been so accommodating.

Nerys was fiftyish, small and slight, with greying hair styled into a neat bob and gold-rimmed glasses. She wore a tailored camel skirt suit and sensible brown brogues, and was carrying a tan leather briefcase. As Alessa greeted her at Reception, the woman put down her case and extended a hand warmly.

"I'm so pleased you've invited me along," she said, her pink-tinted lips spreading into a smile.

"Thanks very much for agreeing to come." Alessa smiled back. "I'm hopeful your input will help us to move things forward."

"I've been following the investigation – from afar, of course.

And I remember the Jessie Lockheed case well." She gave Alessa's hand a little squeeze. "This must all be really hard for you. I do hope I can help."

Alessa led the way up the stairs and into the main office. Most of the other officers were out on calls. A couple of constables sitting at the far end of the room looked up briefly as they entered, then resumed their work in silence.

After reading through various files and listening to Alessa's explanation of everything that had happened so far, Nerys asked if she could use Bennett's room to make notes and digest what she had learned. When she emerged a good half-hour later, she looked pensive.

"From everything I've been told, and through the information gathered thus far, I think the man you're looking for is local."

Alessa's heart sank. This much they had already gleaned.

"Bear with me." Nerys peered over the top of her glasses. "I know that must be fairly obvious to you – I'm just bullet-pointing here." Alessa nodded silently, allowing her to continue.

"He seems to have good knowledge of the local area. It's possible he was brought up round here and maybe moved away." She chewed her lip. "I'm thinking of the Reading connection. Perhaps he's based there now and just passing through."

This made sense. "And he likes a little extra-curricular activity while he's visiting," Alessa said slowly. She gave a small shudder.

"From your own description, it seems the man is in his forties or thereabouts. I suspect he'll be single – it's possible he's been in relationships, but they've been short-lived. There is a pattern to what he does. Every abduction that's come to light appears to have happened during the summer months. Now why would that be?" Her brow creased into a frown. "Of course there's the possibility he lives abroad and this is some

264

sort of annual pilgrimage." She shook her head. "He could be part of a travelling fair or something similar – but I think he's more likely to have a well-paid job. Not white-collar, maybe – but something which requires a degree of expertise in some area. He's smart about how he operates. Cautious. Arrogant, too. I would probably categorise him as a narcissistic sociopath. He'll have plenty of friends, but not one of them will really have a clue what he's like. And he has no conscience at all."

"And what of his fixation with me?" Alessa blurted out, instantly regretting her words.

Nerys studied her face with concern. "I don't think he intends to do you any physical harm," she said gently. "You're just a pawn in his game, Alessa. It's all part of the fun for him. That, and proving he can run rings around the police. He's getting a buzz from it. But the minute he thinks he's going to get his fingers burned, he'll stop. He's too clever to get too close to the flame. Which is why he needs to be apprehended before he disappears back into the woodwork, and you lose any chance of finding him. And I think he's probably on the verge of doing just that very soon."

Alessa accompanied Nerys back down to Reception and thanked her for her help.

"I really appreciate you giving up your time. I'm sure what you've told me will help to eliminate at least some of the people we've been looking into."

"I'm not sure how much use I've been, to be honest," Nerys said, smiling apologetically. "But if nothing else, I hope I've reassured you that you're not in any real danger. I just hope you can identify him before he harms another child."

Spurred on by Nerys's theories, Alessa was keen to speak to Carmel again about it all. Whilst still sceptical about some of the things she'd said, Carmel had definitely made some very astute observations. Alessa was hopeful that, having gained a little more insight from Nerys, anything Carmel could add into the mix would help to build an even more rounded picture of their suspect. It might have been clutching at straws, but they needed all the help they could get.

Both Nerys and Carmel were of the same opinion: that the man was of no real threat to Alessa as an adult; just a sick, depraved individual taking pleasure in her misery. And Carmel had been uncannily accurate about Alessa's underlying tormented state of mind. She'd obviously picked up on quite a lot and, reflecting on it since, Alessa was hopeful the woman might have had further insight into what was going on since their meeting.

Carmel's phone rang out for ages that evening, the hollow tone that tells you no one's home. Alessa dialled several times, but gave up eventually. She felt oddly restless, overcome by a sudden, inexplicable urge to speak to Carmel. She would try to call her again tomorrow.

Things seemed to have reached a plateau at work. One by one, their list of potential suspects had been crossed off. Every line of inquiry was hitting a dead end. With his targets uppermost in his mind, Bennett had begun to focus on other, less serious, cases. Following a particularly trying time at work the next day, Alessa was in desperate need of a solid night's sleep. She'd rung Carmel's number, but still there was no answer. After clearing up the dinner things, she sat with Greta in the living room for a while, but could barely keep her eyes open even though it was only 9.15pm. She yawned deeply.

"I'm sorry, I'm going to have to turn in. I feel wrecked."

Greta's brow furrowed.

"You do look tired, *tesoro*. You carry on – I won't be long coming up myself. Sleep well."

Alessa climbed the stairs wearily. She'd poured herself a glass of wine to take up, and began to run a bath, a luxury she rarely allowed herself, since the water took so long to heat. Despite it being August, the late evening air was cool, blowing a draught through the bathroom window, which didn't exactly enhance the experience. But she'd heard a warm bath encouraged better quality sleep. And whether the wine did or not, she needed it. From along the landing, she could hear the tinkle of wind chimes, which still hung behind the closed door of Joey's room. It was like a gentle nudge, a reminder that he was still around, watching over her. She smiled wistfully.

Slipping into bed after her bath, Alessa let out a grateful sigh. She felt relaxed, and slightly numb from the wine, which was exactly what she'd hoped for. The room was dark and cool, and she pulled the covers tightly around her. Her eyelids were just beginning to grow heavy when she became suddenly aware of something bobbing gently in the corner of the room. And then the waft of petrichor became so strong it made her nose tingle.

Alessa snapped her eyes open, suddenly wide awake. Though she tried not to look, her attention was drawn like a magnet towards the movement.

And it was then that she saw her.

She saw clearly now; there was no mistaking it.

A little girl with long, white-blonde hair, hovering somewhere between the floor and the ceiling. And she was pale, so very pale. Her face was solemn. She lifted a reed-thin arm and turned to face the window, pointing to something in the distance. She appeared to be indicating the main road, in the general direction of Lime Tree Avenue. Turning back briefly to meet Alessa's stunned gaze once more, she faded slowly away, leaving the room feeling like a refrigerator.

Alessa lay still for a time, her heart pounding. Gradually she grew calmer. But sleep was out of the question now. She felt more certain than ever that the spirit was Kimberley Painter. All night, she turned over the little girl's very deliberate gesture in her mind.

What was she trying to tell her?

Thursday, 2 August 1990

Fifty-four days after Kimberley's disappearance

After yet another restless night, Alessa felt ready to drop by the time she reached the end of the working day. Everything kept going through her head and as ever she felt unable to tell anyone. She couldn't possibly talk to Jason about it: she was sure he'd think she was losing her grip. Maybe she was.

As soon as she arrived home that evening, Alessa fished out Carmel's business card once more and dialled, desperate to speak to someone who might understand what was happening to her. She was surprised to hear a man's voice at the other end of the line.

"Oh, sorry! Have I got the right number? I was trying to get hold of Carmel."

There was a catch in the man's voice. "I'm afraid my lovely friend Carmel passed away last week. She'd been very ill for some time, you know."

A stunned silence ensued. Eventually finding her tongue, Alessa spoke shakily.

"Oh. I'm really sorry. That's very sad to hear. I'd no idea she was so unwell. She seemed . . . so full of life . . ."

"Ay, that was Carmel. Never let it show. Even when she lost her daughter, she put on a brave face and soldiered on.

But it must've taken its toll, mustn't it? No one can go through something like that without being torn apart inside."

"I had no idea. I didn't know her well, to be honest. We only met properly the once. She seemed, well, a lovely person."

"She was. The best." The man sniffed. There was a weighty pause. "It tortured her, you know. Carmel's young granddaughter went missing some years ago. They never found her. Her daughter never got over it. Being psychic, Carmel blamed herself for not seeing it coming, not being able to warn her that Sally-Ann was in danger. And then for Carmel to lose her own daughter on top of it all . . . She took her own life in the end, poor girl. Terrible business."

Alessa's mind was reeling. "I'm sorry . . . did you, did you say her granddaughter's name was Sally-Ann?"

"Yes, that's right. Sally-Ann Hughes. You might remember – it was all over the news at the time. The little lass was on a school trip to Oxford one summer – she and her mum lived in Reading. Just disappeared without trace. Doesn't bear thinking about."

So Carmel had lost her own child – and Sally-Ann Hughes had been her granddaughter. How completely tragic. Another innocent stolen from her family. Maybe that was why she had felt the connection with Kimberley; why she'd felt compelled to reach out to Alessa. She recalled the woman's words: *the death of a child is always highly emotive.* The sadness etched onto her face had been heart-rending. Poor Carmel.

"It was the bloody cigarettes that did for her in the end, though – they were her one weakness. She lasted much longer than the doctors predicted, mind you." There was an audible sigh. "Sorry, I'm rambling on. All a bit raw, you know. Can I help in any way?"

Alessa assured the man that he couldn't help, mumbled an apology and hung up. Hot tears pricked her eyes. She rolled the cool blue stone of the kyanite pendant between her fingers, and despite her lack of any real faith, said a silent prayer for Carmel's soul. They'd spent only a short time together, but the woman seemed to have had more insight into what was in her heart than anyone she'd ever met in her life.

And apart from her strange visitation, she'd remembered something she wanted to ask Carmel: it had occurred to her that she'd brought something home which was connected to Kimberley Painter: the proof of her school photograph. She wondered if it could somehow have drawn the little girl to her. But now Alessa wouldn't be able to share any of it with Carmel. She felt strangely bereft.

Wednesday, 8 August 1990

Sixty days after Kimberley's disappearance

Another agonisingly long and fruitless week had dragged on. By now, every passenger from both buses Kimberley had caught the day she'd vanished had been traced and eliminated from their inquiries. Whilst the majority of Bennett's team seemed to be gradually losing momentum, aside from the other cases they were working on, Alessa and Jason continued to work long hours, questioning members of the public and searching painstakingly through archived material about sex offenders and missing children in the Oxford and Reading areas, and beyond. Yet another unsolved case had come to light: a ten-year-old American girl named Carly Swift, who had been holidaying with her family, had disappeared without trace from outside her aunt's cottage in the outlying village of Islip, one Saturday afternoon in the summer of 1982. For reasons unknown, the case had been picked up by the Thames Valley Constabulary in Buckinghamshire, and information hadn't been relayed to their counterparts in the Oxford area.

"This is very odd." Alessa frowned as she trawled through the file which had landed on her desk that morning. "The case was well within our jurisdiction, but it was passed on for some reason." She read on.

Carly had arrived in England with her parents only two days prior to her disappearance. Coming from downtown Detroit to such a quiet rural location, she'd been enjoying the freedom of what her parents had naively considered a safe haven and exploring the locality unrestricted. But walking the hundred yards or so back from the churchyard to her aunt's cottage, she had vanished. The only witness had been Alfred Tuttle, an elderly man from the village, who claimed to have seen her getting into a dark-coloured car and being driven away. Unfortunately, he could remember neither the licence plate number, nor the driver's face. Trawling through the notes accompanying the file, it was questionable whether the man had been a particularly reliable witness, having spent the early afternoon in the local pub and then continuing with more than a few extra cans at home.

Alessa looked at Carly's photograph and shuddered. The child was slight and fair in colouring, similar in appearance to both Jessie and Kimberley. Little golden-haired angels, all of them. Pinning Carly's picture to the bulletin board next to those of the others, Alessa wondered how many more had fallen victim to the same predator. She could still remember that menacing presence, the terrifying sound of his breath, and the

271

thud of his footfall as he had chased her and Jessie along the empty street on that terrible afternoon.

And then it occurred to her.

In spite of everything, she herself had never been in any real danger.

Alessa had always been what her mother described as 'cuddly' as a child. Her thick, almost black hair and the olive complexion inherited from her father didn't fit the mould of the man's preferred quarry.

It had been Jessie he'd wanted all along. Only Jessie.

Even if she'd stood her ground and hadn't tried to escape his clutches, he would have sailed straight past her in pursuit of her friend. It was only ever blonde, petite Jessie who had stoked his unnatural desires. The realisation made her stomach roil.

In the hope that someone might be able to shed further light on the Carly Swift case, Alessa looked for a contact telephone number for the little girl's aunt. The woman was happy to talk to her, although doubtful whether she had any useful information to impart. Galvanised by the thought that she could learn something, Alessa briskly crossed the office to speak to Jason, who was at his desk still going through some paperwork or other that Bennett had generated. Hearing her approach, Jason looked up, his grim expression brightening.

"Hello you. Everything okay?"

"All good. Having fun?" She looked pointedly at the desk, raising an eyebrow.

He pulled a face. "Bloody pointless, all this," he muttered. He darted a look in the direction of Bennett's office, shoving forward the pile of papers on the table in front of him in annoyance. "He's got me going through some ancient traffic offences now. Claims they could be relevant in some way. He's taking the piss."

"For God's sake. What a total waste of your time." Alessa frowned. She was beginning to wonder if Bennett had completely lost the plot. "Jason, I'm going to interview a lady in Islip. Can I use your car?"

He shrugged. "Sure." He opened his desk drawer and handed her the keys, smiling wearily. "Think of me toiling over this lot when you're sailing down those country lanes, won't you?"

She laughed sympathetically, glancing around before leaning forwards to peck him on the cheek surreptitiously. "Good luck with it all. I'll see you later."

*

Imogen Swift was a softly spoken woman in her late forties. Her older brother Michael, Carly's father, had emigrated to the States in the early 1960s, to work in the motor industry. He had met his American wife some three years later and Carly was born in 1972.

Coming from the peace and tranquillity of the Oxfordshire countryside, he had gradually begun to feel homesick, and had hoped to persuade his wife to move back to England with him. The family holiday in Islip was intended to give her a flavour of English rural life to see whether she thought she'd like to give it a try.

"Tragic irony, isn't it? They thought this was a safe place, compared with Detroit. But there was no reason to think Carly would be in any danger, just wandering round the village. It was usually so quiet. Michael was desperately keen to demonstrate to his wife Leigh that it was just what they needed – the crime rate in Detroit was pretty bad compared with here at the time, and he wanted to raise Carly in a better, more secure environment." She shook her head sadly. "She

273

was such a lovely, sunny little girl. It totally devastated them. And then two years later, both Michael and Leigh were killed in a drive-by shooting, back in the US. I have no family of my own. They were all I had."

"I'm so sorry to hear that, Miss Swift. It must have been terrible for you." A lump rose in Alessa's throat. The poor woman had a quiet dignity about her, but the pain of loss was etched into her fine features. Why did life often treat good, decent people so cruelly?

"It's taken a long time to come to terms with. But I have good friends and neighbours. We're a tight-knit community here. Everyone's very kind." Imogen mustered a small smile.

"The day Carly disappeared, did no one else come forward, apart from Alfred Tuttle?" Alessa had been hoping there might be someone else who could add credence to the old man's statement.

The woman shook her head. "Everyone was either watching the football that afternoon, or sitting in their gardens. It was a beautiful day. And old Alf – the man that saw the car – he'd had a few drinks and was a bit the worse for wear. He died a couple of years ago, poor old soul. I don't think anyone really took his statement seriously, though. Certainly not the policeman that interviewed him."

Yet another failing on the part of the force. Alessa felt she ought to be apologising, even though she'd had no part in it. "That's so frustrating to hear. I'm really sorry. Do you happen to know who the officer was that took his statement? Unfortunately the file was a bit vague."

Imogen raised an eyebrow. "Oh, yes. I remember him well. A very unpleasant individual. He really upset Michael and Leigh. Spoke to them almost as if they were suspects."

Alessa groaned inwardly. The MO was instantly recognisable. "Was it someone called DCI Bennett, by any chance?"

Imogen nodded vigorously. "I can't remember his rank, but yes, the name – Bennett. Definitely rings a bell. Michael filed a complaint about the way the man was conducting things and they took him off the case. As I recall, it was another division that took over the investigation after that. Not that they made any more headway than the first lot. It couldn't have helped matters, though, with that buffoon, Bennett or whatever he was called, wasting time at the start of the investigation."

She stared emptily through the window, her eyes filled with sadness. "It was just out there, where she was last seen. So strange. As if she simply vanished into thin air."

Alessa felt something coil unpleasantly in her stomach. It was an all too familiar story.

"Thank you very much for your time, Miss Swift. I won't keep you any longer. You've been most helpful. And I can assure you that the case is still open, even though it's been eight years. If there's ever any news of Carly, you'll be the first to know."

*

Back at the station, Alessa pulled Jason to one side.

"The Carly Swift case – Bennett was in charge originally. He used his usual strong-arm tactics and the father made a formal complaint. He was taken off the case. I did a bit more digging and found out that the Chief Super made some lame excuse about Bennett's mental health, and then sent him off on the sick for an extended period. It was claimed St Aldates was short-staffed at the time and their caseload was too high, so the case was picked up by Thames Valley in the next county. Talk about passing the buck."

Jason raised an eyebrow. "Seems his charisma bypass has got him into hot water more than once, then. I've heard through

275

the grapevine that Chief Superintendent Walker's not impressed with the way the investigation into Kimberley's disappearance has been handled. He'll be feeling the pressure from higher up, so cousin or not, Walker'll be putting the squeeze on Bennett."

"It's no more than he deserves. This is the second missing child case he's led and neither of them look as if they'll ever be solved – largely down to him and his blunders, as far as I can tell. How the hell he hasn't been booted out, or at least demoted . . ."

"Yes, well, I think we know the reason why. And his office is on the second floor . . ."

Chapter 20

Thursday, 9 August 1990

Sixty-one days after Kimberley's disappearance

A hush descended over the office as Chief Superintendent Walker, known to all as their DCI's cousin, swept through the double doors shortly after lunch with a face like thunder.

"Looks like the shit's hit the fan," remarked one PC in a low voice, to no one in particular.

CSI Walker appeared oblivious. His mind was clearly on other things. Barging into Bennett's office and slamming the door hard enough to make the walls reverberate, Walker proceeded to spell things out to the man in no uncertain terms, angrily and loudly enough for anyone on the other side of the partition wall to overhear. Which half the department, all exchanging wide-eyed glances, did.

"Look, mate, I'm getting it in the neck from above over all this. We've other fish to fry, and a hell of a lot of time and resources have been poured into finding this child, without so much as a sock to show for it. It seems our man dangled a carrot with those parcels, and now he's gone quiet on us. And I understand your earlier harassment of the father has done our reputation no favours, either. We're going to need something substantial pretty soon, or you'll have to put it on the back burner. I want results – and fast. Am I making myself clear?"

Walker stormed out of the room, leaving Bennett red-faced and scowling in his office doorway as he looked round at his team, who all dropped their eyes and pretended to be absorbed in something extremely important. You could have heard a pin drop.

Alessa suspected something was afoot when she noticed DCI Bennett and DS Henderson huddled in Bennett's office half an hour or so later. Everyone was fully aware now of Bennett's declining popularity with the powers-that-be and it was apparent from his harassed demeanour that it was getting to him. As Alessa walked past his door, Bennett opened it and beckoned.

"WPC Cano! Just the person."

"Sir?"

"I want you to accompany the good Sergeant Henderson here on a bit of a mission. It's something that needs a woman's touch, if you understand me. We've had a tip-off about a druggie handling stolen goods – TVs and VHS players and the like – in a flat in St Clements, and the suspected culprit has a girlfriend, who we'll need to bring in for questioning as an accessory, plus a couple of young children. Someone ought to be with them while we bring the parents in, and I think you're just the right officer to do it. We won't involve Social Services at this stage. Shouldn't take long to question the mother, with a bit of luck, then we can release her, charges pending."

"But, sir, surely this isn't within our remit?" Alessa was perplexed. Why would Bennett wanted to get involved with yet another petty offence when they were up to their eyes in a missing persons case? Surely this was one for the Crime Squad, or even the Safeguarding Unit, not the Major Investigations Team.

Bennett's meagre lips set into a hard line, the tendons in his neck tightening like wire. His tongue began to probe his cheek in irritation.

"I believe *I'm* the one giving the orders round here, Cano. We are the police and we're here to solve crimes, aren't we? That *is* our role, isn't it?"

Alessa lowered her gaze, her nostrils flaring. She spoke through gritted teeth.

"Yes, sir. When d'you want me to go? It's just that, well, I've got to—"

Bennett raised a palm firmly towards her. "Never mind what you were doing; that can wait. Go along with the sergeant and PC Morris. We've just spoken to one of the neighbours, who's confirmed the suspects are both at home right now, so time is of the essence. Sergeant Henderson, I understand your own car is currently under repair. You can take Shelley's vehicle – he's on desk duty this morning. Someone can follow on and bring you back later, Cano, once the floozy's been returned home to look after her kids."

"All right, sir." Irked, Alessa followed the unusually chatty Henderson to the car. A smirking PC Morris joined them en route to the parking lot. Alessa had almost as much disdain for the man as she had for Bennett. Thirty-something, renowned for his biting sarcasm and cocky manner, she found him self-satisfied and dislikeable. Plus, his personal hygiene left a lot to be desired. Morris clearly had his eye on sergeant's stripes, which meant he bent over backwards to keep on Bennett's good side. She sat, jaw clenched, in the back seat and scarcely uttered a word as they drove the three miles or so to St Clements.

The scruffy flat was in the basement of a run-down four-storey Victorian tenement building, towards the end of the road. Several bicycles were propped against the railings outside. A teenage youth whizzed by on a skateboard, almost knocking Alessa flying.

"Hey! Watch where you're going."

"Fuck off, pig." Already at a safe enough distance not to fear recrimination, the boy cast her a contemptuous look as he sailed away, his middle finger in the air. Alessa narrowed her eyes as her companions glanced at one another and sniggered.

"Morris, go round the back in case the bugger tries to do a bunk. Cano, you come to the front door with me. Have your cuffs ready." Sergeant Henderson pushed his shoulders back, clearly relishing being in charge.

The lank-haired, unkempt male answering the front door would have been in no fit state to resist arrest, even if it had been his intention. High as a kite and with a stupefied expression, he ambled from the property, still in his slippers, mumbling a half-soaked protest as Henderson cuffed and bundled him into the back of the patrol car.

His girlfriend was a different proposition. Morris had burst in through the back door without warning. The young woman, her over-bleached hair scraped into a scrawny ponytail and a small green heart tattooed on one angular cheek, was seated at the kitchen table, engrossed in rolling a joint. Looking up to see her unwelcome visitor, she began to shriek like a banshee, lashing out at him and screaming obscenities. Morris, not known for his diplomacy, was in no mood for her lack of cooperation. He got hold of the girl by her hair and yanked her head back.

"You're nicked, missy," he hissed into her ear, twisting her arms behind her back and restraining her with the handcuffs. "I'm arresting you for assisting in the handling of stolen goods – and I'll be adding possession of class A drugs to that, too."

"I ain't stupid. It's only skunk. I don't do 'eroin or nothin' else."

"Just you give me time, love. I haven't had a proper look around yet. I'm sure I'll find some."

The girl turned angrily, hoicking a mouthful of spit into his face.

"Don't even *think* of trying to fit me up, you wanker. I know my rights!"

Morris delivered a stinging blow to the side of her face.

"Get your fuckin' 'ands off me, you arsehole! I ain't going nowhere with you. I'll 'ave you for assault, you 'ear me?"

From the other room, a child's wails could be heard. Entering through the front of the property, Alessa had been alarmed to hear the commotion coming from the kitchen and furious when she saw how Morris was handling things. She stood in the doorway, wondering if she should intervene. Henderson, returning from the patrol car, barked an order at her to attend to the children whilst he went to Morris's aid.

"We'll sort things out in here, Cano. Go on. They're in the front room."

The tiny boy and girl could have been no more than three and four. Alessa had grown accustomed to seeing people living in squalor, but it never got any easier knowing that young children were being forced to endure such conditions. Seeing the two filthy, painfully thin tots brought a lump to her throat. She did her best to calm them, but the little girl was almost hysterical.

"I – want – my – mummy. That man's hurting my mummy," she sobbed.

"Your mummy will be fine, don't worry," Alessa tried to reassure her. But seeing the woman's bloody nose and cut lip as Morris and Henderson dragged her past the doorway, she was aghast. Their prisoner's blouse was torn, and there were newly inflicted red marks on her arms. What her colleagues had meted out was far in excess of reasonable force. Their behaviour was shocking and completely unprofessional.

The woman struggled to free herself, to no avail. She turned her head towards Alessa, revealing a huge wheal on her cheek, yelling, "You lay one finger on my kids, bitch, and you're dead. You 'ear me?"

"Your children are quite safe. No one's going to harm them."

Alessa took a deep breath. She glared at Henderson and Morris. She wasn't about to say anything in front of the woman, but she had every intention of reporting them for misconduct.

Henderson looked at her, clearly ruffled. "WPC Cano, the situation here is worse than I anticipated. You need to remain with these children until I can arrange transport for them. I'll radio ahead and get someone to contact Social Services immediately. They need to be put into a place of safety."

The woman began to scream uncontrollably. "You *bastards*! You ain't taking my kids! I ain't fuckin' done nothing!"

"Resisting arrest; assaulting a police officer – on top of the stolen goods and the marijuana. No judge in their right mind is going to let two young children stay in this environment. Your goose is well and truly cooked, you stupid tart."

*

Later that night, Alessa lay awake, upset and concerned about the welfare of the poor children, who'd been placed with foster carers for the time being. The parents were clearly unfit, and an emergency protection order had been issued, but that didn't excuse Morris and Henderson's behaviour. Why had Bennett been so keen for her to go along with them? There were other WPCs on duty at St Aldates with child protection experience whom they could have called upon. She had an inkling that there was more to it, and it worried her.

Alessa suddenly remembered the tiny photograph of Kimberley that she'd brought home, intending to return it to the Painters since they now had an enlarged version at the station. For some reason, she'd felt compelled to keep it. She'd wanted to ask Carmel about it, about whether having something that had a link to the dead child, could somehow have drawn the girl's spirit to her. But now there was no one she could consult – or confide in.

Slipping from her bed, Alessa went to the chest and lifted the lid, quietly removing the old memory box, where she'd tucked the picture away among the other things from her past that she couldn't bring herself to part with. But as she peeled open the cardboard flaps, a horribly cold sensation flooded through her whole body. For there, right in front of her, rather than the stack of LPs she usually kept on the top, was her shameful little secret, with Kimberley's smiling face staring from its centre. She certainly hadn't left it like that.

But someone had.

It felt like a rebuke from beyond the grave.

She snapped the box shut at once, and with trembling hands replaced it in the chest, her mind reeling.

Alessa felt sick. The realisation that all of this must somehow be due to her own personal connection to Jessie Lockheed was beyond disturbing. She'd brought it all on herself. As if the torment by the girls' killer wasn't enough – the packages, those taunting words . . .

She was being sucked back into a nightmare she'd hoped was long buried. Now, on top of all this, the niggling thought that something fishy was going on in the background at work began to play on her mind, too. It felt as if her whole life had been tipped on its head. Daylight had started to filter through before she eventually drifted off into an unrefreshing and fitful slumber.

*

Alessa's hunch about work proved to be right. Upon arrival at the station the following morning, fired up to make a formal complaint to Chief Superintendent Walker about Henderson and Morris, she was waylaid in Reception by Bennett, who'd been waiting at the desk. Sharman widened his eyes and threw Alessa a warning look. Bennett appeared oddly smug.

"WPC Cano, can you come with me, please."

It would have been pointless mentioning anything to him about what had happened. She would have to wait until later to speak to Walker.

Jaw clenched, Alessa followed as, without further explanation, Bennett moved briskly up the stairs. There was a distinct atmosphere in the room as they walked through the double doors, a hush descending as though she'd interrupted a private conversation. There appeared to be a full complement of officers, all seated at their desks as though they too had been summoned for some reason. She wasn't aware of any important briefing being scheduled. As she continued behind Bennett, she felt all eyes upon her, and could detect the occasional indecipherable whisper. Her skin prickled. Something was going on – and whatever it was, it seemed she was the only one who hadn't been informed.

Reluctantly, she followed Bennett into his office, where

284

she was surprised to find Walker sitting opposite a pale and agitated Jason, the latter perched on the edge of a plastic chair, wringing his hands and clearly at his wits' end. Hearing her enter, he looked round, his eyes wide. He was shaking his head, his anguished expression conveying that all most definitely was not well. Alessa felt suddenly woozy. She reached shakily for the back of the chair next to Jason.

Chief Superintendent Walker didn't invite her to sit. He shifted in his seat, turning to look up at her and gave a small cough. "I'll repeat what I've just said for your benefit, WPC Cano." His tone was severe. He darted a look from Alessa to Jason, then back. "It has been brought to my attention that, after using PC Shelley's patrol car yesterday afternoon, Sergeant Henderson, whom we know to be a diligent and reliable officer, discovered certain irregular items – items which point to a criminal offence having being committed. As PC Shelley is known to be the regular user of the vehicle, I can only deduce that said items are his property. Pending a full investigation, I have no choice but to suspend PC Shelley and, as his regular co-pilot, you also, WPC Cano."

"What? What on earth are you talking about?" The room seemed suddenly smaller, as if the walls were closing in around them. Alessa's head was spinning. She turned to the smirking Bennett, tongue roaming his cheek as ever, then back to his senior ranking officer, whose expression was stony.

"The use of drugs by any police officer is taken very seriously," declared Walker. He shook his head slightly, raising a hand to straighten his tie. "Naturally we have to uphold certain standards and can never, under any circumstances, condone any form of illegal activity amongst our ranks. I want both of your warrant cards and badges." He rapped the desk as if expecting the articles to materialise miraculously in

285

front of him. "You are both to be suspended from duty, with immediate effect."

"On what grounds? This is ridiculous, sir. Jason doesn't take drugs, and neither do I."

"Then how do you explain the packets of cocaine, complete with straw and razor blade, not to mention the cannabis resin and cigarette papers, discovered in the glove compartment of PC Shelley's vehicle?"

Alessa stared open-mouthed at Jason, who lifted his hands in exasperation.

"I have *never* used drugs, sir. And if any were found in my vehicle, it certainly had nothing to do with me."

"I wish I could believe that, PC Shelley. But it's my duty to investigate, and also to stamp out any whiff of corruption amongst my officers."

"But, sir—"

"Your Force ID, please. Now."

Speechless with rage and indignation, Alessa and Jason handed over their wallets.

"This is unbelievable," Alessa told Jason as they left the building, all eyes upon them. "The only way there could've been drugs in that car is if someone else put them there. And I know exactly who would've done it."

"But what the hell can we do about it? It's their word against ours." Jason clasped his head in both hands, his chin dropping to his chest. "Listen, there's something I think you ought to know . . ."

But his words petered out as Alessa, oblivious, suddenly began to march diagonally across the road, her attention firmly on the public phone booth on the opposite corner. He stepped up his pace to catch up with her.

"Alessa, wait! What are you doing?"

Alessa was so incensed that all she could think about was seeing their humongous prick of a DCI get his comeuppance. She swung open the door to the call box and turned to face Jason, her dark eyes ablaze.

"I wouldn't normally dream of asking him, but I'm going to get my uncle involved in this. It's high time Bennett and his dodgy sidekick got their marching orders."

Chapter 21

Friday, 10 August 1990

Sixty-two days since Kimberley's disappearance

Gregarious and laid-back in nature but with a shrewd business mind, through his charitable work over the years, Uncle Rob had forged useful alliances with several powerful and high-profile people in Oxford and beyond, Chief Constable Raybould being one of them. And Alessa knew that, if the request came from her, he would call on his old friend for help.

Uncle Rob was delighted to hear from his niece, but none too impressed when she told him what had happened.

"You leave this one with me, *piccolina*. I'll get on the blower to Jack Raybould right away."

Alessa remained in the call box, waiting. Jason stood against the open door, his face pale and unsmiling. He stood motionless, studying Alessa, who was still fired up and unable to keep still, hopping from one foot to the other as she guarded the phone as if it were the Crown Jewels.

"They can't do this to us," she ranted. "I don't know what Bennett's game is but he's gone too far."

Jason filled his lungs, lifting a hand to his forehead. "I think it might be—" He was interrupted by the shrill ring of the telephone. Alessa grabbed the receiver with a quivering hand.

The mellow tone of Uncle Rob's Anglo-Italian accent came down the line.

"Can you and Jason meet me at the back of St Aldates in fifteen minutes? Chief Constable Raybould would like to speak to you both. As luck would have it, he's in the area at the moment. Someone will be waiting to show you where to go. Sounds like this Bennett chap's been under internal investigation by Professional Standards. Apparently, amongst other things, it seems he's not averse to taking backhanders to turn a blind eye . . ."

Alessa felt almost triumphant. She replaced the receiver and turned to Jason, her eyes wild. She grabbed both of his hands in her own with a kind of manic energy.

"You, you *knew* he was bent, didn't you? At least it sounds like they're already onto the swine."

Jason offered her a wan smile. "Don't get too excited just yet. We still have to persuade the Chief Constable *we* haven't done anything iffy."

"Yeah, but he's sure to believe us. Especially if Professional Standards are already involved." She leaned forwards impulsively and kissed him full on the mouth, then threw her head back, letting out a long breath. "Thank Christ for that."

Jason gave Alessa a reticent hug. "Don't go rejoicing just yet. Look, what I was going to say . . ." He hesitated, then seemed to reconsider. "Never mind. We'd better get a shift on.

Wouldn't want to keep Raybould waiting. I've heard he doesn't suffer fools gladly."

Retracing their steps to the station, instead of going through the main doors that faced onto the street, they hurried through the car park and round to the more secluded area at the back of the building. As instructed, they entered with caution through the narrow rear entrance, where a solemn plain-clothes male officer greeted them. They were led up a short flight of stairs, through an archway and into a small, windowless waiting area, where they were told to take a seat on a battered black leatherette settee.

"It's all very cloak and dagger," Alessa whispered, casting her eyes around the strangely empty space. A single steel door led from the room and she wondered what was on the other side. Jason, still looking uneasy, managed a brief smile but made no response. He seemed decidedly edgy. It was understandable, Alessa thought. He'd clearly thought his job was on the line only a short while earlier but she was confident everything would be ironed out as soon as they'd given their version of events.

The sound of rapid footfall on the stairs made them both sit up sharply in anticipation. Uncle Rob appeared, his face breaking into a warm smile at the sight of his niece.

"*Ciao, bella!*"

He delivered his usual effusive bear hug welcome to Alessa, kissing her on both cheeks, and shook Jason firmly by the hand.

"Pleased to meet you at last. My sister speaks very highly of you." Uncle Rob winked at Alessa. Impeccable as ever, he was dressed in a navy mohair suit and pale blue cashmere polo shirt, his abundant silver-grey hair swept back from a deeply tanned face. His sharp blue eyes, a mirror image of his older sister's, seemed to take in every detail of Jason's appearance, from his wayward hair and crumpled shirt to his battered Dr Martens

290

lace-ups. Jason appeared unusually flustered and tongue-tied. Alessa thought a distraction might be in order.

"How are you? How was Italy?"

"Hmm. Let's just say Matteo and I didn't part on the best of terms. He can be *such* a spoilt child." Uncle Rob rolled his eyes. "Otherwise, everything was wonderful as ever. The weather, the food. You two will have to come out there with me one day soon. You'd love it."

Alessa smiled to herself. Things always seemed to go awry between Uncle Rob and his boyfriends sooner or later. She wouldn't have said as much, but thought he'd be better suited to someone a little nearer his own age.

The mysterious door opened suddenly and Chief Constable Raybould emerged from the room beyond. He loomed large in the doorway, his shock of closely cropped white hair almost touching the top of the frame. The man was as broad as he was tall, filling the entrance. He stepped forward and greeted Uncle Rob with a genial slap on the back and a wide grin.

"Good to see you, mate. It's been a while." He spoke with a soft Oxfordshire burr. Uncle Rob nodded and returned the gesture.

Turning to the slightly nervous pair, Raybould nodded his acknowledgement of them and extended a huge hand to each in turn, then led the way into the office. It was more spacious than the room they'd just left, but functionally furnished, with a plain grey Formica desk and a swivel chair beneath the window. Venetian blinds concealed its occupants from prying eyes. Parking himself behind the desk, the Chief Constable motioned to the others to sit on the plastic seats provided.

Addressing Alessa first, he adopted a serious tone. "Now then, let's have this story from the beginning. I have to trust you on this one, and let me tell you, if there's any hint of impropriety on your part, I'm a force to be reckoned with."

Uncle Rob opened his mouth to object, but the Chief Constable raised a hand.

"I'm sticking my neck out on this, Rob. I've got to do everything by the book. I don't want any comebacks. Bennett's a slippery customer."

Uncle Rob conceded and allowed Alessa to begin. She proceeded to tell him about Bennett's incompetence, his unjustified harassment of Malcolm Painter and the shoddy way he seemed to operate generally. She revealed her findings about the Carly Swift case, and how it had had to be assigned elsewhere because of his lack of professionalism, which had apparently been covered up by Walker. Finally, she filled him in about the visit to St Clements the previous day, and the brutality displayed by Morris and Henderson; of her suspicions that she had been dragged along under false pretences and how she now realised that it had been an excuse to use Jason's patrol car, to plant drugs to incriminate him.

The man listened in silence, his face giving nothing away. He nodded from time to time, shaking his head when she described the extent of the heavy-handedness displayed by the two officers. All the while he scribbled notes. When she had finished, he turned to Jason.

"And you can corroborate all this, DS Shelley?"

"Absolutely, sir."

"I realise this has accelerated things somewhat. Have you completed your report for Barry Franklin yet?"

"Just putting the finishing touches to it. I've been updating Professional Standards in between. Dr Franklin has filed copies of everything I've given him so far—"

Alessa caught her breath. She fired a look at Jason in astonishment.

"Hold on, *DS*? But you— I thought you said you were a PC? And what's this about a report? Who's Dr Franklin?"

Jason smiled sheepishly, colour creeping up his cheeks. "I couldn't tell you. I wanted to, but I was sworn to secrecy, in case it compromised the investigation. Dr Franklin is a superintendent – head of Professional Standards locally. He's also a doctor of psychology. The Met sent me here to observe Bennett. He's as bent as they come." He paused, darting a look at Raybould before continuing. "We've found evidence that he's been accepting bribes over the years and securing false convictions by foul means to tweak the crime and outcome figures, too. There've been instances of crucial alibi statements vanishing from files of certain cases he's been assigned to, forensic evidence being tampered with, that kind of stuff. I reckon he might've somehow got wind of what I've been doing and that's why he's trying to get rid of me. Of *both* of us. Maybe he thought you were involved, too. But I think Professional Standards have built a strong enough case to dismiss him for gross incompetence, not to mention corruption, once and for all."

Alessa was at once shocked and hurt. "So, how much of what you told me about your background is true, then? Or was it *all* a fabrication to cover up your mission?"

Jason fixed his eyes on her, his brow furrowing. He looked genuinely remorseful. "No. Only my rank, and the purpose of my transfer. I *had* wanted to move back to Oxford to help out at home, as well. It was killing two birds with one stone, if you like. And believe me, I felt really bad not telling you everything. But it would've put you in a very awkward position, apart from anything else."

"So, there'd been suspicions about Bennett for a while,

then." She shook her head as she turned events over in her mind and thought about the appalling way the man had behaved ever since she had started at St Aldates. "And I just thought he was misogynistic and inept. To think he'd stoop so low as to receive bribes . . . and locking up innocent people just to hit targets?" She considered for a moment. "What about Henderson? Is he on the take, too?"

"We don't have any evidence against him at this stage. He does appear to be in the DCI's pocket, although it's quite possible he's not actually aware of Bennett's dodgier activities. I must say, from all the dealings I've had with the man, he doesn't seem very switched on."

Alessa rolled her eyes. The idea that Henderson was capable of anything that required any degree of nous seemed improbable.

The Chief Constable rose from his seat. When standing, he seemed to fill the room like an abominable snowman.

"Well, from everything you've told me, I reckon it's time we brought Bennett in. We'll keep a lid on it for the moment. I don't imagine it'll do much for morale at the station, knowing they've been taking orders from a bent officer. The story is that he's suddenly been taken ill with stress. I dare say it won't be far from the truth, by the time we've finished with the bugger. We're replacing the current Chief Super with Superintendent Gordon, from the Met – I think Walker's definitely outlived his shelf life. Early retirement beckons, whether he knows the extent of what his cousin's been up to or not. No room for nepotism in this job. Time for a clean sweep all round, I think."

"What about us? Bennett's taken our badges and warrant cards, and no doubt told everyone that we're drug users."

"You just leave it with me. You've nothing to worry about. It'll all come out in the wash. And while we're about it, I reckon

Sergeant Henderson and PC Morris could do with being hauled over the coals, too."

Alessa's thoughts turned to Kimberley. "But who'll take over the investigation, sir? We still have a missing child out there, somewhere."

Raybould puffed out his cheeks. "I'm afraid that, owing to Bennett's obsession with Malcolm Painter, we've lost too much precious time on this one. If he'd concentrated his efforts elsewhere when the girl first went missing, we might've had a better chance of apprehending the real perpetrator. The longer things have dragged on, the greater the chance he's going to evade capture for good."

Alessa clapped her hands to her head in frustration. She knew where he was going with this and it wasn't what she wanted to hear.

"But with someone else in charge, a different approach, *surely* we have a better chance of finding him?" Her words came out as a desperate wail.

Raybould grimaced. "I rather doubt it now, I'm afraid. We've missed that sweet spot. Too much time's elapsed and it feels like we've reached an impasse. We'll keep the investigation open, of course, but with what little evidence we do have, sadly I think it's inevitable by now that the child must be deceased." He exhaled, dropping his gaze for a moment. "All we can do is put out an appeal for the public to be vigilant and warn them to keep their children under close supervision."

Seeing Alessa's anguished expression, he hesitated briefly, darting a look at Uncle Rob, who had stepped forward to place a soothing hand on his niece's shoulder.

"There are several other important cases pending and unfortunately there simply aren't sufficient man hours to cover everything, as much as we'd like there to be," Raybould went

295

on. "We have a suitable replacement for Bennett lined up, an excellent DCI by the name of Powell, from Reading."

Alessa felt as though she'd been slapped. "But what shall I tell the Painters? Their whole lives have been shattered."

"I think it's best to say nothing, at this stage. Just keep things as they are; update them once in a while to appease them. If you imply the hunt for Kimberley's abductor is no longer a priority, it won't look good from their point of view."

Alessa was aghast. "But, sir—"

"I'm sorry if that's not what you wanted to hear, WPC Cano. But our time and resources aren't limitless, unfortunately." Raybould drew himself upright and spoke with a firm tone. "And while I know it shouldn't, budget has to be a consideration, too. It's an irritating fact of life. The police force has standards to maintain, and inevitably, particularly in this day and age, crime statistics reflect our ability as officers. We must concentrate our efforts on those offences that we *can* solve, or the public will think we aren't doing our job properly."

"So you're pulling the plug on the investigation?" In spite of herself, Alessa could hear her voice growing loud. So Bennett, apart from being corrupt, had scuppered any chance of their continuing to search for Kimberley by wasting money and resources on his ridiculous vendetta against Malcom Painter. Where was the justice in it all?

"I can understand your frustration." Raybould let out a long breath. "I'm not closing the case – just moving it down the ladder a few rungs. I'm ultimately answerable to the Commissioner, and it's my responsibility to uphold the law for *all* the citizens of Oxford. There are countless other grieving families out there; people who've lost husbands, wives, children as a result of reckless drivers, drug dealers, firearm and knife crime. They all deserve an equal share of

296

our time and effort. I'm sure deep down you'll agree with me . . ."

Whilst Alessa could see his point, she certainly didn't agree with halting the investigation, but knew that trying to argue her case was futile. They parted company with the Chief Constable, having been reassured once more that Bennett would no longer be a fixture at St Aldates, and that their badges would be returned as soon as possible. The other officers, he'd asserted, would be briefed immediately with regard to Bennett's apparent error of judgement about their so-called drug use, and Henderson and Morris would be suspended from duty.

"Well," said Uncle Rob, once Raybould had wished them goodbye and left the building. The three of them stood, discombobulated, outside Raybould's office. "It's been very enlightening. All this subterfuge and intrigue, right on our doorsteps. Who'd have thought it? Jack and I usually only ever chat about golf."

Alessa was still reeling from their meeting with the Chief Constable and made him no response. She, Jason, and Uncle Rob filed back down the stairs and hovered in an awkward huddle outside the rear entrance, unsure what they should do next.

Alessa turned to Jason suddenly, searching his face anxiously. Her relief at hearing about Bennett was short-lived. Now that she'd had time to process what Jason had revealed, she wasn't sure how to feel. He was obviously a good copper. But he had, to all intents and purposes, lied to her. Could she really trust him now? Would his job always come first? Though the thought of not seeing him anymore was unbearable.

"Where does this leave you? *Us?* Your main purpose here seems to be over. Will they move you back to London now? Will we still be able to see one another?"

Jason took her hand in his. "Don't worry. I'm staying put, in

Oxford. That was the agreement. It's possible they'll move me into another department, but I'll still be based at St Aldates. I'll give it a few weeks before I put my stripes back on, though. It'll save answering awkward questions. I'll just tell everyone I'm about to sit my sergeant's exam."

She hugged him, her eyes brimming with tears of relief.

Uncle Rob looked on, a slightly soppy expression on his face. "Let's go and see your mamma. I'm sure she'll be fascinated to hear about all this—"

"No!" chimed Alessa and Jason simultaneously.

"This has to stay between the four of us, Uncle Rob," said Alessa. She looked straight into his eyes, her face serious. "Mamma wouldn't say anything deliberately, but you know how she loves to chat when she gets the chance – to the window cleaner, the lady on the till in the supermarket . . . If she let something slip in conversation . . . well, we can't afford to take any chances. Not until they've secured Bennett's dismissal."

Uncle Rob raised his palms defensively. "Okay, okay. I get it." He glanced at his watch then slapped his hands together. "Well, I don't know about you two, but my stomach's complaining like mad. Let's grab some pizzas and wine and take them round to your house. I'd like to catch up with my big sister – and don't worry, my lips are sealed." He gave the two of them an exaggerated wink.

*

With the threat of suspension now eliminated, Jason and Alessa were able to enjoy a relaxing evening. Uncle Rob was lively and engaging. Greta really seemed to come to life in his company. They made an entertaining double act, and their striking family resemblance, even down to their wildly gesticulating mannerisms, was remarkable. They shared enthusiastic tales of

298

their parents and grandparents in Italy, and of their antics as children.

The free-flowing wine made for a relaxed atmosphere, and Uncle Rob's frequently replenished glass of brandy seemed to loosen his tongue. Quite how the subject was raised, Alessa couldn't recall, but he leaned forward, swirling his glass.

"I could've been heading for a life of crime myself at one time, you know."

Alessa pulled back her chin sceptically. She shot a look at Jason, whose lips were twitching. Greta rolled her eyes, as if she'd heard it all before.

"Don't listen to him. Pinching fruit from outside the greengrocer's when you were ten hardly means you're destined to become an armed robber."

"Yes, but the shopkeeper wanted to press charges. I could've finished up with a criminal record!"

Greta flapped her hands at him. "You were just a silly boy. Still are." She winked at Jason. "What must you think of us!"

Jason looked sideways at Alessa. "I nicked a bar of chocolate once when I was about eight – for a dare," he added. "My dad dragged me back to the shop by my ear and made me hand it back. The humiliation was enough to stop me even considering doing it again."

"Ha! So there you go. Even respected officers of the law have shady secrets." Uncle Rob laughed uproariously.

Jason grinned, glancing at Alessa sheepishly. She arched an eyebrow. "So you were a bit of a tearaway, then?"

"Nah. Just easily led, you might say. I learned my lesson."

"Well, while we're baring all, anyone else want to get anything off their chest?"

Uncle Rob took a swig from his glass and leaned back in his chair, scanning their faces eagerly.

Alessa shifted in her seat. "I think . . . I think I may have seen a ghost recently," she blurted out. The room fell silent. She had everyone's attention now.

"You never said anything," her mother said at last, her eyes widening.

"I suppose I didn't want anyone thinking I was losing the plot, especially with those packages arriving, and everything . . ."

"Tell us more, then." Uncle Rob wriggled to the edge of his seat. "When did you see your ghost – and where?"

"Only in the last few weeks. I've seen something a couple of times now – in my room, late at night. It's hard to explain." She paused, chewing her lip. She should probably have kept quiet. But there was no going back now. "I had the sense of a little girl, very pale with long, fair hair. She looked quite transparent on the first occasion. No definite shape. I thought I was imagining things. But the second time she was a bit more, well, solid, I suppose. And I got the impression she was trying to tell me something. The thing is . . ." She glanced around at her disbelieving audience, unsure how much to divulge. "I've a feeling the ghost may be Kimberley Painter."

Everyone was staring at her. Jason's mouth had fallen open. Alessa turned to him. "I'm sorry – you probably think I'm some kind of fruitcake . . ."

Jason shook his head, pressing her hand firmly. "I think nothing of the sort. I'm not a complete sceptic, you know. And if you think that's what you saw, I'm sure you're right. The question is, *what* is she trying to tell you?"

"That's just it, I don't know. She pointed out of the window, down the road, towards where the Painters lived. And then she just disappeared. I wish I could've asked her, but it stunned me so much at the time, I couldn't speak."

"I had a partner once who was into all that kind of stuff, so

300

I've read quite a bit about the subject over the years," declared Uncle Rob. "Ghosts can't harm us. They're on a different plane of existence. It's just fear of the unknown. So if you see her again, remind yourself of that. Ask her what she wants. Who knows, you might get some useful answers."

The atmosphere in the room had turned unusually cold. With a sharp blast of freezing air, the door burst open. Everyone drew in their breath, their eyes travelling first to the doorway, then towards each other in anticipation. But nothing else happened. The door creaked slowly shut once more, leaving them in stunned silence.

"Enough of this talk now," said Greta, rising suddenly from her chair. She shivered a little, rubbing her hands together. "I must've left a window open upstairs – a draught, you know ..." Her eyes flickered uncertainly. "I'll just go check. More drinks, everyone?"

They drank and chatted late into the evening, the tone of conversation kept deliberately light from then on. Alessa couldn't take her eyes off Jason, who smiled and winked from time to time when he caught her gazing in his direction.

In just a short while, the mood – and the temperature – had, thankfully, lifted considerably. The subject of Alessa's ghostly encounter was no longer uppermost in everyone's minds.

After one more glass of wine, Greta took herself off to bed, stating that she'd have a thumping headache if she drank any more. Without consulting her brother, she'd called him a cab, peeping back round the living room door to announce it would be along within the next fifteen minutes.

"You need your beauty sleep, Roberto," she said pointedly. "And I think you've had quite enough *grappa* for one evening."

With Uncle Rob's reluctant departure, Jason announced it was time he was on his way, too. He staggered a little as he rose to leave, snorting with laughter as he gripped the back of the settee to steady himself.

"Whoa. That brandy your uncle gave me's gone right to my head."

Slightly tipsy herself, Alessa watched him in amusement. "Look, why don't you stay? The bed's already made up – at least you can get your head down straight away and sleep it off . . ." She regarded him for a moment, her head cocked to one side. Even though drunk, he was utterly gorgeous.

He nodded, grinning blearily. "If you don't mind. I'll take a pint of water up with me. Better rehydrate a bit . . ."

They shared a lingering goodnight kiss on the landing and retreated to their respective bedrooms.

But lying awake in her darkened room and pleasantly relaxed after the amount of wine she'd had, the thought of Jason in such close proximity was too much of a temptation. Alessa crept from her bed and padded down the landing. The sound of heavy snoring from Greta's room suggested she was fast asleep. Taking a deep breath, Alessa opened the door to Jason's bedroom, quietly clicking it shut behind her.

"You awake?" she whispered.

The small amount of light filtering through the gap in the curtains revealed that his response was to tug the bedsheet back.

"Come here. Let me warm you up." His voice was hushed, but there was no mistaking the desire in his tone. He sounded suddenly much more sober.

Tingling with anticipation, she slipped in beside him. Jason's muscular arms encircled her, drawing her close. Her cool feet slid between his solid calves. She could smell faded aftershave as she rested her head against his bare chest, and taste the slight saltiness of sweat. The delicious sensation of his warm skin next to hers almost took her breath away.

"Oh God, I want you. So much." Jason laced his fingers through her hair as he pressed his mouth softly to her cheek, his breath warm against her neck.

Alessa let out an involuntary gasp. She raised her face towards his suddenly, a thrill of nerves building from somewhere deep inside her. Their lips met with an urgency she hadn't experienced before. The rise and fall of his chest was becoming more rapid.

Suddenly Jason drew back a little. Alessa could see his face searching hers, his eyes earnest and wide in the darkness. "Are you sure? Is this what you want?"

Alessa pressed a finger to his lips. She sank into him once again, instinctively moulding her body against his. He let out a long breath and ran his hands down her back, then began to move beneath her nightshirt. He kissed her gently from her neck to her breasts. Alessa shivered with delight, and made no attempt to resist. She knew with certainty that she wanted to give herself to him completely. It felt like the most natural thing in the world. This was everything she'd ever dreamed it would be.

For the first time, they spent the entire night together, their bodies entwined. Alessa hoped that this would be the first night of many. She'd been involved with a few frogs in the past— No, *toads* would be more accurate.

Now she'd found her true Prince Charming, she didn't want to let him go.

Chapter 22

Monday, 13 August 1990

Sixty-five days after Kimberley's disappearance

Inspection of CCTV footage of the station car park had revealed a hooded man – later positively identified as DCI Bennett – climbing furtively from Jason's patrol car on the day the drugs had been discovered. With the subsequent expulsion of Bennett and Chief Superintendent Walker, a host of new changes were rapidly implemented at St Aldates.

Whilst declared innocent of any involvement in Bennett's shadier dealings, Sergeant Henderson and the objectionable PC Morris found themselves suspended from duty. An indignant Henderson decided that he wanted a change in career direction, and used his time to research alternative avenues of employment. With an inflated opinion of his own powers of observation and detection, the man resolved to set up on his own as a private investigator. Morris, however, after lying low for several weeks, insinuated his way back in but requested a transfer to Northamptonshire, from where he hailed originally.

DCI Powell was a breath of fresh air. A plump, balding man approaching his mid-fifties, he was amiable, with a dry sense of humour and an easy-going manner. Held in high regard by all of the officers in the department regardless of rank, he was fair-minded and treated everyone with respect. With his arrival, the efficiency of investigative procedures and the public perception of his team seemed to improve almost overnight. Alessa liked him enormously from the outset and felt confident that her own career now had a much greater chance of progression.

Jason was soon outed as a sergeant and given a more far-reaching role, which meant that he and Alessa no longer worked quite so closely together. But as their professional relationship dwindled, their private one continued to blossom. Just six months later, Jason proposed to Alessa, much to the delight of Greta and Roberto.

Greta was brimming with excitement. "We'll put an announcement in the newspaper," she declared. "It's not every day your daughter gets engaged. And we must throw a party. My little girl getting married – and Jason's the *loveliest* young man. I couldn't be happier."

Alessa wasn't really bothered about an engagement party, but was happy to indulge Greta, who seldom had anything to look forward to. For the first time in years, Alessa thought briefly about her father. She knew from things her mother had told her that at one time Greta had been very much in love with Jorge. It shocked Alessa to realise that neither she nor Greta even knew if he was still living. She couldn't speak for her mamma, but Alessa didn't really care – any more than he'd cared about them. Her earliest memories were of lying in bed, shielding her ears from the sound of screaming arguments, the slamming of doors, and all too frequently Greta weeping in her bedroom. All Alessa knew was that once her father had left, her home life felt much calmer. And her mamma began to sing again as she went about the house, as she used to when Alessa had been tiny. Although money had been tight, they'd still had each other, and Uncle Rob, and that was all that mattered.

She wasn't about to let her parents' failed marriage cast a cloud over her own. Even though she'd only known Jason for a relatively short time, she knew she had found a good, decent man.

One who would take care of her.

Friday, 19 April 1991

314 days since Kimberley's disappearance

After months of build-up, the day of the party arrived. At Uncle Rob's insistence, the gathering was being held at his most exclusive establishment, Ristorante Roberto. The huge, elegant orangery at the back of the property, which doubled as a function room, was perfect for such an event. Greta had thrown herself, heart and soul, into the preparations. While Alessa had wanted it to be a low-key, intimate affair, the guest list seemed to have spiralled. Cousins still living in Italy and Alessa's godparents were expected, and Greta was eagerly anticipating their arrival. Eventually Alessa resigned herself to the fact that it was going to be a real bells-and-whistles occasion. But she was happy to let Greta have her moment.

Uncle Rob had invited a handful of his own close friends to share in the celebrations, Chief Constable Jack Raybould amongst them. And Alessa thought it would be a nice gesture

306

to invite Valentina and Alberto, the friendly couple from the pizzeria in Jericho.

Aside from his parents, Jason had no other close family nearby, apart from an elderly aunt and two middle-aged cousins. His sister had sent them a card wishing them well, but she wasn't wealthy and flying over from Canada just for a party was out of the question. He had lost touch with most of his old friends too, although he still kept in contact with one or two of the officers he'd served with at the Met.

It was a beautiful spring evening, and Alessa and Jason stood at the entrance to the restaurant on the Banbury Road, as they welcomed their guests. The imposing double-bayed Cotswold stone structure stood on its own, set back from the main road, its nearest neighbours a bank and a designer boutique. Entrance to the building was via a stone archway through the wall separating it from the pavement. The awning above the doorway and the twisted-stem lollipop olive trees either side of the portico had been decorated with heart-shaped golden fairy lights, with a sandwich-board sign on the pavement outside announcing Alessa and Jason's engagement. Waiters greeted each attendee with a flute of Prosecco as they crossed the threshold. Plates of exotic-looking canapés offered by glamorous waitresses were being regularly replenished and greedily devoured. Despite her initial lack of enthusiasm for the event, Alessa felt happier than she had done for years. The weather had smiled on them and everything seemed perfect.

Jason clasped Alessa's hand. "I can't quite believe this is happening," he said, looking about him in awe. "Never in a million years would I have thought I'd be hosting a bash at this place. We've often driven past – I remember my parents going on about it, years ago. Our neighbours had been once. Their kids treated them to a meal here for their silver wedding anniversary. They gushed for weeks about how wonderful it was. But poor old Mum and Dad could never have afforded it. I'm a bit worried they'll feel like fish out of water." There was a trace of anxiety in his voice.

"Don't be silly." Alessa felt suddenly awkward. She dropped a kiss on his cheek. "We'll all be family soon. Uncle Rob and Mamma will see they're looked after properly. They'll have a great time."

Most of the other guests had already arrived, but there was still no sign of Jason's parents. He kept checking his watch. "I hope there hasn't been a problem. Stress makes Mum's symptoms worse and I know she's been building this all up for weeks. She's not good with changes to her routine."

Alessa looked up, then down the bustling street for evidence of their taxi. A small white florist's van pulled up suddenly at the kerbside. The young, heavily tattooed courier stepped out, squinting up at the building.

"This Roberto's?" he enquired rather vacantly.

Jason's lips twitched. "Pretty sure that's what it says on the sign."

The lad nodded inanely and opened the double doors to the back of his vehicle.

"Delivery for a" – he peered at the tag accompanying a large bouquet of red roses – "Miss Kay-no?"

"Cah-no," corrected Jason. "They'll be for my beautiful fiancée here." He grinned at Alessa, who rolled her eyes.

The boy's face remained deadpan. "Just need an autograph, mate."

Jason signed the delivery note and the driver mumbled his thanks, closed the doors, then climbed back into the van and pulled away.

"They're gorgeous." Alessa was thrilled. She accepted the

flowers as Jason handed them over, scanning the stems for a message. "Does it say who they're from?"

Noticing a handwritten note stapled to the cellophane wrapping, she peered more closely at the wording, then clapped a hand to her mouth in horror. Suddenly the pavement seemed to be coming up to meet her. Staggering sideways, she released her grip on the bouquet, letting it fall to the ground.

"Oh my God."

She had begun to shake like a leaf.

"What the hell? Whatever's wrong?" Jason grabbed her by the arm in an attempt to take her weight. "You've gone as white as a sheet."

Alessa stared at him, open-mouthed. She tried to speak but somehow the words wouldn't come. Her whole body felt like a block of ice.

Jason stooped to detach the tag and scrutinised the message to see why they'd provoked such a reaction. Seeing the wording and familiar unsteadily scrawled script, his face grew pale.

For Miss Sandi Cano. Thank you for all your help.

"The *bastard*." Jason wrapped his arms round the quivering Alessa, who clung to him as though her life depended on it. "We'll contact the florist's to see who placed the order."

Uncle Rob appeared in the doorway, looking slightly apologetic. "We've just had a phone call from your father, Jason. He asked me to let you know. I'm afraid it doesn't look as if your mum's up to it this evening . . ." He trailed off, registering the distress on their faces.

"Everything okay?"

"Alessa just received those." Wild-eyed, Jason nodded towards the bouquet lying on the pavement, thrusting the card

309

into Uncle Rob's hand. Lifting it to his face, Rob looked back at Jason, confused.

"I don't understand. Who . . .?"

"Same handwriting that was on the other stuff that arrived for her. The freak that killed Jessie Lockheed and Kimberley Painter."

Uncle Rob's whole body seemed to tighten. Stepping forwards, he patted Alessa's cheek gently. "Don't worry, *piccolina*. You mustn't let this spoil your evening. Some sicko's having a lot of fun at your expense, it would seem. Don't let him think he's winning." Uncle Rob glanced round sharply, his eyes taking in every inch of their surroundings, every passer-by. He motioned Jason aside, as the stunned Alessa continued to sob quietly. "Did you get the name of the florist?"

"Yeah. I'll ring them now. Hopefully he'll have slipped up." Jason's hands were balled into fists, his knuckles white. He spoke through clenched teeth. "I swear, if I could just get my hands on the fucker . . . "

The muscles in Uncle Rob's cheeks twitched. The colour had drained from his face. "The way I'm feeling right now, illegal or not, I'd happily pay someone to dispose of him if we could track him down. People like that, they need to be wiped out."

But a phone call to the flower shop in the city centre proved fruitless. Apparently, a man had walked in off the street the previous afternoon, paid cash for the bouquet and left delivery instructions, plus the accompanying note, with the young female assistant in the shop. There was no CCTV on the premises and the girl couldn't give a particularly useful description of him, other than that he was stocky, probably in his forties, with a heavy beard and moustache. She didn't see his hair; it had been covered with a plain, khaki-coloured baseball cap, his eyes hidden behind tinted glasses.

The party was as successful as it could be under the circumstances, but things had been ruined for Alessa and Jason. They tried to forget about the roses, and also the disappointment of Jason's parents' no-show, but it was pointless. No amount of alcohol or artificially cheerful conversation could erase the memory of the flowers, and Alessa's spirits were flat. Every time she thought of that cryptic note, nausea threatened. Alessa had had reservations about announcing the engagement in the local press, but Greta seemed so deflated when she objected, she'd reluctantly agreed. And now *this* . . .

Clearly her tormentor was watching her every move, and the knowledge filled her with cold dread. She'd made Uncle Rob promise not to tell her mamma about the unwanted gift, knowing how it would upset her. Greta had been so upbeat and had put so much effort into organising things. Alessa didn't want anything to ruin the occasion for her.

By the time the remaining guests had finally dwindled away, Alessa sank wearily into a chair, her head in her hands. She looked drained. Greta crossed the room to sit beside her, gently tilting Alessa's chin upwards.

"What is it, *tesoro*? You look as if you've got the weight of the world on your shoulders. What a shame Jason's mum and dad weren't able to come. We'll have them round for dinner soon instead, to make up for it."

Alessa forced a smile. "I'm fine. Just really tired, that's all. I've got a headache, too. Probably too much Prosecco."

Greta laughed, content with this explanation. "Well, let's get you home and off to bed, then. A good night's sleep should set you right."

"Yes, I think that's just what I need. Shall we call a cab?"

Jason sat next to Alessa in the taxi home and she rested her head heavily on his shoulder. Uncle Rob tried to make light-hearted conversation, and Greta seemed cheerful enough, but the couple weren't in the mood for chatter.

Uncle Rob was intent on staying at the house that night. He'd given Alessa his word that he wouldn't mention the bouquet to her mother, but seemed anxious about the situation and Alessa realised he felt duty-bound to watch over them. Jason decided, with some reluctance, to head home. He was concerned about his mum and wanted to make sure all was well. The taxi waited as they kissed goodbye at Alessa's front door.

"Don't you worry." Jason cupped her face in his hands, his serious eyes holding hers. "We'll catch up with the scumbag sooner or later. He can't carry on like this indefinitely without slipping up."

"I hope you're right." Alessa could feel the tension welling inside her. "I'm just so *angry* he ruined our evening. After all the hard work Mamma and Uncle Rob put in, too. I keep thinking . . . he's out there right now, laughing at me."

Jason stroked her cheek. "There'll be other evenings." He shook his head. "I don't get it, though. What the hell was he driving at, thanking you? It makes no sense."

Alessa pictured the words on the card and something like an electric shock zipped across her brow. "Who knows? He's completely warped, that much is clear."

Jason nodded. He blew out his cheeks, adopting a more cheerful tone. "Well, it looked like everyone else had a good time. And your mum seemed to enjoy herself."

"Yes, it was lovely to see her looking so happy." She painted on a smile, wrapping her arms around his waist as she rested her head against his chest. "Let's not dwell on it. Tomorrow's another day. Go on – you'd better go. The guy's got the meter running."

Alessa waved as the cab pulled away and went inside, casting about her one last time before locking up for the night. There was no sign of anyone loitering, but the knowledge that the malevolent troll seemed to be constantly aware of their whereabouts and privy to their plans left her with knots in her gut. He was still playing games with her – and at the moment, he had the upper hand. She remembered Carmel's words and clutched at her throat, turning the blue kyanite pendant that the woman had given her over in her fingers. She wasn't entirely convinced even now, but she willed its healing properties to help her; to rid her of this torture once and for all.

Greta had gone straight up to bed, but Uncle Rob was brooding at the kitchen table. He had poured himself a large glass of brandy and was swirling it angrily. He looked up as Alessa walked through the door and rearranged his tense features into a smile.

"How're you doing? You look dead on your feet." He studied her with concern.

She sank into the chair opposite him and lifted her eyes to the ceiling. Uncle Rob had always been the one person she could talk to. But there were some things she felt unable to share, even with him.

"I've just about had enough. Work's been pretty full-on for a good while, and some of the stuff we have to deal with – well, you can imagine." She pressed her face into her palms. "But being targeted like this, it's wearing me down."

"I don't get it." He took a slurp of brandy, swilling it round his mouth. "I mean, I know there's obviously the connection with Jessie, but why make *you* the focus? It's very odd."

"Maybe . . ." Alessa pictured Jessie's grey, lifeless face in the Polaroid snap. The echo of her friend's terrified screams seemed to flood her ears. She gripped the edge of the table.

"Uncle Rob, that day . . . when Jessie . . ." Her troubled eyes sought his for a moment. "It's just . . ." She stopped and shook her head. "Oh, never mind."

"What is it, *piccolina*?" He put down his glass, giving her his full attention.

She cleared her throat. "No. It's nothing." Pushing back her chair, she rose abruptly. "It's late. I'm wrecked. I'm not thinking rationally. Hopefully we'll nail this slimeball soon and I can put all this behind me – behind *us*. It'll be okay. I've got to stay positive." She leaned to kiss her uncle on the cheek.

He caught her gently by the hand. "Are you sure there's nothing else worrying you? All fine with you and Jason?"

The corners of Alessa's mouth lifted. "Everything's great with Jason. He's the one good thing in my life right now."

Uncle Rob nodded, patting her hand. "He seems very decent. Which is exactly what you deserve."

Alessa dropped her gaze and made her way to the door. "I'd love to stay and chat, but I really need my bed."

Uncle Rob studied her with narrowed eyes. He pursed his lips. "I'm always here – if you want to talk. Don't forget."

She nodded, squeezing out a small smile. "I know. And I'm fine – really. Night."

"Good night. I'll sleep on the sofa. Shout if you need me for any reason. See you in the morning."

*

Alessa was emotionally exhausted, but sleep was impossible. Thoughts coursed through her brain as she tossed and turned, constantly adjusting her pillow in a vain attempt to get comfortable. Where was all this leading? The depraved piece of shit knew her deepest, darkest secret and it was as though he was positively relishing tormenting her with it. Even though

Carmel had assured her she was in no danger, she was terrified of what he might do next.

But then there was Kimberley – poor, tragic little Kimberley. Alessa felt suddenly deeply ashamed that she was wallowing in concerns about her own welfare, knowing that a helpless, innocent young girl had fallen victim to the abhorrent fantasies of such a deviant in the most appalling, unthinkable—

And then, as though the very thought had summoned her, she was there, yet again. The temperature in the room had plummeted rapidly, so much so that Alessa could see her own breath hanging like fog in the air. Without even looking around, she could feel the intensity of a pair of eyes staring down at her. Her heart thumped in her chest as she felt tiny, frozen fingers curl around her own suddenly. Steeling herself, and trying her utmost to defy the instinct to pull away, she sat up stiffly and turned slowly towards the window. The frail little girl with the fair hair was standing beside her – right next to the bed this time. She was clearer than she'd ever appeared before, her expression earnest. Again, there was that distinctive, primeval smell in the air – like woodland after rainfall. The scent of nature itself; of decay and rebirth.

Not a word was spoken, but as the ghostly girl gradually turned her face away, it was as though she was imparting something to Alessa telepathically. A picture had been firmly implanted in Alessa's mind: two numbers, seven and eight. It was the strangest feeling. A sharing of knowledge, without any exchange of words.

"What? Wh-what is it you're trying to tell me?" Alessa managed to stammer. Those numbers – what on earth did they signify?

But the little girl just gave the briefest hint of a smile. Then, in a flurry of silver-white orbs, she seemed to disintegrate. Alessa was simultaneously awestruck and mystified as to the meaning of the message. She lay staring at the ceiling. All she could hope was that with time, everything would become clear. Eventually she drifted off, the digits still dancing teasingly through her brain.

1992

Two years had passed, and the investigation into Kimberley Painter's disappearance had been temporarily shelved. The pictures of suspects on the bulletin board had been replaced by those of violent drug dealers and armed robbers. The main people missing in the area these days seemed to have been associated with the drugs scene in one way or another. It was becoming alarmingly common and was a sad and worrying indictment on the way society seemed to be heading.

Alessa and Jason had married and moved into a little terraced house in Jericho. It was far enough away from Greta to give them their space, but near enough so that Alessa could be at Squitchey House at the drop of a hat if needed. But even before moving out, no further disturbing correspondence, or deliveries of any kind, for that matter, had arrived for Alessa, and she began to wonder if the man had moved away – or even if he could be dead. Since leaving home, she had received no more visitations from the ghostly little girl either. Whilst part of her didn't want to dismiss what she was sure she'd seen, much less the powerful emotional connection she felt they had made, Alessa had begun to wonder whether it could, in fact, have been some sort of manifestation brought about by her own fragile state of mind at the time. It was all so incomprehensible.

Other cases came and went, but with every spare moment,

still Alessa continued in her bid to find out what had happened to Kimberley. As time went by, and with the lack of any further leads, she was beginning to fear that they might never find the man who had killed three, possibly four – or even more – little girls. She was desperately sad to learn that Mary Painter had taken her own life. The poor woman had no longer been able to live with her terrible grief. Alessa wanted to visit Malcom but was stopped by her own feelings of guilt and remorse.

We're doing all we can. She remembered telling Mrs Painter those very words. But whatever they'd done hadn't been enough, had it? She believed that the force had let the couple down, and lived in the hope that, one day, she would be able to put that right.

She owed it to them. She owed it to Kimberley.

Chapter 23

April 2007

Almost seventeen years after Kimberley's disappearance

Detective Inspector Alessa Shelley pulled her damp mac around her as she stood on the front step of 37 Lime Tree Avenue. The fine April drizzle had wetted her hair and she frowned at the bedraggled reflection staring back at her from the grimy living room window. Taking a deep breath, she pressed the bell. It had been almost sixteen years since she and Malcolm Painter had come face to face, and she was apprehensive as to his reaction in finding her at his door once more.

The wizened, unkempt creature before her was a shadow of the man she had first met all those years ago.

"Mr Painter? D'you remember me?"

Malcolm stared at her for a moment, and then a glimmer of recognition registered on his face. He smiled – almost wistfully, she thought.

"WPC Cano, isn't it? It's been a long time."

"I'm a Detective Inspector these days, sir." Alessa extended a hand in greeting. "And it's DI Shelley actually. Haven't been Cano for some years now."

Malcolm looked taken aback. "So *you're* the one in charge of the investigation now? That young copper told me a woman had taken over from that idiot Bennett. I wasn't expecting—" He broke off. "Well, you'd better come in. You'll have to ignore the state of the place. Everything's gone to pot since— Well, you know."

Alessa followed him into the living room. Whilst it saddened her to see how the family home had fallen into such a state of disrepair, her overriding emotion was one of anger; that the evil actions of one individual had impacted on the lives of so many others as well as his victims.

"You heard about Mary, I take it?"

"Yes." She felt uncomfortable. "I'm so sorry, Mr Painter. Things can't have been easy for you."

He shook his head. The misery emanating from him was pitiful.

"She just couldn't take it any more. Kimberley was everything to her. We'd waited so long for her to come along that we'd pretty much given up on ever having a child of our own. For her to be taken from us was—" His lower lip trembled, the weight of his and Mary's loss engraved upon his features.

"I've often wondered, you know, if Mary had some sort of premonition. Shortly before Kimberley went missing, she'd had this dream. She wouldn't say quite what it was all about, but it really shook her up. Maybe if she'd told me, I wouldn't have let the littl'un out of my sight. Too bloody late now, eh? Ah, what's the use. No good going over it all time and again. What's done is done."

He looked blankly at the photograph of Kimberley on the mantelpiece, its glass dull and tacky from years of exposure to tobacco smoke residue, and peppered with pensive fingerprints. "Hard to believe so many years have passed. She'd be a young woman now."

He stared out of the window unseeingly.

"Poor Mary. She'd always suffered from depression, you see, even before we had Kimberley. But once our little girl had gone, it was as if it robbed Mary of any emotion at all. She became distant – just sort of retreated into herself. I couldn't get through to her any more. We barely spoke, those last couple of years. She refused to leave the house. And then one day I came home and found her, unconscious on the bed. She'd swallowed a whole load of pills. I called an ambulance and they came right away, but . . ."

Malcolm let out a long breath. He looked up at Alessa and smiled weakly.

"I'm sure you must hear stories like ours all the time in your line of work."

Alessa sighed. "I love my job – most of the time. But sadly there are too many people out there suffering in some way because of others. For my part, I want to help catch those who are responsible. That's why I joined the force – to get justice for families like yours, and for children like Kimberley."

He nodded thoughtfully and indicated the armchair, which looked less than inviting.

"I'm sorry – where are my manners? Have a seat."

"It's okay, I'll stand. I'm a bit damp."

"Suit yourself. Don't mind if I smoke, do you?"

She did mind, but shook her head amenably. "No, carry on."

He screwed up his eyes as he lit a cigarette, then exhaled the overpowering fumes into the already stale air. A dog began to bark outside.

"That's Tucker. I've left him out in the garden. Great dog. Company for me, like. We couldn't have pets with Kimberley – her asthma, you know. D'you like dogs?"

Alessa smiled. "Yes, very much. We – my husband and me – have never had one, though. It didn't seem fair, as we're both pretty much married to the job. We do have two rescue cats though, and they seem fine with the arrangement."

"Oh, your husband's a copper too, then?"

"Yes. He's a DCI now. Jason – you may remember him? We actually met when we were working together on Kimberley's . . . case."

Malcolm nodded. "Vaguely." He paused. "No kiddies, then?"

"Sadly not. The time just never seemed right, somehow." Her thoughts turned suddenly to Joey and how caring for him and then dealing since with his loss, had overshadowed her poor mother's entire existence. Greta seemed to have lost all sense of purpose and her life lacked any real direction anymore. Alessa wasn't sure if, put in her mother's position, she'd have had the emotional strength to cope with any of it. It had been bad enough losing her beloved brother, but as a mother, she felt sure it would have been too much to bear.

"And maybe I'm not cut out for it, anyway."

"It's not for everyone, I s'pose. Being a parent." Malcolm smiled sadly. The dog continued to bark persistently. "D'you mind if I let him in?"

"Not at all."

The bedraggled animal came bounding in through the French window. He ran straight to Alessa, his tail wagging. She stooped to scruff his fur.

Malcolm nodded. "See, he likes you. Good judge of character, animals. Never trust anyone they don't take to, that's what I always say."

Alessa drew a deep breath. "Mr Painter, I've got some news for you. The bodies of another two children have just been found, very close to where Kimberley was discovered. We currently have officers searching the area, in case there are any more remains."

Malcolm sank into his chair, a look of disbelief clouding his face.

"So he's killed more than once, then?"

"It would seem so, yes. We have to confirm it, but I reckon it's all too much of a coincidence. Everything points to it being the same perpetrator. We're currently trawling through missing person files to see who the children could be. I'm hopeful the culprit's slipped up somewhere along the line and left some clue to his identity. We just need that breakthrough . . ."

"So, some other poor souls have had their lives ruined by him too, just like Mary and me. It makes me sick to my stomach to think someone who's capable of – of *that* – must still be walking the streets, free to harm another kiddie. Surely *someone* out there must have an inkling they're living with a predator?"

Alessa shrugged sadly. "Who knows? Maybe he lives alone. Or maybe he's just very, very careful. You'd be amazed how well people can hide their behaviour. It makes you extremely cynical about the human animal, being a copper. Unfortunately, no one's above suspicion."

"Well, I hope you get him. I've no fight left in me now, but I want to see the bastard get his just deserts before I go." He patted the panting dog and gestured with a thumb towards the partition wall between his own house and his neighbour's.

"Tucker here's all I've got these days. Him and old Bernard next door."

"Mr . . . Stephens, wasn't it? I remember speaking to him years ago. Crikey, he must be a good age, now."

Malcolm sighed. "He's in a worse state than me, even. At least I can get out if I want to. I don't know how he keeps going. His wife passed away before we lost Kimberley. Lost his only lad in a car accident some years ago, too. Poor old sod's nearly ninety and I think mine's the only face he ever sees these days. Still sharp as a tack, but he's crippled with arthritis. He refuses to have a 'home help'. Says he doesn't want strangers poking around his stuff. I'd hate to see him go into a home. But I reckon it's probably inevitable, eventually."

He stared at the ground. "'*Life is hard. Then you die.*' Who was it said that? Might sound cynical, but it's bloody true. And for some, it's a damned sight harder than others."

He looked up at Alessa, his eyes misted with tears.

Her heart went out to him. "You've been dealt some really rotten cards, Mr Painter. But I'll do my level best to see that whoever took Kimberley from you, and more than likely robbed other families of their children, is brought to book. You have my word."

As she turned to leave, Malcom went to rise from his seat. Alessa lifted a hand.

"It's okay, I'll see myself out. But I'll be in touch again very soon, to keep you updated. Bye for now."

Closing the front gate behind her, Alessa looked back at the house. She felt all the more determined to see justice done; for Kimberley, and for the other girls and their poor families. Her eyes were drawn to the bedroom window, which would once have been Kimberley's room. Lost in thought, she stared for a moment, not really registering her surroundings. Then something caught her attention in the upstairs window of the neighbouring property, pulling her up sharply. Her heart quickened as, for the briefest of moments, she thought she saw a small figure looking down at the street. But when she looked again, it had vanished.

323

A shiver ran through Alessa. Puzzled, she climbed back into her car and with one last cautious glance at the now empty window, set off purposefully in the direction of The Laurels estate.

Chapter 24

April 2007

The residents of The Laurels were finding the not insignificant police presence in their usually tranquil little corner of Oxfordshire decidedly disquieting. The thought that they'd been living a stone's throw from a murderer's depository was not a palatable one. Curtains twitched incessantly as officers came and went beyond the cordoned area at the edge of the spinney, their distinctive cars and vans monopolising the whole length of the road as far as the blue-and-white plastic barrier.

Alessa's own vehicle was the latest to join the line. The rain had stopped briefly and the air temperature was a little warmer, so she shrugged off her uncomfortably damp raincoat and slung it onto the back seat. As she climbed from the car, she gazed up at the now completely derelict Hill Manor, looming above the housing estate, darkly menacing against the sky's dove grey backdrop. She recalled once more the day she and Jessie had trudged the length of the main road and up to its door, with the intention of seeking out ghosts. How ironic that the search for young Kimberley Painter had brought them here, so nearby. What a terribly bleak place for a child to end up.

Jason greeted her from a few yards away with a solemn nod as, taking a deep breath, she raised the cordon and entered the wooded area.

"Anything new turned up?" she asked tentatively, as he approached her.

"Two of the guys have found yet more remains over there." He inclined his head to one side in the general direction of the air-raid shelter which had concealed Kimberley's skeleton. "The dogs were going berserk. The forensics team have set to work on it now. From what they've said, this latest find could well have been there a couple of decades or so. It's beginning to look as though we've uncovered a proper graveyard out here."

Alessa felt a sick sensation in the pit of her stomach. She knew she needed to examine the discovery but didn't relish the prospect.

"I'd better take a look, then. Is there . . . much to see?"

"Just small human bones, as far as I could tell. They may well have turned something else up while they've been digging. It's taking them ages. I came away a few minutes ago." He sighed. His expression was bleak. "It looks as though he must've discovered the air-raid shelter where Kimberley was found at a later date. But the others aren't that far away from it – maybe he uncovered the entrance after starting to dig another grave and thought it a better hiding place. I hope to God there aren't any more. It's utterly depressing to think of the poor families. I want that son-of-a-bitch strung up."

"You and me both. If there've been several victims, there's a higher chance he'll have slipped up somewhere along the line; left a breadcrumb or two."

Alessa made her way deeper into the copse. Five forensic officers in white hooded paper suits were milling around the site of the latest discovery. One was busily photographing the scene from various angles. A young woman, squatting next to the shallow grave, turned to look at her. She stood up, brushing soil from her latex gloves.

"Interesting find here, ma'am," she said, indicating the dug-over area. "It's a badge – it'd been dropped underneath the remains."

She held out a hand, revealing a small enamel pin badge, ingrained with soil. Alessa leaned forward and peered at it with interest. Emblazoned with the words "Argentina 78" encircling the lower half of the badge, there was an image of a black-and-white football at its centre, framed by pale blue wavy lines.

"World Cup, 1978," she said slowly. A chill ran through her. Alessa turned to look at the pitifully small bones that had been uncovered. The skull was tiny and rounded. The incisors, still protruding from the jaw bone, were a reasonable size, but many of the remaining molars were clearly milk teeth. She tried to picture Jessie smiling – that angelic, doe-eyed expression that she had come to—

Her pulse quickened and she felt her throat tighten. No, she couldn't – daren't – allow herself to think of it. Alessa pushed the thought from her mind.

"Do we know . . .? Can you tell at this stage if the remains are male or female?" she asked the young forensic officer, somewhat brusquely.

"Difficult to say for certain when it's a juvenile, but I'd hazard an educated guess at female," said the girl. "The pathologist will be able to tell us more once we get everything back to the lab." She looked at Alessa curiously. "You all right, ma'am? You've gone awfully pale."

"I'm fine, thank you." Taking a deep breath, she straightened. The pungent scent of damp foliage prickled her nostrils. Her head suddenly began to swim. *Petrichor . . .*

"Get this lot bagged and labelled, and I'll speak to you, or a member of your team, tomorrow, when you've had the opportunity to carry out further analysis."

Abruptly, she turned and headed back out of the woods. The forensic team members stared after her.

The young female officer raised an eyebrow and turned to her bemused camera-wielding colleague. "What the hell's up with her, d'you reckon?"

*

"It's her; it has to be." Distraught, Alessa sat slumped at her mother's kitchen table, her head buried in her hands. She tugged at her hair in anguish.

"But surely that's a good thing? For the family, I mean? They'll finally have closure."

Greta placed a cup of herbal tea in front of her daughter, her brow knitting. "Here, drink this. It'll soothe you."

Alessa looked up at her, tears spilling from her eyes. "Almost thirty years she's been gone. Three decades – and not a day's passed since then that the memory of what happened hasn't haunted me."

"Then surely it will mean closure for you, too? Jessie can be laid to rest properly, and you can move on. And you've helped it to happen. You should feel very proud."

"*Proud?*" Alessa almost spat the word. She shook her head. "You've no idea, Mamma. *No* idea."

Perplexed, Greta raised her hands in the air. "I don't understand. I always thought the main reason you joined

328

the police was to get a fair deal for the victims. To serve the community and make a difference, and all that. And as far as I can tell, that's exactly what you *are* doing."

To assuage my own guilt, thought Alessa. But she didn't – *couldn't* – vocalise her feelings. And the very idea of having to meet the Lockheed family once more after all these years, of seeing Jessie's older sister whose resemblance made her seem more like an older twin . . . She felt suddenly nauseous.

Almost knocking her mother off her feet, Alessa flew from the kitchen into the downstairs loo, her hand over her mouth, barely making it to the toilet bowl in time.

"Are you all right, *tesoro*?" Greta had followed her. She stood anxiously outside the cloakroom as her daughter retched on the other side of the door. "Should I ring Jason?"

"*No*. No, I'll be fine. It's just been a really stressful day, that's all." Alessa stared at her reflection in the mirror. She looked ashen and drawn, her eyes sunken and dull. "I think I could probably do with a few days off, after this case has been put to bed."

"You work too hard. It's not right. I always thought you loved your job. It shouldn't be making you feel like this."

A drained Alessa emerged from the bathroom and attempted a smile. "I do love my job. It's just that every once in a while, things get on top of me. I need to request an extended a break. I'm a bit run-down, I think. Nothing a longer holiday won't sort."

"I do hope you're right." Greta rubbed Alessa's back, her face serious. "Life's too short for you to work yourself into the ground," she said gently. "Maybe it's time you called it a day. Get yourself a nice, easy little job somewhere with no pressure – and more sociable hours."

For the first time in her whole career, Alessa wondered if this might just be a good idea.

More gruesome remains, and the worrying prospect of facing the Lockheeds.

She was turning into a gibbering wreck.

*

Later that night, Alessa and Jason curled up on the sofa with a much-needed glass of brandy. He studied her, his eyebrows slanting with concern.

"This is really getting to you, isn't it?" Jason reached across, stroking her cheek gently. "I know it can't be easy. It must bring it all back for you. At least if they confirm it *is* Jessie, maybe you can start to put this whole thing behind you."

Alessa put down her drink. "I don't—" She stopped. Inhaling deeply, she turned to look at her husband, her eyes brimming with tears.

"Hey, come on." He went to put his arms round her, but she resisted.

"No. There's something I have to tell you. I can't keep it to myself any longer. And if you want to leave me afterwards, I won't try to stop you."

Jason sat back in his seat. He stared at her apprehensively. "What the hell could be so terrible that you think I'd react like *that*?"

"I'm a wicked person. Why would you want to be with someone so bad when you're such a good, kind man?"

"Alessa, you're not making any sense. You're a beautiful person. I should know – I've been married to you long enough!"

"No. I'm really *not*. That's just it."

He tilted his head to one side and gazed at her. "You're a brilliant wife. A thoughtful, loving daughter. Your mum told me how you always had endless patience with Joey. And look at all the strangers you've helped over the years – the effort you put into every case you take on. You always go the extra mile. You've given the job your all."

Alessa looked into his adoring face and began to sob. "I don't deserve you. I never have."

Jason threw up his hands in exasperation. "Fuck's sake. We're going round in bloody circles here. Will you please just tell me what this is all about?"

"It was my fault," she said eventually, struggling to muster some sort of composure. She stared at the floor, unable to look him in the eye. "Jessie should never have been abducted by that monster. As we were running away, she was struggling to keep up with me. She kept grabbing at my sleeve, trying to hang on to me with both hands. I was desperate, and she was holding me back. So I turned around and pushed her – hard. She stumbled and fell. It knocked the wind out of her. And instead of going back to help her up, I carried on running and left her there. On the ground."

Jason slowly released the breath that he'd been holding in.

"But you were only a kid," he said softly. "And you were running for your life. Christ, if we all dwelt on our childhood misdemeanours, we'd make the rest of our existence a misery. You just have to learn from your mistakes and let them go. Not carry them around for a lifetime like a lead weight." He smoothed the hair from her face. "You can't blame yourself for someone snatching your friend. At the end of the day, it could've been you."

"Yes, but it wasn't me, was it? And I made bloody sure it wasn't." She began to sob. "I kept thinking afterwards, would she have helped me, if it'd been the other way round? And then I'd try to convince myself that she would've done exactly the same. Sometimes I wasn't even sure she liked me that much."

Jason drew back his chin. "But . . . I thought she was your best friend."

She nodded. "She was. For years. We were inseparable. But when we got to secondary school, she seemed to change. Wanted to be part of the in-crowd. Apart from anything else, she started making fun of people. I think she thought it was clever. She could be really mean sometimes. She even laughed when some of the other kids teased me, saying I was getting too fat, that I ate too much . . ." Alessa paused, raising her eyes to the ceiling. "But worst of all, she never stuck up for Joey. When the others found out I had a disabled brother, I became a bit of a target. She just sniggered when they mocked him, when they called him vile names. It really hurt."

Jason puffed out his cheeks. "Listen, she was a kid. *You* were a kid. Children can be horrible. Some of them grow out of it; some don't. And puberty's a weird time – everyone handles it differently. Diplomacy is something a lot of people don't learn until adulthood – and even then, plenty of them carry on being pretty gross and insensitive."

"But she *died*. And I knocked her over. I should've gone back, but I didn't." Finally saying it out loud made Alessa's stomach turn over. "It was just a kind of reflex reaction, I guess. But all the same, surely it makes me culpable, even if I *was* just a child. She may have been a little shit sometimes, but she didn't deserve to lose her life. It's tortured me every day since, and now all *this* has happened—" She gesticulated, her eyes darting wildly. "It's brought everything to a head. I'm going to have to face her family all over again. I'm sure they blamed me, even though they didn't know exactly what went on. They wouldn't have said as much, but they must've hated me. They must have wished *I'd* been taken and not their beloved Jessie."

"Surely they'd rather *neither* of you had been taken,"

suggested Jason quietly. He pulled Alessa to him and kissed the top of her head. "You can't change the past. But you've done everything you possibly could to make amends for it. You've got to stop punishing yourself. You didn't kill her. But someone out there did. And we'll find him, sooner or later."

"And there's something else." Alessa stiffened. She drew back suddenly. She wanted to come clean about it all, but the more she revealed, the worse she felt. The admission to her husband that she'd been far from perfect, rather than a relief, was making her feel like a pariah. Her heart heavy, she left the room, returning moments later clutching a small silver bracelet. She thrust it towards Jason, not meeting his gaze.

"What's this?" He turned the bangle over in his hands, examining it with a frown.

"It was Jessie's. I took it."

"Took it? When?"

"I was round her house one afternoon, two days before she was snatched. She'd been particularly unpleasant and I was angry and hurt. So I took the bracelet, just to upset her. It had been a birthday present from her big sister and I knew it was her favourite. She adored her sister. It was always *Karen* this and *Karen* that. A gift from Karen was something to be cherished."

She let out a long breath. "Jessie was almost in tears about it the next day at school and I was glad. It made a change for her to be the one who was miserable and I thought she deserved it. But afterwards, I felt guilty. Once I'd let her stew for a bit, I was going to put it back if I visited again, or slip it into her school bag or something, so she'd think she just hadn't looked properly." Alessa's lower lip began to tremble. "Anyway, when we were leaving school that day – the day it happened – I decided to come clean. I'd calmed down and I felt bad that she was still upset about it. She'd actually been okay that day – more like her old self. We were walking up the road, just chatting, and I was about to take the thing out of my pocket and hand it back when—" She shook her head. "I was too busy trying to save myself. I meant to give it back but I never got the chance . . ."

"But the intention was there." Jason sighed. He cocked his head to one side. "Like I said, we all did daft things when we were kids. And it sounds like you've been carrying a whole load of unnecessary baggage around with you for far too long. Time to stop beating yourself up about it all, don't you think?"

She wrapped her arms around him tightly. "I'm so lucky to have you," she whispered.

"And I'm the luckiest man alive to have you," he responded, pressing his lips to her cheek. "And I'm not going anywhere. Ever."

Chapter 25

April 2007

The results from the forensic anthropologist's tests had arrived. From the dental records on file, they had proved conclusively that the remains were those of Jessie Lockheed. Alessa was sickened to learn that there was evidence of blunt force trauma to the back of the skull and to the lower limbs, almost certainly sustained before death. Although hard to verify, given the rate of decomposition and absence of soft tissue, the cause of mortality was thought to be strangulation, indicated by a fractured hyoid bone. She tried hard to push this information from her mind, to remain detached. But it was impossible not to remember Jessie's outstretched hands as she lay there on the pavement, the fading screams from behind as Alessa ran for her life. It made her gut contract horribly.

Alessa sat hunched over the report laid before her on the desk. She looked down at the photograph of Jessie clipped to the front of the file, then to the smiling face of Kimberley

Painter staring from the bulletin board. Two children snuffed out without a second thought; two families sentenced to lives that would always be overshadowed by a shared tragedy.

"I'll have to go and see the Lockheeds," she told Jason, who was reading over her shoulder. Her stomach lurched. The prospect of meeting them all once again was not one she relished.

Jason squeezed her hand. "I'll come with you. For moral support, you know. I won't butt in if you don't want me to . . ."

"No. This is something I have to do alone." She rose resolutely from her seat and inhaled deeply. "And the sooner I face the music, the sooner it'll be over."

*

Turning left from the Woodstock Road onto First Turn, Wolvercote, Alessa felt suddenly light-headed as the car approached the Lockheed family home. Everything was just as she remembered it. It felt so strange. It was less than three quarters of a mile from her mother's home, yet she had not had occasion to return here for almost thirty years. Although not as impressive as either of the main drags leading into the city centre, the quiet suburban road was one of the more affluent in the area, its houses now commanding a considerably higher asking price than they had done when she was a child. Alessa pulled up and sat for a moment to compose herself. Her stomach was in knots.

This was ridiculous; she was a professional. She had a job to do. Taking a deep breath, she climbed out, adjusted her coat, and strode towards the building.

She pushed open the wrought iron gate, which was newly painted in shiny black enamel. The front lawn was neatly mown and bordered by a glorious profusion of red, white, and mauve tulips in full bloom. She looked up at the semi-detached house, its render painted white as it always had been. It seemed smaller than she remembered – but then, everything always appeared so much bigger when you were a child. The same lace net curtains hung at the windows, pristine and fresh from the washing line. Mrs Lockheed always had kept a very clean house.

As Alessa stood on the doorstep, time seemed to stand still. She was twelve years old once more, calling for her friend to come out to play. Her hand felt like lead as she lifted the polished brass door knocker, but even before she could let it fall, the door swung open. Mrs Lockheed stood before her, grey-haired and sunken-eyed, but unmistakably the same woman she had known all those years ago.

She eyed Alessa with some mistrust. "Yes?"

"Mrs Lockheed, I don't know if you remember me. I'm Sandi Cano – at least, I used to be. I was Jessie's friend . . ."

The woman peered at her from behind tortoiseshell-framed glasses. Her whole face lit up with recognition. She raised a hand to her mouth and stepped backwards in surprise.

"Sandi? Is that really you?"

"Yes." Alessa's whole body tensed. She hovered a moment, anticipating some sort of rebuke. She needn't have worried. Mrs Lockheed opened her arms wide, tears springing to her eyes.

"Come and give me a hug. You naughty girl! Where've you been all these years? It's been such a long time. We've all missed you, you know."

Alessa was completely flummoxed. She hadn't expected to be welcomed, much less so genially.

"I'm sorry. You know how it is – you start off full of good intentions to keep in touch, but life somehow gets in the way." This couldn't have been further from the truth, but she relaxed a little.

"Well, don't stand on ceremony. Come on in." Mrs Lockheed

stepped aside and waved her into the polished parquet-tiled hallway. The older woman's eyes shone as she looked Alessa up and down. She shook her head, almost in disbelief. "Just look at you. All grown up."

She turned and called up the stairs. "Bill! Come on down. You'll never guess who's come to pay us a visit."

Mr Lockheed came slowly down the stairs, clutching the banister. Alessa felt a pang as she saw how time had treated her friend's father. She remembered him being tall and well-built, but his whole frame seemed to have withered. The man had aged far more than his wife and his face was gaunt and lined with pain. He winced as he reached the foot of the staircase, but managed a smile.

"Good grief, it's Sandi, isn't it? Well, well. How lovely to see you." He extended a hand, revealing twisted, arthritically swollen knuckles.

Alessa took his hand in both of hers and shook it warmly. "It's good to see you too, Mr Lockheed." A lump had risen in her throat. She knew she had to raise the subject of Jessie, but somehow the words just wouldn't come.

Mrs Lockheed interrupted her thoughts. "I'll put the kettle on. Bill, take Sandi into the front room. You'll have a piece of cake won't you, love? I've baked a Victoria sponge. You're not one of these silly girls who's always on a diet, I hope?"

Alessa forced a smile. "No, I'm sure I can manage a slice, Mrs Lockheed. I remember you always did bake excellent cakes."

Alessa perched awkwardly on the edge of her chair opposite Mr Lockheed. She looked around the immaculate living room. The contrast with Malcolm Painter's run-down home was stark. It occurred to her the difference was that the Lockheeds still had each other – and extended family besides. Mrs Lockheed had always been very house proud and had evidently maintained her self-imposed high standards. Framed pictures of Jessie at various stages of her childhood were lovingly displayed on the polished mahogany sideboard. In the deep window recess, several more photographs were arranged. One clearly showed Jessie's sister, Karen, in a flouncy white wedding gown and full veil. More recent images of a handsome, dark-haired man with his arm round a slightly older Karen, and two fair-haired children, a boy and girl, seemed to take pride of place at the front. The little girl bore a striking resemblance to Jessie. Alessa felt her heart begin to flutter. She put a hand to her throat.

"You have a lovely home." Alessa felt the quaver in her voice.

"Eileen likes to keep on top of things. I can't do much now – bloody arthritis, you know. But she's got enough energy for both of us. Even does the garden these days. The grandchildren keep us going." He indicated the picture of Karen and her family. "That's them – Jodie and Arthur. Little monkeys the pair of them, but we love them to bits. And Jodie's the absolute spit of our Jessie." He smiled sadly. "D'you have any children, Sandi?"

Before she could respond, Mrs Lockheed bustled in with a tray laden with steaming cups of tea and an impressively well-risen sponge cake. She cut it into generous slices and slid one onto a plate for Alessa, who accepted with a nervous smile. She had never envisaged herself in the Lockheed family home again, much less sitting down for tea and cake with Jessie's parents.

"Help yourself to milk and sugar," Mrs Lockheed said, beaming. "We've often wondered about you, you know. It's so lovely to see you. You've cheered me up no end." She glanced over to the sideboard. "Hard to believe she'd be over forty now," she said, wistfully.

Alessa cleared her throat. "This isn't entirely a social visit. I have some news for you," she began. "About Jessie."

Mr and Mrs Lockheed looked at one another and then back towards their guest.

Her words came tumbling out in a rush. "There's no easy way to say this. I'm a police officer these days. I've been working on a missing child case for some years. It's just that . . . we've discovered some more human remains, and the forensic tests have confirmed that it's Jessie."

Mrs Lockheed emitted a sob. The colour suddenly drained from her cheeks. She clutched at her husband, who sat in stunned silence, staring at Alessa. Eventually he spoke.

"It's finally at an end, then," he said, quietly. "All these years of waiting to bring her home and now, at long last, we can. I thought I'd die never knowing what had become of her. I'd given up on it. At least we can give her a decent burial. That much I'm thankful for."

Mrs Lockheed sat crying softly, her husband's frail arms wrapped round her. "Oh my God. She's coming home, Bill," she wept. "Our baby's coming home to us."

She turned to Alessa, smiling through her tears. "Thank you, Sandi. Thank you, from the bottom of our hearts."

*

"So it went well, then?" Jason looked up from his newspaper as a pale but smiling Alessa walked through the door. She stooped to stroke Bella, one of their rescue cats, who had trotted up to greet her, then flopped onto the settee, emotionally drained but ultimately relieved.

"It wasn't what I'd been expecting at all. I'd built it up for so long – stupid, really. I think they're just grateful they can finally bury her. I'll go to the funeral, of course. I think it'll help me, too. Does that sound selfish?"

"Of course not. It's a burden you've been carrying around

far too long. Hopefully this'll help you move on. Draw a line under things." He slid an arm around her shoulder and gave her a gentle squeeze. "I'm proud of you, you know. That took a lot of guts to go there today. It couldn't've been easy."

"It wasn't. But I'm so glad I went. It was actually lovely to see them both. Poor Mr Lockheed doesn't look at all well, though. I think everything's taken its toll on him. It's so cruel, Jase. And another two families still have to be told . . ." She let out a long breath. "Have they confirmed the identities of the other remains yet?"

Jason shook his head. "Not conclusively. They're pretty sure one is Carly Swift, but they're still conducting tests on the other skeleton. The likeliest at the moment seems to be an eleven-year-old girl called Sally-Ann Hughes, from the Reading area. She went missing after a school trip into Oxford, back in the summer of '86."

Alessa clapped a hand to her mouth. "Carmel's granddaughter."

"Who?"

"D'you remember, years ago, when we hadn't long met and that woman gave me her business card in the White Horse?"

Jason grimaced. "Uh-huh – and then you were snapped by our suspect coming out of her shop and plastered all over the front page of the local rag. I found out later – a couple of the lads said Bennett had gone berserk."

Alessa's cheeks flushed. So Jason knew, then. He'd never mentioned it. "It was stupid of me to go in uniform, I know. It was when I was feeling pretty low. Anyway, to cut a long story short, Carmel passed away soon afterwards. And it was then I learned she was Sally-Ann's grandmother."

His eyes widened. "Really? How did you find out?"

"I'd tried to ring her, but her friend picked up. He told me

341

she'd died after a long illness. Poor woman. It was before my time on the force, but I remembered the news footage, when Sally-Ann first went missing. And then her name cropped up during the investigation into Kimberley's disappearance, when Bennett was in charge. I think Henderson was looking into it. If I remember rightly, the Reading team were heading the investigation. Probably another one Bennett shrugged off." The memory of the man made her whole body tighten. His name left a bad taste in her mouth.

Jason looked solemn. "The mother was a young single parent, on her own with the little girl. Seems she hit the bottle in a big way and was found face down in the River Kennet one morning in November, the year after her daughter went missing. Apparently it would've been Sally-Ann's twelfth birthday."

Alessa felt tears sting her eyes. Her overriding emotion was one of anger. She thought of Carmel and how kind she'd been, and of everything she'd endured in her last years.

"I knew the mother had committed suicide but I wasn't aware of the circumstances. How absolutely *tragic*. I want that monster locked up. There's got to be *something* in this World Cup badge thing they turned up with Jessie. If we could only trace the owner . . ." She shook her head, rubbing her face with both hands. "Christ, it feels like looking for a needle in a haystack after all these years."

She thought suddenly of her most recent visit to Lime Tree Avenue. The odd sense of being watched from above. Alessa sat up abruptly. An unpleasantly cold sensation tingled along her spine, like someone running an ice cube right to the nape of her neck. The hairs stood up on her arms and her heart began to race like a freight train. The cryptic image of the numbers that Kimberley Painter had shown her all those years ago flashed before her once more; so distinctive, in such a unique style. It was as if some sort of riddle had been implanted firmly in her memory.

At first, she would keep turning them over and over in her mind: seven and eight; eight and seven. The numbers had danced round her brain teasingly. But was it meant to be 78 or 87? It had made Alessa's head throb to think of it.

For a long while, she'd wondered if they had somehow been wrong to dismiss any involvement from the paedophile Jerome Wilde; overlooked some vital piece of evidence, perhaps. She'd remembered the address where he had been staying off the Cowley Road: 78 Newcombe Terrace. The idea had tormented her. She'd gone over the files, time and time again. They could find nothing linking Wilde to Kimberley, nor to Jessie – unless, perhaps, there had been a connection with another of the house's occupants that they'd somehow missed. And then there was the tarot reading from Carmel. She'd told Alessa there were 78 cards in the pack. Maybe this was more significant than she'd previously thought?

But like a bolt from the blue, something else had suddenly occurred to Alessa. And now it was all finally starting to make sense.

"I've just remembered something," she said, slowly. "There's someone else I need to speak to again. I may be wrong, but I've a strong feeling they may be able to shed light on something that's been niggling at me for a very long time."

"D'you want me to come with you?" a bewildered Jason called after her, as she headed for the door.

"No, I'll be fine. I could be a while, though. But if you need me, I'll be in Lime Tree Avenue." She lifted her mac from the coat hook, then pulled it on, staring at her reflection in the hallway mirror. "Stupid, *so* stupid! How did I not see it before? I think we're coming full circle."

Chapter 26

April 2007

"I've been expecting you. Not right now, necessarily, but I knew you'd come. Sooner or later."

He sounded weary. Resigned. His face was a picture of misery. He seemed to hesitate for a moment, and Alessa wondered if he was actually going to let her in. But with a sigh, Bernard Stephens eventually stepped aside and made way for her to enter the hallway, closing the door behind her. He followed her slowly into the living room, flinching as he did so. Alessa was alarmed to realise the old man was beginning to hyperventilate. He clutched at the door frame, droplets of sweat covering his face, which had turned the colour of putty.

"Are you all right, Mr Stephens?" Concerned, Alessa helped him to his armchair, where he took a tiny canister from his pocket and sprayed a small amount of its contents into his mouth.

"Touch of angina, you know. Hits me from time to time – it'll pass in a minute." He sat back and took a few deep breaths. Gradually, the colour began to suffuse his cheeks once more. Gripping the arms of the chair, he pulled himself into a more upright position, but still his breath sounded alarmingly rasping.

Alessa hesitated. She had no wish to send the old man to an early grave, but she knew her mission was important. She had to stay focused.

"You said you were expecting me," she began eventually, studying him closely for signs of a relapse. "Can you tell me why, please?"

Bernard sighed. He pointed to the dark wooden bureau in the corner of the room.

"The key's in the lock – just turn it," he said, huskily. "Look in the little drawer at the bottom, left-hand side."

Alessa pulled down the lid carefully, and indicated one of the drawers, turning to look at the old man.

"This one?"

Bernard nodded solemnly. "Yes. Go on, open it."

She did so. Inside was a small, battered brown envelope, folded over twice, with a rubber band securing its contents. She picked it up and glanced over again at Bernard, awaiting further instruction.

"Look inside, then." The old man sounded impatient. He averted his eyes as Alessa removed the band and revealed its contents. She held up a child's cherry-shaped hair bobble, clearly the partner to the one that she'd received in the mail all those years ago. Needles of ice seemed to surge through her veins.

"How did you come by this, Mr Stephens?" she ventured slowly. "I think you know who it belonged to . . ."

"Course I bloody well know. D'you really think if I didn't, I'd have bothered otherwise? With any of it?"

345

Alessa regarded him quizzically. "Any of what, Mr Stephens? You're talking in riddles."

As her eyes scanned the room, they fell on one of the framed photographs on the sideboard near the window, the picture she had only half-registered the last time she visited the old man. She hadn't examined it close up before, but something told her she needed to. She wondered now, with hindsight, whether Kimberley had somehow been leading her here all along.

She had a vague memory – not of noticing the subject because she hadn't looked at him properly at the time – but of the distinctive design of the Argentina '78 T-shirt he was wearing – identical to the logo that appeared on the badge they'd found beneath Jessie's skeleton. Identical to the numbers that had plagued her for all these years.

Alessa walked across to take a better look at the man in the picture. She peered at the image more closely. Somewhere in the recesses of her mind, a terrible memory was stirring. Her heart began to race.

"Who's the man in this picture, Mr Stephens?" As she spoke, she could feel the tremor in her voice.

"I think you know very well who he is. And I think that's the reason you've come here today. Isn't it?" Bernard looked her in the eye challengingly. "Well? Isn't it?"

Alessa sank slowly into the armchair opposite the old man. She nodded mutely. Looking back at the photograph once more, she began to absorb yet more of its content. The background scenery looked strangely familiar. The foliage was sparser, the trees not so tall, but it suddenly dawned on her that the subject was standing in front of the spinney in the grounds of Hill Manor. The one that backed onto The Laurels estate.

Bernard was staring into space. "I found the hair bobble, you see. It was then I knew for sure. It turned up in Derek's car.

346

Not right away, when she went missing, like. It was a couple of years later. I recognised it at once because Kimberley often wore them. She'd pop over sometimes and I'd give her a sweet from my jar. I used to tease her that the birds would swoop down and eat the cherries in her hair one day." He smiled sadly. "The thing was wedged under the spare wheel in Derek's boot. I could've easily missed it. He replaced his cars every couple of years or so. He always brought them to me to service, you see, since I was a mechanic by trade. I liked to think it was because he preferred to entrust the job to me, but it was probably more that he was too tight to pay anyone else, if truth be told." Bernard stared blankly at the floor. "His mother always said he was a wrong 'un. Sent her to an early grave, he did, with the worry of it all. She knew; I think my poor Jean had always known he wasn't right. A mother's instinct, I suppose. I should've listened to her years ago."

Tears filled his eyes.

"We were childhood sweethearts, you know. She was my soulmate. The kindest, sweetest girl you could ever hope to meet. She could've had her pick of the lads but she chose *me*." His voice cracked as he gulped down a sob. "Part of me died when she was taken."

He paused, his gaze travelling once more to Derek's picture. His face hardened, the tone of his voice suddenly harsh. "When *he* took her."

He cleared his throat.

"Derek moved in with a young single mother, pleasant enough woman, in the late seventies," he went on, his eyes staring somewhere into the distance. "She had a little girl – Sarah, they called her. Pretty little thing, she was. Dainty; long blonde hair. That picture of Derek was taken just near the house, on the outskirts of Oxford. The estate hadn't long been built.

347

Anyway, he'd only been with his new girlfriend a few months when something happened. There was a . . . a complaint made against him."

Bernard sat, tapping his fingers on the arm of the chair as he relived the memory.

"We had the police knocking on the door, looking for our Derek. That awful chap – Bennett, wasn't it? – who tried to put the blame on poor Malcom for Kimberley, he was one of 'em. I recognised him when he came to the door. Apparently, the little girl told her mother that Derek had, you know . . . interfered with her; that he'd put his hands round her throat, too. Nothing came of it in the end. I think they decided the child had made it up. The charges were dropped, but the woman took her daughter and moved away – right to the other end of the country, I believe. Derek moved out of the area after that as well. Bought a flat in Reading. Even though he wasn't far away, we hardly ever saw him anymore."

He looked at Alessa, his expression earnest.

"I always wanted to give him the benefit of the doubt. But even though he was my son, our only child, my suspicions were aroused. When I thought about it later, it seemed like too much of a coincidence, these kiddies always going missing in the area, the exact time he came home. And when young Kimberley disappeared . . ." He shook his head.

Absorbing the enormity of what he was saying, Alessa spoke eventually. "You say children went missing when your son came home. When was that, exactly?"

Bernard looked up at her. His eyes had glazed over now, as though he were trying to detach himself from the situation.

"Not regularly, you understand. Every few years. During the World Cup; 1978 onwards. Derek was a salesman – his job was as a marketing campaign manager and he always took annual leave during the World Cup. You know, a break after the hectic promotional schedule he'd just had. He'd be jetting off here there and everywhere, but always popped home just beforehand. I'd sort his car out for him and then he'd be off again." He rolled his eyes. "He'd usually run me to the club, by way of a favour. It was the only bloody favour he ever did do me, mind you."

Bernard laughed bitterly. He looked up at Alessa, his tone suddenly grave.

"After finding the bobble, the pattern began to dawn on me. Only one child at a time that I knew of, in this area at least, but it was always on one of those rare Saturdays, when he'd been home. One little girl went missing every time he'd finished for the season. It was almost as though he was rewarding himself – a treat when all the hard work was over. That was how it seemed to me. I felt ill . . . to think, my own flesh and blood. Doing something like . . . like *that*."

He clapped a hand across his mouth. "I knew I had to stop him. I didn't confront Derek – God knows how he'd have reacted. I might've finished up in a shallow grave myself, for all I know. I couldn't let him do that to someone else's child. He was evil; there's no other word for it. He may have been my son, but he was rotten to the core. He destroyed my lovely Jean and he robbed those poor little girls of their lives. Ruined their families' existence, too. I'll never know why – we always raised him to be a good person. I suppose some people are just born that way – wired up wrong."

Alessa stared at the old man. "What do you mean? That you . . . you had to stop him? What did you do?"

"I loosened all the wheel nuts on his car," he said flatly. "I knew at least one of them would come off once the car picked up pace – and the stupid speeds he always drove at meant it would

349

be a nasty smash. It was a cert he'd be maimed or killed. Either way, it'd put a stop to his wicked behaviour. It was reckless of me, I know. I suppose I left it in the lap of the gods. But I felt it was no more than he deserved. He was warped. People like that never change."

Alessa was aghast. "But someone else could've died in the process! Didn't that occur to you?"

"I didn't really consider the consequences." Bernard looked down at his hands in anguish, as if remembering the terrible thing they had done. "I wasn't being rational. It was all I could think of at the time. I felt sick to my stomach, reeling with the shock – lovely little Kimberley, of all people. And as it happened, no one else *did* get hurt. He was killed outright. The car flipped over and slammed into the central reservation on the M4. The whole thing went up in flames. His body was charred beyond recognition."

He stared at her vacantly.

"I found other stuff afterwards, in his flat in Reading. I went through it all after he died. He'd kept things belonging to the girls – almost like bloody trophies, or that was how it felt. They were in a shoe box under his bed. Hair ribbon; a little sandal; a pair of knickers with an American label – Walmart, or something. I remembered then, an article in the paper about a young American girl that went missing in Islip some years earlier. But, worst of all, there were the photographs . . ."

Alessa caught her breath. "What did you do with them, Mr Stephens?"

He stared at her incredulously for a moment, as though he thought she'd lost her mind. "I bloody destroyed them, of course. They were an obscenity. I burned the lot in my incinerator." He gestured towards the garden. "I kept the bobble, though. I couldn't bring myself to throw it away. I had thought that one day, when I'd gone, someone would find it and make the connection. I decided I had to come clean, though. I owe it to Malcolm."

The old man looked up at her, tears glistening in his rheumy eyes. He exuded utter misery. "But he was my son. He may have been a monster, but once upon a time he was my little boy. What does that make me?"

Alessa's mind whirred as she tried to process this momentous revelation, her eyes constantly drawn to the photograph. Here he was at last: the beast that had haunted her for almost thirty years. The man she'd been so desperate to see convicted for his heinous crimes. And now he would never be punished for the pain he'd inflicted on so many. A ball of anger swelled in her chest. "You do realise I'm duty-bound to arrest you, don't you, Mr Stephens? That's one hell of an admission you've just made."

Bernard inclined his head solemnly. Alessa stared at his wretched face, his pale, paper-thin skin showing every vein. She considered the situation. He was hardly going to make a run for it. Her brain was fuddled with it all and she needed time to digest everything she'd just learned. She desperately wanted to tell Jason. But more than anything, she felt emotionally drained and craved the oblivion of sleep.

Tomorrow would be soon enough to bring the old man in. She would return in the morning with a clear head to read him his rights. And then she would have to break the news to Malcolm Painter.

"I'm leaving now, Mr Stephens." Alessa rose abruptly and crossed the room, pausing at the door. "But I'll be back first thing tomorrow. We both know you'll have to be arrested and charged, and that'll have to take place at the station. I'd like to take the photograph now, though." She drew in a breath. "I want to show my husband the face of the man who abducted and killed my friend, Jessie Lockheed. It's clear he was also responsible for taking the lives of Carly Swift, Sally-Ann Hughes, and Kimberley Painter, and God only knows who else."

Bernard buried his face in his hands and began to weep quietly. Alessa felt a momentary pang of sympathy, but quickly brushed it away. He had hampered their investigation and eliminated any chance of redress for the victims' families. This was no time for sentimentality.

She thought suddenly of the enamel pin discovered with Jessie's remains. The numbers that had baffled her for so long. Even if it had taken decades, everything had fallen into place, just as Carmel had predicted.

"Did . . . did your son own a World Cup badge, by any chance?"

Bernard nodded through his tears. "Oh yes. He always had plenty of official merchandise. There was a different one every season, of course. Very proud of his connections, he was."

Alessa said no more. She made her way through the hallway, clicking the front door shut behind her, then paused for a moment to glance up at number thirty-seven. There was no sign of anyone in the upstairs window now. Maybe Kimberley was finally at peace.

*

Bernard watched through his net curtains as the policewoman climbed into her vehicle and drove away. He knew he'd have to face the music now: that the whole world would find out what Derek had done. What he himself had done. There was sure to be a court appearance. A jail term to serve. But the guilt of filicide notwithstanding, it was as though a huge weight had been lifted from him. He suddenly felt completely exhausted.

Sinking into his armchair, he leaned back and closed his eyes. Tomorrow was going to be a very long day.

*

It was only ten o'clock but felt more like midnight. Alessa hung her coat in the hall, pausing a moment to collect her thoughts. From her handbag, she took out the photograph she'd taken from Bernard Stephens. She stared blankly at the face of the man who had wreaked such havoc on the lives of so many. The frightening thing was, he looked so *ordinary*. Not the spectre of her nightmares, but on the face of it just a regular, normal bloke.

Almost too tired to speak now, she went into the living room. Jason looked up expectantly. "Any joy?"

"Not the expression I'd have chosen. But yes, we've found him."

Alessa exhaled deeply as she handed over the picture, kicking off her shoes and sinking into the settee beside her husband. Her eyes fighting to stay open, she began wearily to relate the details of her conversation with Bernard Stephens.

"So it was the Painters' neighbour, all along?" Jason shook his head in disbelief. "Well, his son, anyway. Didn't Bennett think to question him when Kimberley first went missing?"

"I actually interviewed Bernard Stephens myself once, during the original investigation." She recalled the old man's earnest endorsement of Malcom's good character. Though from everything he'd said earlier, he hadn't been aware of his son's involvement at the time.

"I wasn't present when Bennett and Henderson first went to see him, though. I don't believe Derek's presence in the area that weekend was even acknowledged, if I remember rightly. Absolutely beyond belief, when you think our lot had been to interview his mum and dad a few years earlier, after he'd been accused of molesting that little girl. It must've been on file somewhere, whether there'd been a conviction or not. And Bennett was working at St Aldates when Derek Stephens was brought in for questioning. He'd actually spoken to his parents. The man was bloody incompetent as well as bent. Christ, we might never have found out if it hadn't been for that photo. I can't believe I missed it all those years ago."

"Hiding in plain sight. It's often the way, isn't it?" Jason's brow creased into a frown. "The crafty old sod's been carrying this around with him all this time. And he's in his nineties now, for God's sake. It'll be a miracle if he actually makes it to trial. But it'll be terrible for poor Malcolm Painter, finding out the old chap he considers a friend has known all these years who killed his daughter. Bad enough he'll have to learn it was Bernard's son, let alone the fact that Bernard was aware of it."

The telephone rang out in the hallway. Jason motioned to his wife to stay put and went to answer it. The conversation was brief enough but when he returned to break the news, she had fallen fast asleep. So Bernard Stephens never would face a jury, then. Jason was in no rush to tell her. It would change nothing now, and she was exhausted. Thank God they could finally draw a line under it all. Gently slipping a throw over her, he switched off the light. There had been enough revelations for one day.

Chapter 27

Saturday, 9 June 1990, late afternoon

In her frantic bid to leave, Kimberley had stumbled to the ground in Faye's grandmother's garden in Acacia Hill. She was wheezing now, the asthma having reared its head once more, and fearful in the knowledge that she was completely at the mercy of the irate Faye. The girl stood over her, almost gloating. She paused for a moment. Eventually, Faye thrust a hand into her own pocket and pulled out Kimberley's inhaler.

"This what you're looking for?"

Kimberley looked at her in desperation. She was struggling for breath as she lay on the sodden lawn, staring up helplessly at her friend, who seemed to be taking a sadistic delight in her predicament.

"You dropped it when we got off the bus. I picked it up for you. That's what mates do, isn't it? Look out for each other?"

Kimberley reached out to her imploringly. "Please," she wheezed. "I . . . can't breathe . . ."

Faye hesitated, then suddenly threw the inhaler at Kimberley.

"There you go." There was a look of cold contempt in her eyes. "You can sod off home now. I'll find someone better to come to town with me. *See ya, wouldn't wanna be ya.*"

With an exaggerated wave, she turned on her heel and went back into the house.

Kimberley took a huge puff from the inhaler and sat up. Her breathing slowly started to return to normal, but she still felt weak and light-headed. She rested for a few moments, then staggered to her feet and, putting one foot unsteadily but resolutely in front of the other, made her way out of the gate, trying to remember which way they had come. She could see the end of the road from the alleyway and knew the bus stop wasn't far away. All she wanted to do was get home to her mum and dad. She would have to get the bus back to the stop near where Faye lived and walk from there, as she didn't know which number to catch to Lime Tree Avenue. How she wished they'd just stayed in the house. How she wished she'd remained unaware of Faye's less agreeable side and carried on thinking of her as she always had – her wonderful, audacious best friend. Everything had gone horribly wrong.

*

The bus pulled up at the end of Faye's road and Kimberley alighted, wondering miserably how on earth she was going to explain her unkempt appearance to her parents. The rain was even heavier than it had been earlier. It would take a good ten minutes to walk home and she'd be even wetter by then, if that were possible. Her socks had fallen to her ankles and her feet squelched in her shoes. The blue dye from the leather had stained her feet. She tried in vain to brush the soil and grass stains from her cardigan sleeves and skirt, but they just smudged and looked even worse. Her sopping clothes clung to her skin, making her shiver. Kimberley knew her mother would go berserk. She would have to come clean about where she'd been and then she'd probably be grounded for months. Years, even. She felt utterly wretched.

Kimberley was saddened that her friendship with Faye had come to such an abrupt end. Faye clearly wasn't the person Kimberley had thought she was. She wouldn't tell; she wasn't a snitch. But she didn't want to be her friend now, any more than Faye would want to be hers.

Maybe it wouldn't really matter if she was confined to the house. After all, she didn't have anyone else to play with, anyway. She'd be starting at the secondary school soon enough, she told herself. A year wasn't so long. Hopefully, she would make new friends then. In the meantime, she would just have to keep her head down. She wondered if Faye would just ignore her at school, or whether she might make life unpleasant for her. But then again, she knew what Faye had done. Perhaps she had the upper hand, after all.

Kimberley turned into Lime Tree Avenue. She thought it might be best if she sneaked in round the back. At least if her mum and dad were in the living room, she might be able to tiptoe upstairs and change before they saw her. She ducked down as she passed the front wall and then, once she'd reached the end of the road, hurried breathlessly down the alleyway. The unrelenting rain was becoming even heavier now. Kimberley's legs felt like lead. She reached the garden gate and was about to lift the latch when a voice stopped her in her tracks.

"Well, well. What have you been up to, then?"

Kimberley turned to see Derek, their neighbour Bernard's son, climbing from a shiny blue car parked in the entry. He didn't visit all that often and looked different from how she remembered him. She suddenly realised that it was because he had grown a beard.

"Hello. I . . . got caught in the rain." Kimberley hesitated. He was staring at her a little strangely and it made her feel awkward. His hair was much darker than the last time she'd seen him. It looked a bit odd – almost like he'd coloured it in with a felt-tip pen. He'd put on weight, too. Although probably in his forties by now, she recalled her dad saying he had never settled down with anyone; her mum remarked that maybe it was because he travelled abroad a lot with his job.

Derek laughed suddenly. The sound was jarring and made Kimberley jump.

"I can see that! Come on, you can dry off in our house. And you'd better clean your face, too. Your mum won't be very impressed if you go home looking like that."

Kimberley opened her mouth to decline the offer, but thought better of it. At least if she was dry, there wouldn't be the usual tirade about her catching a chest infection, on top of everything else.

"Thank you." She smiled gratefully and followed Derek up the path. He led her through the kitchen and into the hallway. She peered into the cosy living room, expecting to see Bernard. The aroma of his pipe smoke lingered, but he was nowhere to be seen.

"Is your dad out?" asked Kimberley. She liked Bernard. He always gave her a friendly wave from his window and often offered her a few sweets from a big jar he kept if he saw her in the garden.

"Yes, I've just dropped him off at the social club. He likes a pint or two on a Saturday afternoon. Come on; let's get you out of those wet things."

Kimberley took off her shoes and socks and followed him up the stairs. The carpet felt thick and soft beneath her feet. She was appreciative of the warmth of the house after getting drenched, and looking forward to getting into dry clothes.

Derek opened the airing cupboard on the landing and began rooting through the folded pile on the shelf within. Kimberley hesitated, unsure what he was doing.

"I'll get the hairdryer for you in a sec. It's in the bedroom." He gestured towards the door on her right. "Go on into the bathroom and get undressed, then I'll stick your clothes on a quick wash and shove them in the tumble dryer. They won't take long."

Kimberley peeled off her cardigan, T-shirt, and socks, and unzipped her skirt. Derek's hand appeared round the bathroom door.

"Sorry, here's a towel."

As she stepped out of her skirt, the door was suddenly pushed wide open. She clutched the towel in front of her, embarrassed.

"Don't be shy! Aw, look at you. You're shivering. Here, let me rub you down . . ."

"I'm all right, thank you. I can dry myself."

"Come on. I'll warm you up. You look frozen."

There was something about his voice that made her feel nervous. His pupils were dilated and he was staring at her; not at her face, but at her body. He reached out and stroked her arm slowly in a peculiar fashion. Kimberley began to tremble – not from the cold now, but from a terrible, deep-rooted fear rising within her.

"I-I've just remembered, I need to be home by six. My mum will ground me, otherwise."

Her breathing was becoming rapid and she could feel her

chest tightening. The wheezing was beginning again. But instead of leaving the bathroom, Derek closed the door behind him. He turned to face her and smiled a horrible, lecherous leer. Kimberley was panic-stricken.

"Please, let me go," she whispered. Her chest began to heave with the effort of breathing. The awful wheezing noise was getting louder and her throat felt constricted.

"Of *course* you can go. In a minute though, eh?"

Kimberley tried to scream, but only managed to emit a strangled whistling sound. A hand was clapped hard over her face and she felt herself being pushed to the floor. Suddenly, his eyes looking quite mad now, Derek tore off a huge wad of toilet tissue, balled it up and, prising open Kimberley's jaw, shoved it inside her mouth, clamping it shut once more. She struggled to free herself but was powerless against his vice-like grip. The tissue was hitting her throat, making her retch. She felt the dampness of the mat beneath her, smelled the cleaning fluid from the lavatory bowl. Her heels slid back and forth against the vinyl floor as she tried to fend him off. Kimberley's eyes darted about her wildly. The sinister-looking doll covering the spare toilet roll seemed to be staring down at her from the shelf above the sink. Derek's weight had her pinned to the ground.

Help me. Somebody help me.

She could feel the heat of his rancid breath on her face, the roughness of his beard against her neck. Her little arms flailed helplessly as she tried in vain to push him away, desperate to escape his bulk and the vile, sweaty muskiness of his skin. He was panting and pawing at her, pressing his body against hers. It was nauseating. The room began to swim. All the time she tried desperately to breathe through her nose, but the intake of air was inadequate. Kimberley was suffocating. Random thoughts flashed through her mind: her parents; Faye; the safe haven of her own room; the comfort of her beloved teddy bear, Barney . . .

A pair of hardened, clammy hands closed around her throat, squeezing tighter, tighter. She let out a final wheezing gasp, then a cloak of blackness seemed to envelop her.

Kimberley felt a peculiar rushing sensation and was suddenly propelled upwards. Disorientated, she looked around her. She noticed with mild curiosity that she seemed to be floating, up on the ceiling. Or was she looking *through* the ceiling? She couldn't be sure. Very strange, but somehow liberating, too. Looking downwards, she was puzzled to see a man pulling himself to his feet, staring at the ground beneath him. What he was staring at appeared to be a large rag doll, lying there on the bathroom floor, motionless and limp.

Kimberley was shocked to realise that the rag doll was her.

Chapter 28

June 2007

Kimberley Painter's funeral was a low-key affair. Naturally, Malcolm wanted her to be interred with her mother, Mary. There would be space in the family plot for him, too, when his time eventually came.

The service was simple and moving. A handful of people, mainly Malcolm's immediate neighbours and a couple of his old work colleagues, were gathered in the small church where Malcolm and Mary had married over forty years earlier. Alessa and Jason sat in the pew behind Malcolm, Alessa dabbing her eyes with a handkerchief at the pitiful sight of the tiny white coffin containing Kimberley's mortal remains. It was, in a way, a homecoming; after seventeen years of agonising uncertainty and anguish, the return of a beloved daughter to her grieving father, reuniting her in death with the mother who had been unable to bear the pain of her loss.

The hymn sung was the uplifting "All Things Bright and

Beautiful", one of Kimberley's favourites. The vicar read a touching eulogy about Kimberley's short life, before the coffin was carried out by Malcolm to the strains of "Love Survives", a song from the soundtrack of the animated movie *All Dogs Go To Heaven* – a film that Kimberley had loved.

At Alessa's suggestion, everyone involved in the case had chipped in to pay for white doves to be released after the interment. She had discovered the practice after Joey's passing, and arranged for the same at his funeral. Both she and her mother had found it very comforting. The symbolic liberation of Kimberley's spirit seemed pertinent after her remains had been imprisoned for so long in that awful, foetid tomb. Alessa hoped fervently that the little girl was finally at peace.

A few prayers were said at the graveside, and then people gradually began to drift away, Alessa and Jason among them, to leave the quietly weeping Malcolm alone with his thoughts. The earlier watery sunshine had given way to the falling of soft rain, but he seemed oblivious to it as he stood, staring down at the little casket strewn with soil and pink roses that had been cast by some of the mourners. Alessa noticed he had yet to part with the clod of dampened earth gripped in his palm, almost as though he couldn't bear to throw it onto his daughter's remains.

As Jason and Alessa walked slowly from the grave, she noticed a tall, slender young woman standing under a tree, observing the funeral's attendees. Suddenly, a spark of familiarity lit the girl's face and she crossed the lawn towards them, clutching a posy of mauve freesias and pink and white carnations. She carried herself proudly, almost like a mannequin, but there was an air of deep sadness about her.

"WPC Cano?"

The young woman was dressed elegantly in a tailored black skirt suit and heels, her glossy brown hair twisted into a chignon and secured with a black velvet bow. Alessa studied her for a moment, and then recognition dawned.

"Faye? Is that you?"

The girl nodded, smiling disconsolately. "I had to come. I felt so terrible for poor Mr Painter, being all alone now. I wasn't sure he'd want to see me, but I wanted to say goodbye. The last time Kimberley and I met, we parted on such bad terms . . ." Her voice cracked suddenly. She broke down, rivulets of tears streaking her flawless foundation. Alessa fumbled in her bag for a tissue, pressing it into her hand. After a few minutes, Faye managed to compose herself but continued to stand staring emptily across at Malcolm's lonely, hunched figure.

"I look back on it now, since I've had a daughter of my own, and realise what a horrible child I really must've been." Faye shook her head. "If it hadn't been for me and my stupid behaviour, this would never have happened. My little friend Peanuts might be a grown woman now, with a family of her own, like me. Her mum might still be alive, and who knows . . ."

Alessa placed a hand gently on her arm. "Who knows anything? We can never tell what fate has in store for us. Any event can have completely different consequences if it happens only moments earlier or later. Kimberley was in the wrong place at the wrong time. It had nothing to do with you. It was sheer bad luck. You can't blame the person you used to be, and you can't torture yourself with a lifetime of 'ifs' and 'buts'. I should know. I've been there."

She cast her mind back to Jessie's funeral only weeks earlier. How wretched she'd felt initially, seeing the Lockheed family huddled together in the front row of the church, heads bowed, united in their grief. And yet, as Jason had pointed out, she had been instrumental in helping them achieve closure. She couldn't go on blaming herself forever. She had been alone briefly with

Jessie's remains in the mortuary before the lid to the coffin was finally screwed down in readiness to transport her to the chapel of rest, to allow the family to visit and say their goodbyes. Though Jason insisted there was no need, it had been a long-awaited opportunity for Alessa herself to say sorry. And to slip a small, silver bangle into the folds of the casket's white silk lining.

Alessa looked back at the grave. Malcolm was still gazing down at the gaping hole in the ground, lost in thought. Alessa wondered what would become of him now. She hoped this might bring him some closure, and that he had at least found peace of mind, now that his daughter had finally been returned to him.

Turning back to Faye, she gave a firm but encouraging nod. "Go and lay your flowers, sweetheart. Pay your respects. And then let her go. Life goes on."

Alessa watched as Faye, with some trepidation, walked slowly towards Malcom. She tentatively placed a hand on his shoulder. The man looked up, a look of confusion on his face, and there was a brief trading of words. A lump came to Alessa's throat as she watched the two embrace. They stood locked together for a few moments before drawing back. Tears, then smiles, were exchanged and they began to talk. Alessa knew they had both made their peace. It gladdened her to think that Faye could now move on, for she, more than most, knew what a terrible shadow the whole affair must have cast over the girl's life.

She took Jason's hand and they continued walking from the cemetery. Casting one last look over her shoulder, Alessa caught her breath as she thought she saw a flicker of movement in the tall shrubs at the edge of the graveyard. Her eyes sought the source but it had ceased.

It must have been a trick of the light.

365

Epilogue

Johannesburg, South Africa

Friday, 11 June 2010

*Twenty years and seven days after
Kimberley's disappearance*

The bloated, grey-bearded man sat beneath an umbrella beside the pool, sipping an ice-cold beer and people-watching. Much of his face was shielded by the peak of an oversized camouflage-patterned baseball cap, more suitable for a teenager than someone approaching his seventh decade. His mirror sunglasses reflected the shimmering water. For those unable to attend the game, the opening match of the World Cup was due to be aired in half an hour on an impressively large poolside screen provided by the hotel's proprietor. Quite a crowd of the resident families was beginning to assemble, and the shallow end of the pool was filled with laughing children jumping onto inflatables and splashing one another gleefully.

"I don't like the look of that one." The woman stretched out on a sunlounger on the opposite side of the pool had been observing the man from behind her huge Dolce and Gabbana shades.

"Hmm?"

"That guy over there. He's taking far too much interest in the kids. I noticed him yesterday at breakfast. He's on his own, too."

Her husband put down his book and looked up. "Jesus, you can't accuse every unattached middle-aged bloke you see of being a perv, Tracey. Lighten up, will you."

"I'm telling you, there's something not right about him."

A little fair-haired girl of about nine or ten climbed from the pool and ran towards the entrance to the bar, her wet footprints on the paving slabs drying almost instantly in the unseasonably hot sun. The solitary man peered at his wristwatch, rose from his seat, and casually walked towards the building, glancing back over his shoulder as he did so.

The woman sat up immediately and nudged her husband's arm with some urgency. "Go after him, will you. Make sure he's not up to anything."

"He's probably gone to get himself another beer."

"David, will you just bloody humour me and check he's not going after that little girl. *Please*."

The husband let out an exasperated sigh and slid his feet into a pair of plastic mules. Self-consciously sucking in the unsightly overhang of his ample stomach, he shuffled towards the building, keeping the grey-bearded man in his sights. Entering the bar, he squinted as the darker interior momentarily blurred his vision. As his eyes adjusted, he looked around, but the man had vanished. Suddenly the little fair-haired girl came skipping back through the bar, her hand clasped safely in her mother's. Relieved, David smiled to himself and returned to his anxious wife.

"It's okay. She's with her mum. That chap's disappeared. Maybe he's gone to watch the match in his room. He might well have had enough of the screaming kids, too."

Tracey lay back and closed her eyes once more. "Well, I'm glad he's gone. He was putting me on edge. Bloody weirdo."

*

From the seclusion of his balcony, the man in the baseball cap looked down at Tracey with distaste. He'd noticed her watching him earlier, and now the nosey mare had obviously said something to her husband. Not much got past him; he'd become adept at reading people's body language. It had been too risky on this occasion. He would bide his time. He'd waited long enough. It had been twenty years since the Painter girl – almost to the day, he suddenly realised. An anniversary would have felt appropriate. But a few more days, or even weeks, wouldn't matter. It would just make it all the sweeter. There would always be other opportunities. *All things come to he who waits.* He smiled to himself. His extended holiday stretched ahead of him, with no work to worry about for weeks. And how much better still the weather was this side of the equator compared with perennially rainy England, even though it was officially winter in South Africa.

How he wished he'd moved out here decades ago, when he was still a young man. Fun in the sun – that was what it was all about. He thought back to how he'd come to be here in the first place. More by default than design since he couldn't chance staying in the UK any longer than necessary. South Africa had seemed far enough away and as good a place as any. And now, of course, they'd landed the World Cup: it felt as if it had all been pre-destined. Europe was too close to home – more risk of running into someone who recognised him. The passport he'd managed to get his hands on, even to the trained eye, looked like the real deal. Amazing what was available these days.

Thank God he'd never reported the car stolen. He'd suspected the net would close in on him eventually and wanted to get out while the going was good. It had just been tough shit for the sap who'd taken it. Probably some hapless druggie, since the guy obviously hadn't been missed. And what a favour he'd done him. No one was going to be looking for a dead man. He was free to do just as he pleased. It was *extremely* liberating.

It had given him a real kick, sending those parcels to that Sandi Cano. And leaving a key inside a plant pot? Who in their right mind would do that! Well, they were asking for someone to break in, weren't they? He hadn't been able to resist it. She must have been shitting herself.

It was immensely gratifying to think – no, to *know* – he'd put the wind up her. It hadn't been hard to find out the Canos' phone number, either. He'd called the uncle's restaurant under the pretext of being an old family friend who'd lost his address book, and the dopey girl he'd spoken to had let him have it readily. The man really should be more careful about who he chose to employ.

He'd first spotted Cano hovering in the background of the press conference when they began the search for Kimberley Painter. It was always easy for him to get into those things with his connections. He had an acquaintance who worked for the gutter press, and the guy had been only too happy to provide him with a pass in exchange for free tickets to a big game. He used to sit at the back and watch. It had always amused him to observe the proceedings from a safe distance as the bungling police stumbled at every hurdle. Cano wasn't the fat dollop she'd been as a child, but he recognised her straight away. He never forgot a face. Silly little tart. She'd obviously made it her purpose in life to seek out the likes of him after her own experience. How transparent. How *noble*.

At first, he'd been on pins, thinking she might have been able to identify him. The police were all over Lime Tree Avenue – one look at those photos in his dad's house and the game could've been up. He'd even toyed with the idea of getting rid of her. It probably wouldn't have been that difficult. But when she looked straight at him as they filed out, there wasn't a glimmer of recognition. It bolstered him, and that was when he'd had the idea of sending the video tape to shake her up a bit; to let the bitch know he was on to her.

After all, she had unintentionally helped him when she pushed the Lockheed girl over. She'd made his mission *so* much easier. And she wouldn't have wanted *that* to come out, would she? Oh, the irony . . .

His confidence had swelled further after ringing his dad only to find out she'd been to the house. That writing pad he always kept on the phone table in the hall – if Cano had bothered to look more carefully, she'd have had a record of his movements for pretty much that whole summer. Very sloppy for a copper. His dad always jotted everything down whenever he phoned him. Saturday, 9 June – *Derek visiting*. Monday, 2 July – *Derek passing through*. Tuesday, 10 July – *Derek servicing car*. It would have placed him in the area for all the relevant dates. And he'd written plenty in there himself when he'd been home, too: phone numbers and things. Just out of habit, but a bit careless really, now he thought back. He'd been so meticulous about everything else. But Cano *must* have seen the photos in the front room, unless she was totally blinkered. Maybe she really *had* thought it best to keep her mouth shut. Still, he would have loved to continue his vendetta against the copper and tip her over the edge completely. It had given him such a sense of *power*. But common sense prevailed. He couldn't afford to be complacent. The odds of the police catching up with him were sure to increase, the more risks he took. Best if he got out before he did something careless, before someone cottoned on. The last time he'd gone by Cano's house, he'd clocked the new alarm system – and more worryingly, the security cameras. It had given him a jolt. He couldn't be sure they hadn't been there the time before and he'd started to panic. He'd lain low in Reading after that – until that stunt with the engagement flowers which he hadn't been able to resist. One last go before he left for good. Well, the knees-up had been announced in the *Oxford Mail* – it would have been rude not to . . .

He'd been planning to abscond for months anyway, and the car had been an unexpected gift. Everyone believed him deceased now – and that was how he wanted it to stay.

He peered down at the increasing number of people gathering by the pool. There she was again, the girl with the fair hair. She looked quite a lot like Kimberley Painter. And every bit as ripe for the taking. He ran a lascivious tongue over his dry lips. There would be more chances; he still had plenty of time. But perhaps not today . . .

He sat back in the wicker chair, smirking conceitedly to himself. He'd always got away with it; he knew he'd get away with it again. Patience and tenacity was all it took – and he had more than his fair share of both. But he'd been in retirement for long enough now. He'd decided to test the waters once more.

Just one last time. His swansong.

371

A roar went up from below as the match kicked off and his heart soared. Oh, how he *loved* the World Cup.

Rising from his seat to fetch a beer from the mini-bar, he halted abruptly, confronted by the sight of a small blonde-haired girl staring at him solemnly through the voile curtain, from the other side of the balcony's patio door. His initial surprise and delight turned to sudden horror as recognition dawned. As he backed away, the child drew nearer, her eyes unblinking, a smile spreading slowly across her face . . .

*

The cheers from the crowd turned suddenly to screams as, limbs flailing, a man's screeching body plummeted from one of the balconies overlooking the pool. It landed with a sickening thud on the paved terrace beneath, scattering the horrified spectators. The man lay motionless, arms and legs askew, his wide, lifeless eyes staring skywards, the face contorted in terror. A dribble of blood pooled at the corner of his mouth, and yet more had begun to spread out in a gory puddle behind his head, sullying the jet-washed paving slabs.

In the ensuing mayhem, no one noticed the tinkle of childish laughter, and the diminutive figure of a pale, fair-haired girl watching from above, then fading gradually from view.

Acknowledgements

It's so important to remember that any book is a collaborative effort, so I must begin by thanking my wonderful editor, Rachel Hart. Once again, her patience, support and guidance throughout have been invaluable and greatly appreciated. Thanks also to Lydia Mason for her meticulous copyedit and helpful suggestions. Many thanks and a big shout-out to the lovely wider team at Avon Books, who work their socks off behind the scenes to create the final polished article and act as tireless cheerleaders to bring the book to the attention of readers everywhere. All credit to those unsung heroes working away in the background – you are absolute stars!

A special thank you to the multi-talented Angie Weiland-Crosby for the kind permission to use her poignant quote as the book's epigraph. She is a gifted wordsmith and her beautiful prose really resonates with me.

As always, huge gratitude to the many fabulous bloggers and reviewers who are so incredibly generous with their time – we authors have so much to thank you for. Also to all the brilliant writers and friends on X who are unfailingly supportive and encouraging – you are a lovely lot!

Thanks as ever to the people central to my existence, my wonderful family: to my husband, Mark; my children, Gemma, Natalie and Christopher; and my grandchildren, Olivia, Josh, Isaac, Noah, Oliver and Gracie. You are all what makes everything worthwhile!

Finally, and most importantly, a massive thank you to every reader who has bought and read this book – your support is invaluable and I'm eternally grateful to you all. This has been something of a new direction for me with the inclusion of a paranormal twist, and I really hope you've enjoyed the story.

When a young widow's little girl vanishes, could a dark family secret hold the answer?

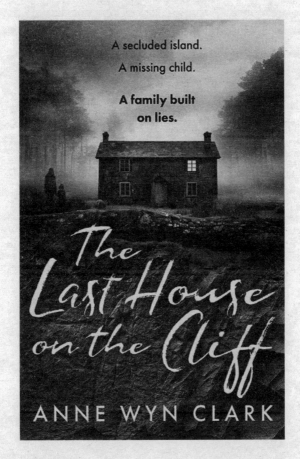

A secluded island.

A missing child.

A family built on lies.

The Last House on the Cliff

ANNE WYN CLARK

A terrifically dark and twisty tale that asks:
can you ever really trust those closest to you?
Perfect for fans of Ruth Ware, Cass Green and C.J. Tudor.

A mysterious figure.
A whispering community.
A deadly secret . . .

Your dream family home?
Or your worst nightmare?

Whisper
Cottage

ANNE WYN CLARK

A haunting, twisty story about the power of secrets and
rumours, perfect for fans of Ruth Ware's *The Turn of the
Key* and Lucy Atkins's *Magpie Lane*.

A missing child.
A broken community.
A horrifying secret.

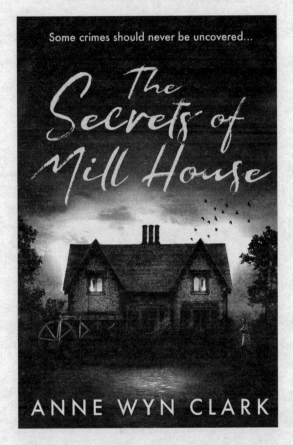

Some crimes should never be uncovered…

The Secrets of Mill House

ANNE WYN CLARK

The chilling, stay-up-all-night suspense thriller for fans
of C.J. Tudor, Riley Sager and Stephen King.